THE THRILLING LIBRARY:

VOLUME 4

BY
NORVELL W. PAGE
AND
NORMAN A. DANIELS

THRILLING PUBLICATIONS
2017

TABLE OF

CONTENTS

THE BLACK BAT'S DRAGON TRAIL

CHAPTER I

THE DRAGON STRIKES

IT HAD been raining lightly. Down in Chinatown the wet pavement and cobblestones reflected the lights from a thousand windows and neon signs. It shimmered upon elderly Chinese, with hands tucked in their sleeves in patriarchal dignity, shuffling along with a younger generation in American clothes. It gleamed upon dozens of others threading their way in and out of the cafes to blend with the restless human tide—opulent folk in search of food and exotic entertainment, panhandlers from the slums in search of handouts, and sharp-eyed, swarthy-faced men with upturned raincoat collars, hat brims pulled low over their eyes.

At the narrow entrance to a dim alley one of the raincoated figures, moving casually as he approached, paused to light a cigarette. It gave him a chance to sweep his gaze up the street in both directions over his cupped hands and to look at the diamond-studded wrist-watch within inches of his eyes. There was a large diamond stickpin in his tie while still another stone glittered on a finger of his left hand.

"Eleven-thirty," the man muttered under his breath. "The others oughta be showin' up any time now if they ain't already here. Yep—here comes one of 'em."

He turned and stepped swiftly into the alley, melting into night that was Stygian. The second man paused a moment to glance furtively about him, then he, too, disappeared as though whisked from sight by an invisible hand. There came a muffled curse as he stumbled over some refuse underfoot. The anathema was followed by a chuckle from somewhere up ahead.

Within ten minutes several more men appeared in the alley. Presently several husky Chinese also approached and followed on the heels of the Americans. They made their way along the alley that was so narrow there hardly was room for the two big, sleek laundry trucks parked at the back of a ruined building that was windowless above. The white placards of a house wrecking company were pasted on the red bricks.

From the darkness a voice speaking in Cantonese from somewhere beside the trucks directed the Orientals to the front truck. The American mobsters who had gathered got into the second one. As the last man came in, a Chinese driver at the wheel of the rear truck stuck his head out and again whispered directions.

"If you will open the two back doors of the truck, Dragon," he said to one of the gangsters, "you will find your friends inside."

The man obeyed. He crawled in, fumbling around for a seat. From the darkness up near the front came a growled complaint.

"I don't like joinin' up with a secret Chinese society one damned bit. This is the first time the boss has sent us on a job and not told us what it is. I think he's nuts, if you ask me." He sniffed audibly. "Besides I like workin' with guys of my own kind."

THE BESPECTACLED Chinese sitting at the wheel of the truck turned in the darkness. He spoke in English that was cultured, and without a trace of accent.

"The Chinese members of the Dragon feel the same way, Flash, except myself," he said. "But they realize that what we are about to do would be utterly impossible without your specialized talents. I still think it is foolish of Duke to endanger the profitable—ah—laundry business my little establishment has built up during the past two years by joining the Dragon. But like all Americans he's unable to resist a quick clean-up. A large sum in cash offered by the Dragon Master for a single job tonight fired Duke's greed. It is indeed regrettable."

"When are we gonna meet this guy we're supposed to address as 'Master?'" the man called "Flash" asked complainingly.

But the bespectacled laundryman at the wheel did not answer. He was too busy. The truck ahead, in which the Chinese rode, had begun to roll toward the opposite end of the alley, and he was quickly following.

Both shiny trucks rolled out into the street, and for three quarters of an hour their drivers worked their way across town by darkened side streets until at last they came to a building sitting alone at the edge of a small city park. Years before, the park and the building had been the private grounds and museum of a multi-millionaire. On his death, it had been willed to the city.

It was dark with the loneliness of midnight around the building, near which the trucks presently stopped. Up ahead one of the Chinese got out and disappeared into the night. Ten minutes later he returned as silently as he had come, getting in beside the driver again.

"Everything is quiet," he informed in sing-song Chinese. "I saw nobody. There is a light in the watchman's cubbyhole at the back. Drive straight ahead without lights and pull up near the large door at the back."

Inside the marble halls of the building an elderly watchman in striped overalls made his rounds, punching his clock at regular stations along the dimly lit corridors. It was about twelve-thirty and time for him to lunch. He punched in the last station, went back among the glassed-in cases to his little room at the back, sat down on a bench in a corner, and opened his dinner pail.

As he ate, a new sound suddenly obtruded itself. The watchman paused, cocking an intent ear to listen. Again it came—a faint clicking from in back. He could not recognize the sound, for he could not guess that it was made as Flash probed the vitals of the locked door with an instrument as delicate and as specialized as those used by a brain surgeon. Already Flash had located the wires of the alarm system and burned them out with a torch.

The watchman put down his lunch and hurried out into the main building again, padding along with revolver in hand. He slipped through a room whose walls were covered with modern paintings and into the hallway leading to the back. He had almost reached the rear door when a menacing voice came from somewhere behind him.

"Just drop the roscoe, pal, like a good guy."

The watchman whirled, making one single motion to lift his gun. He never got it up. The big .38 Police Special in the hand of the determined man who had spoken, rose and fell against his skull. The watchman's muffled cry was cut short, and the man who had attacked him caught him as he slumped.

He shoved the bleeding watchman to two other men who appeared dimly in the shadows.

"Take him back to his place and stay with him," he ordered gruffly. "If he wakes up whack him over the head again. Flash, get a couple of those Chinese to give you a hand with your cutting outfit. According to one of the guys who shows the rubbernecks around, the vault is downstairs. Come on."

THE TWO mobsters each took the watchman by a wrist and began dragging his limp form back along the polished floor. Flash directed two of the husky Chinese to pick up the huge, heavy suitcases containing his acetylene and oxygen tanks. He himself carried the torch and it was no ordinary one. It had cost him exactly two thousand dollars.

Down two dark flights of steps the party moved cautiously and silently. Bringing up the rear were several Chinese carrying ordinary canvas stretchers. Once they stopped and held flashlights while Flash knelt before a door and inserted an instrument into the lock. After a few moments' expert manipulation it clicked. They went down still another flight into a vault room deep beneath the earth's surface.

One of the Chinese who made up one half of the queerly assorted group looked dubious at sight of the massive door of the vault with its chilled steel. Flash saw the look, and chuckled, low in his throat.

"Sure, it's burglar-proof, pal, but don't worry," he said, and grinned broadly. "It takes heat to make steel burglar-proof, maybe you know. So all you got to do to cut it is to get something hotter. That's why this torch cost me two thousand slugs. It was made in Berlin by a screwy little professor. One of them scientific birds."

"You are quite sure the alarm system has been disconnected?" the Chinese who appeared to be in charge of his coterie asked uncertainly.

"He knows his business, buddy," growled a burly gangster impatiently. "Hurry up, Flash, and get that toy of yours busy."

The "expert" put on goggles, stuffed cotton plugs into his ears, adjusted the two gauges to more than four times the ordinary pressure on the short red and green hoses, and snapped a flint lighter to the torch. Yellow flame lashed out, then shortened, giving way to a blue light with such hissing intensity that it grated painfully into eardrums, like steel scraped across glass.

While the others stood around with palms over their ears Flash Mega, who long ago had gained a reputation with the police for the facility with which he could handle just such a situation, set to work with the torch. Steel that would withstand the bite of an ordinary flame as though it were nothing but a lighted match soon began to gin way as the torch ate viciously into metal. The white-hot stuff bubbled and foamed and ran down to splatter on the concrete floor in molten drops. For five minutes the cracksman worked the torch in a circular motion that ate a three-inch-wide hole deeper and deeper into metal.

Only an expert welder could have cut such a hole more than six inches deep into metal, due to back heat melting the tip of the torch. Yet presently the flame ate through, started a circular cut around the spokes of the vault door handle, and completed it. Flash shut off the torch, picked up a tiny crowbar that was almost a jimmy, pried loose the mechanism, and let it crash to the floor, leaving a gaping hole two feet in diameter.

The laundryman who had been so dubious stared in disbelief. Flash had cut through eighteen inches of solid burglar-proof steel! The cracksman grinned at Chow Seto, the Chinese who on other occasions than this was known as an innocuous laundryman, but said nothing.

The vault door swung open, and the master cracksman packed up his outfit. Chow Seto, followed by the others, went inside the vault. Several small crates were stacked in a corner. The bespectacled Chinese laundryman took a single look at the contents of one, then nodded to the others.

"This is it, gentlemen," he announced. "In these boxes we have a treasure worth approximately ten to eleven million dollars."

A BIG mobster who had been called Joe—Joe Mega, the brother of the expert Flash—gave a harsh laugh as he bent and picked up a green object from a box. It was of corroded bronze.

"A ceremonial vase of the Shang Dynasty, seventeen hundred and sixty-six to eleven hundred and twenty-two years before the coming of Christ," informed Chow Seto blandly. "One of the few things I learned at Columbia University before finding out that the—ah—laundry business pays better than a knowledge of the value of things of great antiquity."

"You mean to tell me that dopes pay millions for this junk?" demanded Joe in disbelief, juggling the precious vessel up and down in his hands. "Well, pal, it's a good thing the Duke didn't put me wise when I cased this joint for him or I'da told him he was nuts!"

Chow Seto almost winced as he quickly took the treasure from the hood's careless hands. He delivered rapid orders in Cantonese and the men brought in the stretchers. Quickly and efficiently the Orientals picked up the small crates and placed them on the stretchers to carry to the waiting trucks. In that treasure were altar pieces from the Sixth Century, a T'ang filigree gold crown once worn by an empress. Sung paintings on silk that rolled up like papyrus, delicate white Ting Yao pottery, and other antiques for which a collector would have sold his soul. Case after case was carried up the stairs and outside, where it was loaded into the guarded trucks.

Two of the mobsters were the last to come out of the building. They climbed into a truck and Joe's voice called to them from the front sharply:

"What about that watchman, Manni?"

"You never did know your own strength, Joe," came the laconic reply from the gangster called Manni, who among his intimates—and to the police—was known as Manni Torrio. "The guy's dead, Joe—that's all."

The trucks got under way, leaving behind a gaping back door. Silence descended over the place that had become a hall of death for an elderly watchman whose only crime had been that he had tried to fulfill his duty. The Dragon had struck!

CHAPTER II

THE DRAGON STRIKES AGAIN

THREE QUARTERS of an hour later the trucks were back at the place from which they had started. One of the Orientals knocked on the back door of the house beside the alleyway, and it was opened shortly by an elderly Chinese. Low orders were voiced and again the Orientals got busy.

Within short minutes the door had swallowed up crates, stretchers, and men. Chow Seto's two trucks rolled out and departed. The Chinese gunman himself, however, did not accompany them.

Inside the building the six American gangsters made their way along an ordinary passage where ancient boards creaked underfoot. The art collection had been taken away hurriedly, ahead of them. The aged Chinese led them through a door and down a flight of steps and along still another passage, the musty air of the catacombslike place filling their lungs, half choking them.

The narrow way was lit by a dim electric light bulb over another door. This door, the trained eyes of the mobsters saw at once was made of steel.

"Where's Chow?" asked Flash, before they reached the door. "I thought he was with us."

"Search me," Joe growled, and shrugged.

In front of the steel door the party came to a halt in a single file while the aged Oriental reached out a foot, unseen, and pressed twice on a thin, purposely warped board. Beneath that board was an electric button that sounded a buzzer inside. Two rings would cause that door to open. But woe to him who stood before it unaware that his weight was sounding a warning that an enemy was without!

For a moment nothing was heard except the rasping breathing of the men standing in the cramped, musty passage, with heads bent to

The Black Bat

avoid scraping the rafters above. Then, there came a metallic click as an electrically operated bolt was withdrawn and the door swung inward.

Flash, directly behind the aged Chinese, gave a muffled gasp of admiration as he peered over the old man's head.

Standing demurely with hands tucked in the sleeves of her embroidered pink silk Oriental costume was a Chinese girl of breath-taking beauty! About nineteen or twenty, Flash quickly judged.

"The Dragon Master welcomes the new members, Dragons," she said in English, and in a cultured voice. "You will follow me."

She turned and led the way.

"Get a load of that baby, Joe," Flash Mega muttered to his brother over his shoulder. "But hands off her! She's mine."

"Nix," his burly brother grunted, scowling. "It's bad enough to take a blood oath in a damn Chinese secret society without you muffin' the works by fallin' for a good-looking dame. You go monkeying around with her and you'll get in trouble. Dames and business don't mix. You know what Duke's orders are—keep our mouths shut and obey the orders of this Dragon Master guy we're goin' to see."

The mobsters followed the girl down a short flight of broad stone steps into the basementlike room, which was some forty-five or fifty feet square. Its floor was two stories below street level—and stepping into that room was like stepping into another world.

The place was decorated like a secret worship room in some ancient palace of old China. Rich drapes of Oriental splendor hung from the walls and thick rugs of untold value covered the concrete floor. There were no chairs. With a wave of her hand the girl directed the mobsters to sofas.

There were at least thirty Chinese present, as well as some Americans, though Chow Seto and the group of Chinese who had been in the trucks were missing. Some of the Chinese men were young, with American haircuts, and wearing American clothes. These Orientals held various positions in private homes, in cafes, and in laundries and art shops throughout the city. Others were little shopkeepers in Chinatown, and they wore the raiment that was their ancient heritage. And one Oriental's horny hands proclaimed him a farmer who had come from outside the city.

FLASH MEGA'S black eyes watched speculatively as the girl moved lightly across the room toward other broad stone steps leading up to an opening in the drapes. Joe saw the look on the face of his brother, and quickly realized its import.

"Lay off, Flash!" he growled again, jabbing a sharp elbow. "Dames are gonna get you in plenty trouble some of these days."

The girl who held Flash Mega's attention to the exclusion of all else crossed the room and ascended the short flight of steps. Here was a sort of stone altar surmounted by a carved dragon's head, in whose two eyes glowed two tiny red electric bulbs. The girl disappeared through the drapes.

The red bulbs forming the dragon's eyes above the men blinked three times and it grew quiet in the smoke-filled room, the sing-song Cantonese of the Orientals instantly dying down: The drapes parted again and a man stepped through, bowing low in obeisance to the dragon altar, his long-nailed hands outstretched. Robes of green silk covered him from neck to the floor, and a weird green mask in the shape of a dragon's head concealed his features.

He straightened and his eyes surveyed the silent watchers below. When he spoke it was in a curiously high-pitched voice.

"I am the Dragon Master," he intoned. "Tonight the Dragon has performed a great service. Recently there was brought to this country from China certain priceless works of art to the value of many millions of dollars. The money was to be used as a war chest to buy badly needed airplanes for our country in her fight against an aggressor.

"Eight bankers and other financiers looked over the collection, and then formed what was known as 'Eight Incorporated' for the purpose of purchasing the treasure. However, these financiers quickly became victims of their own greed. Their art experts appraised the treasure at only eight millions of dollars, instead of the ten or eleven millions suggested as their worth by Dr. Ling, whose ability to fix an evaluation cannot be doubted."

The figure in green paused. Flash Mega spoke to his brother in an aside. His lips did not move, and his narrowed eyes were intent on the Dragon Master.

"That guy's voice is disguised, Joe—I'd lay a bet on it. There's something familiar about it, too. You reckon that's why Duke ain't here? You reckon it's him playing this Dragon business? Or do you think that the guy in that green thing is Chow Seto?"

He got an elbow jab and a surly, low-voiced growl for an answer, and the Dragon Master went on.

"It was then that I enlisted the services of our new American members," the high-pitched voice droned. "Tonight, with the aid of these new brothers, we have done the impossible. We have taken the treasure from a vault that was impregnable, and we will hold it until these evil eight are made to realize their foolhardiness. We shall again demand that ten millions in cash immediately be raised for its return, the money eventually to be paid over to proper representatives of the Chinese Government."

"Just supposing they call your bluff like they did on the first note, pal?" put in Flash Mega, a disdainful grin crossing his face. Flash was not the sort to be impressed even by this pageantry before him.

"You underestimate the new society of which you are now a blood brother, Dragon," the Dragon Master said coldly. "Of course they again will refuse. So I have planned accordingly. They must be given proof that the Dragons mean business. Already I have selected the—shall we say victim?—whose ultimate fate will bring them to their senses. In this city lives one of the evil eight—a blind man who once was a district attorney. One Tony Quinn by name. He lives alone in his mansion with a single man servant. Perhaps you have heard of him?"

A snarling, bitter curse rumbled deep in Joe Mega's heavy chest. Rage sent the dark red blood into his swarthy face, and his merciless eyes blazed.

"I oughta know the damned district attorney!" he shouted. "He sent two of the mob up the river before his eyes were put out by acid thrown at him. One of the guys was a special pal of mine. Duke's got it in for him, too—been swearing to get even with Quinn ever since!"

A chuckle came from the Dragon Master, though there was nothing pleasant in the sound.

"I think Duke need not trouble himself to seek revenge any longer. That will be done for him most efficiently, and you two may come along to witness it. As you possibly know, when the collection first was appraised, Harvey Belmont and the other men comprising Eight Incorporated presented Quinn with a little green jade Buddha in appreciation of certain of his former public services. It seems that he had broken up a gang attempting to blackmail Mr. Belmont and some of his friends. Tomorrow morning Quinn's body will be found, his neck broken and the jade Buddha beside him. Wrapped around the Buddha will be a note with our demands that unless the full ten millions, on which they first agreed, is paid at once, that the others will suffer a like fate."

"Supposing they don't come up with the dough?" put in Manni Torrio, also dubious.

"Then one by one the financiers whose greed was responsible for what has happened tonight will die violently and at once," the Dragon Master said without a single change in the monotone of his voice.

"Listen, pal," Flash Mega sneered, "I'm with you to the limit, and I sure want to be present when that ex-district attorney goes on his last ride. But don't go getting any foolish ideas about Commissioner Warner and his cops. One false move on your part and we'll all end up doing a Chinese fandango in the hot squat."

The Dragon Master did not answer that, but clapped his long-nailed hands twice.

"Observe!" he intoned.

THE DRAPES behind him parted and the most astounding person the mob had ever set eyes upon waddled through on dwarfed, crooked legs!

The man—or was he actually man?—was a Chinese not more than four and one half feet in height, yet weighing a full one hundred and sixty pounds. His pinhead with its huge ears was shaved slick until it glistened, except for a tiny topknot of black hair. The creature had no neck. Only a lump of muscle that looked to be as hard as iron was humped at the base of the small, bullet-shaped skull. It disappeared into shoulders that were a mass of muscle. The arms were abnormally long, almost touching the floor.

The brown monstrosity was stripped to the waist, the dwarfed legs being encased in black silk knee trousers cut short at the huge, knotted calves. No shoes were on the huge, twisted feet. Something in the set of the grotesque and misshapen body with the long dangling arms was remindful of a giant chimpanzee. The abnormality looked about with a pair of keen, intelligent, close-set eyes and then up at the Dragon Master.

"This is Ohmo," announced the man in green. "Do not be misled by his looks, for he is a most valuable asset to us. Ohmo is a mute and understands no English. He is quite harmless if left alone, but will blindly obey any order given by me."

"I get it!" The cracksman grinned, then laughed aloud. "You're sending this guy to pay a call on that ex-district attorney, huh?"

"He will be taken to pay a call on the honorable ex-district attorney," corrected the Dragon blaster. "The rest of you Dragons will return to your respective positions throughout the city, unless you"—he looked directly at Flash Mega—"care to go along. For the rest of you, there is much work to be done. One Dragon already has his full instructions which will be carried out upon word from his Dragon Master. That particular Dragon will know who I mean, for he serves as personal servant to Harvey Belmont. That is all. You may go."

He spoke in Cantonese to the pinheaded monstrosity and it waddled back out of sight on short, bowed legs. The Dragon Master then stepped back a single step, bowed low to the altar again, with his long-nailed hands outstretched, and disappeared through the curtains.

The Dragon Master was gone.

CHAPTER III

MONSTER IN THE NIGHT

I **N THE** well equipped gymnasium of his home that evening Tony Quinn, stripped to a pair of white trunks, stood locked toe to toe, and struggled with all his strength to break the hold of the man whose clean-shaven head gleamed under the ceiling light. The man's underslung, aggressive jaw was clamped tight and nothing could be heard but the harsh breathing of the two struggling men. Then the former district attorney relaxed and let his weight sag.

There was a final grunt, a heave, and at the moment Quinn stopped long enough to get a fresh breath he unexpectedly went sailing through the air to land with a thud on the thick wrestling mat.

"How did that happen?" he complained, as he sat up, looking startled.

Jack "Butch" O'Leary, his wrestling mate, straightened his massive shoulders and grinned at the ludicrous look of surprise on Quinn's face.

Silk

"That's what you get for not shifting your weight like I've been drumming into you, Boss," he said, chuckling. The result was no surprise to a former boxer like O'Leary. "Just another case of keeping one jump ahead of your opponent," he said offhandedly. "Or, as you've heard it said—Jack Dempsey's famous remark, remember?—not forgetting to duck. You learn that in boxing as well as wrestling. Sorry I had to pull that one on you, Boss, but it'll teach you never to be off guard. You've learned fast."

"I've learned enough for this evening, anyhow, Butch," Quinn said, snapping upright in a flip-up. "As a ju-jutsu teacher you're tops. Anyway, it passes the time, doesn't it? Not much else to do. It's been pretty quiet lately."

"Quite right, sir," put in Silk Norton, Quinn's ever-ready right-hand man, valet and confidante, who had been standing by quietly watching the lessons in the ancient Japanese art of ju-jutsu. "For myself, I'm satisfied. There have been plenty of times since I've been trying to master this rather strenuous avocation of ours when I've almost wished for the peace of my former profession."

Quinn smiled at that, for before Silk Norton's reformation the little man had been a safe cracker *par excellence*.

Quinn was still smiling as he got into the glassed-in shower, watching his unconventional valet lay out blue silk pajamas and a red silk dressing gown. The little ex-confidence man who, hungry and desperate, had come in the night to rob him and had remained to become a faithful valet and valued friend would no more be content to play a role of idleness when it came to facing the foes of law and order than the others who made up the former district attorney's little circle. Beneath that high, bald forehead and the air of general slipperiness that exuded from him lay a keen brain that loved excitement. More than a score of times that brain had proved a valuable asset to Quinn in the strange role Fate had destined him to play.

Quinn turned on the water. Seen under the flying spray his body was not strikingly muscular, but it was tall and well built. Strength and speed were packed into the supple lines that were deceptive.

To the world that knew about him, Anthony Quinn, once a virile, upstanding representative of law forces whose name had held terror for evil doers, was now an impotent blind man whose sight had been permanently destroyed by acid thrown at him in a crowded courtroom, and whose face was horribly scarred about the eyes. Day by day he could be seen tapping his way about the grounds of his estate or along the street near his home, sometimes led by the faithful Silk.

But for a long time he had seemed to live in a world apart. To those who paused long enough to give him a fleeting thought, the former brilliant and public servant appeared to be a retiring man hiding himself from the world and his former friends because of deep disgust with life and sensitiveness over his affliction.

SUCH ACTUALLY had been the case during the long months when Tony Quinn had lived in a sea of blackness. But Nature had been as kind as possible, giving him something in return for what had been taken from him. As a result he had since realized that his senses of feel, smell, and hearing were far more acute than formerly. Under his sensitive fingers whatever he touched had begun to tell strange new stories. His sense of smell had sharpened. His ears had become the ears of a hound, picking up with ease and sifting multitudinous sounds that once had been inaudible.

More months had gone by until, in the darkness of a lonely night, a girl with golden hair and blue eyes had come in through an open window like an angel out of nowhere to offer him hope where eye specialists had said there was no hope. Through a delicate operation by an unknown small town surgeon the corneas of the eyes of Carol Baldwin's policeman father—dying from paralysis brought on by a gangster bullet—had been given to him.

An extraordinary thing had occurred. When at last Tony Quinn had been allowed to remove the bandages he had been astounded by the miracle that had happened. His were the eyes of darkness as well as the eyes of day!

His were the eyes of a—black bat!

Because he had recognized this himself it had given the former district attorney the inspiration for his life work. And now the name of the Black Bat that he had taken for himself in a self-imposed crusade against crime had become almost legendary. By night he had become that figure of terror to the underworld—the Black Bat who prowled wherever evil stalked, and met it on its own grounds.

Unhampered by the red tape that tied the hands of men who were sworn to preserve law and order, and with professional ethics of his former position shuffled off, he had become a shadowy Nemesis of crime who brought panic to the underworld. Gangsters who long had been waxing fat and rich behind the protection of high-priced lawyers found themselves unprotected and at the mercy of a terrible avenger who, unknown and often unseen, fought them tooth and nail. The Black Bat met threat by action, intimidation by retaliation.

Quinn, fresh and virile, with nothing physical to indicate that he was the Black Bat, came out of his shower, dressed, and went into the living room to his favorite chair by the open fireplace. The damp, early summer night was warm and Silk Norton had pulled back the heavy drapes and opened the French windows to let in the night's damp coolness. After Butch O'Leary, the other man of the trio who were Tony Quinn's two closest personal allies, had gone out through the secret tunnel to his boarding house a few blocks away, the slippery little valet came in carrying a glass of cold milk.

"Could I get you anything else, sir?" he asked, as he handed it to the supposedly blind man.

Silk was about forty, and a master at makeup and voice imitation. His perfect imitation of Quinn's voice more than once had fooled Captain McGrath, of Homicide, when the keen policeman, long suspicious that Quinn was the Black Bat, had phoned while the Black Bat was on the prowl.

"You can bring the new book on Chinese art you got for me, Silk," answered Quinn, setting down the empty glass. "I've become quite interested in the subject. I'm going to read a few hours before turning in."

"Very good, sir."

Silk brought the book from the library and then retired on noiseless feet, seeming to glide from the room. Quinn settled himself deeper into his chair to read into the small hours of the morning, as was his custom.

The house grew deadly quiet. Midnight came and still Quinn read on. From somewhere off in the night came the faint, gloomy boom of a clock striking two.

QUINN DID not quite know when the first foreign sounds penetrated his sensitive ears and told him he was not alone in the room. But the half raised book suddenly slid down beside him in the chair. At the same time there came a strange human smell to his sensitive nostrils.

Then a huge hand reached over the back of the chair as he ducked and shot up, wheeling to face a sight that sent the hair raising itself along the nape of his neck.

Standing at the back of his chair was a grotesque caricature of a human being, naked to the waist, and looking like some abysmal brute out of the Neanderthal Age. Its glistening pinhead was sunk deep between the enormously wide shoulders like the sharp, slick head of a monster sea turtle protruding from its shell. A Chinese, undoubtedly, Quinn saw at that first swift glance, and the horrible being had paused for a split second, the green jade Buddha he had taken from another room clutched in one of the creature's oversized hands. But only for a split second.

Now, as Quinn faced it, the Thing dropped the Buddha and sprang through the air like a giant chimpanzee!

Quinn's right foot unconsciously had sought the cleverly hidden light switch that Butch had placed under the edge of the carpet for just such an emergency. His slippered foot clicked out the lights and plunged the room into darkness.

And the moment the lights went out Tony Quinn, ex-district attorney, became the Black Bat!

He flung himself sideward as the Thing cleared the distance separating them. It struck the exact spot where he had stood, a faint whistling sound emanating from its nostrils as it landed. He guessed then that the monster was a mute. It wheeled to pounce again upon its prey but the prey had become a flitting shadow. The Bat melted into the folds of the drapes, against the wall.

The Thing's keen ears, however, caught the faint rustle inaudible to ordinary human ears and it whirled, leaping toward the spot. This time it caught its quarry. A hand with fingers like steel prongs closed over the Bat's wrist and crushed down. The bones almost gave way under the pressure. Quinn had not called for help—it had all happened too swiftly. Besides, the lessons Butch had so painstakingly taught him during the past weeks were standing him in good stead.

He let his weight sag against that of his attacker for a moment, just as Butch had done earlier in the evening. An arm shot out at the deformed body. Then, in the pitch darkness of the room, there was a flurry of bodies, that faint whistling sound from the mute thug again, and the Thing hit the floor flat on its back with a jar that shook the house.

Such a terrific fall would have knocked the wind from an ordinary human and broken its grasp, but the monster's steel-banded fingers encircling the Bat's wrist only clamped down the harder—crushed until the bones threatened to crack. A moan of pain burst from the Bat's lips and he opened them to shout. But before he could call out, the Thing's other hand shot out from the floor and grabbed his ankle with the same crushing force. The hand jerked, and the Bat went down. His wrist was released and a paralyzing blow that almost broke his neck caught him just below the ear.

Ju-jutsu!

The whole world spun crazily before Quinn's pain-filled eyes. He was lifted as though he had been a child and thrown across the Thing's shoulders. As agilely as a monkey the Oriental monstrosity went out through the open French window to the ground, carrying the jade Buddha clasped in one huge hand.

It set off at a rocking run across the grounds, and even in his half paralyzed state, Tony Quinn found himself amazed that even a half human Thing like this, with such short, bowed legs, could move so fast. It slipped through the shrubbery, peered furtively about the dimly lit street, then loped on with its human burden across a back lot. Presently a large laundry truck loomed up near a row of trees.

A MAN got out from under the wheel and stepped to the ground as Quinn was carried to the truck. There was something vaguely familiar about this man but, half-dazed as Quinn was, it eluded his memory at the moment. And when still another man got out of the rear of the truck, his looks also touched some chord of recognition uncertainly.

Then the ex-district attorney had it—when he saw the diamonds! These two were the notorious gangsters Flash Mega and his brother Joe! He had reason to remember them only too well during the time he had been in office—and to know the leader of the gang to which they belonged. "Duke" Kasini! For some reason Quinn had been kidnaped by a Chinese thug who was being aided by members of Kasini's big mob!

Flash chuckled softly in the darkness as he held open the doors of the truck for Quinn to be carried inside. Not for a moment did one of those over-sized hands of the distorted Oriental relax its grip on the captive's pinioned ones, and in them was the strength of a gorilla's hands. The Thing straddled his captive on the floor of the truck, looking inquiringly toward the muffled figure in green silk robes sitting on a seat near the front. The Dragon Master—though Tony Quinn could not yet know that. He did, however, recognize the man's speech when he murmured his approval in Cantonese.

"Master," Flash Mega said with a chuckle, "I take off my hat to this monkey man of yours. But he didn't kill him—yet—did he?"

"Ohmo never disobeys the orders of the Dragon Master," the man addressed intoned, in a curiously high-pitched voice. "I ordered him to bring this man alive, that you might witness but one of the many things I have taught him. Now, to the City Hall."

Joe Mega got back under the wheel. The creature now identified by the name, Ohmo, held Quinn in a deadly grip as those steel-banded fingers held his pinioned wrists as in a vise. As the truck eased away into the early morning darkness Quinn's bat eyes saw the Dragon Master take a piece of paper from his green robes and wrap it around the jade Buddha, snapping it snug with a rubber band. A note that probably would be left beside his body, Quinn knew instinctively.

For Tony Quinn was certain that Kasini and his mob, joining up with some kind of a secret society of thugs, had helped kidnap him only because they meant to leave him dead on the steps of the City Hall, or somewhere nearby.

Those two gangsters had good reasons for wishing him dead. Quinn well realized that. During his term as district attorney he had prosecuted hood after hood and sent them up the river. Some of the men had talked. Among things Quinn had learned was that Duke Kasini made regular trips to China to buy huge shipments of opium and smuggle it in by way of Marseilles and other European ports. He was well known in Shanghai where he worked hand in glove with dealers in the poppy.

Of course this information had been passed along to the Federal Bureau of Narcotics at Washington, but nothing had come of it to date, though men had been working on the tip assiduously. Knowing that a man was guilty, and securing enough concrete evidence to bring him to trial were two entirely different things.

The truck jolted on, working its way by devious side streets toward City Hall. Quinn had not moved. By now Flash had climbed over into the front seat beside his brother. And by now the grip on Tony Quinn's pinioned wrists had relaxed a trifle.

Joe Mega turned around then in the front seat, and spoke to the sinister figure in green.

"The City Hall's just around the block," he said. "But I still think—" and the mobster, callous murderer that he was, suppressed a slight shiver—"that a roscoe would do the job better. I don't mind bumpin' guys off, but that ape gives me the creeps."

The laundry truck swung sharply around a corner, swaying. The Dragon Master spoke in Cantonese to the half naked Chinese still astride Quinn's pajama-clad body. Quinn moved then. He snapped up and heaved hard, grabbing at the jade Buddha beside the green-robed leader. As Ohmo fell sideward and turned like a cat, the jade piece in Quinn's hand smashed him alongside his shaved head. He fell like a log.

"Look out," yelled Flash Mega. "The guy's blind, but he's dangerous!"

His gun came up, but Quinn already had made a headlong dive and landed atop both Flash and his brother, at the wheel. The gun went clattering. Joe Mega fell over the wheel and the truck lurched wildly, smashing a front fender against a street light standard. The impact threw open the left door just as Quinn grabbed at the handle. He fell out over Mega, tumbling headlong to the pavement. He caught a brief flash of concrete coming up, heard the sudden wail of a siren as a police car shot into view down the street, and then stars exploded in his brain.

He was still sprawled unconscious on the pavement in his silk dressing gown, with the jade Buddha beside him, when more police cars and an ambulance arrived. In one of the cars were Police Commissioner Warner and Captain McGrath, of Homicide.

CHAPTER IV

DRAGON MASTER'S ULTIMATUM

AT TEN o'clock the following morning three police cars conveying two black limousines drew up in front of the curb at Tony Quinn's estate. A number of men, including two Chinese, got out of the two shiny machines and came up the walk to the house, followed by the uniformed police who stopped to wait outside on guard when the others entered. Two more policemen patrolled the grounds.

Silk opened the front door and ushered the visitors into the spacious sitting room hung with heavy, expensive drapes.

"How's Tony, Silk?" asked rugged, gray-haired Commissioner Warner as the valet murmured for them to be seated.

A worried frown crossed the little man's sharp, pointed face.

"A very bad fall he had, sir. But he's managed to get out of bed to see you and give you more details of his unfortunate experience. Permit me to thank you, sir, on my own account for such quick action on the part of the police after I heard the commotion and discovered that he was missing."

Silk disappeared and Captain McGrath, always suspicious of Tony Quinn, whom he firmly believed, but could not prove, to be the Black Bat, let his eyes rove around the room as he reached for a cigar. McGrath was beefy-faced, and heavy-shouldered, with the tenacity of a bulldog. Duty was a fetish with him, and it was for this reason that he was determined, sooner or later, to catch Tony Quinn red-handed at his night-prowling activities, much as he liked the man. But such was Captain McGrath's stern creed that, had such evidence to warrant it been placed in his hands, he would have arrested his own brother for an infringement of the law as quickly as he would run in the lowest criminal in town.

"Maybe he's not hurt as bad as he's letting on," the captain grunted, biting off the end of the cigar. "The ambulance surgeon said it was only a bad lick on the head."

Before Commissioner Warner could answer, Quinn, guided by his valet, came in, tapping his way with a cane. From beneath the white bandage on his head his dead-looking eyes stared lifelessly ahead like two pools of colored glass. His face was pale and drawn—thanks to some ministration on the part of the clever Silk, though the visitors would never have guessed this. He looked ready to collapse, though waving away Warner's apologies for having brought him out of bed in this condition.

"By all means don't discourage the captain, Commissioner," he added, his voice weak and uncertain as he almost collapsed into a chair. "By the way, did he buy that rubber reducing belt I suggested?"

A LAUGH at McGrath's expense went around the room. His rapidly expanding middle was as sore a spot in his mind as his corns sometimes were to his feet. He bit down viciously on the unlit cigar.

"Go ahead and laugh," he growled. "But here's something you won't laugh off. I'm betting a month's pay that, after last night's little affair—

you getting slugged right after we get news about that big museum being robbed of millions—that the Black Bat goes into action again."

Commissioner Warner had already briefly informed Quinn of that huge robbery, in which Quinn himself had a personal interest, since he was a member of Eight Incorporated who had contracted to buy it.

"And I'm betting another month's pay," the captain added grimly, "that this time I slap the cuffs on him. Any takers?"

"Captain, this is too good for an invalid to miss, so I'll take both bets," answered Quinn, smiling wanly. "And now, Commissioner, what can a helpless blind man do to help you gentlemen?"

Warner made the introductions, presenting the two Chinese first. Colonel Wang was thin, bespectacled, an army officer who appeared to speak but little English and this brokenly. His object in coming to America was twofold, he had told the commissioner, who relayed the information. He had accompanied the fabulous treasure that had been brought to this country from China a month before, so that its sale should help the Chinese Government to purchase more guns, ammunition and planes. The Chinese colonel had been in charge of the armed Chinese guards who had guarded it with their lives. His second mission here was to select and test-hop the military planes that were to be bought and shipped back to China.

Professor Ling, the other Chinese, was a scholarly-looking little man in high white collar and business suit. With his wispy gray mustache and thin chin whiskers he looked much like a masquerading Mandarin patriarch who would have felt more at home in heavily embroidered robes of state. He owned an art antique shop in Chinatown and at one time had been curator of Eastern arts at the museum where the collection had been stolen.

Walter Dugro, one of the American visitors, was still tanned and rugged in spite of his fifty or so years. Some time before, he had taken over a bankrupt light plane factory and reorganized the business for the production of military planes. It was his deadly new experimental twin-engined bomber that Colonel Wang had been putting through its paces.

Warner introduced Paul Chivor next. About thirty-five or so, affable, and a flying soldier-of-fortune, Chivor was a handsome man who appeared to be well educated, cultured, and who spoke Cantonese fluently. For the most part he acted as interpreter for Colonel Wang.

Naturally Quinn knew the four bankers. Harvey Belmont, thin and aristocratic, was their recognized leader, and the others were Thompson, Harrison and Heffner. When Quinn had been district attorney he had broken up a blackmail gang that had tried to swindle them, though he

Carol

had small personal liking for any of them. They were all too eager for profit.

Quinn himself had wanted them to pay the full ten millions for the treasure, even though he had intended to turn over any excess profits he should make from the transaction to the Chinese Government when the treasure later would be sold for a still higher figure.

That was all an aside now, in Tony Quinn's mind, for his attention was on Commissioner Warner whose chief interest, at present, was in what had happened to the former district attorney the night before.

"First of all, Tony," the commissioner said, "you weren't in condition to tell coherently what happened when we brought you home at four this morning. So I'd like you to relate everything now to McGrath and myself."

He took from his pocket the green jade Buddha and put it on the table.

TONY QUINN could have told more the night before, had he cared to. He had deliberately declined to do so for two reasons. He wanted McGrath to think he was more badly hurt than he was, and he had wanted these men to come here, just as they now had come.

He told again of the attack, but omitted certain details. He did describe how he had been carried, half paralyzed, on a pair of naked shoulders to the truck from which he had eventually escaped. But he made no mention of having recognized his kidnapers. Despite the fact that the

Bat usually made every possible effort to coöperate with the police to the fullest, he felt on this occasion he was justified in withholding this information. To give it would be to invite a renewed attempt on his life. He wanted the killer mob to feel secure for the moment.

He told of overhearing their plans, however, of happening to grasp the Buddha in his struggle with the thug, and of his blind dive toward the front of the truck in a desperate effort to cause a smash-up. The bulldog McGrath interrupted.

"How'd you know which end of the truck was the front?" he demanded suspiciously. "You were struggling with this ape Thing and you say you were confused—"

"McGrath," gritted Warner in downright anger, "this is the last straw. I've warned you time and again that my patience would run out. Well, this morning, you're going on a plainclothes beat in Chinatown to direct the dragnet of officers down there—captain or not. We'll see how your feet like that for a while."

"But, Commissioner," interceded Tony Quinn, wanting the Homicide captain any place except down there, "please don't be so harsh on the captain. I'm sure he means nothing personal."

But Warner stood pat.

"And now, gentlemen," he said to the others around him, "you again see what you're up against. Naturally we're making every effort to recover the treasure. Suspects at the rate of nearly a hundred an hour are being brought in by the police dragnet. So far we've found nothing, nor do I expect to. After reading the note from this Dragon society which has been defiant enough to admit they were responsible for the robbery, I know we're not up against amateurs.

"Whether or not you wish to pay the money they demand is your affair, though I advise against it. I brought you here to listen to Quinn's story, so you'll know the risk you're taking. It's plain enough to me he was kidnaped, as the most available of you members of Eight Incorporated, meaning to kill him to serve as an example to the rest of you what to expect, if you held out.

"It seems unbelievable that an up-to-the-date vault of burglar-proof steel has been cut open. But the fact remains that it has been, that the treasure is gone, and that the city, as owners of the museum, is responsible to the Chinese Government and its ambassador for several millions of dollars. And now, Tony, perhaps you would like to have me read that note for you."

He opened the note and read:

To Those Concerned: Honorable greetings and a final warning from the Dragon. You have been given one chance to pay to a beleaguered country the full value of the treasure, ten millions of dollars. You have been given one warning of what would happen should you fail to do so. Should the honorable morning papers carry the story that the guilty Eight Incorporated refuse our just demands, then others will suffer the Death of the Dragon before another day dawns. Your police protection will be of no avail.

The Dragon Master has spoken.

A short silence followed. Tony Quinn sat woodenly, his dead eyes in his bandaged head staring lifelessly into space. Finally McGrath spoke up again.

"Are you real sure you can't identify something about those guys— something they said or did?" he demanded. "You didn't by any chance feel a diamond as big as a coconut on the hand of one of them, did you?"

QUINN HAD to admire the tenacious officer. McGrath already had catalogued every cracksman in town who might have been able to have opened that supposedly impregnable vault. And a logical conclusion had been Flash Mega, always identifiable by his diamonds.

"If you're referring to Duke Kasini's mob, Captain," Quinn said, "it wouldn't hurt to look them up. Though I gather from what my valet has read to me that they've been laying low since Federal agents from the Narcotics Bureau recently confiscated nearly a quarter of a million dollars' worth of their opium aboard a tanker. As I understand it, however, it could not definitely be pinned on Duke as the man who had brought it in, so he was freed again."

Harvey Belmont spoke up then, twisting and gripping his thin fingers nervously. But the eyes that went to the worried police commissioner were stubbornly uncompromising.

"Gentlemen, I'm going to speak bluntly," he said. "My colleagues and myself—aside from Quinn—are business men, not philanthropists. As chairman of Eight Incorporated, I organized the concern for the purpose of buying the Chinese art collection and holding it for later sale under more favorable conditions. Naturally I'm upset that the city must be held responsible for the loss, since my colleagues and myself always have had an active hand in affairs of civic betterment. I, myself, arranged for the treasure to be placed in that particular vault, since everyone was certain it was entirely burglar-proof. It was a vault which, as most of you know, was willed to the city by one of my late business associates.

"But Dr. Ling, here, a foremost authority on Eastern arts, appraised the collection at a value of eight millions of dollars, in company with our own experts. I am still willing to go through with the agreement at that figure. But we are not paying the money to any secret society of thugs who cover their nefarious activities under the cloak of a comic opera name. How do we know we would ever get the collection back from them, for one thing?"

Dr. Ling spoke up then, nodding his wise head.

"Mr. Belmont is right. While the treasure is indeed worth two millions more under more favorable conditions, I advised the sale at the other figure in view of China's pressing need."

Belmont shot him a look tinged with irritation. In those few words the banker and the others had been revealed as men eager for a quick two millions in profits.

Thompson, however, nodded his bald head in agreement. He was a hump-shouldered man with discolored false plates of cheap make, and sat with his clammy hands clasped over his round little paunch. He wore cheap hand-me-down suits to save money and was notoriously a miser. He had objected strenuously to the others presenting the jade Buddha to Tony Quinn. Quinn could not see it anyhow, he had argued, so why waste the money it would bring?

"If the city wishes to gamble ten millions to get the treasure back, that's their business," he grumbled. "Anytime they do I'm still willing to go through with the original agreement to pay eight millions for it."

Warner's brow furrowed with anxiety. That meant a big loss to the city should the demands of this Dragon society have to be met. Of course, there would be the insurance, but it would nowhere near cover the two millions extra now demanded, and which would have to be met by the city. The morning newspapers already were howling at his heels like a hungry wolf pack, demanding that the thieves be caught. Two millions meant a great deal to already overburdened taxpayers. City editors were demanding to know a lot of things, especially who had been responsible for the collection being placed in the vault.

So was the mayor who, oddly enough, had not been consulted about its temporary disposal.

Warner had spent two weary hours in the chief city official's office before calling on Quinn. Publicly, the mayor could not countenance the paying of the ransom by Eight Incorporated, but privately he, as well as Commissioner Warner, was hoping that they would be frightened enough by the Dragons' threat to do so.

WALTER DUGRO, the plane manufacturer, had been sitting quietly, taking little part in the conversation. Now he spoke up.

"Well, gentlemen, this unfortunate affair is having repercussions in more ways than one. While it's true that the emergency bills for home defense which have been passed in Washington will soon set my factory to humming, the delay on this order for my new bomber will mean a lot to the employees now not working. Had this affair not come up, I had hoped that a quick approval of the new ship by Colonel Wang would set us to work on orders to a country I admire for defending herself against a ruthless aggressor.

McGrath

"But we have no proof that even after any monies are paid to this Dragon society, which professes to have purely patriotic motives, that the collection will be returned. I can only hope, however, that a solution will be reached soon. China is desperately in need of those planes, and my laid-off employees could use the work that will take them off Government relief rolls until other factories get into full swing."

They discussed the matter for another three quarters of an hour. Harvey Belmont and the other three members of Eight Incorporated were plainly a bit huffed that their business transaction, with its attendant two to three millions in quick profits, had been so openly discussed with outsiders. Quinn himself merely smiled, taking a passive attitude. His co-members were leaving the matter in Warner's hands, and demanding full police protection until the commissioner could wipe out the menace of the Dragon society and get back the treasure.

Most of the time Paul Chivor said nothing, though occasionally he bent over and conversed in Cantonese with Colonel Wang in a low voice.

Finally Thompson rose to his feet and reached for his hat where he had placed it on the table.

"I see no reason to waste further time," he said to Commissioner Warner a trifle coldly. "After all, this is your affair. Our position in the matter has been made quite clear. I shall tell the newspapers flatly that we are not paying a single cent to this group of thugs. Good day, gentlemen."

The others rose and went out too, after shaking hands with Quinn who had tried to rise but could not seem to make it. He sat with outstretched hand as each came by. McGrath was purposely last, sticking out his own powerful paw. But instead of taking Quinn's hand he merely held his own within an inch of it, hoping—as he did hope time after time—that he would get proof that the man he was certain was not blind would forget himself and clasp it.

But Tony Quinn's dead-looking eyes only stared straight ahead.

"Are they all gone, Silk?" he asked his valet.

Commissioner Warner answered from the doorway.

"Not all, Tony. There's still a stubborn jackass Homicide captain standing there hoping you'll see his hand—when he ought to know you're as blind as a bat."

"Yeah, a Black Bat," McGrath said significantly, following his harried superior. He turned in the doorway. "Y'know, Quinn, I'm kind of glad the chief put me on the Chinatown detail. I've got a hunch that's where the Black Bat will show. So long."

Silk closed the door and watched until he was sure that all had gone. Belmont, plainly worried that he might be a victim of the Dragon society, was driven away by his Chinese valet under police escort. Police also went with the others.

Then the nearly bald little man who posed as a valet turned to Quinn.

"I'm a little worried about McGrath this time, sir," Silk said. "With him in charge in Chinatown this afternoon he'll give every officer special orders to be on the lookout for the Black Bat."

"I wouldn't worry too much about it, Silk," Quinn said carelessly. "The police know quite well that there's a thousand to one chance of the collection being down there. That's probably the last place it would be taken. By nightfall they'll have all suspects picked up and questioned. It will be reasonably quiet in Chinatown by then—I hope."

"What now, sir?"

"Call in Butch and Carol through the tunnel."

HALF AN hour later the four of them sat together in a locked room. Silk was no longer the obsequious servant. He never was when attending such conferences, but gloried in being one of the Black Bat's trusted confidential allies. He sat comfortably in a big chair, with one of the highballs in which he occasionally indulged within easy reach.

Butch lounged in another chair and watched Quinn like a huge St. Bernard eyeing its master. Carol Baldwin, the golden-haired, blue-eyed girl who had brought back sight to a blind Tony Quinn, lay curled up like a soft young kitten on a nearby divan. Her face was filled with excitement.

"I think this calls for you to make the first move, Butch," Quinn was announcing to the former boxer. "First, I want you to study the pictures of Kasini's mob that I have in my private rogues' gallery. Take them along with you if necessary. Go down to Chinatown this afternoon and play the part of the panhandler around the laundries and cafes. You might possibly be able to spot the laundry truck used to kidnap me, though I doubt it. The lettering was, of course, false; as were the license plates. But even if you don't see it, you may be able to stumble onto something."

"And I?" asked Silk, sipping at his cold drink.

"With two policemen on the grounds, Silk, you'd better stick close to home. But you can get me Dr. Ling's home address. I may decide to call on him. Also get all the information you can on Paul Chivor—when he learned to fly, and all that. I'm not quite sure about him yet. He's a little too suave and quiet. As for you, Carol, you'll be in Chinatown, too—for a rendezvous with Butch and myself. And now for a little surprise."

He reached into a pocket of his smoking jacket and brought forth three little silver whistles. He tossed one each to the three. Carol picked hers up, examined it briefly, then blew experimentally.

No sound came forth, but across the room Quinn put a hand to his ear and rubbed it. Her face brightened instantly.

"Ah! So that's it, Tony? These whistles are pitched too high for the average human ear. I've heard of such things. They say that Doberman-Pinscher police dogs in service in foreign countries can hear these whistles up to three miles."

He nodded. "Good girl, Carol! You don't read for nothing, do you? Yes, Silk and I have been experimenting with these whistles for two weeks. During the long months when I couldn't see I had to depend upon my senses of feel, smell, and hearing, you know—especially my hearing. I was astounded to find my ears getting sharper and sharper until I've almost the uncanny hearing that is to be found among certain animals. That's why I can hear these whistles.

"I can't hear them as far as a keen-eared animal could, but I have been able to hear them, if repeated often enough, up to a distance of several blocks. It's a little idea of mine in case some of you need help. Your signal will be one blow on your whistle, Carol. Yours will be two blasts, Silk. And, Butch, if you get in a tight spot blow three times and keep on blowing. Conceal them on your persons in such a manner that no ordinary search will reveal them."

For more than an hour more the Black Bat discussed details of the crime which he hoped to solve. As he finished, the telephone rang. Silk answered.

"Just a moment, Commissioner," he murmured, "and I'll connect you with the phone in his bedroom."

Quinn went in and picked up the receiver.

"Tony," Warner's voice called, laughingly, "I didn't take that jade Buddha with me, but left it on the table."

"I'll ask Silk about it, Commissioner. If it's here—"

"No need to ask," came the chuckling reply. "That's why I called you up. Thompson took it. Picked it up under his hat when he left and showed it to me after we got out of the house. He says he feels it his 'duty' to return it to Dr. Ling until the collection is found, in view of recent events. I really couldn't ask the darned miser to return it, so I'm sure you'll understand."

"Quite. Think nothing of it, Commissioner."

Thompson was more of a miser than he had imagined, Quinn was thinking as he hung up, a smile touching his lips. But he was not giving up that jade gift so easily. The Black Bat was going to pay a visit to Dr. Ling's home above his art shop and collect a certain Buddha.

CHAPTER V

BUTCH BECOMES A PANHANDLER

D **OWN IN** Chinatown Butch moved along the narrow, crooked streets for a while to get the lay of the land, and then got busy. Fortunately—for the appearance he wished to create in his panhandler role—he had not shaved for a couple of days. That fact, and a touch of dirt that had been smudged into his whiskers gave him a decidedly unwashed appearance. He wore a cast-off suit that long ago had seen better days, and a ragged, crumpled cap.

Inside his coat pocket were the pictures he had been studying in Quinn's private "morgue," as such reference collections are called in newspaper offices. The ex-boxer was fully aware of his limited mental capacity and that he could scarcely depend on his unsupported memory, so was taking no chance of muffing such an important mission for the Black Bat.

He walked into an art shop, his homely face and aggressive, under-slung jaw making him look more than a mere panhandler. He looked positively frightening.

"Got a nickel for a cuppa cawfee, buddy?" he mumbled to the elderly Chinese proprietor.

The Chinese waved him out.

"Go 'way!" he shouted. "You get out or I call police."

Again and again the same thing happened. Butch was just beginning to congratulate himself on not being forced to beg for a living when a heavy hand fell on his shoulder from behind. He turned and looked into the glowering face of Homicide Captain McGrath, whose aching corns had not improved his acid temper any.

"Beat it," ordered the captain tersely. "We got a city flop-house for you guys. Don't let me catch you around here again or I'll run you in."

Butch mumbled apologetically—and obeyed by heading right around the corner to resume operations. He spotted the Chow Seto Laundry again just as a man got out of a cab up the street and entered the place. Butch recognized Joe Mega easily. The "panhandler" unhesitatingly followed him in.

Mega was talking in a low-voiced tone to a scholarly-looking Chinese wearing shell-rimmed glasses. Even Butch's slow-thinking mind had no difficulty in recognizing that Oriental as Chow Seto, whose pictured face was one of the photographs in the former boxer's pocket. On the counter between the gangster was a tin container with a slot cut in its sealed top. Printed on the can were the words:

PLEASE HELP THE CHINESE WOMEN AND CHILDREN
MADE HOMELESS BY THE WAR

As Butch came in he saw Joe Mega's fingers dropping a bright object into the can. A message of some kind, maybe.

Chow Seto looked up and saw Butch. It was the second time Butch had been in this place.

"Get out!" screamed the laundryman. "No comee back, I told you all same—"

"What's eating you, Chow?" demanded Mega of the Oriental. "Cut out the pidgin English with—"

Then he saw that the Chinese was talking to someone else and turned.

"Come on—get outa here, ya big ape," Joe Mega growled at Butch.

In his faithful way, Butch, the slow-witted, was a man of direct action. He knew that Joe Mega had been the driver of the laundry truck in which Quinn had been kidnaped, for Quinn had told him so. Mega also had taken his orders from the mysterious leader of the Dragon, who had been present on that death ride.

Therefore, to Butch's single-track mind Mega had dropped into the container a note meant for the Dragon Master.

Butch acted automatically. He stepped half to one side and forward as Mega's hand went beneath his coat, and let drive with a right hook that had carried him high in the heavyweight division. His iron-knuckled fist smacked against the mobster's swarthy jaw and Mega fell like a pole-axed ox. Butch snatched up the can containing the message.

BUT HE had not counted on Chow Seta. Like a streak of light the slender Chinese snatched up a small replica of an old-fashioned bung starter from beneath the counter. His brown hand lashed out and the weapon caught Butch alongside the head. The can fell and went rolling across the floor as Butch crumpled on top of Mega. Chow Seto leaped nimbly over the counter, jabbering in Cantonese to two other Chinese in back.

He rolled Butch aside and got Joe Mega to his feet. The mobster was cursing savagely.

"I'll get the police—have him locked up for assault," said the Chinese. "Hold him here until I return."

"Don't be a damned idiot!" snapped Mega. "They might take a fool notion to search this place, like they've combed most of the other joints around here. I'll just beat this bum up and throw him out into the.... For the love of Mike! Look there on the floor, Chow!"

He grunted expressively as he pointed to several objects that had dropped from Butch O'Leary's pockets as the Black Bat's emissary had fallen.

He bent swiftly, then straightened up with several rogues' gallery photos of Duke Kasini, some of his men, and some snapshots of several Chinese. Joe Mega's lips tightened menacingly as he studied the pictures.

"I get it," he said at last, glowering down at Butch. "The law says the cops can't search a place without a warrant. So they sent this big dumb-looking bird around as a bum. Come on, help me lift him in back before somebody sees him."

"Do you think he's a Federal man snooping around?" demanded the Chinese as they carried the recumbent ex-boxer into the back room.

Butch

Into his almond eyes behind the spectacles had come a look of uneasiness. "Ever since we lost that big shipment off the tanker I've been half expecting something like this. Those Federals never give up, Joe, don't forget."

"Well, you can forget that," growled the burly gangster. "He's only a flattie and he won't be a live one long. We're in the clear. Stop beefing. I'm banking nobody saw him come in here. They don't send men around on the tails of their own men."

Joe Mega let Butch O'Leary's legs drop heavily, then straightened up, looking at Chow Seto.

"I just brought you another customer," he said. "That was what I dropped in the can. The bellhop working for us over at the Lamont Hotel lined him up. Here, lift up that trap door. We'll shove this bum down...."

In the meantime, Tony Quinn waited impatiently until darkness, then slipped out through the tunnel to the gatehouse back of his home, leaving the two unsuspecting patrolmen on guard about the grounds and Silk Norton near the telephone. He got in the coupé that the ex-boxer had parked for him some distance away, and drove to Chinatown. At a street corner not too well lighted he parked and got out, strolling around with his hat brim pulled low over his eyes for a look at Dr. Ling's art shop and the living quarters above it.

When he reached the place he noticed that a pretty Chinese girl of eighteen or nineteen had crossed toward the shop from the other side of the street. He noticed something else, too. Flash Mega was tailing her. The gangster appeared to be interested in a window display, but he was not taking his eyes from that girl.

The Black Bat turned swiftly and got back to the corner without attracting undue attention. There was a fire-escape overhead. He leaped, caught the bottom and pulled himself up. Slipping up four flights of the narrow iron steps of the fire-escape he came out on the roofs above Chinatown. From the shadow of a chimney he looked over the edge of the building into the street. Apparently the girl had disappeared inside the red stone building, for Flash Mega was following boldly.

Tony Quinn slipped out of his coat and put on the Black Bat outfit which, because of its construction, could be folded into a small, flat package and carried in a cleverly concealed pocket. He patted the two .38s into place under the ribbed and scalloped wings, then like a flitting shadow he cat-footed across until he came to Dr. Ling's roof. To his vast relief there was a skylight that afforded an entrance, thus not necessitating a swing over the edge of the roof for a try at a window.

HE RAISED the skylight, ears cocked, then slipped noiselessly into a room on the fourth floor. Apparently the art curator, Dr. Ling, was quite well off, for the room appeared to be the quarters of two or three servants. None were here now, however.

Down another flight of carpeted steps the Black Bat made his way to the third floor. No sounds of life here, either, and from this vantage point he could have heard voices from below. Perhaps Mega had not followed the girl inside after all, or had already been sent packing.

Then to the Black Bat's keen ears there came sounds from the pad of feet up the stairs toward where he crouched in the curtained hallway.

He melted back against the wall, looking about him. There was a door behind him and he tested the knob, his eyes on the stairs below. A Chinese woman servant was coming up. The Black Bat's hand twisted the knob and it turned without difficulty. He eased himself into a bedroom—a woman's bedroom judging from the faint perfume in the air.

The Black Bat waited, half expecting someone outside to turn the knob. But the servant passed on by and ascended the last flight to her own quarters on the top floor under the skylight. The Black Bat waited a couple of minutes to make sure.

He opened the door a trifle, and this time he heard voices below. One voice apparently was that of the young Chinese girl he had seen on the street. She spoke in well modulated tones and in them was the iciness of a frozen mountain stream.

"What do you mean by coming to this house?" the Bat heard her demand of someone. Flash Mega, in all probability.

"Take it easy, I-tso," came the cracksman's roughly persuasive voice. "It ain't every doll I bother to follow home. How's about you and me for tonight, baby? You know, some Chinese eats, and—"

"Get out!"

But the gangster did not get out. He must have come boldly toward the girl for she started swiftly up the stairs. Flash Mega's heavy tread pounded after her.

"Get out, I tell you," she ordered again, though there was a touch of fear in her voice now. Flash was coming right on up.

"If you don't get out of here, I'll call the police," she said for the last time, and the fear in her voice was undisguised now.

The Black Bat looked hurriedly about him. That this bedroom was hers, and that she meant to take the sanctuary from the gangster here he had no doubt. He looked about him again for a place of concealment for himself, but saw nothing promising. The heavy drapes about the walls would not hide him, once the lights were turned on.

Quickly the Black Bat crossed over in the darkness, loosened the bulbs from the two lights, then melted behind the drapes as the door opened. The girl tried to slam it shut but Flash Mega's foot caught it. He chuckled in the darkness when she snapped the switch and nothing happened.

"Listen, baby, you're gonna be nice to me when I try to date you up from now on," he said, a hint of threat in his voice. "It would be too bad if your father found out his precious daughter was a member of the Dragon society, wouldn't it?"

"I give you one more chance to go," I-tso said coldly to the mobster whose grin could be seen in the dim light of the hall. "I knew it was a mistake to enlist the help of such as you in our cause. Unless you go at once the Dragon Master will hear of this."

Flash Mega's answer was to push her into the room. He grabbed her by both arms and his voice grew ugly. He was living up fully to his reputation for surliness now.

"Nobody gives a damn about your Dragon Master," he said sneeringly. "That's got nothing to do with you and me. If it hadn't been for me that museum vault never woulda been opened. There wasn't another mobster on earth who coulda cracked that—"

"That will do, Dragon!"

FLASH MEGA drew in his breath with a rasping sound and whirled toward the door. How that green-robed figure in the dragon mask had got there he could not guess. But the figure was there just the same. The man in the green robe pointed a long-nailed finger in Flash Mega's face.

"You fool!" the Dragon Master accused thunderously. "You stupid, thick-witted fool! You dare endanger our cause by a silly infatuation for one who is a thousand times too good for your kind? To disobey me means death—the same kind of death that was dealt out to one of the evil eight tonight at dusk."

The Black Bat looked at that weird figure in the dragon mask and long, green silk robes. So he had made good the threat that had been made in the note, despite police protection for the eight? Was it Belmont he meant? He was the most likely. Had Ohmo somehow slipped through the cordon of police around Belmont's guarded mansion and dealt out death?

The Bat detected an undercurrent of murderous rage in Flash Mega's next words, though he apparently was trying to placate the Dragon Master.

"Honest, Boss—I mean Master—I was only kiddin' the dame—"

"Silence! I came here to see if Dr. Ling was in, hoping he might go to the remaining evil ones and persuade them to save themselves by paying the ransom. There soon will be only six, for another is about to die."

"Who?" whispered the cracksman softly.

"Harrison. He ought to slip out of town tonight in a plane flown by Paul Chivor. The plane will take off, yes. But neither Harrison nor his foolish pilot will arrive at the Harrison country estate alive. But that is not all. Harvey Belmont also must be taught a lesson."

The Black Bat's eyes narrowed. So Belmont had not been the first victim of the Dragon society. Who, then?

From beneath his green robes the dragon-masked man took a sealed envelope. He handed it to the mobster who slipped it inside his coat, as the Dragon Master, apparently through with his chiding for the time being, gave some low-voiced, hurried instructions.

The Chinese girl had gone over to the shaded light beside her bed, fumbled at the bulb, and discovered it to be loose. She screwed it tight again. The Black Bat knew then that he was about to be discovered.

He had hoped that things would turn out differently. It had been his intention to find out all he could, then leap across the room in the darkness and snatch the weird green mask from the Dragon Master's face. Now he waited, his hands on the .38s.

"In this envelope are sealed orders for one whose name is written," the Dragon Master was saying to Flash Mega. "I had intended sending them by another. But it is just as well. You will be interested because it concerns your friend, ex-District Attorney Quinn. We'll see if we can't complete the job this time. Now go."

It was at that moment that I-tso Ling managed to click on the light. And it was at that moment that a voice from across the room said quietly:

"Gentlemen, stand fast!"

Flash Mega's hand was still under his armpit where he had placed the letter in an inner coat pocket. It came up with a gun as a startled cry burst from his thick lips.

"The Black Bat!"

Then gun thunder drowned out the sound of his voice.

CHAPTER VI

DR. LING'S DAUGHTER

S **NAPPING REPORTS** of the Black Bat's twin .38s filled the room, the sound mingling with the Chinese girl's scream. The gangster had jerked his own gun free, but the stream of slugs sent his way ripped it from his hand. The Black Bat could easily have killed the younger Mega. The mobster deserved killing. He was a thug without a spark of mercy in his heart and had been a party to the cold-blooded murder of an elderly watchman. Of that, the Black Bat was sure, even if Flash had not been the actual murderer himself—which the Nemesis of the underworld knew was a possibility.

But the Black Bat did not want to kill Flash Mega. He preferred to incapacitate the mobster and make him talk. Moreover, he wanted him out of the way now while he jerked the dragon head mask from that weird figure in green and took him prisoner.

The Black Bat had not counted on any interference from the girl. But as his deadly shots sent Flash Mega's gun spinning I-tso flung herself straight at the man in black, with arms outspread. Behind her

the Dragon Master moved fast, diving through the door, with Flash Mega on his heels.

"Run, Master!" screamed I-tso Ling, throwing her arms around the man whose appearance always sent terror through those members of the underworld who had the misfortune to meet him.

The Black Bat flung her aside and leaped for the door to follow his quarry. Flash however, showed lightning presence of mind. Before the Black Bat could reach the door he heard the click of a key in the lock. Running feet pounded down the stairs. The Black Bat was locked in—with a pretty Chinese girl—unable to pursue the wily head of the Dragon society and his henchman.

He sheathed his guns and looked at I-tso. She stood with her back to the wall, arms outspread, and now that her impulsive protective movement to save the Dragon Master was over, a fear she could not

A stream of slugs
ripped the gun from
the gangster's hand.

fight down began to show itself in her soft, almond-shaped eyes. She shrank back from the man who so much resembled a huge black bat.

"What are you going to do with me?" she whispered huskily.

"You should be turned across a knee first, I think," he answered sternly. "You have just allowed one murderer, probably two, to escape."

"What right have you to talk?" she demanded with sudden spirit. "Why do you try to thwart a just cause?"

"I deal out justice, instead of working against it," he told her, coming a step nearer. "This Dragon Master is not a patriot. Patriots do not hire gangsters. Who is he?"

"I don't know," she whispered in a low voice. "No one knows. He has a way of changing his real voice."

From outside the door came the sound of the hurried patter of footsteps coming down the stairs from the upper floor, and the servant's shrill voice came in Cantonese. I-tso answered back. The sound of the running footsteps receded toward the shop below.

"I told her to bring the police," I-tso said. "They must have heard those shots anyhow."

The Black Bat paid no attention.

"Who is the Dragon Master," he repeated sternly. "Your father?"

"No—no, I swear he isn't!" she cried, a note of hysteria in her voice.

"How did he get in here?"

"I don't know. I didn't know he was here until he spoke. Perhaps he told the truth. Perhaps he did come to see my father, who left the shop a little while ago at closing time."

To the Black Bat's question about where the treasure had been taken she shook her head.

"I think the Dragon Master himself took it away," was all she said.

"Where a patriotic cause is concerned, no man commits ruthless murder as this man has done," he told her firmly. "And he intends to commit more. Such a man would not hesitate to take your own life once the money has been paid. You are being duped—if you will only realize it."

From down below where the servant had unlocked the shop door came voices. Police were entering. A voice the Black Bat recognized was bellowing down there. McGrath's! The Black Bat grinned to himself and raised the window.

HE WENT back, clicked off the light, and his hands caught the Chinese girl by the shoulders.

"Until this Dragon society is broken up you and I must be enemies, I-tso Ling," he said firmly. "But if you'll help me I promise that once the treasure is returned, the full amount of its value will be used for the purpose intended."

And with that he was gone through the window to the roof above. He wanted to plant the seeds of distrust of the Dragon Master and his cohorts in this girl and in any others he could. Through that he might find a chink in the masked leader's armor and thwart his murderous scheme. But he had to work fast. Already one man was dead, according to the Dragon Master, two more were slated to die in a death plane within the hour, and there was to be another attempt on his own life this night—or at least on the life of blind Tony Quinn, former district attorney.

The Black Bat was grinning broadly as he climbed the fire-escape to the roof. He had an idea what would happen in that Chinese girl's bedroom as soon as he left. And, as if the Black Bat had the gift of second sight, as well as his actual double sight, things were happening there exactly as he visioned.

I-tso Ling turned on the lights as feet pounded up the stairs. McGrath, followed by two other police officers, unlocked the door and yanked it open. He gave a start at sight of the Chinese girl there alone.

"Where is he?" he roared.

"Who?" she countered innocently.

"Don't hand me that!" snapped the captain. "You know blamed well who, young lady. The Black Bat!" He barged in past her, looking sharply around. Then he glowered at her. "Go look in the mirror!" he commanded sternly.

She went to the mirror and looked. Squarely in the center of her smooth forehead was the insignia of the Black Bat, a tiny black bat with outspread ribbed wings. She removed it and turned. McGrath was looking out of the window.

"What was he doing here?" he snapped at her.

"I don't know," she confessed honestly. "But I do know that I'm glad he came. A—man—followed me into the house."

She made no mention of the Dragon Master, but the seeds of suspicion that the Bat had sown were beginning to bear fruit....

Reaching the roof unseen in the dim light, the Black Bat melted into the shadows like a fleeting ghost, thankful that the soles of his specially made shoes were as soft as felt and made not a sound. In the lee of the chimney again he changed into his light topcoat with the specially constructed pockets to conceal his Black Bat outfit, then hurried to the street by way of the fire-escape. The change had taken but a short time, less than five minutes having elapsed since he had left I-tso Ling's home. Yet hardly had he started toward the corner when a taxi shot out of an alley a short distance behind him.

The Black Bat instinctively darted into a doorway, hands near his guns. He suppressed a start of surprise at sight of Dr. Ling's daughter and a man she evidently had hastened from the back of the house to meet. The bespectacled Chinese was Colonel Wang!

Rounding the corner then, the Black Bat walked quickly toward the heart of Chinatown for his rendezvous with Carol Baldwin. No one noticed the man with the wide-brimmed hat pulled low over his eyes, at least giving him no more than a casual glance. Least of all Captain McGrath who had barged out of Doctor Ling's house, flagged a passing cruiser, and was piling in beside the two husky police officers.

"To Tony Quinn's house and step on it," the Black Bat heard him order. "The only way he'll beat me there this time is to fly."

A young Chinese school boy of about ten, in rumpled cap, short-sleeved shirt, and knee breeches came down the street with a bundle of papers under one arm. The youngster waved a paper at the Black Bat.

"Wuxtry! Wuxtry! Read all about it! Big Banker knocked off in his office by the Dragon mob! Wuxtry!"

THE BLACK BAT bought the proffered paper and by the light of a street lamp saw Thompson's picture on the front page. The miserly financier, working late in his big office as was his custom, had been throttled in the washroom while his chauffeur and two uniformed policemen waited outside his locked door to take him home. There had been not a sound of a struggle from within, but finally the chauffeur, growing uneasy, had summoned a guard to unlock the door. Thompson had been found on the floor of the washroom with his neck horribly twisted. A jade Buddha that was known to have been in his possession had been missing.

The killer—Commissioner Warner, in giving the story to the news-hounds had made no mention of Ohmo—had made his entrance and exit through a forced window, despite the fact that it was three stories above the ground.

It wasn't hard to visualize what had happened. The deformed Chinese thug probably had been driven in one of Chow Seto's closed laundry trucks to an alley somewhere nearby. Most likely Ohmo had made his way unseen across rooftops, like a huge monkey, to the top of the squat stone building housing the offices of Belmont and his associates. In the gathering dusk, he had climbed down like a human fly, opened and wriggled through the window into the washroom. There, he evidently had crept upon Thompson from behind and broken the financier's neck with a few wrenches of those monstrous hands with their iron strength.

"I wonder if Ohmo took the Buddha with him, as the commissioner seemed to think, or whether Thompson already had sent it to Dr. Ling's house?" muttered the Black Bat, as he tossed the paper into a trash container.

He hurried across the street to a cigar store on the corner and quickly located the office telephone number of the Dugro plant factory. There was no answer, and he tried the man's house. Somebody had to warn Dugro of what was about to happen to that plane. But again the Black Bat got no answer.

"I'll have to go myself," he said, under his breath. "I can get there about as quickly as McGrath can. Besides, I'll have to detour McGrath elsewhere."

He dialed again and got Commissioner Warner on the wire.

"Greetings, Commissioner," he said, smiling to himself. "This is the Black Bat. I've just missed renewing my friendship with my old friend McGrath in the house of Dr. Ling. The Dragon Master was there, in green robes and a dragon mask. So was Flash Mega, one of Duke Kasini's men, and a cracksman extraordinary if there ever was one—as you know. I regret to say that both escaped, but I believe that's a clue to the looted museum vault, though I've heard that McGrath also had an idea Flash was involved, but somehow managed to wriggle out of the net of suspicion."

"Where's McGrath now?" barked the gray-haired police veteran.

The Black Bat chuckled. "In view of his hasty departure in a police cruiser I rather imagine he's speeding toward the house of former District Attorney Anthony Quinn. I would advise, however, that you call him by radio and detour him to Belmont's home. In giving orders to Flash Mega, this Dragon Master mentioned something about the financier being 'taught a lesson.' Good night, Commissioner."

He hurried out to another phone, not daring to risk Warner tracing the call. He had made no mention of the threat upon his own life, preferring to keep as many police away from his home as possible. Those two on guard were more than a source of worry already.

HE DIALED a third time and almost immediately Silk Norton's familiar voice answered. Quickly he told Silk what had happened and that McGrath undoubtedly would show up there sooner or later. He also told of the new death threat to himself.

"I'm hurrying to the airport, Silk," he said. "I'll call or come home as soon as possible. If McGrath shows up stall him somehow."

"I'll do my best, sir. Commissioner Warner called a little while ago. My imitation of your voice worked quite well. He's been checking up on certain men. What he found out about Paul Chivor coincides with what an aviator friend told me a few minutes ago over long distance from California. Chivor's reputation as a pilot is hardly spotless, sir. His regular transport pilot license was taken away from him out there quite a number of months ago for stunting a plane while drunk. He went to China but was prevented by the consul from enlisting for military service in a foreign army. I believed he stayed intoxicated most of the time. A sort of black sheep, as I understand it. My friend even had reports he was hitting the junk."

"Good heavens, Silk! Anything more?"

"Yes, sir. Chivor might possibly have met Duke Kasini while in China. At least word was circulated among the flying fraternity that he hung around the hotels in Nanking and Hankow where the opium dealers gathered, mooching drinks, until he finally wheedled himself into a job with the Chinese Government as some sort of aviation adviser. Then according to what Commissioner Warner told me, believing he was talking to you, Chivor came over with Colonel Wang with the treasure as a sort of assistant to help supervise packing and shipping the military planes back to China. Also to act as interpreter. Since then he's stayed in his hotel most of the time, drinking."

"And now he's flying Harrison out of town to his country estate in a plane that has been marked for destruction by the Dragon Master, Silk," the Black Bat said grimly. "I'm on my way."

He hung up and slid out into the night again. Carol was waiting at the place he had told her he would park the coupé. Something in her lovely face told him she had bad news. She showed him a copy of the paper.

"I know," he said, nodding. "Carol, Harrison is taking off for his private estate upstate shortly in a plane flown by Paul Chivor. He's trying to slip away from this Dragon gang but is only hastening his death. The ship has been turned into some kind of death trap."

"You're going out there now?" Carol asked anxiously.

"As quickly as possible. You meet me here when I return. Try to contact Butch in the meantime, as we all agreed."

"He wasn't there, Tony!" Carol cried sharply. "Oh, I'm so afraid something has happened to him!"

"We'll have to chance it for the moment," the Black Bat said, shaking his head. "At least until I get this present important matter attended to. The place I'm going to is only two miles out, and I'll be back almost at once. I've got to talk to Chivor. Perhaps he can help us."

CHAPTER VII

BUTCH MEETS THE DUKE

B ACK IN a low cellar somewhere in the rabbit warrens of Chinatown Butch O'Leary regained consciousness under a deluge of cold water thrown in his face a second time. He blinked his eyes and opened them as the slender Chinese laundryman who had slammed him put down the pail.

Big Butch's head was aching terribly. There was a peculiar smell in the air that was foreign to him, but Butch judged from the appearance of the place it was some kind of an underground storeroom. Nearly a dozen gangsters were crowded in the place with the Chinese, who seemed to be in charge.

"Feeling better, my hulking friend?" inquired the Oriental, sarcastically, solicitously.

He came closer to test the bonds that held the powerful prisoner in a straight-backed chair that had wooden arm rests.

"I feel like hell, and I'm not your friend, you slant-eyed hunk of chop suey," growled Butch. At least he could still give vent to his feelings. "And if I ever get loose I'm gonna crack that dome of yours so hard they'll think it's an earthquake in Hong Kong."

"You aren't going to get loose," was the bland reply. "But your funeral shall be worthy of one of your station. A cement coffin to preserve you in the water for years to come, a nice new laundry wagon for a hearse, a dozen men here to act as mourners, and flowers of a wondrous kind— poppies."

Joe Mega came over and looked down at the victim or Chow Seto's blow with the wooden mallet. Mega's own jaw was still aching from the sledge-hammer blow that had knocked him cold. His open palm lashed out and caught the helpless Butch a terrific slap on the cheek, leaving livid fingerprints on the dirty skin.

"Who sent you down here, flattie?" he growled angrily.

"Go to the devil!" mumbled Butch, fighting the hardest battle of his life to keep calm. It was easy to realize what had happened, when he remembered the pictures they must have found on him. He had blundered! But they would get no information from him.

Joe Mega changed his tactics abruptly. In an effort to be cunning he let a genial smile break the lines of his surly face. He reached out and patted Butch gently on top of his shaved head.

"Now look, pal," he began wheedlingly, stroking Butch's bullet-shaped dome with the palm of his hand. "I'm a softie at heart when you get down to it. I wouldn't hurt a fly, see? Why, I even go out into the country once in a while to Chow Seto's brother's farm just to watch the birds and the bees, because I got a sentimental streak in me. But you take a guy like Duke now—the feller I work for. He ain't got none of them finer sentiments in him like I have. Why, pal, I've seen him stick slivers whittled from a match under a guy's fingernails and then set 'em afire when the guy already had spilled, just to listen to him yell. He'll be here pretty soon, too. Why don'tcha just tell old Joe a few things before the boss comes in?"

Butch told him plenty—all of which concerned Mr. Mega's ancestors and where they undoubtedly had gone after the demise. He also suggested that Mr. Mega could go there.

"And you won't need your winter underwear either," the ex-boxer finished belligerently.

The ring of mobsters roared with laughter at Joe's expense, and so did the Chinese.

But Mega stepped back, his swarthy face contorted with rage. The temper he had made such a valiant effort to control had snapped. With a snarl he yanked out his gun and flipped the barrel into his hand for a handle. Butch braced himself for a brutal beating about the head and face by a gun butt, but he was stubbornly determined that it would not make him open up. What difference would one more beating make anyhow? He was probably doomed already. Unless—

The door opened abruptly and a man came in from some underground passage, moving with the effortless ease of a black panther. He wore an expensive blue suit, dark shirt, and a straw hat set at a rakish angle on his slick, greased-down black hair. He caught sight of the prisoner the instant he entered the room, saw what was about to happen.

"Hold it, Joe," he ordered sharply. "Where'd you get him? Who is he?"

JOE MEGA grunted an explanation, pointing to several pictures on the table which the new arrival went over to examine.

"He had 'em on him," Joe Mega said. "Maybe Chow Seto was right. Maybe this guy is a Fed after all."

"Well, we'll soon find out," answered the mob leader seating himself on the edge of the table with a leg draped over it.

He straightened the crease in his trousers, took out a gold-plated nail file and began to manicure his long, carefully polished fingernails. Carefully he looked over the pictures, each of which had the rogues' gallery number attached. The candid photograph of himself was a wide contrast to the man sitting on the table.

Finally he leaned forward toward the immobile prisoner. His voice was gentle but his eyes were those of a tiger.

"You're gonna talk, brother," he informed, "whatever and whoever you are. Before I get through with you you'll beg me to let you spill. You can save yourself a lot of trouble by doing it now. What were you doing snooping in Chow's place?"

"My socks were dirty," growled Butch. "I wanted him to wash 'em."

DUKE KASINI—FOR the dark-haired man was the notorious mob leader—sighed and rose from the table, slipping the gold plated nail file into his pocket.

"Blackie," he ordered one of his men, "you and Manni lash his hands palm down to the arms of the chair where he can't move 'em. Sharpen ten matches about an inch long to shove under his nails one at a time. When we start lighting the heads he'll talk."

Butch felt the cold sweat break out and begin to bead on his upper lip. He did not fear the devil himself, and he knew he would die before uttering a word that would endanger the cause of Tony Quinn, but this match business was a little hard to stomach. There would be plenty of pain before he lost consciousness.

But he refused to let himself be frightened into a panic.

He threw his weight backward and the chair tipped. It hit the floor with a crash and rolled over against several burlap bundles from which that strange odor exuded. Butch's face came close to several tins with Chinese writing on them, and one had been opened. That was why the odor was so strong, and Butch knew enough to realize that the stuff was opium, from which heroin and other drugs were made. What he was staring at right now meant that the information District Attorney Anthony Quinn had been given by a couple of convicted mobsters about Duke Kasini was true. This looked like the gangster's storeroom for his contraband. But what could Butch O'Leary do about that now?

The two gangsters who had been called Manni and Blackie hauled him upright again, cursing, and shoved the chair nearer the table. While they untied one arm at a time and struggled to lash his palms down flat on the wooden arm rest Joe Mega methodically began sharpening matches to sliver points about an inch from the beaded tip.

Then from somewhere outside there came the sound of feet hurrying along a passage. Flash Mega, followed by Chow Seto's two partners, came in. His swarthy face was a trifle paler than usual.

"I just come from the Dragon Master in Dr. Ling's house, Duke," he panted, shoving an envelope at the sleek mobster. "He said give you this…. And, Duke—the Black Bat was there!"

All talking and other noise suddenly ceased as Flash Mega babbled his story of the hooded Nemesis who invariably appeared when a new crime wave struck the city. Gunmen looked at each other nervously. This meant more than simply dodging the police now. The Black Bat did not follow the rules laid down for the legally appointed minions of law and order. He made his own rules, for there was no reason for him to have to abide by legal red tape. Worst of all, everybody knew he could see in darkness as well as in day.

"That's not the worst of it either," put in one of the Chinese, his almond-shaped eyes showing his uneasiness. "I just heard a short-wave broadcast, for we've been tuned in on all police calls since last night. The order has gone out to round up Duke Kasini and every one of his mob for questioning!"

KASINI SHOWED remarkable coolness. He knew what that meant, and it was an old story to him. It had happened again and again in his life.

He had been reading the note brought by Flash Mega, and now a slight sneer crossed his thin lips.

"Take it easy, you dopes!" he said coolly. "Don't we always get pulled in when something breaks? Haven't we always got our iron-clad alibis fixed up in advance? Let 'em pull us in. They've picked up about five hundred guys all over town today. Now cut out playing old women and listen."

He took a match from his pocket, snapped his thumbnail to the head, and let the flame lick at the envelope held between the fingers of his other hand. He dropped the burning note to the floor, then looked his men over, one by one. A hard grin crossed his handsome face.

"Belmont has just been snatched!" he told them. "The Dragon Master sent Ohmo right in after him when the Chinese valet squawked and brought the cops running. Some of us are to go over and pick up Belmont now. Then we're to go after Tony Quinn again, as a warning to the others—all that are left. They'll pay up soon."

"You or even that monkey man couldn't get within two blocks of Quinn's house now," Flash Mega said positively. "Why, the whole place will be crawlin' with cops!"

"Personally I hope they are there," answered the mob leader, with a shrug. "And at Belmont's, too. You guys didn't think we rung in with this Dragon outfit only because of a cut on that collection, did you?"

"Meaning what, Duke?" asked Blackie softly.

"Brighten up, Blackie. Every cop in town will be over in that district tonight. I knew they would be when this Dragon business broke. I figured it that way from the start. It's our chance to settle a little business with Old Whiskers—or the Feds who work for him—and grabbed that load of junk off the tanker. Come on!"

CHAPTER VIII

DEATH PLANE

ONCE OUT of the heavier city traffic, the Black Bat made good time toward the airport. It lay less than two miles out beyond the city limits in a broad field just off the highway. Here, too, squatted the low, serrated buildings of Walter Dugro's plane factory. Once the field had been a municipal airport until increased traffic had necessitated a move to a larger one. Now it served merely as a test field for Dugro's planes and a few privately hangared jobs.

There were few lights about the place, except dim ones in Dugro's factory, which was not yet running night shifts for Government contracts in the new emergency program. From somewhere outside of the factory came the sound of an idling airplane motor in the night. That, the Black Bat thought swiftly, would be the plane that Chivor would pilot, taking Harrison to his country estate. The Black Bat must reach them before that plane took off!

He leaped from his car and hurried toward a high wire fence that surrounded the plant, looking this way and that along the deserted stretch of buildings. There was no sign of life, though two or three parked cars were down near some darkened sheds. Probably one of these belonged to the watchman, and possibly another was the car of Paul Chivor who had unsuspectingly come out to fly a plane to his death.

The Black Bat tested the fence and found that it had not been charged. He had hardly believed it would be, since the Dugro factory was not yet actively engaged in building Dugro's new bomber for the Government. Then the Black Bat's lithe muscles carried him up and over the fence. He dropped lightly to the ground and at a swift, noiseless trot set off for the corner of the building.

Out front the plane motor was still idling. He rounded the corner and came onto the edge of the tarmac. A door in one of the Dugro buildings was open and it was from this that the plane evidently had been rolled before being warmed up. Now as the Black Bat paused suddenly, to ponder his next move, he saw a movement in the pilot's compartment of the high-winged cabin monoplane. A man's head was outlined for a moment—then the idling motor suddenly broke into stronger life!

With a roar of power it spun around on one wheel and taxied off down the side of the field toward the end of the runway to turn around for the take-off. The Black Bat leaped from his hiding place and tore out after the trundling plane. For fifty yards he raced it through the darkness, its twin landing lights throwing long fingers ahead on the darkened airport.

The man at the controls saw a weird figure burst out of the night and come in under the bobbing wing. A startled cry broke from him. His hand came up and jabbed out through the window. Flame lanced from it. Above the roar of his motor came the sharper, snapping reports of an automatic pistol. But the Black Bat had seen him and had ducked aside, his cry of warning drowned out.

Then the ship spun around on one wheel into the runway, the powerful motor burst into full life, and under its eighteen hundred revolutions per minute the sleek, high-winged monoplane went skimming down the oiled runway and rose gracefully.

The Black Bat could only stand helplessly panting, and watch there in the darkness below. The plane was circling for a safe altitude before heading off cross country. It was now a thousand feet directly above the field. The twin landing lights set in the leading edge of the wing had been shut off.

Picking up two small objects his night-trained eyes discerned lying on the ground, the Black Bat promptly forgot them as a new thought flashed through his brain. The radio! That plane might have a radio. He set out at a run for the open door through which the plane had been rolled. He reached the edge of the building again and hurried along. The lights on the edge of the roof, shining down on the tarmac, blinked out and a uniformed watchman began rolling the door shut.

The man at the controls saw a weird figure burst out of the night.

THE MAN gave a startled cry as a weird figure in a black hood and winglike appurtenances under its arms appeared in the opening.

"Quiet!" commanded the Black Bat, his automatic out and covering the watchman. "I mean no harm. On the contrary, I'm trying to save two lives. I tried to telephone here to warn them, but got no answer."

"The office is at the other end of the building," the watchman said, swallowing hard. "There is no—"

"Never mind. Has that plane that just took off got a radio?"

"Y-yes, sir," gasped the man, still badly frightened. "But it's been out of commission the last few days. They been meaning to have it fixed, but haven't got around to it."

"But there must be some way to get in touch with it! There's got to be! That plane is a death-trap, man! The pilot must be warned!"

"I'm sorry, sir, but there is no way I know of. You say there is something wrong with the ship?"

"More than wrong. You've heard of the Dragon Master who killed the financier Thompson in his office only a short time ago this evening? Well, that passenger being flown away is Harrison, Thompson's associate, and Harrison has also been doomed to die! Something is going to happen to him and to Chivor, his pilot!"

The watchman's face blanched with horror as he stared at the Black Bat.

"My God, sir, this is terrible!" he cried. "Mr. Chivor is not flying that plane! Mr. Dugro himself is at the controls!"

It was the Black Bat's turn to stare. He grabbed the man by the shoulders and shook him.

"Are you sure?"

The watchman nodded vigorously.

"Yes, sir. I just talked to him."

"Where's that Chivor fellow, the pilot who was supposed to fly Harrison?"

"I think you'd better come with me, sir," suggested the frightened man, hurrying back through the building.

The Black Bat followed him. They went into the huge interior, through a big sliding door of sheet metal, and into a big hangarlike room with an office at the back. A shiny new twin-engined light bomber stood before the door, its three-bladed metal props glinting dully from the dim lights overhead. This was the job that Colonel Wang had been testing recently. The published reports were that it would do better than three hundred miles an hour.

"Wait a minute," the Black Bat snapped sharply, leaping to the plane and looking inside the sleek fuselage toward the two pilots' seats. "Is this thing ready to fly?"

"Why—yes, sir."

"Then come on!" cried the Black Bat and hurried the man on toward the office. "Maybe it isn't too late, if Chivor is still here. Maybe we can catch them! It's worth a try."

The watchman, however, merely stepped inside the office and pointed to the swivel chair back of a battered desk.

"There you are, sir," he announced disgustedly.

Paul Chivor lay sleeping soundly in the chair, his long legs and scuffed flying boots outspread on the desk top. He lay slumped back in the chair, reeking with the smell of whiskey. His head hung to one side and saliva drooled from a corner of his mouth. He was snoring loudly, his good-looking face anything but handsome now.

"He came in about a half an hour ago—reeling," the watchman explained to the Black Bat. "I've never seen any man with so much in him and still able to keep his feet. He made me help him wheel out Mr. Dugro's plane, but wouldn't tell me what he was going to do. He kept mumbling something about it being a secret. I managed to slip away while he was warming the motor and telephoned Mr. Dugro on the shop phone.

"He said there wasn't time to get another pilot, so he jumped in his car and came right out. By that time Mr. Harrison had arrived. So Mr. Dugro flew him himself. He—he was going to spend the night at Mr. Harrison's country estate and fly back in the morning in time for Colonel Wang's final tests on the new bomber."

THE BLACK BAT shrugged. He could do little else. Once again the man in the green robe had made good his insidious threats. The Black Bat grabbed Paul Chivor and began to shake him. Chivor gave a strangled snore and opened his eyes.

"Uh-agh-w-what is it?" he mumbled.

"Get up!" commanded the man in black, shaking him again.

"Go 'way!" mumbled the pilot sleepily, pushing at the hands on his shoulders. "Don' wanna get up. Wanna go to sleep."

The Black Bat turned to the watchman and asked if he had any coffee. The man quickly unsnapped his lunch pail and brought out a black thermos bottle. He unscrewed the cap, poured it full, and handed it to the hooded man. Five minutes later Chivor was sitting weakly in the chair, blinking his eyes and sipping the last of the coffee. He was sobering up now, the sight of the grim, hooded figure above him helping to bring him around.

"Who the devil are you?" he finally grunted suspiciously.

"The Black Bat," was the grim reply. "Tonight you were supposed to fly Harrison to his estate up country a hundred miles or so. Why—"

"Well, what of it?" Chivor snapped testily. "I stopped in at a cocktail bar on the way out and took on a couple too many. I can fly better when I'm high than when I'm cold sober, any day. But Dugro came out here to the field, cursed me for getting blotto, so I came in the office here for a nap."

The Black Bat told him then what had happened, and that Dugro was now flying a death plane. Chivor's face turned dark with anger and resentment.

"What am I supposed to do—weep about it?" he snarled. "It's my neck I saved. If I hadn't have got crocked where do you think I'd be in the morning?"

There was truth in that, and nothing to be gained by further questions. The Black Bat stepped from the office and vanished. It took him only moments to slip out of his Black Bat outfit, stow it safely in its special pocket, and start his car. But all the way back to town he was frowning thoughtfully.

"That man was not as blotto as he pretended to be," the Black Bat concluded. "I saw a flicker of surprise in his eyes when I first shook him, and the coffee brought him out of it a little too quickly."

As soon as he got back to town he telephoned Silk Norton. He asked about McGrath.

"No, sir, McGrath hasn't put in appearance yet," Silk informed, "but I've some bad news that just came over the radio. Dugro's plane exploded in the air about five miles south of town. The tail is believed to have been blown off by a small time bomb. Harrison was found dead in the wreckage beside the highway when two state troopers dashed up right after it spun into the ground."

"But Walter Dugro himself was flying that death-trap plane, Silk. What happened to him?"

"He jumped, sir, after vainly trying to get Mr. Harrison to. But it seems that Mr. Harrison was too frozen with fear. According to the newscast, Mr. Dugro crashed down through the limbs of a tree and was injured. The two state troopers who saw the plane crash beside the highway phoned for a police ambulance."

THE BLACK BAT could see how clever it had been. Harrison had told his associates that he was being sneaked out of town in Dugro's private plane. Somehow the Dragon Master had found out about it and had contrived to have a small time bomb placed in the tail of the plane, set to explode right after the take-off.

Who besides the dead man's associates knew about it? Only two men of whom the Black Bat could think—Paul Chivor and Colonel Wang. The bespectacled Chinese who had accompanied the collection to America had been at Dugro's factory for days testing out the new twin-engined fighter, and quite naturally would have been in a position to know what was happening.

And now the time bomb had exploded, the plane had crashed in what ordinarily might have looked like an accident, Harrison had been killed and Dugro had been badly injured.

"Silk," the Black Bat said to his eagerly listening valet, "do you think you could get through a police guard that's been placed about Harvey Belmont's home, and open his private safe? Just a hunch I'm playing."

"I should be glad to try both, sir. As you know, I've been studying the science of—er—safes for some time. But what about Captain McGrath? Suppose he should show up here while I'm gone?"

"I've been thinking of that, Silk. Now listen carefully. I'll get hold of Carol and send her to you in the coupé. You meet her in the tunnel beneath the gatehouse with your makeup kit and a nurse's outfit you'll find in the closet. Make a nurse of her. She'll then arrive at my house in the regular way and explain to the two policemen on guard that I'm having a restless night and that she has come to relieve you. If McGrath shows up she'll positively refuse to let him disturb me. As soon as she arrives you let her in, then explain to the officers you're leaving her in charge and that you're going for a long walk, to try to shake off the effects of a hard night."

"I quite understand, sir. What am I to look for on my—er—walk?"

"I'll try to meet you. If not, see if there is a record of stock lists, or of various companies Belmont has a hand in. I certainly would have less reason to suspect a man of being the Dragon Master if a stock list showed his millions to be anything but paper millions. I don't suspect Belmont particularly, but he is still alive, and I have to take every possibility into consideration. We simply can't afford to overlook any bets."

The Black Bat found Carol on the street corner where she had agreed to meet him. Her face showed undeniable anxiety. She came hastily to meet him, placing a hand on his arm.

"Tony, I'm frightened about Butch," she told him, low-voiced. "He didn't meet me here. Furthermore, I saw two men I'm positive were Kasini mobsters come out of the Chow Seto Laundry around the corner with bundles under their arms. Perhaps it really was their laundry they were taking home, but they went into a ramshackle hotel next door. Tony, I think they've got Butch!"

CHAPTER IX

CHINESE LAUNDRY

QUINN WENT with Carol back to the coupé. He got in and sat down, leaving the door open.

"Silk is expecting you, darling," he told her, and repeated what he had already told Silk. That was a habit with the Black Bat, in order to impress his instructions. "You're to hurry to Silk at once. He'll meet you in the tunnel beneath the gatehouse with his makeup kit. He'll also have a nurse's outfit taken from the closet where we keep such things. You're to put it on and then come to the house the front way, through the police guard. Explain that I'm having a restless night and you've come to relieve Silk. McGrath will undoubtedly show up. When he does you're to refuse him admittance to my bedroom absolutely, on the grounds that the patient can't be disturbed."

He started to get out to leave her, but again she touched his arm.

"Please be careful, Tony," she said, low-voiced. "And—haven't you forgotten something?"

He bent swiftly, kissed her, then got from the car and faded into the night. He hurried through a dark alley, cut across a brighter lighted street, worked his way through the crowd until he rounded the corner and came to Chow Seto's Laundry.

The front door was locked and the place dark. The Black Bat, now in ordinary guise, went on to the corner and came in through the alley. In pitch darkness that was almost like day to his bat eyes he slipped from his light topcoat and donned the Black Bat outfit. A hundred alley smells and sounds out of the night penetrated his keen senses as he leaped over a high board fence and came into the back yard of Chow Seto's place of business. He recognized it by the narrow gate where the laundry delivery trucks backed up to the rear door.

The Black Bat inspected the back windows, found them latched from within. No chance of entrance there unless he broke the pane. He replaced the thin steel tool he had taken from a scalloped rib of his bat outfit, brought forth a handful of keys, some of which were paper thin.

He inserted key after key in the lock of the door next. When he found the right one he sprung it, and pushed—only to find a bar across the door from within.

Because the window, though latched, was not barred, however, the Black Bat guessed that someone was in the place night and day. Either that, or the very fact that the place was easy to enter might be a clever blind.

The Black Bat looked swiftly about him. He went to a nearby trash barrel and brought out a discarded newspaper, soaking it at a dripping hydrant at the back of the ramshackle building. He pasted the sheets of paper to the window pane near the top. The dampness made them cling enough so that when the Black Bat pushed gently the pane gave way with but a faint tinkle. He reached through the hole, unlatched the window, and slid through.

His night-trained eyes already had taken in the room before entering. It was an ordinary back room such as might be found in any Chinese laundry. There was a gas plate, a table on which food could be served, and a bunk in one corner. Shirts by the hundreds hung everywhere on drying lines in both the back room and the larger one up front.

The Black Bat ducked under the flapping laundry and began exploring the front room. A peculiar smell came to his nostrils—one that he quickly recognized. He ignored it while hurriedly exploring the place, a .38 automatic in one hand. After all, it was not so unusual to pick up the odor of opium in a Chinese place like this. There were probably a hundred or more pipes near here, being smoked this minute by addicts of the poppy.

His eyes at once located the cleverly hidden trap door in the back and he opened it up. A flight of narrow steps led down about eight feet into a cellar that was empty except for a few broken and discarded canned goods boxes. The concrete floor gave off no sound and the cracked walls were bare.

FINDING NOTHING in the cellar, he went back upstairs again, grimly thoughtful. That particular odor was still strong, and suddenly it gave him an idea. Many other things were done with opium except smoking it in pipes, in its crudest form.

In a corner of the front room of the establishment were dozens of packages of laundry tied neatly and ready for delivery. The Black Bat went over there and brought a package down from the shelf, and the string made a loud popping sound as it broke under his fingers. He pulled aside the wrapping paper.

The bundle contained half a dozen ordinary white shirts, ironed and folded neatly as only a Chinaman could do it. But unfolding one and shaking it, the Black Bat made a discovery. Several wafer-thin packages fell out of the collars and cuffs and the front pocket yielded more.

Dope! Whether it was heroin, morphine, codeine, cocaine or other derivatives of opium the Black Bat could not tell from the looks, but all were equally contraband.

The Bat went through a couple of other packages of laundry. More paper envelopes. More white powders.

"So that's the connection?" the hooded man mumbled under his breath, a bit startled himself as the enormity of the scheme began to unfold itself.

Whatever these powders were they were derived from the alkaloid substance of opium. Opium smuggled in by Duke Kasini beyond any doubt!

The Black Bat's unerring diligence had at last uncovered the distributing plant of one of the biggest retail dope rings in the country!

He had started to replace the packages on the shelf when two things happened almost simultaneously. From behind him through the trap door from which he had just emerged himself came a movement, and from somewhere below in that same empty cellar there came blast after blast on the high-pitched whistle he had given Butch.

The Black Bat wheeled with the speed of a startled cat and was already falling to the floor when he saw the Chinese beneath the raised trap door pointing a gun at him. His own .38 exploded and the Oriental's gun went flying. He made a dive forward at the Chinese who ducked back down the steep steps.

The Black Bat came in on top of him almost head first, and together he and the Oriental he recognized on the instant as one of Chow Seto's partners crashed into the empty cellar. A startled yell came from the Chinese who had been behind the Black Bat's attacker.

Flame spurts lashed out in the cellar as the door thumped shut and one Chinese began screaming orders in Cantonese. The Black Bat's dive to one side in the darkness caused him to stumble over a box underfoot, though he could see plainly. The clatter made him a perfect target from less than five feet.

He saw a gun swing up, and his own snapping .38s gave back a death-laden answer. A stream of slugs poured into the Chinese dope peddler. He dropped in his tracks, but the other partner had leaped in from the side with a long-bladed knife in his hand. He thought, of course, that that grim, hooded figure could not see, and that error in judgment proved fatal.

THE BLACK BAT disliked to kill at any time, even in self defense or in defense of his helpmates, but there was no choice now. And he also knew the misery and human suffering put upon the world by these dealers who had waxed rich through the terrible hold they had upon their victims. Sanitariums were filled with such victims trying to fight their way back to normalcy or some semblance of real living. So he shot the knifeman three times and then it was quiet in the cellar.

"Butch!" he called, searching the place for signs of a door. "Butch!"

There was no answer. Not in Butch's voice—but that whistle was still blowing blast after blast in the agreed signals from somewhere back of those four walls. The sound, pitched too high for an ordinary human ear, was coming from nearby.

Then the Black Bat noticed the place where he had stumbled over and knocked aside the box, with a resultant racket that might have been his undoing. Beneath it, barely discernible even in daylight probably, was something that looked like the head of a ten-penny nail. The Black Bat's foot pressed down on it. Almost at once a block of the concrete wall swung in. What he had thought, when examining the place, were cracks in the cement, actually were the cunningly concealed outlines of a secret door.

A short, narrow passage ran back about twenty feet to another door. The whistle blasts were coming from beyond it, and the Black Bat's hands slipped fresh clips into his automatics as he darted back.

He did not even hesitate. His muscular shoulder hit the wooden door and it gave in under the impact. He almost fell into a low, cellarlike room.

Butch was alone and presented a startling sight. The massive-necked former boxer had been tied in an ordinary wooden chair but it no longer resembled one. He stood erect on his bound feet, the remains of the broken wood hanging from him in splinters.

"BOSS!" BUTCH cried. "I knew you would come—I knew it!"

He grinned delightedly, crow-hopping around on his tightly lashed feet.

"Boy, am I glad to see you!"

"Here, let me get at those bonds," ordered the Black Bat. "We've got to get out of here in a hurry. Someone might have heard those shots."

"Where's those two Chinese pals of that Chow Seto guy?" demanded the prisoner belligerently, flexing his muscles. "I'm gonna knock some heads together."

He looked disappointed when the Black Bat told him that they were beyond caring whether or not their heads were knocked together.

"Lucky for them," grunted Butch. "Say, they was workin' in with Duke Kasini, Boss. He left them here to watch me while he took his gang and went out to do some jobs."

Quickly he related all he had overheard and finished with the information that the banker, Harvey Belmont, had been kidnaped. The Black Bat nodded.

"I expected something like that," he said. "The Dragon Master said in Ling's house that Belmont needed a lesson. I have a feeling though, Butch, that they're going to be very careful not to hurt him. If Harvey Belmont really is the richest of the group who were to buy the treasure—as he's supposed to be—this Dragon Master is far too cunning to kill the goose that lays the golden egg. It's good psychology they're using, too. If Belmont is frightened enough, and sees that his partners are being killed, one by one, he'll put his life before his money. He'll pay up, eventually.... How did you get loose?"

Butch grinned and unconsciously flexed his iron muscles again.

"They were getting ready to give me the works with lighted matches shoved under the fingernails. They thought I was a Fed, or something looking for junk. But you know what them dopes did, Boss? They had already untied my hands from my sides and lashed 'em to the arm of that chair. But when this guy with the diamonds came in with some more orders from the Dragon Master they left those two Chinese to watch me and hit out.

"Pretty soon these two Chinese dope sellers hear a noise on a buzzer they got rigged up and they hit out. That was you upstairs, of course. Anyhow, being left alone a minute was all I needed. I gave one good heave and split off them chair arms like they were dried match sticks. The whistle was in the cuff of my sleeve so I started blowing while I rolled around and busted that chair to pieces. I didn't know if it was you upstairs, but I had a kind of hunch it was, and I was sure hoping so."

The Black Bat made a hurried inspection of the place.

"Think of the set-up, Butch," he pointed out. "Kasini smuggled in the stuff from China via Mexican or other ports, and this Chow Seto and his two partners probably picked it up in dirty laundry some way. From here the stuff went out to victims all over the city."

They hurried out through the door again, anxious to get away from this place, but sirens already were wailing to a stop in front of the laundry. They were likely to be trapped!

"Quick, Butch—out the back way!" ordered the Black Bat. "Head for home. Hurry, before they come around. Someone must have heard, and turned in an alarm as soon as that first shot was fired!"

He jumped quickly up the steps and cautiously raised the door an inch. Butch crowded behind him, stumbling in the Stygian blackness.

But already flashlights were playing out front, and there were the sounds of more police as other cruisers jerked to a stop outside.

"Hurry, Butch!" the Black Bat repeated. "It will take them a minute or two to find their way up that dark alley—they can't make it in the cruisers—and we must beat them to it! We've got to be gone before they get there!"

Even as he spoke in a hoarse whisper he was leaping through the hidden entrance in the cellar wall he had found, and up the steps to the laundry, closely followed by the massive-necked Butch. Hidden by the lines of drying shirts, they cat-footed to the rear room where the Black Bat had left the window raised.

The next instant they were cautiously emerging through the window in the alley where the Black Bat hastened away in one direction and Butch scuttled away in another.

Hidden by a high board fence a safe distance away, the Black Bat quickly shed his black, hooded garb. With his soft hat pulled down shieldingly low he slipped into the street where he found a passing cab, ordering the driver to an address on Pine Street.

After a time he got out at the address given, one in the middle of a block of residences. He waited until the taxi's tail-light had vanished back in the direction of Chinatown, then walked up the street. Three blocks away lay the smart home of Harvey Belmont.

On the next block over, the Black Bat cut in between two houses. But the man who emerged only moments later was an entirely different one. He had become a hooded black shadow.

From the back of the Belmont grounds the Black Bat leaped over a hedge into the shadow of an arbor. Only one patrolman was in sight, but even that alert bluecoat never realized that a flitting shadow passed within fifteen feet of him. The Black Bat went in through a cellar window, climbed a flight of stairs to a large kitchen and paused. Only silence greeted his keenly-listening ears.

On noiseless feet he moved into the dining room, then on into a living room beyond. A quick search disclosed no wall safe, unless one were hidden back of a sliding panel. Still as silently as a shadow he moved on into a luxurious library. Here, above an open fireplace, a panel had been slid back. The safe door was cracked partly open. The Black Bat smiled grimly behind his mask. And the smile became a wide grin when his keen eyes caught the outline of a shoe behind a heavy chair in a corner.

"All right, Silk, you can come out," he whispered, chuckling softly through the darkness.

CHAPTER X

MYSTERY EXPLOSION

GRINNING, **SILK NORTON** rose from behind the chair. He looked the part of a typical yegg in felt-soled shoes and rumpled suit. He came across the room to the Black Bat, carrying his tool kit.

"Oh, so it's you, sir," Silk whispered. "I'd just got the safe door open when I knew someone was in the house who had no business here. I can't say I heard anybody—it was more like I felt somebody had come in. I was pretty certain it was you, but when a man is doing a job like this he mustn't take chances."

Silk was taken completely by surprise at the news that Belmont had been kidnaped. Finding that no one was here when he had arrived himself, he had thought that perhaps the financier had changed his mind and gone to confer with the others of Eight Incorporated, since they now had such vital matters to confer about.

"I couldn't listen in very much on the radio," he explained, "so haven't been able to keep up with everything that's been going on. One of the two officers on guard at our place insisted on being in the house most of the time. I kind of suspect it had something to do with personal orders from Captain McGrath, though the sandwiches and coffee might have been a contributing factor. Never have I seen such appetites! No wonder I was forced to stay in the kitchen a good deal of the time."

Silk had not taken anything from the opened safe as yet, so now the Black Bat began to sift the papers he saw there, not just certain of what he would find or what he might learn. He only knew that from Harvey Belmont's suite of offices in the squat building where his associate Thompson had been throttled, that the banking genius spun a financial web that spread all over the country, in various corporations.

The Black Bat soon found ample proof of how wide-spread was Belmont's money schemes. The financier kept a sort of record of various holding companies, bonding companies, insurance utilities, and a list of stocks of other companies in his home safe, probably copies of others in his offices.

Only two of the list were of more than passing interest to the Black Bat. One notation showed that he owned the controlling stock in the Dugro Aircraft Company. Another memorandum proved the financier to have been the sole owner of the Asiation Import and Export Company, of California.

"Here's an odd one, Silk," Quinn whispered to the little valet. "Asiation Import and Export. I've never heard of such a name."

"Sounds rather unusual, sir," Silk commented.

"A combination of Asiatic and Aviation, I imagine…. No—wait a minute, Silk! It's coming back to me now. When the revolution first broke out in Spain there was a scramble on to buy up good used airplanes suitable for military service. They were sold to the Loyalists as well as to Franco, and some of the outfits like this one got into trouble with the State Department. I recall this one now in particular. Hmm! Our friend Belmont certainly has his fingers in a lot of pies, but he must have lost a pile of money before he got out of this one."

Abruptly the Black Bat paused and went rigid, his restraining hand on Silk's arm. Then he heard it again. Footsteps were creeping through the dining room. He motioned for Silk to replace the contents of the safe and close it. Gun in hand, the Black Bat slipped like a wraith to the door and stood watching as a shadowy figure came into the living room. It moved over to the window, saw the patrolling officer on duty there, unconscious that anything amiss was going on in the house he was guarding, then the wraith crept on toward the library.

It was at that moment that the Black Bat's voice whispered pleasantly from nearby:

"Good evening, Miss Ling. Visiting?"

THE GIRL gave a stifled gasp and turned to face the weird figure in the hood—the same she had met in her own bedroom earlier in the evening.

"So we meet again," said the Black Bat, coming closer to her. "And still enemies, I'm sorry to say. What are you doing, may I ask?"

"I've been hiding and waiting a chance to get away unseen," she answered.

"That's not a direct answer, I fear, though it sounds frank enough. You should know by now that my interest is China's interest insofar as this stolen art collection is concerned. Why did you come here? Who sent you? Your murderous Master?"

She shook her head, knowing he could see in the darkness.

"No. He did not send me. But you heard him say in my father's house why he had come there—to get him to act as an intermediary for the others. After he left—"

"—out the back way presumably, you hurried out and joined Colonel Wang," the Black Bat finished.

A startled look came over I-tso's oval-shaped face. She tried to peer through the darkness into this man's hooded face, even coming a bit closer. The fear his appearance usually aroused in others was completely lacking.

"You know everything, don't you?" she whispered.

"No indeed, but enough to know that immediately after the Dragon Master disappeared from your father's house you left also, and rode away in a cab with the colonel. Why?"

"You probably wouldn't believe me if I told you," she answered quietly.

"I'd like to, I-tso Ling. But up to now you've given me little reason to do so. You're a Dragon and helped the murderous leader of that blackmailing crew to escape. He was in your house. That means that quite possibly your own father or Colonel Wang was present."

"No—no!" she cried in a strained whisper. "I swear that isn't true. They couldn't be. You see, since I met Wang a short time ago we have— well, we've come to mean much to each other. But my father wants me to stay here in America. He's violently opposed to my marrying someone else and going back to live in China when he—he already has another man picked out as my husband. I've been meeting the colonel secretly. That's what he was doing tonight—waiting for me."

"Where did you go then?"

"We rode around a bit, talking over our personal affairs, and I finally came here—after I left him."

"But at his suggestion, possibly. Naturally he's anxious for the ten million to be paid."

"Of course he is! After all, put yourself in his position. He came over with the treasure and may be held responsible to his superiors upon his return. I—I had to do something! So I came here to see Mr. Belmont and beg him to accede to the Dragon Master's demands tomorrow. But no—no!—Colonel Wang knows nothing of that! When I slipped in here, though, there was an uproar out front. Mr. Belmont had been kidnaped! From what I overheard them say, Mr. Belmont's valet—he is a Dragon, too—had sounded an alarm and drawn the officers to the front of the house. By the time it was over Ohmo had Mr. Belmont and was away. The valet fled, too, and joined Ohmo. I had just come in, unnoticed, and found myself unable to leave. I've been hiding here ever since, trying to get away unseen."

Instinctively the Black Bat knew the girl was telling the truth. Had she known of the orders to kidnap the financier she would have had no reason for coming here at this particular time. And she appeared to be entirely frank. Under his questioning she told of how the Dragon society had been organized three weeks previously by the man who wore the green robes and the green dragon's mask, and that none of them knew who he was. She had been horrified by the murders, and no one had seen the art collection since the robbery. It had vanished.

AFTER TALKING to her a while, the Black Bat was certain that I-tso definitely was on his side now. With her as an ally he might be able to recover the treasure. He asked her to help him.

"It will mean death for me if I'm found out, but I'll do it," I-tso Ling told him unhesitatingly. "And I promise not to tell the colonel or my father. I think there will be another meeting of the Dragon society tomorrow night in the hidden cellar deep beneath those condemned buildings. I will be there—and do all I can."

There was nothing more to do but let the girl slip away and let Silk follow, without her having been aware that the little valet had been hiding in the library. The Black Bat took I-tso to the back of the house, pausing at the door.

"Wait here until the police officer reaches the front of the house," he instructed. "Then hurry away. Find out what you can about this man who calls himself the Dragon Master."

"How can I get in touch with you?" she whispered.

The face beneath the hood broke into a smile.

"You can't. The Black Bat has no friends or confidants. But I'll get in touch with you. We'll meet again—so don't lock your skylight."

His method of letting her and Silk slip away was simple. He went to the front of the house and slipped out through a window. He chuckled at the look of surprise on the face of the officer when he found himself covered by the Back Bat's guns.

Presently there came to the Black Bat's ears two blasts from Silk's whistle—blasts that the patrolling police officer could not possibly hear—informing the hooded man that Silk Norton was safely away from Harvey Belmont's deserted mansion. The Black Bat left the officer with his back turned, backed away under the trees, and then disappeared. He found Silk waiting and the two of them hurried toward the estate of Tony Quinn, not many blocks away.

"It's been quite an evening, sir," ventured the little valet, covering his baggy suit with a light topcoat and replacing the cap with a hat. "May I ask what now?"

"We'll go home now," the Black Bat said. "That Dragon Master is a devilishly cunning man, Silk. So far he's made good on every threat he has made. He said one of Eight Incorporated would die within hours—and Thompson was killed in his office. Harrison tried to pull a sneak—and died in the wreckage of the plane taking him to safety, a wreck that almost cost Dugro his life also. Belmont has been kidnaped, and they're out for Tony Quinn's scalp. Maybe there's something doing right now at my house."

HIS WORDS seemed almost prophetic, for when they approached within two blocks of the Tony Quinn estate the Black Bat saw something that happened too fast for words to describe it in the happening. A laundry truck rounded the corner some distance away and paused for not more than five seconds. Its rear doors opened, then slammed shut again. Quickly.

Then it shot away, and from the direction of Quinn's house there came a heavy explosion!

"Silk, follow that truck!" shouted the Black Bat. "Take that car!" He pointed to the coupé where Carol had left it. "Hurry!"

Silk kept running toward the car and the Black Bat sprinted unseen to the gatehouse. The little valet jumped in, spun the starter, and was off as an alert police cruiser shot around a corner ahead and took out in pursuit of the speeding laundry truck with the police cruiser coming up fast.

The police car gained like a hound on a rabbit. Silk slammed the accelerator to the floor and tried to keep up, cutting across a side street with tires screeching a protest. A couple of minutes later he came out of a side street and caught sight of the laundry truck under the street lights, with the cruiser coming up fast.

But once again the back doors were opened from within, and were closed again almost at once. It was enough. There was a shattering roar, a flash, and what had been a shiny new police car went rolling up over the curb in a mass of shattered steel with two inert things inside that once had been men in blue.

CHAPTER XI

A BLIND MAN'S
NURSE

PROBABLY THE most disgusted man in the entire city at about the time the sound of the mysterious explosion in Tony Quinn's house went rocking away through the night, was Captain McGrath of Homicide.

McGrath was dazedly picking himself up off the grass outside of Tony Quinn's house with his ears ringing and a few dozen stray stars shooting all through the ozone. Nearby was a hole that looked like a small shell crater.

In a lifetime of police work it had been by far his most disastrous day. It had started with the special afternoon assignment the commissioner had given him in Chinatown. His work had been to direct the efforts of various cruisers and regular officers combing that section, while he himself circulated through the streets with an eye out for suspicious characters. But by late afternoon, when nothing had been uncovered, the hunt had cooled down and most of the cruisers had been directed back to their regular beats.

McGrath had just eased up a bit, keeping a weather eye on Dr. Ling's house because of the little Chinese scholar's connection with the case of the stolen treasure when he had answered a servant's alarm and gone in with two officers to investigate. The first thing that had greeted his eyes when he had opened the bedroom door of Dr. Ling's daughter had been a Black Bat insignia pasted squarely in the center of her forehead.

This had been too much. McGrath was tired and in bad humor. His corns were giving him hell, and to top it all off the Black Bat had shown up and projected himself into the case—and, as usual, had disappeared before the captain could lay hands on him.

So the doughty officer had hurried out, hunted up a police cruiser, and ordered the officers to drive him to Quinn's house. But hardly had he got under way when that personal broadcast to him had come over the police radio, and Commissioner Warner's voice had dripped sarcasm. It had not made it easier for McGrath to know that every radio car in town was tuned in to that sermon and that the policemen occupants of the cars were grinning.

That realization had made his ears burn, for his attempts to get the Black Bat were well known to all the men in the department. The fact that he had never yet been able to put the cuffs on the elusive figure brought too much muffled laughter to suit him.

There had been nothing to do but order the two sober-faced radio officers to drive to Harvey Belmont's home. He had arrived just in time to find the place in an uproar over Belmont's kidnaping, and a dazed officer phoning Headquarters to broadcast the alarm that the Dragon Master had struck again.

By then McGrath knew that the Black Bat—if he was Tony Quinn— as the captain so firmly believed—probably was safely at home away from Chinatown. But Captain McGrath was a stubborn man. He had set out to go to Quinn's house, and all hell and high water was not going to stop him. He went, ordering the two officers in the cruiser to stop about two blocks away.

"Stay here until I get back," he grunted, as he got out of the car. "Keep an eye out for any suspicious cars cruising around."

He crossed over to the shrubbery, started through, and found a gun barrel squarely in his face.

"Hands up!" ordered the alert officer behind it. "No monkey business."

"Never mind—it's McGrath," growled the disgruntled detective, though he was secretly pleased at such vigilance on the part of the men he had personally instructed to keep an eye on Quinn. "Just came over for a routine checkup. Anything new?"

The bluecoat sheathed his pistol.

"Quinn hasn't left the house, sir. One of us has been in the kitchen and the other about the grounds all the time. But that pussy-footed valet of his went out. He sent for a nurse to relieve him tonight. She's inside."

McGRATH'S SUSPICIONS promptly soared. A nurse, eh? Sure, Quinn had had a bad bump, but not that bad. He no more needed a nurse than McGrath himself did. The officer went to the front door and was admitted by a neat woman in white. She was quite pretty despite her streaked gray hair beneath the perched cap.

"Yes, what is it?" Carol asked crisply—though he could have no idea she was Carol.

He bit off the end of a cigar and looked her over.

"I'm Captain McGrath, of Homicide," he said. "How's Quinn coming along?"

"I gave him a hypo a little while ago," she murmured, "and he's finally dropped off to sleep. He'll be all right in a few days. All he needs is plenty of rest, and not to be disturbed."

"Maybe I'd better take a peak anyhow," suggested the bulldog captain. "You never can tell about those things. There have been threats against his life you know, from the same gang he got away from last night."

"No, no, you mustn't see him," she said firmly, shaking her head. "He can't be disturbed."

"I won't disturb him," said the doughty McGrath, and stalked into the house.

He headed straight for Tony Quinn's bedroom and opened the door enough to peek in. Carol held her breath. But from the bandaged head visible under the edge of the covers there emanated regular snores. In fact, quite loud ones. Butch could sleep any time, anywhere.

McGrath closed the door, his face almost registering disappointment. But the bulldog in him would not let him give up. He eyed the nurse up and down, openly suspicious.

"Say, haven't I seen you somewhere before?" he demanded bluntly. "In a crowd or on the street or something?"

Carol blushed prettily and gave him a coy smile. In doing so she exposed two horrible buck teeth and a whole mouthful of others capped with gold. Her jaws looked like a pawnshop window filled with the stuff. He restrained his instinctive shudder.

"Why, Officer, you're rather old-fashioned in your technique, but then I guess we can't be choosey at our age," she told him, exposing those awful hash pounders again. "I'm off next week, so I could meet you downtown almost any night. We can have a good dinner, take in a show, go to a couple of night clubs, and—"

McGrath's face changed color. He almost fled from the house and started back to the waiting cruiser, reaching for a match.

The match was never lit, nor was the cigar. From some place nearby the very lawn itself seemed to erupt in a tremendous explosion that knocked him down and sent him rolling. He managed to scramble up, but reeled and fell again, choking on the cigar that had been rammed halfway down his throat. Falling on his face in that way, he had almost swallowed it. He was spitting out the mangled remains and cursing when Donovan and the other officer came running.

"Donovan!" he bellowed. "They threw a bomb or something!"

"Yee-ow!" yelled Donovan. "Look at that hole in the ground!"

The three of them broke into a hurried run to search the grounds, with guns out. From down the street came the wailing of a siren as the two alert officers he had just left in the police cruiser glimpsed the laundry truck nearly three blocks distant from the house and set off in hot pursuit on what was to be their last chase.

McGrath and his men found nothing in their hurried search. The police captain's guess was that someone had sneaked in along the hedge and tried to throw a bomb through one of the French windows. The nurse's white-clad figure was there now, in plain sight. McGrath raced for those windows, but could not guess that Carol went cold all over as the big officer dashed in.

SHE WAS fighting the hardest battle of her life to keep calm. Always she had dreaded what she feared would be the inevitable day when McGrath would find out the facts about Tony Quinn, that in truth—as the bulldog-minded police officer so keenly surmised—the former district attorney was the elusive Black Bat. Time after time Captain McGrath had missed beating Quinn into the house only by split seconds, but Carol had known that it could not always go on like that. The odds had to fall the other way sometime.

"What happened?" she demanded of him breathlessly, as he barged into the house.

Instinctively she placed herself between the big officer and the door leading into Tony Quinn's bedroom.

"An explosion!" barked McGrath. "Some rat sneaked up and tossed in a bomb!" His jaw shot out belligerently, "I want to see Quinn, sister—now!"

"You can't!" she declared defiantly. "You mustn't! He's had too much of a shock already."

"Out of my way!" he snapped, shoving her aside. "Hey, Quinn!" he bellowed, pushing past Carol who tried vainly to cling to his massive arm.

And then the sweetest sound that Carol Baldwin ever expected to hear in life came from that sick room. There was a loud clatter, the stumbling fall of a body, and Quinn's voice began calling wildly:

"Silk! Silk! Where are you? What's happened?"

When Captain McGrath burst into the bedroom Quinn, in pajamas, was down on the floor beside his bed, getting to his knees. His dead eyes were staring all about while he fumbled with outstretched hands for some familiar object that would orientate him. In the dim glow of the nightlight on the medicine table Carol ran to his side and helped him up.

"Is that you, nurse?" he asked. "Where's my valet? Didn't I hear McGrath's voice?"

"Here, let me help you back into bed," she said soothingly, straightening the bandage she had fastened so that it fitted like a cap. "Your valet went for a walk, Mr. Quinn. And, yes—Captain McGrath is here."

"What happened, McGrath?" repeated Quinn dazedly. "I had just dozed off when the whole house shook as if there had been an explosion. It almost knocked me out of bed. I tried to get up—I guess I fell—"

McGrath hurriedly explained, then strode into the other room of Quinn's private suite to the telephone. One of the officers came in to report that there had been another explosion some blocks away. The burly detective ordered him to bar all people from coming into the grounds, and dialed Headquarters. Quinn could hear him explaining to Commissioner Warner.

"Oh, Tony, I've never been so frightened as I was when he came through that door!" Carol whispered breathlessly, as she bent over to straighten the covers. "My whole body seemed to turn to ice. How on earth did you do it? Butch was in that bed asleep only two or three minutes ago."

"I'm under it now," came a muffled voice from below, followed by a strangled sneeze. "And I'm not asleep. That bomb woke me up. He rolled me out just after it went off."

"I had my pajamas on under my clothes, Carol," Quinn told her, in an answering whisper. "I made it here by a split hair. And, Carol, that was no ordinary bomb. Silk and I were a good two blocks from the house when we saw a laundry truck pull up under a street light nearly another block away. All we saw was the back doors open quickly then as quickly close. The explosion came almost instantly, yet the men responsible for it were a good three hundred yards away."

"What are you going to do now?" she asked quickly.

"I want you to get rid of everybody as quickly as possible," was all he could say then, because McGrath came back into the room.

AS THE big officer entered, Quinn lay flat on his back again with the covers tucked up beneath the chin, around his bandaged head. His dead-looking eyes stared straight up over the foot of the bed.

"I just had Commissioner Warner on the phone," announced the captain. "He's sending more guards to patrol the grounds, though little good it'll do now. They won't come back."

"Is the commissioner coming here?" Quinn asked in a hollow voice.

McGrath shook his head. "He says he can't make it, and for me to take charge. He's having a meeting at Dugro's house tonight. They took Dugro straight there after his accident, instead of to the hospital. Professor Ling and that Wang fellow will be there for tonight's meeting, along with some others. They're going to decide what to do about the ransom."

Quinn would have liked to ask if any word of Belmont had come to the police, but sick and injured Tony Quinn would not know about that kidnaping yet. Carol, however, instinctively guessed that Quinn might want to know the latest developments in the case of the financier.

"Oh, Captain," she said, "I heard over the radio about that horrible kidnaping of Mr. Harvey Belmont by his Chinese valet for the Dragon Master monster. Isn't it terrible! Has there been any word of Mr. Belmont yet?"

McGrath shook his head, absently reaching for a cigar.

"Not yet. But we'll probably hear soon." He saw the inquiring frown on Quinn's face, and told him the details of the kidnaping, briefly. "Somebody's bound to get word of, or from Belmont soon," he repeated. "Probably with a ransom demand of some kind concerning that treasure, for that's the only reason for the snatch. If they'd have wanted to kill Belmont the Chinese could have done it easily."

As he finished, he lighted his stogy. Quinn began coughing weakly when he caught a whiff of the cigar smoke. That was Carol's cue to get McGrath out of the room, which she did with vigor bordering on professional indignation.

"And furthermore," she told the big man as he let himself be shooed out, "I'm locking this door and keeping it locked the rest of the night! Nobody else gets in. If your men must make an investigation of this attempt to murder Mr. Quinn, kindly order them to do so quietly. He's a sick man."

McGrath agreed almost humbly, and went out. Already half a dozen police cars were racing up to the curb beyond the lawn. Uniformed cops were scouring the neighborhood. And it was only a short time before one drawn-faced bluecoat had arrived breathlessly with a story of one thing that had been found. The face of the big Homicide captain was drained white as he listened. His springy step was gone and his bull voice subdued as he went with the bluecoat to the waiting cruiser and got heavily into it.

They drove some blocks down the street to where a curious crowd was being shooed back by several grim-faced police. McGrath got out, forced his way through the crowd and looked down at what was left of the new police cruiser.

The entire engine and front wheels had been blown away and the rest of the car was only twisted steel. McGrath's bulldog jaws clamped down until the muscles in his cheeks stood out like iron lumps as he looked at what was inside. Only minutes before those two mangled things had been men who had driven him to Quinn's house.

"I'll get 'em, Fitz!" came soundlessly from between his clenched teeth. "I swear to you and Murphy that I'll get the hell's spawn who did this if I have to team up with the Black Bat!"

CHAPTER XII

A RAID ON MR. WHISKERS

HURRIEDLY TONY QUINN got himself dressed. Except for that small shaded light on the medicine table, his bedroom was dark. As soon as he was ready he called in Carol and Butch and sat on the edge of the bed talking to them. In his hand was a plain metal disk. Butch had managed to grab it from the can with the slotted top before leaving Chow Seto's laundry, for oddly enough it had been set in place again on the counter after being the object of contention that had almost cost Butch O'Leary his life.

Quinn examined the lettering and numbers stamped on it. They read:

PLEASANT HOTEL. SHANGHAI—
0894-A ROOM 5930

"There's something phony about this," announced Quinn, turning the object over in his hands. "No hotel in Shanghai has nearly six thousand rooms."

"Perhaps it's a code of some kind," suggested Carol, her hand on his shoulder.

"Quite likely. Those last numbers look like telephone listings. We know that Chow Seto retails narcotics, and this may be something that has to do with it."

"Maybe it's some kind of a system like a friend of mine used during prohibition days," Butch suggested, brightening. "He used tags like the shoe repairman gives you when you leave a pair of shoes to be mended. You know—he tears it in half and writes your name on it beside a number. When you come back after 'em you got to give him the tag. That's the way my friend worked it. When a customer phoned in he had to give his name and his number, and it had to check with a file my friend kept beside the telephone. That way no cop could phone for a quart to be delivered and then pinch my friend when he showed up with it."

Quinn chuckled, but his eyes brightened.

"Butch, I believe you've hit it!" he exclaimed. "Let's take a look at this thing again. Pleasant would mean—"

"Placid," replied Carol promptly. "The telephone number is Placid five-nine-three-o. That's down in the Chinatown district, too."

"Chow Seto's probably." Quinn nodded and sent Butch for the telephone directory. He opened it and thumbed through. "Yes, here it is. Chow Seto Laundry. Placid five-nine-three-o.

"What about the other number then?" put in Butch. "You mean—"

"The other one is the drug user's number. I think it means that a new customer was added to the huge number who get their 'laundry' done at Chow Seto's establishment. His number is o-eight-nine-four-A. Quite simple now that you think of it, yet the average person would never connect the numbers with anything out of the ordinary."

Quinn got to his feet and slipped on the light coat that, with the broad brimmed black hat he wore, always so effectively served to disguise his features to the casual observer.

"I'm going to Dugro's house to see what I can find out," Quinn told his two aides, again looking through the directory for an address. "Luckily the other car is parked on a side street, instead of being in the garage. Silk has the coupé.... Keep this bedroom door locked, Carol, and don't let even Warner himself come in should he arrive. I rather imagine, though, that at this minute he's with Dugro, waiting for the others to show up."

His final instructions given, Tony Quinn went out through the tunnel and came up under the gatehouse. Police were on guard everywhere and he had to wait for several minutes before emerging through the hidden door.

Crowds were gathered along the streets. The explosion had rattled windows everywhere around and word had spread that another attempt had been made on the life of injured Tony Quinn.

"Must be kinda tough on a guy blind like that and flat on his back, to have them go heaving hand grenades at him," Quinn heard one man remark to another.

"Yeah," was the reply. "It musta been some of the mobs he sent up the river when he was D.A."

"And you don't know how near right you are, my friend," Quinn muttered under his breath as he passed by.

REACHING THE parked car, he set out for Walter Dugro's house, taking a circular route across town to avoid traffic as much as possible. There was always the chance of some slight accident due to some reckless driver, and of a policeman making a routine inquiry, asking to see a driver's license. Blind men were not supposed to have licenses, or to be driving at all. And Tony Quinn was supposed to be home, injured, and living in a world of blackness.

As he headed the car on a roundabout way along the warehouse district along the waterfront, he saw that the section was deserted. Not even a watchman was in sight.

"I'd better stop off and phone McGrath about Chow Seto's place right away," he decided. "It's possible that the art collection might—"

He broke off with a low exclamation and slowed down. A hundred yards away in the Stygian blackness between two big warehouses there was a faint glow. But it was not that that attracted the former district attorney's attention so much as did the trucks. Two of them were backed up to an open door—exact replicas of the truck in which he had been kidnaped. And standing on guard at the back of them were two mobsters with machine guns. Others were hurriedly tossing packages into the back of the waiting trucks.

Quinn rolled his car on past, and parked unobtrusively at the curb not far away. Soon a fleeting shadow merged with the deeper ones around the building as a hooded figure with batlike wings under his arms moved toward the trucks.

Then the Black Bat's retentive memory clicked. This building was a warehouse leased by the Government to store certain types of contraband goods seized by customs men until proper disposal was made. It all came back now. For months Narcotics men had been smashing one ring after another in hauls all over the country. In the last raid, in the Black Bat's own city, a quarter of a million dollars' worth of stuff had been seized off a tanker.

It had been discovered that the dope smugglers had concocted a clever scheme. In the guise of plumbers some of them had come aboard carrying long sections of two-inch pipe to replace rusted ones in the ship's hold. The new pipes had been installed, the rusted ones filled with narcotics, the ends plugged, and the smugglers had blandly carried the stuff out past the customs men. The dope had been found—but not the smugglers. Kasini, who had been suspected, had been rounded up and questioned but had had an iron-clad alibi.

"I always thought that confiscated narcotics were given to hospitals," the Black Bat was thinking now. "But Kasini seems to have reason to believe that contraband is in that building. Perhaps his supply is getting short and he's desperate."

The two men with sub-machine guns stood on guard near the trucks were talking in low tones.

"Did you see anything?" one of them suddenly said uneasily. "I thought I heard something brushin' by me. Sorta slithering."

Already the Black Bat had recognized that speaker, both by face and voice. The man was Manni Torrio, one of Duke Kasini's chief lieutenants.

"You oughta lay off the snow," the other man growled to Manni. "Ever since this Black Bat showed up at old Ling's house the whole mob's been jittery. Even the China boys were showing it when Duke went with them to pick up Belmont."

"I'm plenty jittery," Manni Torrio muttered, shifting his short weapon. "Every cop in town's on the lookout for us since we lifted that art collection. They're foaming over the old duck at the museum getting his head bashed in by Joe. That's a burn for everyone of us if we get caught. And now Duke sends us to knock over Old Whiskers' warehouse because he got tipped off his junk the Feds took off the tanker is still in here."

THE BLACK BAT had awaited his opportunity and had slipped inside. He paused beside a stack of crates. So it had been "Joe" who had killed the elderly watchman at the museum! That would be Joe Mega, of course.

Over at the other side of the room was a monster safe of a kind the Black Bat had not seen in years. Almost as large as a vault, it stood nearly seven feet high, and presumably had been installed when the ancient red brick building was erected. Now Flash Mega's torch had found it like soft butter. The cracksman had already finished packing up his outfit while others hurriedly carried packages to the trucks.

The Black Bat flitted toward the door again, guns out. Someone caught sight of his moving shadow and cried out a warning as a spurt of fire lashed out. Flash Mega's angry curses at the nervous mobster were drowned out in the snapping reports of the Black Bat's two .38s. The mobster went down and hell broke loose in the warehouse as Manni Torrio opened up with his chopper.

The hail of death sprayed across the warehouse and the Black Bat dropped flat. The spray of .45s sieved a line of holes in the wall across the room. From outside came shouts, orders, curses, and the roar of starting motors.

"You fools!" yelled Mega's rage-filled voice. "Now you've done it. Get outa here quick!"

"It's the Black Bat!" screamed another mobster. "Come on, you guys!"

But for Mega to get out of that door was a problem. The Black Bat had worked his way to a spot where he was under cover himself, and had part of them cut off. Mega was behind the safe, cursing. He made the mistake of exposing a hand carrying the big suitcase containing his oxygen tank and one of the Black Bat's .38s spanged off metal as the bullets ripped holes through leather.

Mega dropped the suitcases and broke for the door as the Black Bat's guns clicked empty. He snatched out the clips and replaced them with loaded ones, but the delay had given the cracksman the brief chance he needed. Under a hail of protecting slugs from Manni Torrio's deadly chopper Flash Mega made the trucks. Back doors were slammed shut.

From outside came the wail of a siren, followed by a second. The Black Bat looked about for a means of escape back to his car. But the car was nearly a hundred yards away down the street, and at about the spot where the police would stop. There wasn't a chance to get back to it and get away without being pursued.

He ran forward through the pitch blackness as the trucks pulled out. But not before he had bent swiftly above three men he had downed, his hands brushing them lightly in the darkness. He wanted to identify his work to the police so there would be no mistakes.

He leaped at the right rear fender of the second truck, his own momentum carrying him up on top of the shiny big vehicle. The truck shot out of the gate as two police cruisers came screaming down the waterfront, followed by another car. Men leaped from the third car and ran into the warehouse. It was deserted now except for the three dead or wounded men on the floor.

"The Black Bat," one of them, a Federal man, said significantly, as his flashlight played over the insignia pasted in the center of each man's forehead. "And he's certainly making things hot for the Kasini mob, whoever he may really be."

"Yes, but this one is on us, boys," commented another Federal agent. "We're a little late to close the trap. Through a fluke that wouldn't happen again in a lifetime that mob sprung the trigger and got away without getting caught. Ever since District Attorney Quinn tipped us off two years ago that Kasini was running in narcotics we've been on his trail. I thought we had him cold this time. Come on, let's see how the police are making out."

THE POLICE were not making out at all, for the luck of some evil god seemed to ride with the drug-running members of the Dragon society that night. On top of the truck doing nearly seventy miles an hour the Black Bat saw the two cruisers coming up like sleek greyhounds. Then as the officers opened up with a fusillade, Manni Torrio opened the back door of the rear truck and poked out the short snout of his sub-machine gun. It burst into snarling flame and a hail of slugs peppered both front tires of the nearest car.

It began to skid wildly, there came a rub-a-dub of deflated tires on the pavement, and the car almost overturned. The second cruiser coming up close behind and trying to get around into the clear, hooked fenders and began to skid sideward also. It swerved wildly with a squall of tires, tried to straighten out, and crashed against the curb with front wheels bent.

By the time the Federal men arrived in their own car, the two trucks had cut through a side street, shot across a main stem, ducked into an alley on the edge of town, then headed out the other direction into the country by a seldom used narrow road.

CHAPTER XIII

SILK RUNS INTO TROUBLE

CAUTIOUSLY FOLLOWING the truck that had just brought death to two policemen in their smashed car, Silk Norton was horrified at what he had just witnessed. As he drove with one hand he took a simple makeup kit from a hidden compartment in the coupé and began to work at his features, using the rear view mirror.

Porcelain caps cleverly, though hurriedly, set in place changed the shape of his jaws. A rubber pad back of his lower lip made it full and protruding. He streaked his hair gray. And a pair of thin glass eyecups did the rest. They changed his pale eyes into snapping black ones.

As he worked, and sped along after the death vehicle, he kept tuned to the police broadcasts on the car radio, tense with dread of what he might hear. For all he knew Quinn's home might be a shambles by now, with Carol and the faithful Butch dead in it. But to his relief he soon found out differently.

Silk shut off the radio when he heard the gratifying news, and sighed his relief. The bomb had missed the house, falling short on the grounds. No one had been injured.

For nearly half an hour Silk followed the truck that was heading boldly back toward Chinatown. The Chinese driver was clever. By devious side streets and dark alleys he drove slowly, taxing Silk's wits to the utmost to trail him unnoticed. Presently when the truck cut around a corner, Silk was faced with the alternative of stopping or boldly following.

He slowed up, and finally drove around the corner into a dimly lit street. But the truck had vanished into thin air!

The little man headed the coupé toward the next corner and pulled up to the curb. Still no sign of his quarry going either direction on the cross street.

Where Silk got out of the car, he was decidedly puzzled. The driver of that truck couldn't have had time to round another corner a block further on. So Silk stuck his hands in his pockets and nonchalantly strolled back the way he had come. Halfway down the street he came to an opening so narrow it hardly would admit the passage of a car. It hadn't looked like an alley at a casual glance.

Silk took a look up and down the street, then stepped into the little alley. The narrow space lay between the backs of several high buildings. Above him were the faint outlines of an ancient type fire-escape.

A white card on the wall took his eye and he ventured a quick look from a lighted match cupped in his hands. The placard was that of a house wrecking company. That told him that these buildings had been condemned and were untenanted—were in the hands of wreckers.

For nearly a hundred feet the little valet moved on noiseless felt soles up the narrow alley in darkness that was like black fog. Then, without warning, he came upon the outlines of the truck ahead.

He started to melt into a gaping doorway. Too late he became aware of a movement somewhere close by. He wheeled and tried to duck, but from out of the night the monster already had leaped. It looked like a bull ape out of the jungle as fingers that were like iron grabbed him by the throat and sank deep, shutting off his wind.

He tried to struggle, flailing his arms in the Thing's steel grasp. But it merely struck him a paralyzing blow that left him half conscious, then tossed him into the truck, where he was covered by Joe Mega's gun. He

Silk was thrown inside the barn like a sack of potatoes.

also recognized the Thing, as Butch had earlier, since Silk Norton also had studied that collection of pictures from Tony Quinn's private rogues' gallery.

"CHOW," JOE MEGA said, and chuckled, "this monkey man gets better all the time. We could use him in the mob after the Dragon Master gets done with him."

Mega threw the rays of a flashlight into Silk's face for a moment.

"He's pretty runty for a flattie. Maybe he's a Fed. We'll find out all right when we get inside. Now we can make two sing."

"It isn't coincidence that two men were caught prowling after us within the past hours, Joe," said the bespectacled Chinese who was Chow Seto, though Silk did not know that. There was a note of anxiety in the Oriental's voice. "There's something in the wind."

Joe Mega's voice took on an ugly tone. "Sure, there's plenty in the wind. A cut on a two million rake-off from that treasure. You're not going yellow on the mob, are you, Chow?"

The slender laundryman's voice had something dangerously razor-edged in it.

"You know me better than that. I've worked with Duke's mob too long. We were getting along well, just as we have for two years, until this Dragon business came up. I knew it would center the attention of the police on Chinatown and endanger us. But Duke's been getting too confident. It was stupid for him to send the others to raid a Government warehouse to get back a confiscated shipment. That doesn't ring true to me. Who ever heard of Federal men leaving such a cargo in—"

"Forget it," Mega cut in impatiently. "Let's get over to the laundry."

Leaving the deformed Thing who had attacked Silk in the condemned building, Chow drove the truck into the alley behind the laundry and backed up to the rear door. The doors that had opened and spewed out death to two police officers now opened again and Mega ushered Silk Norton out. Silk was bound and gagged with his own necktie and handkerchief. With his wrists behind his back he was taken inside.

Chow Seto had lifted a cleverly concealed trap door in the back room and descended into the cellar. Silk managed to follow somehow, and Mega came last. On the floor the Chinese suddenly stumbled over something and fell against the wall in the darkness. Mega chuckled but the sound turned into a snarl of hate and fear as he flashed his light on the floor. Lying there with Black Bat insignia on their foreheads were Chow Seto's two partners.

With curses dripping from his lips the gangster leaped to the other side of the room and pressed the nail head that swung the secret wall section inward. The other room was empty—except for the scattered remnants of a broken chair and Duke Kasini's picture on a table with the insignia of the Black Bat pasted across it.

Chow Seto looked at it and turned to Joe Mega. There was a look of terrible fear in the eyes of the Chinese dope peddler.

"Well, Joe?" he whispered.

Joe Mega covered his own shaken feelings with a sneer.

"Don't go off half cocked."

Chow Seto shrugged and picked up a five-gallon can of gasoline that was in a corner. Then the disguised Silk saw the murderous look that came into Joe Mega's cruel eyes as the gangster's gun came up, pointing squarely at the back of the Chinese. Silk could not even cry out because of the gag that had been shoved into his mouth.

The Chinese drug peddler was still turning when Mega shot him. He fell, and the gangster walked over and bent down. The gun roared twice more within inches of the Oriental's chest.

"You were pretty good in your way, pal," the gangster said softly, straightening with the gasoline can in his hand. "I sorta hated to bump you. But when guys start getting the chill up their backs they're dangerous to the mob."

HE BEGAN sloshing gasoline over the table and burlap bags in the corner. With a jerk of his head to Silk to walk ahead of him, he poured a trail of the liquid in through the passage to the cellar, up the steps, and into the kitchen. Warning Silk to stand pat he sloshed more gasoline all over the front room and almost everything in it. Something seemed to strike him as funny, for he began to chuckle.

"It'll be a joke on the guy who owns the hotel next door," he said to Silk. "All the mob had rooms there for hideouts. Most of the time we came in through another underground passage. Too bad we can't stick around to watch it burn, pal."

Prodding Silk outside, he ordered the little valet into the front seat of the waiting truck. He climbed in himself and started the motor. From his coat pocket he took out a nondescript cigarette lighter and carefully polished it until no vestige of fingerprints could be left. Then he snapped a big thumb down. The flaming object arched through the air and fell through the open window into the gasoline-soaked rear room of the laundry.

What followed then was almost an explosion. As the truck shot out of the alley and got away a sheet of flame went up inside the building and roared through the two rooms, turning them into an inferno. The glassed front gave way and fire shot through into the street. Cries began to fill the air. Someone raced to the corner and turned in an alarm just as two big cars dashed up and spilled out several men.

Mega, looking back, uttered a curse, but his tone was a mixture of amazement tinged with relief.

"Those fellows are Feds, pal, or my eyes are getting bad," he muttered. "Another minute and you'd have been okay.... Hey, don't choke on me now!" For Silk seemed in imminent danger of doing just that. "Here, I'll take the gag out—somebody to talk to anyhow. But you'd better not try yellin'."

Behind them now flames threw a glow into the sky above Chinatown.

"I rather gather," Silk said dryly, when Joe Mega had jerked the gag from his mouth, "that Mr. Kasini's retail business will suffer something of a temporary set-back."

"Shut up!" growled the killer beside him. "I gotta think. I gotta think harder than I ever did before in my life. Every move we've made tonight has been busted up by that Black Bat. He nearly got Flash in old Ling's house. He slid into Chow's place and cleaned house there. No tellin' where he'll show next."

He drove on with his bound prisoner beside him, half muttering. Silk knew it would be useless to try getting the door open and jumping. Mega could handle him with one hand, or shoot him in the back before he got far.

Silk was still turning over in his mind a possible solution to what had seemed to him to be a terrible new explosive weapon unleashed by the Dragon Master. When he first had been thrown into the truck by the pinheaded Chinese thug he had half expected to find some kind of new infernal machine there. Actually there had been nothing he could see.

Presently, after they had driven out of the city, Joe Mega turned the truck into a dim road that led back among some trees. Ahead lay a ramshackle house with sheds and farm implements scattered about. Beyond was the flat outline of a small truck farm. Joe Mega drove up without lights and braked to a stop behind the house, shutting off the motor.

"All right, pal, it's the end of the line for you," he growled at Silk, gripping him by the collar and shoving him out.

A man loomed up out of the night and spoke sharply in Chinese.

"Talk English," Joe Mega growled.

"A thousand apologies, Dragon," the Chinese farmer replied. "I thought you were my brother, Chow Seto. I just caught a police broadcast from the city. All cars are searching for the men who robbed a warehouse and got away. All except three. They were found with a Black

Bat insignia on their foreheads. One Dragon who was sent here earlier to me with a message will help you now."

WITH JOE MEGA'S blistering curses in his ears Silk was shoved toward a ramshackle barn. He was thrown inside like a sack of potatoes while Joe Mega and the gangster the Chinese had mentioned menaced him with their guns.

The place was foul and unsanitary beyond description. The rank smell of manure filled the air, and a lantern burned dimly. At one of the stalls Joe Mega placed his burly shoulder against an old work horse's hip and shoved the animal aside. He bent over the manger, fumbled in the darkness with one hand, heaved hard and lifted one end. When he picked up the lantern a narrow flight of stairs leading down was revealed.

They descended into a cellar below the barn where Silk was shoved toward a chair. As in the cellar room in the laundry, burlap bags were piled up in a corner. Silk's eyes, however, were on several small stacked crates. He would have paid them scant attention except for their effect upon Joe Mega. The gangster's jaw was sagging.

Those were the crates that had been taken from the museum less than twenty-four hours before!

CHAPTER XIV

BLACK BAT
TO THE RESCUE

RIDING ATOP the cab of the big laundry truck the Black Bat still had held his precarious position as the machine sped out of town by a little used road and entered the country. Up ahead of him the leading truck clicked off its lights and crept on for a short distance, before finally turning off among a group of trees. The second truck with the Black Bat atop the cab followed. Tensed and ready, the Black Bat waited until the truck lurched into a rut, then swiftly slid to the ground.

He arose to his feet and sped toward the house. His night-piercing eyes saw a third laundry truck parked in back of a ramshackle house. Aside from that, there was no sign of life about.

The Black Bat melted into the shadows of the Chinese farmer's home. No lights were visible as he slipped inside the house. The eyes behind the hood flicked over a small kitchen in a state of general untidiness.

Near the stove were two objects that gave evidence the farmer who lived here spent much of his time in the kitchen. One was a dial telephone on a stand by a chair and the other was a high-powered radio adjusted to pick up police calls.

The Black Bat picked up the receiver and a silk-gloved finger dialed the telephone number of Walter Dugro. Dugro's voice itself answered.

"Good evening, Mr. Dugro," said the hooded man. "This is the Black Bat. I'm calling from the kitchen of a Chinese truck farmer about three miles out, I think, and I've called you because I understand Commissioner Warner is at your house. I've just arrived—unseen—with several members of the Dragon society after a raid some of the contingent made on a warehouse down in the dock district. I did my best to break it up, and at least caused Flash Mega to leave his safe-cutting equipment."

"The commissioner is here with me now, and has just heard the story from Headquarters," answered Dugro. "Just a moment—he's cutting in on a branch phone."

The gray-haired police official's crisp voice came over the wire.

"You, Black Bat, what's this about the Dragon society?"

"They've just gone into a barn out here, Commissioner, that I'm positive is too small to hold them all and the loot they're carrying. There must be an underground room of some sort. Here's the telephone number of this place. Trace the address. A flying squad of officers may be able to get out here and nab the entire outfit. All except Kasini and some of the Chinese members. I rather imagine they're the ones who have Belmont."

He gave Warner the number and told the official what had happened in the laundry in Chinatown when he had visited it, naturally omitting any mention of Butch. And he now learned that Chow Seto's place as well as the rickety hotel next to it had gone up in roaring flames just as a squad of Federal men had swooped down. The fire was still uncontrolled.

"I should have phoned about Chow Seto sooner, Commissioner," the Black Bat said, with regret in his voice. "However, I don't suppose it really matters. If you can get some men out here in a hurry you can nab a number of the Dragon members red-handed."

The Black Bat quickly hung up the receiver as a sound came from somewhere behind him. Footsteps clomped onto the low back porch. Someone was coming. The Black Bat turned to step out of sight but stepped on a round stick of stovewood that acted like a roller. Even his catlike muscles could not save him in time.

He hit the floor to the accompaniment of a clatter of rattling pans. Someone shouted excitedly in Chinese and a porch switch flooded the kitchen with light. A husky Chinese farmer leaped through the door.

The Black Bat came up fast, then dived at the Chinese as the man reached for a button hidden beneath a two-by-four back of the door jamb. A buzzer of some sort. He caught the Oriental's wrist as the farmer began to scream a warning. The Black Bat's hard fist lashed out and silk-covered knuckles smacked hard against the man's jaw. But the heavy Chinese had the strength of a bull. His head rolled to one side with the blow and he tried for a ju-jutsu hold.

BUT SUCH tricks were no secret to the Black Bat and they went down in a flurry of flying arms and legs. A foot sent the table crashing. The radio went rolling with a tinkle of broken tubes.

The hooded man tried to get out his gun but the wily Chinese held his wrist and was threatening to break it as he tried to bend it back. Both men were panting so desperately with the exertion that the Oriental was unable to cry out.

The single warning he had been able to give, however, had been enough. From outside came shots and the pound of running feet. The Chinese began to scream again, on his back on the floor. A brown hand snatched up a stick of stove wood. It went flying, then both men snapped to their feet again. For all his bulk, the Chinese was as quick as a cat. He plunged at the hooded figure as more feet hit the back porch, but in doing so he laid himself open to the kind of fighting that the Black Bat had learned from Butch O'Leary. The Black Bat's right fist came up in a short bone-snapping blow that numbed it to the elbow. The brother of Chow Seto went down and lay still.

The Black Bat wheeled toward the back door as men dived in. His twin .38s met fire with fire. One wild bullet shot out the light and chaos broke loose in the kitchen. A mobster went down in the doorway and another fell on top of him. The others who had come running whirled and dived back out into the night. Once again Kasini's mob were screaming to each other that the hooded devil was after them. He couldn't be shaken off. They were beginning to believe that no matter where they went that grim Nemesis would appear almost at once.

"That guy ain't human, I tell you!" Manni Torrio was shouting as he ran for the truck to get his chopper.

Inside the upset kitchen it was beginning to quiet down again as the last of the mobsters fled out, backing away and shooting. The Black Bat, however, was no longer there. He had ducked out the way he had come in. His hooded form flitted toward the truck where Torrio was emerging with his sub-machine gun. Before the mobster realized what had happened the Black Bat had swung a hard blow at his jaw and grabbed the weapon, as Torrio screamed in fear and fell. From the protection of the truck's front the deadly weapon began a staccato barking.

Crouching under cover whenever possible the Black Bat began working his way toward the barn. The mobsters themselves had fled to various vantage points. But the Black Bat had to see what was in that barn. As he reached it, and dodged inside, yellow light was coming from an underground room through a manger. The Black Bat slid over to the manger and looked down a lantern-lit opening—straight into the disguised face of Silk Norton who was coming up the rough stairs. Left alone in the commotion Silk had managed to get himself loose from his bonds.

Swiftly Silk related what had happened. He told tersely of his capture by Ohmo in the alley, of the murder of Chow Seto, and of Mega bringing him to the farm.

"The farmer is Chow Seto's brother, sir," the little man said. "I gather they use this place as a second storeroom for their drugs. And the stolen art collection was brought here! All the crates are downstairs."

"Good! McGrath's on his way out here now with a flying squad. He can put a heavy guard over that treasure until morning."

"I'm afraid it would do little good, sir," the valet said wryly. "There seems to have been a slight switch made. When Joe Mega broke open one of the crates all he found was an ordinary vase of baked red clay. It's now smashed into about a thousand pieces. Mega was that angry."

That clinched the suspicions about the Dragon Master that the Black Bat had imparted to I-tso Ling. He had been sure that the man in green had no intention of returning the treasure, but was using the others as dupes. Of course it was the Dragon Master who had made the substitution.

"We've got to get out of here in a hurry, Silk," the Black Bat said as they hurried toward the door. "We'll take one of the trucks and you drive. I'll cover us with the machine gun."

THEY GOT away in the same truck Silk had been brought in. As they pulled out the Chinese farmer came staggering out of the house shouting that he had heard the Black Bat telephoning the police. And at that information the mobsters were too busy with their own affairs to do more than fire a few shots at the escaping truck.

"We hadn't been in the barn but a little while," Silk finally said, as the truck sped along far ahead of the shooting, "until the others showed up with the loot they'd taken from the warehouse. And the minute they had opened some of the stolen cans you should have heard them yell! Those tins didn't contain dope, sir—there was nothing in them but ordinary mud! Which made me think that the tip Duke Kasini got about any contraband being in the warehouse was a trap set by narcotics agents."

"It looks that way. Yet for some unexplainable reason the Federal men arrived just a bit too late."

Silk nodded, his eyes on the road ahead. "So it would seem, sir. But those Dragons were really upset when they found the treasure was missing. Mega stormed and cursed. Somebody suggested that Kasini had double-crossed and framed his own men. But they were all wild, sir—and scared to death."

The Black Bat nodded and smiled beneath his hood.

"Things are beginning to happen, Silk—plenty," he said....

A GROUP of grim-faced men were in the living room of Dugro's home when Captain McGrath returned from a dash to the farm of Chow Seto's brother at instructions from Commissioner Warner. He reported to his superior that all the gangsters had fled, though some undoubtedly would be rounded up. Heffner, one of the remaining members of Eight Incorporated, angular, bony-faced and with a clipped gray mustache, sat on a couch, his mental stress plain in his eyes. Dr. Ling was there, and the little art expert had been horrified at learning that the Dragon Master had been in his own home. Colonel Wang and Paul Chivor were also present. Chivor was mostly silent, as usual, speaking only occasionally in low-toned Cantonese with Colonel Wang.

Dugro was in pretty bad shape. His left ankle was bandaged and rested straight out on an ottoman in front of his armchair. His head was swathed in bandages that covered a cheek which had been ripped open by a broken limb when he crashed down through the tree branches in his parachute.

"Those twenty-four-foot service 'chutes weren't built for joy-riding, but only to get a man down safely," he explained. "If I had seen the tree sooner I could have slipped the 'chute and missed it. Lord, what a night!"

"The question is, what is to be done now," spoke up Dr. Ling in his precise English. "In view of the Dragon Master's unexpected appearance in my house to ask me to act as intermediary, I have decided to assume that responsibility. Some settlement must be arranged about the treasure, for already two lives have been taken because of it, and more are threatened."

Heffner looked at Commissioner Warner.

"What do you advise, Commissioner?" he suggested.

The police veteran shook his head.

"I'm not advising, Mr. Heffner. The decision as to whether the demands of this Dragon Master shall be met rests with the members of Eight Incorporated who are still alive."

A pleasant voice came from the doorway.

"Exactly my sentiments, Commissioner Warner. Good evening, gentlemen."

LAST WARNING

E **VERY MAN** in the room twisted about to look at the hooded figure in black who stood in the doorway. He held an automatic in one hand and the gun seemed to be pointed more in Captain McGrath's direction than at any of the others. The Black Bat smiled at the expression on the big officer's face.

"How'd you get through those cops out there?" demanded McGrath as the Black Bat came in and placed himself so that he could watch all doors.

"It's not their fault, Captain. Now that I am here I want to say that I'm sorry you didn't get those birds out at that farm before they had flown tonight. I'm more disappointed about the treasure. I thought we had it."

"So did I," growled the detective disgustedly. "But there wasn't a thing in a single crate but red clay pottery. But we got the Chinese farmer who owned the place. Found him hiding out in a ditch in the field. He broke for it and one of the officers downed him. He talked before he died. Said he had helped the Dragon Master bring the stuff from somewhere in town and exchange it. Then the leader in the green robes took it away."

"Unfortunate," said the Black Bat. "That farmer, Captain, was the brother of Chow Seto, the laundryman from whose establishment Duke Kasini's drugs were retailed. Chow Seto was killed by Joe Mega tonight, shot in the back when the Chinese became frightened. Incidentally, Captain, you can swear out a murder charge against Mega for the clubbing to death of the museum watchman when the treasure was stolen. Witnesses were Manni Torrio and Blackie, other members of the Kasini mob. I heard them discussing it at the warehouse robbery tonight."

THE BLACK BAT'S DRAGON TRAIL 87

"Well I must say that I owe you an apology, Black Bat," put in Dugro warmly. "Had I known of the service you're rendering in this case I'd never have fired at you when you tried to stop me taking off in that plane, frightened though I was. Naturally I thought you were one of the Dragon Master's men, after Harrison.... You think then that these Chinese are members of Kasini's mob also, as well as of that Dragon society?"

"It's my theory that only four Chinese in this case are actual criminals—the three who worked Chow Seto's laundry, all of whom are dead, and likewise Chow Seto's brother, whose farm evidently was used as a drug cache. The rest of the Orientals have been duped into believing they're doing a great patriotic service for their mother country. There is one exception, of course. The monstrosity known as Ohmo."

"That's the ape Thing that grabbed Quinn in his house and also got Belmont," said McGrath, biting down viciously on his ever present cigar. "According to the officers on duty when I got there after the snatch, Belmont's Chinese valet began yelling from the front room, and they all responded except one man in the back. He turned just as the Thing grabbed him and almost broke his neck with a blow of its hand. It paralyzed him. Then the Thing went on, and a minute or two later was out again, carrying Belmont like a baby. By the time it got away that damned, double-crossing Chinese valet had run through a door leaving the officers in the front room, snapped the lock, and then beat it out the back way before they could break through."

"That Thing, as you so aptly call it," said the Black Bat, "undoubtedly is possessed of hyper-senses and the cunning of a jungle beast. Furthermore, I'm certain it or he was the instrument of destruction that killed those two police officers tonight."

Warner had been watching the Black Bat with vivid interest, and now he leaned forward in his chair tensely.

"Black Bat," he said tightly, "if you would tell the police who killed Fitzgerald and Murphy and how this green-robed madman did it, I'd almost write you a clean slate."

"Thank you, Commissioner, but I haven't been able to solve that riddle yet. All I'm certain of is—"

HE STOPPED short as from somewhere outside came the voices of two or three police officers, followed by some man's voice speaking angrily. Then footsteps sounded on the front porch.

"I'm all right, I tell you," snapped Harvey Belmont's voice. "You'd better remain outside."

The door opened and the financier strode in. He closed it behind him and stalked over to Commissioner Warner. Warner had risen, trying to mask his surprise at this sudden appearance of the financier. Moreover, Belmont looked anything but the victim of a kidnaping. He was dressed as though for the office, immaculate and dapper.

"You were supposed to give me protection, Commissioner?" he accused hotly. "What kind of a police force have we got in this town when a man is snatched from his own home under the noses of half a dozen officers?"

"Sit down, Mr. Belmont," said the commissioner quietly. "Suppose you just begin at the beginning and let's get this kidnaping business straight."

The financier sat down. He pulled out a handkerchief and mopped his face.

"It happened early this evening," Belmont began to tell the commissioner, twisting his thin, nervous hands as he had in Quinn's house. "As you know, I had sent away all servants except my Chinese valet. Quong, I knew was loyal—he has been with me for seven years. I was getting ready to call Harrison and find out if he still meant to leave town or had decided to stay. Then came that horrible—Thing! I caught one glimpse of its pinhead and naked shoulders before it almost broke my neck with some kind of a ju-jutsu blow. It slung me across its shoulders and ran like the wind across the grounds to where a laundry truck was waiting in the darkness."

"Who was in it?" cut in McGrath.

"I—I saw only some Chinese. That monster Thing threw me in the back and jumped right in with me. Someone taped my eyes. They kept cursing the avaricious Americans who were cheating China in her hour of need. We rode for quite some time until we came to a house. I've no idea where. The tape was never removed from my eyes. I was cursed and mauled and threatened but was not harmed otherwise."

"What became of your valet?" the commissioner asked. "We'll be able to pick him up easily."

For the first time, Harvey Belmont's eyes showed emotion. Into them came a look of sorrow. He shook his head.

"They shot him in that house they took me to, to insure against that very thing. It seems unbelievable that he would have been a party to such a thing as this Dragon business hold-up game. The poor fellow idolized me. Why, he'd even taught me to speak a few words of Chinese—like good-by and good morning and things like that.

"I was held in that house and threatened until I finally agreed to their demands. As soon as I did they took me out again and set me loose somewhere in the city. Two radio policemen found me stumbling along with my eyes still taped and my hands tied behind my back. I made them take me home first before bringing me here."

He reached into his pocket and brought forth a small object that all of them in that room had seen before. It was a little green jade Buddha with a note snapped around it, by rubber bands—the same Buddha that had been taken by Thompson from Tony Quinn's house. The financier handed the jade piece to Commissioner Warner.

"There are the demands, Commissioner, to which I've already agreed," he snapped, and added bluntly: "What else can a man do when he can get no police protection?"

QUIETLY THE police official took the note from around the Buddha and opened it. He read:

> To Those Concerned: This is the last warning from the Dragon. This is the last chance for those remaining members of the evil eight to accede to our just demands. Ten million dollars in cash must be collected at once and held in readiness to be delivered at the prescribed time and place. As soon as indications are given that these instructions are being followed, arrangements will be made for the return of the treasure and the money turned over to responsible representatives of the Chinese Government.
>
> The Dragon has spoken.

Commissioner Warner passed the note around for the others to read and when it was returned to him he put it in his pocket. He said nothing for a moment. Finally he spoke.

"You say you've agreed to raise the money, Mr. Belmont?"

Heffner's face expressed angry indignation. He shot the official a hostile look fraught with meaning.

"Eight million and not a cent more, Commissioner!" he snapped. "Threats or no threats!"

He turned to look defiantly at the Black Bat as he hurled his ultimatum, but the window drapes near which the man in black had stood hung emptily. The Black Bat was gone.

CHAPTER XVI

SURPRISE VISIT

WHILE TONY QUINN breakfasted on Silk's incomparable waffles stripped with bacon, and coffee early the following morning, he perused the early editions of the newspapers. He sat in the kitchen in his dressing gown while the little valet attended to the dishes and kept an eye out for the two officers on duty about the grounds.

The papers were filled with the story of Belmont's kidnaping and subsequent release, though the banker had been tight-lipped to reporters on all details concerning the treasure or any statement concerning payment to the Chinese society. But there was one other account of significance. Heffner's home had been damaged by a mysterious explosion in the early hours of the morning! But the only damage done was to tear away a large section of an enclosed back porch.

"Did you read this account of Heffner's home being bombed, Silk?" asked Quinn.

"Yes, sir. I went through the papers before you got up."

"I see also where the body of Belmont's Chinese valet was fished out of the river early this morning," remarked Quinn. "A barge captain tied up at a pier saw it and notified the police. They recovered two bullets for the ballistic experts."

"That at least is something, sir." Carol padded in from the spare bedroom she had occupied during the night, having difficulty keeping a pair of Quinn's house slippers on her feet. Her pretty face, minus the clever makeup Silk had applied the night before, rose above the folds of one of Quinn's silk dressing gowns beneath which she wore a pair of his pajamas.

"I'm starved," she announced. "Furthermore, I think it rude of you not to awaken me."

While she ate the breakfast, Silk quickly prepared for her, Quinn discussed the case with them both, and what their next moves should be. Then Butch slipped in through the tunnel.

"Nope, no breakfast for me right now," he declined, at Silk's look. "I had a snack—two plates of ham and eggs and toast and four cups of.... Well, all right, I'll drink another cup of coffee with Carol. What's on the fire for today?"

"You, Carol, will stay on here as nurse," Quinn instructed. "And, Silk, I want you to find out where Paul Chivor is staying."

"Commissioner Warner has already mentioned that he and Colonel Wang are at the Hotel Lamont, sir. I believe it's not far from Chinatown."

Later in the morning Quinn and Butch left the house by the tunnel, Quinn wearing his usual broad-brimmed black hat pulled low over his eyes. A telephone call to the Hotel Lamont asking for Chivor in Room One Twenty-eight had elicited the information that Chivor's room was Two Twenty-six and that he was out.

Tony Quinn, the Black Bat now that he was again on the prowl, even in the bright morning hours, headed his car in the direction of Chinatown and the Hotel Lamont.

The hotel at which the flying Chinese colonel and the American pilot were staying proved to be a brick affair some five stories high. Butch stopped the coupé a short distance away and Quinn got out, his collar turned up. No one paid particular attention to the man who strolled along the sidewalk and then suddenly vanished. Quinn's lithe muscles carried him up over a board fence and into a small yard paved with brick. Overhead was a fire-escape. He leaped for the lower rung, pulled himself up and went up to the second floor. He stepped into a carpeted hallway lined with doors on each side. Two Twenty-six was three doors down on the right.

QUINN'S SKELETON keys quickly extracted a lock's secret and he slipped inside of the room occupied by Paul Chivor.

He began a quick search of the man's belongings. The two steamer trunks, however, were protected by a lock of some devilish combination so small that even Quinn's keys were helpless against them. He gave it up and looked about him.

The dresser drawers revealed nothing, so he went to the clothes closet. A low exclamation came from him as his silk-clad fingers felt a small metal object in a pocket of one of the suits. He brought forth a numbered disk, that was an exact duplicate of the one Butch had taken from Chow Seto's place the night before!

"So Paul Chivor is a drug user," the Black Bat said under his breath. "Probably started hitting the stuff in China. When he came over here with Wang and the treasure he had to find a new source of supply. So he contacted Chow Seto's Laundry and this is his identification which—"

He broke off in his soliloquy, his hyper-sensitive ears warning him that someone was in the hall.

"No, sir, Mr. Chivor," he heard a woman's voice say. "I haven't got to your room yet but I will right away."

Quinn stepped into a corner. With remarkable speed he slipped from his light coat and hat into the Black Bat outfit. He rolled his discarded clothing into a compact bundle and stowed it away just as the Black Bat rig had been. Footsteps were coming down the hall.

But to the Black Bat's surprise Chivor's soft footsteps on the thick carpeting went right on past his own door and down the hall toward the fire-escape through which the Black Bat had entered. The Black Bat risked cracking the door a trifle. He saw the pilot stop in front of a corner room, glance casually about, then unlock the door and step inside.

Paul Chivor was sneaking into Colonel Wang's room!

The Black Bat opened the door wider, glanced up and down the hall. The maid's brooms and linen cart stood outside a door further down. From inside the room came the hum of her voice as she cleaned the room. The Black Bat stepped out, became a flitting shadow down the hall, pausing before Colonel Wang's door.

Gently he turned the knob. He slid into the room, a .38 automatic on one hand as Chivor, a cool look on his face, turned and faced him.

"Good morning, Mr. Chivor," greeted the Black Bat quietly.

The cool look left the pilot's face instantly and gave way to something resentfully surly. His handsome features grew dark.

"You certainly seem to get around, don't you?" he grunted.

"Sometimes it's unavoidably necessary," replied the Black Bat. Then his voice grew suddenly stern. "Why did you find it convenient to become intoxicated the other night when you were expected to save a man's life by flying him out of town?" he demanded.

"I told you why," Chivor said grumpily. "I stopped in at a bar and just happened to take a couple too many."

The Black Bat smiled beneath the black hood hiding his scarred features from this man who was so much of an enigma.

"I'm afraid I hardly can believe that, Mr. Chivor," he replied softly. "When I shook you awake in the chair in the watchman's office out at the hangar your eyes showed undeniable surprise at sight of me when you opened them. You quickly closed them to keep from showing it, feigning sleepiness due to overindulgence in alcohol. Further, you sobered up with remarkable speed on the coffee I gave you."

"Which means what?" growled Chivor, his eyes narrowing speculatively.

"That you had some reason for not wanting to fly Mr. Harrison in that death plane. You either knew that that plane was carrying him to his death or you had some other reason for not wanting to leave town."

Slowly the Black Bat's hand unclosed. A bright disk was lying in his black, silk-gloved palm.

"Mr. Chivor," he said, looking the man straight in the eyes, "would it by any chance have been that you had just put in an order to Chow Seto's laundry for some heroin or other dope earlier in the day, and were waiting around for a new supply of the 'snow' to show up?"

Chivor refused to answer.

CHAPTER XVII

A CALL ON A LADY

UTTER SILENCE blanketed the room for a moment. The Black Bat was swiftly turning over in his mind the facts that Silk had found out about Chivor's life in California, of how the man had had his regular transport pilot's license taken away by a civil aeronautics inspector for stunting when he had been drinking too heavily.

The Black Bat also was remembering that the Asiation Export and Import outfit which Harvey Belmont now owned was a West Coast concern. Or had been before getting into trouble with the State Department over the shipment of planes to European belligerents as military fighters. That meant Chivor had known Belmont before seeing him here.

The hooded investigator tried a shot in the dark.

"Mr. Chivor," he said, "as you probably know, Harvey Belmont owns a good deal of the stock in Mr. Dugro's present factory, presumably having been his financial backer. That means you undoubtedly knew Mr. Belmont while you were flying out on the Coast, and possibly Mr. Dugro as well, since one of their principal concerns out there was the Asiation Export and Import Company. Could your present dislike for Mr. Dugro—which has been plainly evident to me ever since you showed no concern that he might have been killed in that exploding plane—have any connection with your having been grounded while flying for them out there?"

The pilot's eyes began to grow hard and more speculative. Otherwise he displayed nothing more to express the evident surprise the Black Bat's question had caused.

"I'll say one thing for you, Black Bat, you really do find out things, don't you?" he admitted begrudgingly. "If you want to know the truth I *was* flying for Dugro out there before he sold the outfit to Belmont. Dugro went to China to sell new ships to that Government. But that didn't pan out, so he came back and got in touch with Belmont again. As near as I can find out, Dugro was sorry about Belmont losing so much dough in the company through him. In other words, Dugro had sold ships to Spain as fighters before he realized he was breaking the law. By the time Old Whiskers caught up with Asiation Export, Belmont was left holding the sack.

"Anyhow,"—he shrugged—"Belmont turned right around and backed Dugro in this new venture, to get back the dough he'd lost. This present Chinese plane order will do it, with a couple of millions profit for Belmont."

"If Colonel Wang okays the Dugro bomber," supplemented the Black Bat.

"If the colonel okays the ship," Chivor repeated, nodding. "But I might as well tell you—that bomber is no good. It's a death-trap. I've tried to tell Wang so, but he's one of those methodical Chinese who's got to find out things for himself. He'll find it out, too, if he ever puts her into a spin with a load test. She'll wind up like a corkscrew. It's in the design of the wing."

The Black Bat then asked Chivor bluntly why he had entered Wang's room so surreptitiously. But Chivor only growled something about being Wang's friend, and refused to answer further. Under the muzzle of the Black Bat's .38, Chivor left the room and entered his own. As soon as the pilot had closed his door the Black Bat, left in the dim hall, stripped off his hooded disguise and hastily donned his coat and hat, leaving again by the fire-escape....

"What did you find out, Boss?" Butch demanded eagerly as the car was headed back toward the estate.

The Black Bat shook his head and frowned.

"Nothing of importance, except that Chivor is the new customer whose number was added to that of the laundry's customers."

"You think maybe he could be figuring on grabbing the dough all for himself when it's delivered?" suggested Butch.

"I wish I knew what has been decided about that payoff," was the Black Bat's only answer.

THERE WAS only one way to find out, and as soon as the Black Bat was again Tony Quinn, safely home and in his bedroom, he called Commissioner Warner on the telephone.

"Good morning, Commissioner," he greeted, his voice that of the sick man he was supposed to be. "How are you?"

Commissioner Warner's voice told how he was. From its tone Quinn judged that the gray-haired police veteran had not slept much.

"Frankly, Tony," he told Quinn, "I'm on edge. With the money to redeem that treasure being raised this morning, and—"

"How much?" Quinn interrupted.

"Ten millions. Belmont and his associates are drawing on banks all over town. Of course you'll be called on for your share—if you haven't been already. Heffner has changed his mind most decidedly and is having more brought in by a special plane this morning. From out of town banks. He is frightened stiff. That explosion which tore off the corner of the back porch of his house came too close for comfort."

"Silk read me the account of it, Commissioner," Quinn said. "Wasn't there any clue of any sort?"

"Not a thing. Just a pile of splintered wood and broken glass. The grounds were alive with police officers, too—and they didn't hear a thing until the explosion came. There isn't a trace of any wiring, or any metal fragments of a bomb, to be found by our experts. The thing seemed to come right out of thin air, just as it did at your place."

Quinn asked about developments in the apprehension of Duke Kasini and his now decimated mob.

"They've disappeared as though swished right off the face of the earth, Tony," Warner informed, and sighed heavily. "We've combed this town with a fine-tooth comb—and not a sign of them."

Tony Quinn spoke a few minutes longer, then waited through the day, lying in bed and reading, though he was on tenterhooks, impatient to take a hand in the game. He was willing enough to put up his share of the redemption money, if there wasn't any other way, but he much preferred to get the treasure back.

There would be a reasonable profit for him and the remaining members of the Eight, later, even by paying ten millions, but he wanted that money to go to the proper channels. He was not thinking of profit for himself.

As soon as it was dark, the Black Bat went on the prowl again.

Once more when the Black Bat reached the locality, a blanket of darkness lay over Chinatown. Neon signs from a hundred cafes and other places threw their iridescent glow against the night as though trying to push back its enveloping folds. On the crooked, cobblestoned streets the tide of humanity moved on, as ceaseless as the flow of a river.

From the darkness of a rooftop the Black Bat stood peering down a moment. Then on his felt-soled shoes he moved like a wraith across the roofs toward Dr. Ling's home.

As the Black Bat had suggested to I-tso Ling, she had left the skylight unlatched. That meant that she also had disposed of the servants temporarily, so that there would be none to be frightened by the Black Bat's sudden appearance. His silk-gloved fingers raised the lid and there came a rustling sound as he went down the steep steps into the upper hall.

He crept on noiseless feet to the second floor below. At the door of I-tso's bedroom he paused a moment, listening. From somewhere down in the shop on the ground floor came a faint murmur of voices. The Black Bat's hand turned the knob to the girl's bedroom and he went in.

She was not there. But in the darkness his night-trained eyes soon saw the piece of white paper tucked in the shaded lamp beside her bed. He crossed the room and unfolded the note. There was no need for him to turn on the light. Her writing was as plain to his eyes as though it had been broad daylight. She had written:

> Black Bat,
> If I'm not in when you come, I'll try to be in my father's shop down-stairs.
> I-tso Ling.

THE BLACK BAT took time to burn the note behind cupped hands before leaving. As he started down to the shop floor he discovered that the stairs leading down into the shop came out on a small balcony landing before going on down. From this the proprietor could see over his wares from above, as well as observe any customers who might have entered while he was out.

From this landing the Black Bat now looked down to where I-tso Ling, her patriarchal little father, the professor, and Harvey Belmont were speaking. Strangely enough no lights were on, and the front shades were drawn tight.

Harvey Belmont was exhibiting extreme nervousness. In the darkness the Black Bat could see him twisting his thin hands as he usually did when under stress.

"I got the message just a few minutes ago," he was explaining to Dr. Ling. "I came right on down alone at once as I was instructed. There are no police about, the guards all having been withdrawn from us as the Dragon Master ordered."

"To say that I am horrified at what you have told me is a weak state-ment, Mr. Belmont," said the little Chinese art expert. He touched his daughter on the arm. "And now, my child, you will go upstairs to your room. This is a matter that does not concern one of such tender years. Mr. Belmont is here on a very grave mission. Go."

The girl obediently turned and felt her way up the steps. She made her way along the landing toward the second short flight leading up to the floor above. As she did so a hand crept out of the drapes and lightly touched hers. She gave a faint little gasp of surprise.

Then the Black Bat's whisper came softly in her ear. "Wait for me in your room."

The girl went on up the stairs and the Black Bat moved unseen down into the shop. He stood within five feet of the two men, yet neither were aware of it.

"But that's the orders that I received, Dr. Ling," Belmont was saying. "I was to come here to your shop and look for the instructions."

"May I ask what instructions, gentlemen?" asked a pleasant voice.

Belmont gave a half strangled cry of fear and stepped back, almost stumbling over a stone Buddha on the floor behind him. He recovered, however, as he seemed to recognize their visitor.

"How did you get in here?" demanded Dr. Ling crisply.

"A part of my—er—professional ethics, Dr. Ling. I believe that Mr. Belmont has been given orders by the Dragon Master to come here and look for instructions—right?"

"And I've been warned that if I make one false move I'll die by being blown to bits," the financier said quickly. "There was no mistaking the menace in that voice that spoke to me on the telephone. It said that I was to come here to Dr. Ling's art shop and look for a little green jade Buddha that was part of the collection of stolen Chinese art. It was an exact duplicate of the one that was presented to Anthony Quinn."

"In that case, gentlemen, you need not bother to turn on the light," the Black Bat told them, and moved quickly away. "If you'll just stand there for a moment I shall be glad to get it for you."

It took him less than two minutes to find the familiar-looking little Buddha. It was back among a number of other art pieces on a small shelf. And when the Black Bat picked it up, he discovered that a folded note was on the underside, held in place by rubber bands. The Black Bat returned with it.

"Here it is, gentlemen," he announced gravely.

"Now come with me, both of you," said Dr. Ling.

IN A back room that served as office for the little Chinese, Dr. Ling switched on a light. Harvey Belmont took the Buddha and unfolded the note. The Bat, peering over his shoulder, read:

> The Dragon is pleased to see that you have come to your senses, Mr. Belmont. It is regrettable that your two foolish colleagues were not so wise. The money you have raised today will be placed in a large suitcase. You will do this alone and without telephoning the police. At precisely ten o'clock tonight you will return to the Ling's shop and deliver this suitcase there. I left your instructions here so that you would have no trouble in finding the place when you deliver the money. To disobey means death.
>
> The Dragon has spoken.

"But, gentlemen," gasped Dr. Ling, when he also had read the note, his almond eyes going first to one and then the other of his two unusual visitors, "this would appear as though I myself am a party to this insidious scheme. And I swear that never has that jade piece been in my humble establishment before this night."

"Quite likely it was left here by one of the many people who came in during the day to browse," suggested the Black Bat. "But it shows a devilish cunning on the part of the Dragon Master. By the time the money is delivered here it will be ordered taken to some other person. That way only one person will know where the final delivery to the Dragon Master himself will be made and in what manner. Very clever, gentlemen."

"Too clever," shot back Harvey Belmont, in a rage. "To think that a man would spend his life building up something only to have it taken away by some gangster from whom the police can't protect him! It's—"

But he spoke only to an empty doorway where the Black Bat had stepped back, for the hooded figure had vanished.

CHAPTER XVIII

DEATH OF A RAT

CAUTIOUSLY THE BAT slipped upstairs and opened the door to I-tso's bedroom. The girl was waiting in the darkened room.

"I'm frightened, Black Bat, very frightened," she confessed to him, coming nearer to him as though for protection. "You haven't forgotten I told you there's to be a meeting of the Dragons tonight at the regular place deep beneath the block of condemned buildings sometime near midnight?"

"I looked for an entrance last night after leaving the farm of Chow Seto's brother, but found only a steel door two flights down," the Black Bat said. "I had a pretty good idea that it is wired, so I did not go too close to it. I tried to find another entrance, but found none."

"There is one more—which I will tell you about," the girl whispered quickly. "But about this meeting—only Duke Kasini and his men will be present, except for the Dragon Master. They are to be paid off for opening the vault. The Chinese members who have been hiding them from the police have already been disbanded. The Dragon society is no more."

"Then why are you frightened?"

"Because," she said, "at ten o'clock tonight I have been ordered by the Dragon Master on pain of death to me and to my honorable father to take a certain suitcase full of money and deliver it to the home of Anthony Quinn!"

For an instant that was a startler for the Black Bat, but he showed nothing of his surprise. Here was a strange new twist, but he would be able to straighten it out all right, particularly now that he was forewarned.

"Don't worry too much about it," he told the Chinese girl. "I'll try to be around the Quinn house when you arrive, so I can telephone Commissioner Warner as soon as I find out where Quinn is going with that suitcase you deliver."

After a few more words with the girl he went up through the skylight again. Down in the street he sought the nearest telephone booth, and called the commissioner. The harried police official was still in his office.

"Good evening, Commissioner," the hooded man in the closed booth said. "This is the Black Bat. Have there been any new developments in the treasure ransom case yet?"

"Only one," answered the commissioner, who was always secretly glad to coöperate with the Black Bat. "Belmont has been ordered to deliver the money personally to some other person tonight. He couldn't—or wouldn't—tell me who that person is."

"I think I can enlighten you, Commissioner. The ransom is to be delivered by Harvey Belmont to Dr. Ling."

"Ling?" The commissioner's voice was startled. "It doesn't seem possible that—"

"And that isn't all," the Black Bat cut in. "Ling doesn't know it yet, but his own daughter has been ordered, on a threat of death, to take the money to Tony Quinn's house immediately upon its delivery to her father."

An explosive growl came from the other end of the line.

"The devil you say! But that means I'll probably get orders through Belmont to pull off the guard around Quinn's house—with that Dragon outfit after Quinn. If I pull off that guard I may be a party to Tony Quinn's murder!"

"It's something we'll have to risk, Commissioner. I can't imagine who Quinn is expected to contact with the money. Have you any knowledge of Paul Chivor's whereabouts?"

"I telephoned his hotel—the Lamont—a little while ago but he's not in. Neither is Colonel Wang."

"Well, anyhow, here's some news of the utmost importance, Commissioner. Tonight the remaining members of Duke Kasini's fugitive mob are assembling at the orders of the Dragon Master. They'll be in a secret room deep beneath a group of condemned buildings on Exeter Street in Chinatown. If you'll wait until they all gather and then surround that building with picked men, you probably will be able to bag the entire lot. Good luck, Commissioner."

QUINN LEFT the telephone booth and headed toward Exeter Street. The Chinese girl had given him exact instructions in the matter of effecting an entrance through one of the two passages. He wanted to find the thug Ohmo and, if necessary, put an end to the murderous monstrosity before it took more human life. And I-tso had told the Black Bat that Ohmo lived deep below the buildings when not on his grim errands for the green-robed Dragon Master.

Presently the Black Bat crawled in through a gaping window yawning in the night. He made his way along a crumbling hallway that had felt the passage of a thousand tenants. The floor was littered with refuse and fallen plaster and crumpled newspapers. Small wonder that the entire block of ancient slum edifices had been condemned by the city. Small wonder, too, that the Dragon Master had had a meeting room hastily prepared there when organizing the Dragon society.

And he had taken just the right way to draw the Chinese members into that murderous organization. The Black Bat knew Chinese psychology, knew how secret meetings, a green-robed leader, and a just cause to aid the mother country in her hour of need would appeal to the Orientals. Though most of them had taken little part in the affairs of the Dragon society, aside from helping in the kidnaping of Harvey Belmont. One Dragon had been a servant in the Belmont house.

The Black Bat moved into the small kitchen of an ancient flat to an ordinary trap door that led to a cellar. He raised it and went down. Through an underground passage he went on beneath three or four of the condemned tenement houses.

In the last of several cellars he passed through he paused. He knew he now was beneath the main building and somewhere near the meeting room. A peculiarly offensive odor came to his nostrils. It came from behind the next door.

The Black Bat's automatic came out as he grasped the knob. He opened it slowly, stepped into a room that he at once knew was the living quarters of Ohmo, the deformed Chinese. There was a pile of dirty blankets in a corner that served as bed, and a conglomeration of food-stuffs on a makeshift table in another corner. But the mute was nowhere about.

As the Black Bat looked about the room, voices came from somewhere nearby. He went out and turned into another short passage. There were heavy drapes ahead. He parted them with a finger to look through—and felt cold chills of surprise at sight of I-tso Ling talking to Flash Mega in front of a makeshift altar surmounted by a dragon's head! Beyond and below was the main meeting room.

How could I-tso have reached here ahead of him, he wondered. Then he remembered that after leaving her he had lost a little time making his telephone call. Evidently she had hurried here immediately. Why? Had she come to prepare a trap for the Black Bat in obedience to orders from the Dragon Master? Or could she have come to help him, in case he ran into trouble?

The fugitive gangster was far from the flashy character he had been only two days before. His swarthy face registered the fact that he was well aware that Duke Kasini's mob was in a tight spot. Even so, at the moment his black eyes were all for the girl. He had a coil of fine electric wire in one hand.

"Listen, baby, I've been trying to see you," he was saying to I-tso. "We're getting paid off tonight. Only the Dragon guy is giving me and Joe all the mob's dough for wiring this joint with nitro. He's gonna blow all the rest of 'em into a thousand pieces. I ain't told Joe yet. But do you know what that means? With all the dough I'm gettin' tonight it's South America for me. But you're gonna be a fugitive, too—you're in on this Dragon business—so I've got the cute idea that I'm taking you with me tonight."

BEFORE SHE could express the contempt for the mobster that was plain in her eyes a buzzer almost over the Black Bat's head sounded twice. Someone was at the steel door at the opposite side of the room. The Black Bat melted back as Flash Mega's diamond-studded hand reached inside the curtains within inches of the Black Bat's face and pressed a button. From across the room came the click of an electrically operated bolt and the door swung open. Then the green-robed figure of the Dragon Master himself entered!

He came over to the altar to the other two. The girl shrank back in spite of her obvious efforts to remain calm.

"What are you doing here?" he demanded of her. "Did not I order you to remain in your room until ten o'clock?"

"Master, I wanted to be sure of my instructions—"

"You lie! Your punishment will be decided later. Go!"

Obediently she went to the steel door at the opposite side of the room, pulled back the handle on the electrically operated bolt, opened it and disappeared. The green-robed figure turned to Mega.

"You have wired everything according to my instructions?" he demanded.

Flash Mega gave the Dragon Master a hard grin.

"Everything," he said boastfully. "It's a neat job too, pal—I mean Master. I was a pretty good radio man in my punk days. Boy, are a bunch of guys in this town gonna get a surprise tonight!"

The figure in green nodded.

"More than you think," the Dragon Master said coldly. "You disobeyed my orders again by your silly infatuation for one who is a thousand times too good for you." In a movement almost too swift for the eyes to follow, he whipped out an automatic. "You fool—to think I'd let you live now that you're no longer useful to me!"

The automatic spouted a snake's tongue lick of flame and Flash Mega's cry of surprise ended in the thud of his body to the concrete floor in front of the altar. But from the curtains over the doorway the Black Bat had stepped through and now his own .38 added its din to the other, deafening in the confines of the room deep under Chinatown. The Dragon Master's gun went spinning from his hand. He started to bend down after it, froze rigidly at the sight of the grim figure who had smashed all his plans.

"I think I've got you this time," the Bat informed him coolly. "I—"

He broke off as a strange, tinkling sound came to his ears. It was the sound of a whistle pitched too high for ordinary human ears—the same sort of whistle with which the Black Bat had supplied his own aides. And it was coming from inside that weird dragon mask!

From behind the Black Bat there came a rush of a body, and he wheeled just as Ohmo plunged through the curtains. The Thing took one single glance at the Black Bat as the Dragon Master shrieked orders in Cantonese. Then it sprang through the air straight at the intruder.

The Black Bat's .38 poured a stream of slugs into Ohmo as he ducked aside to avoid that rush. Ohmo, however, grabbed him with one of those iron hands as he fell. A little bubbling sound came through the gorillalike nostrils that told of blood pouring into lungs. Yet as they fell together, the Black Bat trying to get out his second automatic, he knew that unless he worked loose Ohmo would crush the life from his body, even in dying.

And the pinheaded monstrosity was dying. The Black Bat could hear the strangle in the labored breathing. But the Thing was true to its master to the last. It had been ordered to kill the hooded Nemesis, and those terrible hands were summoning the last of their fading strength to obey.

A hand with fingers of steel closed over the Black Bat's right bicep and worked up to his neck. He flung himself this way and that knotting his hard-muscled body as he strove to get out his other gun. At last he got it out, and as that huge hand found his throat, he began pumping bullet after bullet into the monster's naked body. It gave a final strangled sigh and relaxed.

Then the Black Bat was up and looking about him, shoving in fresh clips, wondering why the Dragon Master had not come to his killer monstrosity's aid. But the Dragon Master was gone.

A groan came from Flash Mega. The Black Bat bent over the dying gangster. Flash opened his eyes, looked up at the hooded Nemesis above him, and a faint, ironical grin broke his hard features.

"Joe always said I'd get in trouble on account of a dame," he mumbled, and died.

The Black Bat got out of the building as soon as possible. Where the Dragon Master had gone he had no idea. It was too late to hunt for him now.

He hurried home and went in through the tunnel. Once in the house, he called in the others and told them of what had happened. After that there was nothing to do but wait until I-tso Ling arrived.

She came shortly before ten. The hidden Quinn, watching through a window, saw a car pull up at the curb below.

He focused his glasses on the driver, pulling him up close. The man at the wheel was Colonel Wang!

CHAPTER XIX

DEATH FLIGHT

VASTLY INTERESTED, Silk hurried down and helped the Chinese girl bring up the suitcase containing package after package of bills in the biggest denominations printed. Silk brought the girl into the bedroom where Quinn was tucked under the covers, wearing the cap made of bandage.

"Mr. Quinn?" I-tso inquired in her soft voice, taking the chair Silk offered her. "I've been ordered by the Dragon Master to bring this suitcase to you with a message."

"To me?" he asked weakly. "Why should he send you to a sick man?"

"That I do not know. I only know that had I not obeyed my father would have paid with his life—as perhaps you know others have paid for disobedience to the Dragon Master's commands. Here is the message I was to deliver to you."

She handed him a note which Silk took from her.

"As you must have been told, Miss Ling, Mr. Quinn is stone-blind," said the valet. "Shall I read it to you, sir?" At Quinn's weak gesture he opened it and read it aloud. The message stated:

> Greetings from the Dragon, Mr. Quinn: Knowing your interest in the cause of justice in spite of the fact that you also have an interest in Eight Incorporated, I know that you will be most eager to offer your humble services to China. You are to take this fund to which you have undoubtedly contributed and deliver it to Mr. Dugro, who has been given some instructions. This enclosed letter which you are to hand him will give him further instructions about what to do with the redemption fund. Mr. Dugro is waiting at the airport.
> The Dragon has spoken.

"Well, of course I shall do everything possible to coöperate," said Quinn from his bed. "Though I had not expected to be called out of a sick bed. Thank you very much for coming, Miss Ling."

As soon as Silk showed I-tso Ling from the room Quinn leaped up out of bed and grabbed a pencil and paper. Hastily he printed a few sentences on it and slipped on his Black Bat outfit. Silk already had been told to keep the Chinese girl talking for a few minutes, and so it was that when she started back toward the car she was startled to see the Black Bat appear out of the night and hand her a note.

"Act on this immediately," he told her in a low voice. "Tell him the Black Bat will deliver the money. I'm going to—er—hijack Tony Quinn."

With Butch driving the coupé, the Black Bat presently saw the outlines of Dugro's plane factory buildings shape up. No lights at all showed. An air of gloom permeated the place. The Black Bat ordered the impatient Butch to stop some distance away, announcing that he would go on alone.

"Aw, Boss," pleaded Butch, "can't I just go in there with you and crack *somebody's* head?"

"Not this trip, Butch."

He took the heavy suitcase and, carrying it easily, went in through the gate and around the corner. The new bomber was sitting on the darkened tarmac, and Walter Dugro was pacing up and down not far away. He was not aware that anyone was near until the Black Bat spoke pleasantly.

"Good evening, Mr. Dugro."

Dugro whirled with an exclamation, then saw the Black Bat.

"Whew, you gave me a start, Black Bat! I—I was expecting Tony Quinn."

"I relieved him of the money, quite forcibly, on his way out here," the Black Bat said coolly. "I thought it best to take his place."

"Thank heaven you have it, anyway!" exclaimed the airplane manufacturer. "I received telephoned orders a little while ago to wait here with the ship ready. That was all."

"Right. I have your orders as to how and to whom you will deliver the ransom. If you'll step inside a moment you can read them."

DUGRO SLID back the steel sliding door for them to enter. He opened the note and read it by the light of the match held by the Black Bat.

"Good lord!" he breathed.

"Bad news?"

"As far as any hope of thwarting this Dragon Master fellow is concerned."

"Suppose I go with you?"

Dugro pulled out his handkerchief and mopped his sweating face. His hand shook slightly as he returned it to a pocket.

"It will mean my death to disobey orders, Black Bat, but I'd feel a lot safer if you would," he said in unconcealed relief. "Just promise me you'll keep down out of sight when we land."

Dugro showed the Black Bat the note with the instructions. The airplane manufacturer's orders were to fly south to the Silverton Country Club and make a landing on a three-hundred-yard stretch of level turf on the golf course. Here he was to toss out the suitcase, then fly back again.

Donning parachutes, Dugro and the Black Bat went out to the ship. Then they were in the air, climbing up into the black night.

Dugro sat in the left-hand seat, the wheel in his expert hands. The Black Bat stood further back in the fuselage.

"You say we're to land on the golf course at Silverton?" the Black Bat asked, above the drone of the motors. "Isn't there danger of a crack-up with no ground lights?"

"I can handle her all right—I think. She lands pretty slow and I've got good landing lights in the wings."

"I suppose this Dragon Master would like nothing better than to know that the Black Bat was aboard," the hooded man suggested, with a dry chuckle. "With him out of the way the head of this sweet racket would have nothing to fear."

Dugro nodded. "That's right. The Black Bat almost spoiled everything for him. He would never be safe as long as the Black Bat was alive."

"Which, I think, is why you were so eager to let me come along," the Black Bat said coolly. "I became certain of that after noticing that your compass is *not* pointing south."

Dugro whirled in the seat, whipping out his gun with one hand. The plane lurched wildly. But the Black Bat had made a flying dive forward and grabbed the man who had been masquerading as the Dragon Master, pinioning his arms.

"Quick, Wang!" he yelled over his shoulder. "Come up here and get these controls!"

With motors roaring the ship went into a dive while the Black Bat struggled to unsnap Dugro's belt and drag him free of the controls. Leaping from where he had been lying prone behind ballast sandbags, Colonel Wang fell headlong down on top of both men and got into the pilot's seat.

When the Bat had printed that message and given it to I-tso Ling he had suspected that the bomber might play some part in this intricate extortion scheme, after the money should be delivered to Dugro, and the contents of his note to Wang had sent the Chinese racing to the field where Dugro was waiting. When Quinn had drawn Dugro inside the hangar to read the message it had given the waiting Chinese time to hide himself back in the fuselage.

Dugro was fighting now like an insane man.

"I knew I should have shot you the moment you appeared," the airplane man panted. "That's what I was going to do later—then knock myself out after returning the treasure to the proper people." Somehow he seemed to be taking a keen joy in making this boastful clean breast of things.

"You're not trying to say that you actually intended to return it?" demanded the Black Bat.

DUGRO WAS subdued now. He lay on the floor of the droning ship as Wang circled and headed back toward the field.

"Yes. It is hidden in some empty motor crates in my factory. It was this way—Belmont didn't know that this bomber is a death-trap should it ever get into a spin with a load. I knew he'd never advance another penny for some corrections necessary in the wing design. In his greed to get that ten million dollar order he kept pressing me until I was desperate. I also knew Wang was going to find out the truth.

"So I had to stall them both—Wang on the tests, and Belmont. The only way out was to steal the treasure, force them to pay ransom for it, then use the money to have a dummy buyer buy out Belmont's share after telling him the plane was no good. That way I would have got control of my factory again, would have money to redesign the wing, and—" He glared at the Black Bat as he shouted wildly: "And I'd have done it too if it hadn't been for you!"

Wang circled the field at less than five hundred feet and let down the wheels. He brought the ship in for a landing. By now the front of the hangar was lit up, and as they rolled to a stop the Black Bat saw men emerge from it.

Dugro moved then, taking the Black Bat completely by surprise. He wrenched his right hand free and caught the hooded man with a terrific blow along the side of the neck.

The Black Bat's whole lower body went half paralyzed and his legs gave way. He tried to get up as Dugro leaped over him, dived through the fuselage door, and broke into a run.

And the Black Bat, trying to drag himself toward the door, saw him go—helpless to do a thing.

Then from the pilot's compartment behind him came the snapping reports of a 9mm Luger. Wang shooting through the open window.

Dugro stumbled and went down, tried to get up, and lay still as more bullets from the Luger poured into him.

A familiar figure detached itself from the group emerging from the hangar. McGrath! He ran forward, poking his head in the door.

"Well, Black Bat, I knew I'd get you some day," he stated in a matter-of-fact voice to the prostrate figure on the floor of the fuselage. He brought out his handcuffs. "You should have known that. Here—stick 'em out."

A cool voice in broken English cut in then, its owner lining the Luger pistol at McGrath's thick middle.

"So sorry please," said Colonel Wang apologetically. "No take him tonight. Velly good fliend of Wang."

CHAPTER XX

CHECKMATED AGAIN

NOT TEN minutes later the Black Bat still sat in the doorway of the plane talking to Chivor, Belmont, Dr. Ling, and McGrath. I-tso Ling, who had come to the airport with Wang, had put in appearance and was up in the pilot's seat with him.

"And so, gentlemen, that's about how it happened," said the Black Bat, finishing the long, detailed account he had been giving. "Dugro's Asiation Export outfit had been exporting planes to belligerents from California. He saw trouble brewing and tricked Mr. Belmont into buying him out while he skipped out to China until things quieted down. Later he came back and got Mr. Belmont to back him in this present plant. But the bomber was a failure and Dugro knew it. He had known Duke Kasini in China, and when he heard of the art collection being brought over he conceived the idea of settling all his troubles by a big coup. He organized the Dragon society merely as a front for his activities."

The Black Bat looked at Paul Chivor who was with the others.

"I still don't know where you fit into this, Mr. Chivor," the Black Bat said. "Somehow, though I'm convinced you're not such a scoundrel as I was inclined to believe."

"Thank you," replied the pilot. "As a matter of fact, I'm with the Bureau of Narcotics. Before I joined the Bureau I was a pilot. I was flying for a California concern—Asiation Export—when word came from my superiors that a District Attorney Anthony Quinn of this city had a lead to the fact that Duke Kasini was smuggling in huge quantities of opium from China. We had been after him for years. My new assignment was to go to China and try to ferret him out from that end.

"So to make it look good I stunted a plane, got myself fired, and we arranged to have my regular license revoked. After which I pulled the drinking act and went to China. It took months and months, but I finally traced Kasini's shipments to European ports and finally here on a tanker. We got that last one, but he was too clever to put himself in the open. We laid a trap. I got word to Kasini that his confiscated shipment of drugs was in an old warehouse, hoping he'd try to hijack it. I also contacted Chow Seto's laundry as a customer, to clinch my evidence.

"We waited and waited at the warehouse for Kasini to make his play. Nearly three weeks. He never seemingly took the bait. Finally, last night, one of our operatives telephoned that the whole mob had been seen near the Chow Seto laundry—around the hotel next door. We decided to take the gamble of grabbing them off there and convicting them on the evidence we already had. So we raced to the place, only to find it in roaring flames. By the time we got back to the warehouse the mob had struck—a fluke that wouldn't happen again in a hundred years."

"And now we've got them all surrounded down beneath those condemned buildings," Commissioner Warner said grimly. "If they don't come out we'll get them with tear gas."

"No—no, Commissioner!" the Black Bat shouted, and swiftly told how Flash Mega had wired the place with nitro. A startled look came over the commissioner's face as he swung to McGrath.

"Get on the phone and tell them to hold off!" he barked sharply, urgently. "Hurry!"

I-tso Ling moved hastily over to the Black Bat and bent with her lips to his ear. She whispered something in it. He turned to Warner and the others.

"It seems that Miss Ling was informed by the Dragon Master—Dugro—before she went to Quinn's house with the treasure that he had ordered Flash Mega to fix up some kind of devilish contraption that could be exploded when Dugro broadcasted on an unused wave length. I'm also assuming, of course, that after my departure the Dragon Master came back and removed the bodies of Mega and the thug so as not to arouse suspicion on the part of the others when they assembled to be paid off."

McGRATH HAD disappeared at a clumsy gallop, but shortly reappeared. He came up to Warner and shook his head.

"Too late, Chief. One of those condemned buildings went up about ten minutes ago. It just rose up a bit and then settled back again into a mass of bricks, Headquarters just told me. Fireman are digging in the wreckage for bodies. Dugro musta fixed it for that to happen right after he took off in the plane. He was a clever guy—just clever enough that we'll never know how he managed to almost blow me to kingdom come. And those two poor guys, Fitz and Murphy—"

The Black Bat rose to his feet in the doorway, still wearing the parachute.

"I think I can enlighten you, Captain," he said. "You will recall that after the explosion on Quinn's lawn only tiny splinters of wood were found by police experts. I also remembered then that Flash Mega was a nitro expert. My suspicions took shape when I found a strong bow and several arrows in the underground room of Ohmo, the Chinese thug. When the metal arrow head was unscrewed it revealed a tiny vial of nitro inside, with a nail plunger sticking out through the tip.

"Since an arrow has been fired a distance of several hundred yards it was an easy matter to place one on Quinn's lawn as a warning to Eight Incorporated. The police car was blown to pieces in the same manner. You will receive that peculiar arrow weapon by messenger tomorrow, Captain, along with the pistol I shot from the Dragon Master's hand in their underground meeting room tonight."

He took from his pocket the shells he had picked up on the airport the night Dugro had fired at him as he took off with Harrison. Compared with shells fired from Dugro's gun, they would be final, conclusive proof.

McGrath took them and shoved them in his own pocket. Automatically he took out a cigar and bit off an end.

"All right, Black Bat, that winds up everything," he said. "All we need to do is have Mr. Belmont and his remaining associates buy the treasure with all this money they'll get back—and maybe buy a new vault door for the museum—and everything is clear. All except between you and me. I don't shoot sitting game. But there's nothing to prevent me hitting the breeze for Tony Quinn's house right now in a police cruiser to do a little settling of my own."

And the doughty officer hurried away. Belmont had taken little part in the conversation. He was too relieved at the return of the money. He looked at the Black Bat now.

"Could I give you a lift to town?" he asked politely.

The Black Bat shook his head, smiling.

"No thank you. But I'm going to ask Colonel Wang to see that I get home. I'm sure he won't mind."

He got inside the plane and closed the door. I-tso Ling translated to Wang in rapid Cantonese, ignoring her father's gesticulating commands to come with him at once. Wang nodded and spun the starter on the two motors. The speedy bomber roared down the runway and lifted into the night. The Black Bat directed Wang to fly at less than a thousand feet over a certain section of town. Even the Chinese girl, confused by being in the air, would not know where he landed.

As Wang shut off the motors only short minutes later and the Black Bat braced himself to jump through the door, I-tso Ling did something that was entirely American. She leaned swiftly and pressed her lips to his cheek.

"That is from the future Mrs. Wang in appreciation for saving my husband's 'face,'" she murmured. "Yes, I'm returning with him to China. When I tell my honorable father that I may be apprehended some day as a Dragon I'm sure he won't object."

Then she said something else that sounded to him like *"Tangtze."*

"I beg your pardon," said the Black Bat.

"It's one way of saying good-by in Chinese," I-tso Ling told him.

He braced his body against the door, held shut by the force of the slipstream, and tumbled out. A world of darkness rushed up at him. He counted five, pulled, and the big 'chute snapped him upright four hundred feet above the ground. As he landed and hurriedly rolled up the parachute there came the sound of a distant siren.

LUCKILY THE Black Bat had landed within two blocks of his own estate, on a vacant stretch of ground. He dashed for the gatehouse with the 'chute wadded in his arms, dropped in the tunnel and sped into the house just as Captain McGrath pulled up in front.

"Tony, where have you been?" cried Carol.

"I'll explain later," he said, laughing as he yanked off his clothes that were over his pajamas and jumped into bed.

"Here—give me that bandage, and get rid of those garments. McGrath's outside."

The big officer came barging in. Carol barely had time to open the bedroom door, before he pushed past her and stopped short at sight of Quinn's bandaged head.

"Well, I'll be—be—dammit to hell!" said Captain McGrath in most unofficerlike fashion.

Tony Quinn looked up at him with his dead eyes and inquired in a weak voice:

"Is that you, McGrath? Did you catch the Dragon Master?"

"You know blamed well I did, but that I didn't get the Black Bat!" yelled back the disgruntled McGrath.

"I rather got that impression from the way you came charging in here. I believe that means you won a bet from me in saying that the Black Bat would show up in the Dragon case. But you also lost one by not capturing him. So I gather that we're even."

"Don't worry—we'll meet again," was the reply as the disgusted Captain McGrath headed for the door. "I'll get you one of these days. So long!"

"*Tangtze,*" Tony Quinn said coolly.

"Huh?" demanded McGrath suspiciously, abruptly, turning in the doorway.

"It's one way of saying good-by in Chinese," Quinn informed him laconically.

"Bah!" snapped Captain McGrath, slamming the front door as he went out.

XI

THE BLACK BAT'S JUSTICE

CHAPTER I

DEATH IN THE SKY

CAPTAIN McGRATH of the Headquarters Squad was a man with a mission. Anything that interfered with it became dull, uninspiring work, like waiting for a plane from Europe to land with five million dollars' worth of diamonds aboard. McGrath would have freely given—if they were his to give—all of those gems for the privilege of peering under the domino of the Black Bat.

McGrath's intention to capture this crime fighter was just as strong now as it had been when he had been a Homicide Squad sergeant. He admitted that the Black Bat's work had given him a lot of undeserved credit, for which he had been lifted up two notches in a year. But McGrath still swore to land the Black Bat.

"No man," McGrath had often stated loudly, "can flout the law even if he is on the side of the police. The Black Bat is guilty of breaking and entering, of assault, maybe of murder, though I guess it's true that he shoots only when the rats shoot first."

McGrath trundled his bulky form into the dispatcher's office and sat down.

"When is she due?" he asked.

"In about twenty minutes." The dispatcher was leaning closer to his instrument board. "I've been trying to raise the pilot. There must be something wrong."

"Don't get excited," McGrath said calmly. "That plane will come in okay. She's flown in the sub-stratosphere all the way from Europe. Now I ask you, who could get at those rocks up there? We've had more than twenty bad diamond thefts lately, but this is different. The rocks are miles up in the air."

"Mechanical troubles can happen anywhere," the dispatcher replied abstractedly.

"Oh," McGrath leaned back. "Mechanical stuff doesn't interest me much. All I have to do is make sure nobody gets his hooks on those five million dollars' worth of diamonds. You tell me when she's circling to land."

He shoved his hat down over his eyes, let his cigar dangle from his fingers and started to dream. As usual, his dream concerned men who wore black hoods and capes that were ribbed after the fashion of a bat's wings.

"Captain!"

The dispatcher's shout brought McGrath out of his semi-coma.

"What is it?" he blurted.

"Weak signals from the plane!" the dispatcher cried in horror. "The pilot can hardly speak. Grab an earphone—right over there."

McGrath pressed the phone to his ear. He heard a man's voice, speaking slowly, as if it required great effort.

"Something… haywire. Coming in… fast. Think I… can make… it…. Everyone aboard… dead or… asleep. Co-pilot just… dropped off. Using… oxygen. Can't…."

The last word seemed to occupy the space of a full minute.

McGRATH DROPPED the earphone and raced out of the office. He yelled to the eight-man squad of picked detectives assigned to protect the diamond shipment. Running toward the long dock jutting out into the basin where the transatlantic air liners came to roost, McGrath yelled for boats.

He got them just about the time the plane was seen glistening like a polished silver bar as it cut through clouds. The pilot was bringing her in, all right, but not too smoothly. As the minutes went by, McGrath found that his throat had gone dry and that he was sweating in anticipation of the ghastly certainty.

The plane's wings banked sharply and one of them shot up a spray as it cut through the water. Apparently the pilot used all his waning strength and skill to right the ship. Its pontoons slapped the water and the motors simultaneously died out.

McGrath waited a moment or two, until he was sure the pilot either couldn't taxi to the dock, or refused to do so for some reason. Then he jumped into one of the waiting launches, waved his men to join him with the other boats. As they streaked toward the helpless, drifting plane, McGrath's worries grew by the minute. If engine trouble had caused the plane to land so dangerously its crew should be trying to attract help.

The launch came alongside the plane and one of the detectives clumsily held it fast with a boat-hook. McGrath jumped to the huge wing, made his way across it and finally reached the cabin door. He yanked it open, surprised at its weight. But when he peered inside, he gave a half-strangled cry of horror.

The steward, clad in his white coat, lay sprawled in one of the passenger's seats. A navigator, uniformed nattily in blue, was curled up on the floor. Two men were seated side by side aft, their heads touching one another's, their eyes glassy.

"Get a doctor—a lot of doctors!" McGrath yelled.

He reached the steward and slid a hand beneath the shirt. There was no heart beat. McGrath made similar examinations of the other passengers. All were dead. The two men in the rear of the plane wore steel handcuffs. From their left and right wrist, respectively, a strong chain led down to a black satchel between their legs.

They had been chained to five million dollars in diamonds, but it seemed that all precautions had proven useless....

McGrath tried to open the bag, found it securely locked. He picked it up and rattled it. There was a slight sound from outside, but the lightness of the bag indicated that its most valuable contents must be nothing more than air. He hurried forward as rapidly as possible and yanked open the door leading to the pilot's quarters.

One pilot was slumped half-in, half-out of his seat. The other, with an oxygen tube still clamped between his teeth, held both hands on the controls as if he had managed the descent of the ship despite death.

McGrath traced that length of tubing. It curled around toward the oxygen tank. Near the door, he saw that the tube had been slit by a sharp instrument. McGrath was not a fool. He stuck his head outside the cabin door.

"You men in launches, head out to sea and look for a floating parachute! Stop every craft you come across and hold everyone on board. The diamonds are gone!"

HALF AN hour later, two police surgeons came into the cabin. They went to work immediately, while McGrath kept officials of the air line out of the way. One doctor slipped his stethoscope down to his neck and slowly sat down. There was a puzzled frown on his face.

"This is just a guess," he announced, "but personally I'd say that all of the victims were strangled, even though there isn't a mark on them."

"How long have they been dead?" McGrath queried.

"Hard to judge. Not long, though—certainly not over an hour. The pilot at the controls probably brought his ship down, but expired before he could taxi to the dock. As soon as you're finished, Captain, we'll rush the bodies to the morgue for autopsy. Perhaps it was a poison. We won't be certain till the autopsy."

THERE WAS nothing McGrath could do but follow the routine measures. He had pictures taken, directed fingerprint experts to dust every inch of the plane's interior.

It was growing dark when morgue men transferred the bodies to a police boat. McGrath climbed aboard, too. He buttonholed one of the surgeons.

"It must have worked pretty fast, whatever it was, eh, Doc? The way that pilot grabbed his oxygen tube proves that maybe it was gas. What do you think?"

The doctor shrugged. "You've forgotten that this is one of the newest planes. It flies in the sub-stratosphere and its cabins are automatically ventilated and hermetically sealed. When the atmosphere becomes dangerously attenuated, oxygen is automatically released in the cabin. But the pilot may have been using the oxygen tube all along. My suggestion is that something happened to the oxygen supply."

"Yeah." McGrath stared at the dock where Commissioner Warner and a horde of police officials were waiting. "Something happened to five million dollars' worth of diamonds, too. Don't forget that."

Warner jumped aboard and stood with McGrath as the six bodies were whisked into waiting ambulances. Warner was a white-haired, slender and dignified-looking man. His was no political job. He had risen from the ranks and his promotion to his high office had been expected and deserved. There was hardly a more astute police officer in the world.

"Well, Captain," he asked, "what's your idea about all this?"

McGrath emitted a long sigh. "All I know is that everybody was dead and five million dollars' worth of ice escaped. I can't figure it out. The plane was specially chartered because it could fly higher than those fighting planes and bombers that play tag all over Europe's skies. There was a stop at Lisbon for refueling, but it was done quickly, and those two Hollanders with the satchelful of diamonds didn't stir from their seats.

"There must have been a seventh passenger hidden aboard somewhere. That guy killed everyone else, took the diamonds and parachuted to the water. It must have been arranged so a boat would be waiting to pick him up. But tell me, how did that seventh passenger get aboard? The whole plane was supposed to have been completely searched. What killed everybody, and why didn't it kill the seventh passenger?"

"I can't answer your questions yet," Warner said quietly. "Everything about this plane's departure, passengers and cargo was kept a strict secret. We've succeeded in keeping this from the newspapers so far, but the man to whom the diamonds was consigned has to be notified. That's your job, Captain. He's *Mynheer* Van der Veer. Since coming to the United States a month ago as a refugee, he's been living on Whately Avenue.

"He is an intelligent man and very wealthy, so don't browbeat him or you might get smacked back. And for heaven's sake, Captain, don't stop on the way if you see a shadow that happens to look like a bat. Right now we're faced with a problem that's even more important than the Black Bat. We've been having a wave of diamond robberies that refuse to be solved. They may be linked up with this one."

McGrath saluted and went ashore. Sliding behind the wheel of his police cruiser, he muttered to himself as he drove away.

"This is one swell case for the Black Bat. I'm stuck before I've even started. Those small breaks and now this…. Five million bucks! I wonder if he—"

"Get a doctor!" McGrath yelled.

The captain exhaled in weary defeat. Certainly the Black Bat might help, and his ability to see things that were practically invisible to McGrath would be an undeniable help. But McGrath shook off the idea reluctantly. How could he ask the Black Bat to coöperate after the way he had been trying to run him down. Why, if the newspapers got wind of it, he would be laughed right from behind his captain's gold badge!

McGrath thought he knew who the hooded mystery man was, but it was just an idea. He had never succeeded in finding out beyond question. Every time he figured on outwitting the Black Bat and exposing him as blind Tony Quinn, something happened to make such an accusation impossible.

All the doctors had declared that Tony Quinn was totally and hopelessly blind. McGrath had always thought so, too. He well remembered the horrible day when Tony Quinn, one of the cleverest district attorneys ever in office, had been accusing a gangster of serious charges. The crook's men had filtered into the courtroom. In an attempt to destroy important evidence with a corrosive acid, they had hurled the acid into Quinn's face. As a result, he had immediately become blind and his face still bore the horrible scars which the acid had left.

That was one of the reasons why McGrath suspected Quinn of being the Black Bat. The eerie being always wore a black hood covering his face completely, except for slits through which he could see. Was that hood meant to conceal those telltale scars?

McGrath spotted his destination, rolled to the curb three minutes later. He forgot all about the Black Bat. He certainly had a more important problem.

CHAPTER II

MYNHEER IS DEAD

CAPTAIN McGRATH lived in a modest suburban bungalow, so he was used to the simpler comforts of life. Places like the mansion which Van der Veer had rented, with its chandeliered ceilings and thickly carpeted floors, always made him snort in contempt. By living in this place, *Mynheer* Van der Veer publicly announced his wealth. McGrath could see at a glance that Commissioner Warner was right. This Dutchman would have to be handled with kid gloves.

McGrath strode up to the porch and jabbed the bell button. The door was promptly opened by a man of about fifty, dressed in a butler's uniform. He glanced at McGrath's badge, bowed slightly and motioned toward a chair in the spacious reception hall, McGrath sat down, twiddling his hat and feeling ill at ease. Then he cocked his head to one side. He could hear voices from a room down the corridor.

"It is the police, *Mynheer*," a rather low, somewhat servile voice said. "I am afraid your theories were right and something has happened to the shipment of diamonds. Shall I show him in?"

"But yes," a booming voice replied. "Are you a fool to keep him waiting? Hand me the report from Amsterdam, quickly. Then bring the policeman in."

McGrath jumped to his feet as a young man hurried out of the room. He was clean-shaven, had light blue eyes. He rubbed his hands fawningly as he stepped before McGrath.

"You have news of the diamonds? Something has happened to them? They should have been brought here long ago."

"I've got news all right," McGrath said. "Bad news. Who are you?"

"*Mynheer* Van der Veer's American manager. My name is Paul Hawley. What has happened? Speak up, man! Those gems are worth five million dollars."

"Well, they're gone," McGrath reported. "Just what happened, I'm damned if I know. Your two messengers are dead and so is everyone else who was aboard that plane. I'd better see the boss, eh? He might be able to help."

"Of course, of course." Hawley was rattled and showed it. "Follow me. He's waiting inside."

McGrath was right behind Hawley as they stepped into a big living room. There was a desk at the far end of it and behind it sat a strange-looking man. He was near sixty, McGrath estimated, but the fiery red beard he wore and the contrasting coal-black hair made his age difficult to determine. He was slender of build and he was engaged in reading the sheaf of stapled papers he held in his hand. Hawley walked over to the desk.

"The police officer, *Mynheer*. He has bad news, I am sorry to say."

Mynheer Van der Veer did not bat an eyelash. He kept on reading the papers as if he were quite alone in the room. McGrath grunted. Big shot or small, Van der Veer couldn't disregard a police captain. McGrath bustled forward.

"Your shipment of diamonds has been stolen. Your agents are dead—murdered. We want you to come down to the morgue and identify them, also to examine the suitcase in which the jewels were supposed to have been placed. Say, will you please—"

McGrath's voice trailed off. His eyes were riveted on Van der Veer's right hand. It was swollen and looked as though it had been held for a long time on a red-hot pipe. Then the captain noticed that the Hollanders eyes were not shifting from left to right.

He hastened around the desk, laid a hand on the diamond merchant's shoulder. Van der Veer's head slumped down lifelessly, to loll against his chest. The body started to slide out of the chair.

McGRATH GRABBED him accidentally, touching the dead man's wrist as he did so. The reflex of horror made him let go, for the flesh was hideously cold. Yet the body was not rigid in rigor mortis. It was quite supple, as though the man had just died.

"Get away from the desk!" McGrath snapped at Hawley. "Your boss is dead. I want nothing touched."

He examined the seared wound on Van der Veer's hand. It was a burn, all right, and a serious one. He looked up sharply at Hawley.

"Okay, you came out of this room a couple of minutes ago. Nobody could possibly have entered it. The only door leads into the hall where I was standing. I know he's been dead for some time, because his flesh is stone-cold. Which means, mister, that you have an awful lot to explain."

McGrath wrapped the telephone in his handkerchief and dialed Headquarters with the end of a pencil. Then he escorted Hawley into the hall again.

"You might as well start talking," he warned. "Van der Veer must have been dead when you came out of the room. So who was that talking in there? Who was the guy with the booming voice? Where did he go?"

"That—that was *Mynheer* Van der Veer," Hawley stammered, his face ghastly white. "I swear it was! He asked me to give him the report on those gems. He wasn't—dead when I left him. In fact, just as you rang, he sat down in that chair. How—how could he be cold and dead now? I don't know what's happened, but I swear I had nothing to do with it!"

"Yeah," McGrath grunted. "Park, and stay parked. Smoke if you like."

McGrath had seen slippery characters before and murderers who could pretend innocence in a way that would put dramatic actors to shame. Hawley seemed to be one of those. True, he didn't look like a killer. But except in the case of gangster executions, few murderers look as though they have just taken a human life.

"The law says you don't have to talk if you don't want to," McGrath stated. "But it might do you some good if you did. What did you kill him for? How'd you do it and where did he get that burn on his hand?"

Hawley shuddered and closed his eyes.

"I didn't kill him. He was all right when I came out to meet you. He didn't have that burn, either. Why not ask Mankensen? He's the butler. He was talking to Van der Veer not five minutes before you arrived."

McGrath was puzzled. Naturally the butler might be in on this mess, but he could certainly furnish a good alibi for Hawley. McGrath looked around for the bell and rang for him. The butler came downstairs, walking with slow deliberation. Though he glanced at Hawley and was startled by the man's pallor, he turned to McGrath and bowed respectfully.

"When did you see Van der Veer last?" the police captain demanded. "I mean when he was talking and moving around."

"He asked me to prepare a mixture of Holland gin and hot water, sir," Mankensen replied unemotionally. "I was upstairs after the liquor— it's very special, sir, and he keeps it locked in his bedroom cabinet. He gave me the key at that time, sir. When he left me, he walked directly into the library to talk with Mr. Hawley. Why don't you ask Mr. Van der Veer, sir? And am I suspected of something?"

"Your boss is dead," McGrath said bluntly. "His flesh feels as if he's been dead for hours. You know—cold and clammy."

THE BUTLER closed his eyes as if he were unbearably tired. His set expression of dignified reserve changed to one of extreme sadness.

"I have been with him only a few weeks, sir, but I found him to be one of the most understanding men I have ever had the privilege to serve. Would you tell me what happened to him, sir? He always appeared to be in the best of health?"

"Sit down and relax." McGrath jerked his head in the direction of a chair. "I don't know what killed him. We're waiting for the medical examiner now, but it looks bad for Hawley. He's the only man who could have killed the old bird."

Dr. Thorpe of the coroner's office arrived in a few moments. He went into the library and the others trooped behind him. Thorpe made a long and careful examination. Then he took McGrath aside.

"Damned weird, Captain," he said in a low voice. "I've been at the morgue and I saw them do autopsies on the victims from the plane. This man seems to have died of the same inexplicable cause. Up to the time I left, we found absolutely nothing which might have caused death. There seemed to be a lack of oxygen in the blood, but that was all. We'll know about that soon. But the latest victim? All I can say is that he has been dead for about twenty-five minutes."

"What?" McGrath asked incredulously. "I thought guys not dead very long stayed warm. That stiff is cold as a frozen fish."

"He can't be!" Dr. Thorpe hurried over to the corpse, reached down and touched it. "You're wrong. He is quite warm and there certainly is no rigor present."

McGrath felt the limp wrist and let out a long gasp. The skin was warm. The clammy chill he had felt several minutes ago was gone!

"I can't understand that burn on his hand," Dr. Thorpe said. "It's a serious one, but it could not have caused death—unless he had a very weak heart and the shock of the actual burn was too much for him. There are also minor and less evident burns on his left hand. He'll have to be shipped to the morgue, of course. Looks like you're having yourself a sweet mess of trouble, eh, Captain? Murder seems to be following you around. Do me a favor and stay away from my house."

McGrath brought Hawley into the next room. While a squad of experts examined the room for clues and prints, he asked his suspect countless questions.

"Okay, you told me Van der Veer was alive when you stepped into the hall. I can't prove he wasn't. You claim that booming voice I heard was Van der Veer's. How can I be sure?"

Hawley got up quickly.

"In my office upstairs are several dictaphone records. I can absolutely prove he dictated them, because there were witnesses. You've got to hear them, officer! I didn't kill him. Why should I when his being alive meant the best job I've ever had? Please listen to them!"

McGRATH NODDED and followed him upstairs. Hawley slipped a cylinder into the transcriber. Instantly McGrath heard the same booming voice that had come from the library.

"All right," he granted, collecting the records and turning them over to a detective. "You'll have to go downtown, though. Nothing to be afraid of if you're innocent. Get your hat and coat."

"Can I send a cable to Amsterdam?" Hawley asked. "I must report Van der Veer's death and the theft of the diamonds. His offices there have to be notified."

"Sure, you just go along with Murphy. Tell the D.A. everything you know—and tell the truth! We always find out when a man is lying."

"I've got nothing to lie about," Hawley retorted. "Thanks, officer, for the consideration you've shown me. There isn't a trace of the diamonds, is there?"

"Not even a sparkle. Beat it, will you? I want to think."

McGrath slumped into a chair and tried to figure it out. The mystery seemed beyond comprehension, though he was inclined to believe

Hawley. After all, the man had no apparent reason to murder his employer. That booming voice certainly indicated that Van der Veer was alive after McGrath had entered the house. But what had killed him so quickly? What of that strange burn on his hand?

McGrath had already made certain that neither Hawley nor anyone else could possibly have installed a machine by which Van der Veer's voice could be reproduced when in reality he was dead. But that eerie coldness of the flesh had vanished in a space of only a few moments. How?

"This job calls for a dozen dopes like me," McGrath groaned. "Why did they have to assign me to guard those diamonds? I'd rather have the Black Bat chasing me around in circles than be stumped like this and— The Black Bat! Why the hell should I think of him every time I get in hot water? The guy ought to hate me. He probably does, but he always comes through when there's something big in the wind.

"Maybe…. Plenty of breaks, and now five million gone. I'll do it! Damn what anyone says. This case calls for the Black Bat. Maybe I'll get a chance to prove he is Tony Quinn, too." McGrath made a wry face. "If I call him into this mess, I guess I can't try to expose him."

He hurried downstairs, gave orders to the detectives to keep the house under guard and to have the butler brought to Headquarters. Then he got his car and drove toward one of the finest residential sections in town.

Captain McGrath felt compelled to do something that rankled deep in his proud heart. He intended to confess his bewilderment and ask help of the man he thought was the Black Bat.

CHAPTER III

A MATTER OF COÖPERATION

TONY QUINN sat before the dying embers of a fire, contentedly enjoying the heat, and puffing on a blackened meerschaum pipe. Before acid had been thrown on his face in a crowded courtroom, he had been a decidedly handsome young district attorney. Now the deep scars around his eyes were almost horrible to look upon. His eyes, too, were dead and staring, glassy with the sightlessness of the blind.

Quinn could see better than the average man now, but he knew what it was to be blind. There had been long months of it, but Nature had compensated for the loss of his sight. She had sharpened his other senses, making his auditory, tactile and olfactory powers as keen as those of a jungle beast.

But one lonely night a girl with golden hair and blue eyes had brought him hope where eye-specialists had stated there was none. Carol Baldwin's policeman father lay dying from a gangster bullet. He had made her offer his corneas to Quinn, and an unknown country doctor had performed the spectacular operation. And when the bandages were finally removed, Tony Quinn could see as well in darkness as in light! Nature had indeed rewarded him for his long months of lonely agony.

A dying man had given his eyes so a Nemesis of crime might see a clear path through the dark maze of the underworld. And Nature had made the fingers of civilization's avenger so sensitive that whatever he touched told strange new stories. His delicate nostrils could identify the most elusive odor. His sharp ears could shift from deafening clamor the one sound he wished to hear and classify.

To his self-imposed crusade against crime, Tony Quinn brought all the eerie powers of detection of—a black bat!

With all of these sensory aids, Tony Quinn had chosen to pretend blindness so that he might carry on his campaign against the underworld. He preferred anonymity, for it terrorized his enemies more when they realized that anyone could be the Black Bat. Besides his natural desire to avoid publicity, there was also the fact that occasionally he had to employ slightly irregular methods, and acting as a recognized agent of the law would have eliminated those unpleasant but necessary methods by tying his hands with red tape.

Three people soon rallied to the Black Bat's banner. They were also odd avengers of society. "Silk" Kirby had once been a confidence man. He slipped in to rob Tony Quinn one night and stayed to become his valet and general helper. Silk, with his smooth tactfulness and ingenuity—which accounted for his nickname—always remained with Quinn. Carol Baldwin, however, had no outward connection with either the Black Bat or Quinn. A resourceful, intelligent girl, she had often been a great help to the Black Bat.

Then there was Butch O'Leary, a hulking giant of a man who was never happier than when his fists were flying in defense of the law and the aid of the Black Bat. Butch was none too intelligent, but faithful and loyal. What he lacked in brains was overbalanced by his incredible willingness to risk death and his enormous strength.

These three made up the Black Bat's clique of associates. They alone knew of his dual identity and that he only pretended blindness.

Silk Kirby came in with a tray of sandwiches and milk. Quinn always maintained his blind-man pose even when no one was around. He turned his head in Silk's general direction.

"Thanks, Silk. Inactivity makes me hungry, I guess. By the way a car has just pulled up in front of the house. It is a heavy car."

"Really, sir?" Silk started toward the front door. "I didn't hear a thing." He peered through a small window set beside the door. "You're right. It's McGrath. When he shows up, it means bad news. He certainly looks angry at something."

Silk waited until McGrath punched the doorbell a couple of times. Then he opened the door and bowed with exaggerated politeness.

"Captain McGrath, the master will be delighted at your social call. May I have your hat, or don't you ever take it off?"

"Where's Quinn?" the captain demanded. "I've got to see him quick. Out of my way!"

He barged into the living room instead of waiting for a reply. Quinn still sat before the fireplace, his dead eyes staring sightlessly at the embers.

"Sit down, Captain," he offered without lifting his head. "You sounded worried. Is there something wrong? Don't tell me the Black Bat has been up to his old tricks. And please don't make an accusation against me, because I've been right here at home for hours."

"Look, Mr. Quinn." McGrath dropped into a chair. "I know I've been a little rough on you sometimes. That's because I think you are the Black Bat and that you're not blind at all. I still think that way, but this time I'm not coming here to make any accusations. I want your help. I've got to have it!"

"Of course." Quinn turned his head, but his eyes looked far to McGrath's left. "But only as Tony Quinn, attorney and ex-district attorney. For the Black Bat's aid, you'll have to get in touch with him."

"Maybe you're not the Black Bat, but you seem to be in touch with him. A plane came over from Europe a few hours ago. It was specially chartered to fly two men and five million dollars' worth of diamonds to a guy named Van der Veer. His first name is something like *Mynheer*."

"That is not a first name," Quinn corrected gently. "It has the same meaning as our 'Mister.' Go on."

"Well, the pilot of the plane radioed that he was in trouble. When the plane landed, everybody on board was dead and the gems were gone. The doctors couldn't find out what killed those men, so I went to Van der Veer's place. When I walked into the hall, I heard him talking. I got proof it was his voice. Two minutes later he was dead as an ice-cold mackerel. Then by the time the doctor showed up, he was warm as if he'd just died.

"I haven't got a clue. The suspects I sent to Headquarters are innocent. I know they are. I need the Black Bat's help. I've got to have it, Quinn! Forget all the trouble I made for you. I've been a damned fool sometimes. Give me a break on this. You can have a free hand an—"

"A free hand?" Quinn broke in wryly. "I'd rather have a pair of healthy eyes. Your story is most interesting, Captain. I wish I could help you, but two things prevent me. First of all, I am quite blind. Secondly, I am not the Black Bat. I don't know him, nor can I get in touch with him. I'm sorry."

McGRATH'S FACE dropped and he got up slowly.

"All right. Maybe you aren't the Black Bat and this has just been a waste of breath. But if you are— Oh, what's the use? You look blind as a bat to me. I—I'm sorry about that last crack, Mr. Quinn, but this case has got me down. I've been working since early this morning and then the case has to bust. By tomorrow night I'll be half-crazy, so I guess I'll go home and get some sleep. If I go nuts, I want to do it without being tired. Good night and I hope the Black Bat hears about the case."

As McGrath spoke, Quinn's cane tapped the floor steadily, as if the story made him nervous. Silk, standing out in the hallway with both ears open wide, received a message from those taps. It ordered him to stall McGrath as much as possible outside the house.

When the captain reached the porch, Silk hovered near him, flicking imaginary specks of dust from his shoulders.

"Still think Mr. Quinn is the Black Bat, Captain? Perhaps for the right kind of offer, I might be able to solve that problem for you."

"Yeah?" McGrath brightened. "It's worth ten bucks. Come on, he is the Black Bat, isn't he?"

"For ten dollars"—Silk grinned slyly—"he is not."

"Fifty," McGrath offered.

"Fifty do grow webbed wings—but that's all, Captain."

"Oh, damn it—three hundred! That's all the cash I can raise quick."

"Well, I suppose that will do."

Silk looked around nervously and McGrath took a firm grip on his nerves. He was going to learn the truth after all. He had always suspected this smooth article of a butler was a crook, and McGrath could infallibly detect crooks.

"That's three hundred you owe me," Silk whispered hoarsely. "You want to know if Quinn is the Black Bat? Well, the answer is—no, he isn't."

McGrath blinked, growled an oath and made a grab for Silk. But the wily ex-confidence man ducked easily and laughed in quiet derision. McGrath jammed his hat down, scowled and headed for the car.

"Sucker!" he told himself irately. "That's what he made out of me—a plain, ordinary sucker."

"Don't forget the three hundred you owe me," Silk called out. "I answered your question, didn't I?"

McGrath almost ground the teeth off the gears as he started away. His helplessness enraged him. Why couldn't he determine, one way or the other, if Tony Quinn was just a helpless blind man or the Black Bat? McGrath simply didn't know any more tricks. He had held a lighted match close to Quinn's eyes more than once and never got so much as a flicker. Quinn must be blind, all right. Those expensive doctors insisted that nothing short of a miracle could restore Quinn's sight, and McGrath was no believer in miracles.

He headed for home. A man had to sleep sometime, and the cots at Police Headquarters were particularly uncomfortable torture devices. Anyway, he couldn't do much until all the autopsies were finished and toxicologists had examined the bodies for poison.

McGrath turned a corner three blocks from the bungalow he called home. He jammed on the brakes, for two cars blocked the street. They had been traveling in opposite directions when their bumpers tangled.

He groaned and got out of his car. He closed his eyes fast to be sure he wasn't seeing things. An immense figure of a man had loomed up. A girl, neat and pretty, but completely overshadowed by the giant, was arguing fearlessly.

"NOW WAIT a minute!" McGrath snapped. "I'm a police officer. By the looks of things, both of you were to blame. Call it all off or I'll hustle you both down to Headquarters. And get those crates out of the road. I want to go home."

"Show me your badge," the giant rumbled.

McGrath gulped and decided it might be healthy to produce it, so he did. The giant took one look, grinned sheepishly and kicked at the road with an immense foot. The girl smiled prettily.

"I guess you're right, officer. I was just mad at this big oaf because he shouted at me. I'll forgive him. Perhaps you had better help move the cars."

"Him?" The giant looked down at McGrath. "Haw!"

Casually he ambled over to the cars, seized the bumper of one and lifted the front end almost completely off the ground. The tangled bumpers scraped free. He pushed the other car several feet away with hardly a grunt.

"If that's your car, lady, I'd advise you to get in it and scram," McGrath said. "That big guy could pulverize both of us and I'm too tired to be mopped around. There's been no damage done, so let's just forget the whole thing."

McGrath drove his car between the two others. As his tail-light vanished, the giant leaned out of his coupé and grinned from ear to ear. The girl signaled that all was clear.

"Nice work, Butch," she called out. "We stalled him eight whole minutes. Now you get back. He may need your car."

"Sure, Miss Carol," Butch agreed. "And I hope he's onto somethin' big and serious. I'm gettin' covered with dry rot from sittin' around."

"It's big, all right." The girl drove closer to Butch O'Leary's car. "He sounded unusually excited over the phone when he asked me to get your help in stalling the good captain. McGrath doesn't know it, but he's having a visitor tonight."

"Yeah," Butch grunted. "A guy with wings and he ain't no angel. See you later, Miss Carol."

Carol Baldwin took an opposite direction, for it was not so important that she return quickly. She wondered what had excited Quinn. McGrath, actually asking Quinn to help him, indicated that it was serious and baffling. Still, there had been nothing of interest in the newspapers yet. Carol constantly checked all editions of important papers from all over the country. Because of her thoroughness, secret files in Tony Quinn's house bulged with all manner of facts about crime and criminals.

She returned to her apartment, not far away from Quinn's house. She sat down beside a telephone table and waited. When things broke, the Black Bat usually maneuvered his forces through her.

She smiled at the way McGrath had been fooled. Quinn had him delayed long enough to don the Black Bat's regalia and slip out of the house via the secret tunnel that led from the laboratory to the garden-house at the rear of Quinn's estate. There a car was always kept waiting and ready. The Black Bat would have had plenty of time to reach Mc-Grath's home.

Carol's eyes grew bright whenever she thought of Tony Quinn. She was glad that the opportunity had come her way to help him create the Black Bat. But there was also an element of sadness in those memories.

Her father had died to turn a helpless blind man into an overwhelmingly efficient Nemesis of crime. She could not have had both Tony and her dying father, of course, yet somehow it was almost as if she did.

Her father was dead, but his eyes still lived to help society strike back against the ruthless killers and devastators of the underworld. Through Tony Quinn, he remained alive to her....

CHAPTER IV

BATTLE AT SEA

M **cGRATH PUT** his car away, walked around to the front of his house and let himself in. His wife was away, so he proceeded directly to the kitchen. There he got himself a glass and swore when he found there were no ice cubes to drop into it. But he headed for the dining room, where the supply of rye was kept. The instant he reached for the light switch, he froze. His hand almost broke the thin glass in its convulsive grip.

"Good evening, Captain," a quiet voice said from the darkness. "We won't need lights, thank you, and I'm afraid you're slipping as a detective. A short time ago I took the ice cubes from your refrigerator and put them in glasses. I mixed a brace of highballs for us. You should have wondered why the cubes were missing."

"The Black Bat!" McGrath said softly. "I can't see you, but if you have a gun in your hand, put it down. This is one time you're as welcome as the drink you say you fixed. Where is it?"

A strong hand grasped McGrath's arm and piloted him safely through the inky darkness until he found that his favorite chair had been pulled up beside a small table. He sat down with a sigh. "I've been looking for you," he said as he fumblingly picked up the glass. "How'd you get here so fast, Tony Quinn?"

The Black Bat chuckled. "Still on that tangent, eh? Forget it, Captain. Quinn is as blind as my namesake. Don't ask me how, but I heard about what happened this afternoon. Your department is keeping this matter hushed for the present, so I thought I would come here and see you for the facts. This robbery is obviously more important that a casual glance would indicate. Tell me what happened."

McGrath smiled slyly as he rotated the ice cubes in his glass.

"Mind if I strike a light?" he asked. "I want to smoke."

Before he could be stopped, he scraped a match, held it directly over the glass. Then he raised it to illuminate the man who sat undismayed in a chair beside him. He saw, first of all, the heavy automatic resting in the black lap. Slowly he raised his eyes to survey the weird man who wore a snugly fitting black hood and a cape that gave the illusion of a bat's wings.

"All right," McGrath grunted. "I was just using some of that power of observation you keep accusing me of not having. The ice cubes in my glass are small, and my drink is very cold. It would take some time for the cubes to melt and chill the drink, proving you've been here a long while and that you didn't make tracks for this house right after I left Quinn. That is, if you were Quinn.

"I'll give you the whole story. Brother, I never thought I'd be working with you, but this time all rules have to be off. Five million dollars' worth of jewelry is missing, and seven men have been killed. The past few days we've been having a regular wave of jewelry store robberies, and diamonds have been taken mostly. Warner thinks the big robbery and the little ones tie up somehow."

Continuing from that point, McGrath gave all the details of the case. All through his story, the Black Bat was so quietly intent that McGrath peered into the darkness to see if he was still there. Each time a word assured him that his eerie visitor had seen his movement and had read the doubt in his face despite the dark.

"Burns on the hands," the Black Bat muttered finally. "Flesh cold one moment, normally warm the next. I won't bluff you, Captain—I can't account for it yet. About the plane, though, your theory seems the only safe one to assume. Someone boarded the ship in Lisbon, killed everyone aboard, grabbed the gems and parachuted into the sea, where he was picked up by prearrangement. A risky affair, Captain—so much so that I can't figure it out.

"Crooks rarely have much nerve, unless it's backed up with a gun. It takes courage to use a parachute, and that's something weasels don't have. We may be dealing with a superior rat, however. I'd like to see that plane, if it could be arranged without a couple of dozen policemen trying to bring me down. Perhaps I may find a clue where you failed to do so."

McGRATH HESITATED, his broad face unhappy.

"I wouldn't mind working with anybody else, but you? Before this is over, you'll probably break every law on the books. Well, I've got to risk it. I'll fix things so the guard at the plane is removed. It will take about an hour. I promise I won't interfere with your work, as long as you don't leave too many bodies strewn around. It's tough trying to explain them.

"Speaking not as an officer sworn to uphold the law but as an ordinary citizen, I wish you luck, whoever you are. Just as long as this case lasts, we'll have a truce, you and I. But when it's over, watch your step because I'll be looking for you."

The Black Bat's quiet laugh was terrifying in the silence of the room.

"We've had our truces before and they usually produced results. And I'm not swooning in terror of your pursuit once the case is finished. Good night. I hope I didn't make that drink too strong."

When McGrath clambered to his feet, everything began to spin. He grabbed the arm of his chair to steady himself. Then he grinned foolishly, amiably.

"That drink was pretty near straight rye and a tall one, too. But, boy, it sure makes a man forget his troubles!"

Somehow he managed to call Headquarters and give intelligible orders that the guard was to be withdrawn from around the plane. Then he reached his bed and fell across it. McGrath never imagined that the Black Bat had purposely made the drink strong so he would remain out of the picture for the time being. He also gave no thought to the possibility that those ice cubes could have been melted under the hot water tap in his kitchen.

The Black Bat slipped out of McGrath's house silently as a ghost, fled through several neighboring yards. An ordinary man would have stumbled and fallen a dozen times, for the yards were littered with rakes, lawnmowers, chairs and children's toys. Yet those objects were not concealed by darkness from the Black Bat's eyes. He reached the car that he had parked well away from McGrath's house. In a few moments he was driving toward the waterfront.

He had stowed his hood in a pocket and pulled down a black, wide-brimmed hat to conceal his features. Tony Quinn, operating as the Black Bat, was in constant danger of recognition, for every patrolman in the city knew those horrible scars on his face. But it was impossible to keep the hood on at all times.

The transatlantic plane had been hauled in, but it was a safe distance from the pier. The Black Bat slipped through the darkness, made sure the pier was not guarded. Noiselessly he dropped into a small motor launch that was moored so conveniently nearby that he figured McGrath must have provided it. There were oars in the locks and he used these in preference to the noisy motor. He welcomed the slight fog, for it aided him.

As he neared the plane, he suddenly shipped the oars. There was another motor launch tied up to one of the plane's wings. From shore it could not be seen. A furtive flash of light proved that a prowler was inside the ship.

THE BLACK BAT drew a gun, laid it on his lap and silently resumed rowing. He quietly threw a line around a strut on the opposite side, held his gun ready and stepped onto the wing. His rubber-soled shoes made little noise and clung well to the slippery surface. He crouched suddenly, for a man had stepped out of the cabin, holding something in his arms. Before the Black Bat could move to prevent his abrupt action, the man hurled whatever he had into the sea. Then he started for his motor launch.

"Freeze!" the Black Bat hissed. "There's a gun trained on you."

The mystery man stopped dead, then took a startlingly quick flying jump that carried him into his launch. The motor roared. A gun cracked and the bullet whistled past the Black Bat. Impeded by the narrow footing, the Black Bat was slower in reaching his own boat. But before the mystery man's launch was more than five hundred feet away, he was in swift pursuit.

He opened the throttle wide and the boat skimmed across the water at top speed. Suddenly he ducked, for a jet of flame and the roar of a gun almost coincided with the thud of a bullet against the bow. He raised his head cautiously, rested the automatic against the roof of the small cabin and drew a bead on the fleeing launch. In rapid succession, he sent three bullets through the darkness. A wild curse in a distinctly accented voice indicated that he had come close. He smiled and fired two more shots.

The fleeing craft adopted a zigzag course. Occasionally a slug smashed into the Black Bat's launch. They were heading out to open sea and those shots were probably not heard ashore. The Black Bat wondered why this particular direction had been chosen, unless there was a larger craft moored somewhere to pick up the killer.

Then he saw his quarry slow down considerably. With a sharp inhale of elation, he grasped his automatic tighter in his black-gloved fist and prepared for action. It came—but not the way he expected. A rattle of gunfire, a series of flashes from the launch ahead of him turned the odds lethally against him.

The killer, knowing he had no chance to outstrip the Black Bat's craft, was using a sub-machine gun to send a fusillade of lead at the launch. The Black Bat flattened to the deck. Suddenly the motor sputtered and died. A bullet had probably ripped the gas-line.

He heard a hoarse, taunting laugh from the darkness as the killer began turning his boat around to put in a few final licks. Even the Black

Bat could not face a tommy-gun and live. That realization made his agile mind work desperately. He stripped off his cloak, propped the oars against a seat and draped the robe over them. From a distance it looked like a crouching man. Satisfied, he scrambled down the small companionway.

The killer's craft came alongside and the machine gun ripped a hundred holes in the Black Bat's cloak. The same taunting laugh at last showed that the killer was content. He roared away, but the Black Bat, cautiously watching from below, had caught a glimpse of the man's face. Those uncanny eyes of his had penetrated the darkness and seen a jet-black Vandyke beard and a shock of dark hair.

Slowly the Black Bat put his robe on again, grimacing at the bullet holes. He was far away from the plane, but he settled down for the long row. That bearded, black-haired killer had won the first round, but the Black Bat always stayed in the ring until the final bell.

REACHING THE plane at last, he made sure no one had been attracted by the shooting. Then he boarded the ship once more. What had the mysterious attacker thrown overboard? McGrath had stated that he had examined the ship carefully. Whatever had gone into the sea had certainly seemed big enough to have been noticed.

The Black Bat spent almost an hour prowling around inside the ship. In the extreme darkness, he looked thoughtfully at the slit in the oxygen tube. Disagreeing with McGrath's opinion, the Black Bat believed the tube had been crushed by something heavy and not cut with a sharp instrument. The black satchel, of course, was gone and the baggage compartment revealed nothing of interest. He thrust inquisitive fingers beneath the padding of the various seats without success, then examined every inch of the floor.

"Not a clue," he muttered. "Nothing but that object dumped into the water, and that doesn't do me any good. Looks like McGrath was right. This is a tough nut to crack."

Obviously, without a trace by which to guide his actions, the next step must be to trace the five million dollars in missing gems. They had to be disposed of if the thief wanted to make a profit from his murders. But since they were stones of average size, there was nothing outstanding about any of them.

Van der Veer had owned diamond-cutting plants in Amsterdam. He had been one of the most successful merchants in the world until a man named Hitler blasted normal life and business into minute fragments. Then he had hidden most of his valuable stock and fled to the United States. His agents in his overrun country had shipped the stones to

Switzerland, where they had immediately been placed on board the chartered plane.

"The Nazis!" the Black Bat gritted. "They'd risk a lot to lay their hands on so many gems. Diamonds would be invaluable for making their tools with which guns and parts are machined, or even to be used in international trade."

The Black Bat determined to make an investigation of that phase. Nazi agents had traveled far for lesser sums than this. He returned to the crippled launch and rowed it ashore.

McGrath's orders still held sway and no one was about to intercept him, and the Black Bat was hardly visible in the darkness. Everything he wore was black, so he seemed to blend with all the shadows and become a part of them.

He approached the spot where his car was parked, but the Black Bat was always cautious. Before actually getting into it, he crouched behind a watchman's shack and used the supersensitive eyes and ears that nature had given him. A private patrolman, assigned to guard the waterfront warehouses, ambled up the pier. The Black Bat heard sudden scampering, as if several people sought better hiding places.

The mysterious man he had chased over the water must have contacted the shore somehow—perhaps by radio—and detailed a squad of men to watch for the return of the other launch, just in case the man in it was not dead. The Black Bat reasoned that they might attack if no one was about. But it was more likely they would merely trail anyone who came from the plane and use their guns in a spot from which escape was less possible.

The shack behind which he was hidden carried telephone wires running down its side. The Black Bat crawled around to the narrow door, examined the padlock on it and drew a small instrument from under his cloak. It took him hardly a minute to open the door. He slipped inside, found to his satisfaction that the phone was dial-equipped and had a direct outside connection. He called Carol Baldwin.

"We're up against one of the most difficult cases we have ever encountered," he told her. "Contact Silk at once. Tell him to put on a simple disguise, get into Butch's car and drive to the pier at Clark Street. Have him park at a convenient spot and watch. I'll come out, and unless there is a gun battle, someone will be trailing me. The moment I shake them, Silk must hang a tail on them."

CHAPTER V

UNEVEN ODDS

S ILK KIRBY got Carol's call and immediately went to work. He required no more than ten minutes to change into a loud suit and don a tie and shirt that could best be described as flamboyant. He quickly changed his facial appearance with an assortment of pigments and small mechanical devices. His cheeks he made rounder, his nose more predatory and his lips fuller. When he was finished, he looked like a young man from some small town. He used the tunnel which led from the hidden laboratory to the garden house. Butch's battered old coupé was parked at the curb. The registration of this car would have surprised the police, for the name and address on the license was also engraved on a tombstone at the address that had been given—a cemetery. Old as it was, there was plenty of power under that shabby hood.

Silk drove the car onto the river highway, followed it until he reached the street which the Black Bat had indicated. He looked around, doused the headlights and coasted slowly down the gradual incline until he could see the Black Bat's car. Then he backed into a driveway and waited, his eyes glued on the car parked at the pier.

Abruptly a fleet black shape seemed to fly toward that car. The motor roared and the car flashed by the spot where Silk was parked. For a fraction of a second the dashlight was lit. Silk caught a glimpse of a wide-brimmed hat and a driver hunched forward over the wheel. It was the Black Bat!

Silk held his breath. There had been no gun battle. If the Black Bat's suspicions were correct, the criminals would be trailing along any second.

They flashed by in a sleek black sedan. By the dim street lights, Silk saw two men in front and two in back, all leaning forward anxiously. He pulled out of the drive and took up the chase. But he stayed well back, for much depended on his evading detection. The killers would be intent on watching the Black Bat's car and not imagine that they themselves were being followed, but Silk took no chances.

The Black Bat deliberately began heading away from the city, indicating that he actually dared these men to do their worst. When the city lights cast only a red glow over the sky and traffic grew thinner on the highway, his car suddenly gained speed. Silk whipped an automatic from his pocket. It felt comfortingly heavy in his lap.

The murder car was gradually gaining on the Black Bat. That far from the city a blasting fusillade of shots could be poured into the coupé and the murderers be miles away before the shooting was even discovered.

Silk wanted to draw closer so that if the fireworks began, he would have a chance to help the Black Bat. But he had his orders, and they were uncompromisingly explicit. His job was to trail these men after they had shown themselves to be members of the murder mob. Therefore he eased up on the gas slightly and dropped back. At a safe distance he extinguished his lights, leaned out of the window and guided his car by means of the white line in the center of the highway.

He heard the rattle of guns, looked up and saw the Black Bat's car swerve dangerously, straighten out and put on a burst of speed. The sedan continued to gain on it and the bullets were pounding at the coupé at a terrific rate. Silk smiled. Though the coupé certainly bore no resemblance to an expensive armored car, it was just as impervious to ordinary gunfire. An unusually high-velocity rifle bullet might penetrate the thick steel hide, but no other slug could do more than dent it.

A SECOND later, though, Silk became worried. It looked as though the Black Bat had been hit, for the coupé began zigzagging all over the road. It gave a final, screeching turn off the main highway and started up a dirt lane. The murder car turned swiftly after it. Silk bit his lip, debating whether he ought to follow the battle.

He turned off the road and guided the car behind a tree. The branches effectively hid it. Slipping out, he seized his gun and started running toward the spot where the glow of headlights revealed the location of the two cars. When he peered through the brush, his heart was hammering against his ribs.

The Black Bat's car had rolled off the lane and come to a stop with its nose in a ditch. Four men with drawn weapons were warily closing in. Silk lay prone, rested one elbow on the ground. Supporting his automatic on his forearm, he drew a bead on one of the men, ready to blast him into eternity if things had gone awry with the Black Bat's plans and he was still inside that car. In the silence of that deserted wooded section, the voices of the men carried to Silk's alert ears.

"If he wasn't croaked, he'd be lettin' us have it, wouldn't he?" one argued. "The boss says he did plenty of shootin' out on the water, so he must have a gun. Jules, you sneak up and open that door. Go on, what're you scared of? We'll blast that crate to pieces if the guy inside tries anything."

Between his eyes would be the seal of the Black Bat.

The man called Jules carefully approached the car, running forward in a crouch. Finally he reached the side of the car, turned the handle and yanked the door open.

"Hey!" he called back in awe. "There ain't nobody in this jalopy!"

The others ran erect, now that the element of danger was past. When Silk could hear them cursing and quarreling over what had happened to the driver, he smiled. He should have known better than to worry whether the Black Bat's trick had missed fire. Hastily he returned to where Butch's coupé was parked, got in and waited.

After several minutes the sedan nosed out of the lane to his surprise, the driver nosed it away from the city again. Silk held far back, but never lost the two red lights of that car for a single instant. It kept traveling for another four miles and then took a cut-off for five miles more. At last it slowed, made a sharp left turn and proceeded up a private lane bordered by tall trees.

Silk followed at a safe distance, his headlights still out. The trees prevented even starlight from lighting his way, so he had to drive with great caution. When he least expected it, he caught sight of the murder car, which was also traveling at a slow rate of speed. But suddenly the driver stepped on the gas and the sedan roared out of sight. Silk pushed down the gas pedal, gripped the wheel firmly and prayed that he would stay on a road he could hardly see.

He was doing forty-five—a terrific speed for this narrow, dark lane—when all hell seemed to burst loose. Something hit the front of the coupé, flung it back with frightful force. Silk hit the wheel and the wind was knocked out of him. One tire blew but violently and both fenders and bumper were demolished.

Still dazed by the unexpectedness of the accident and dizzy from the pain of his collision against the wheel, Silk was easy prey for the three men who abruptly surrounded the car. Two carried rifles, the other a nickle-plated revolver. Flashlights almost blinded him. He made a grab for his gun just as the door beside him was jerked open. On impulse, he jammed the gun between the seat cushions. A rifle barrel struck him viciously across the forehead. He groaned once and went limp.

"The sap!" one of the men growled. "When Jules and the boys passed by, we just tightened that big chain and it got him. Now maybe you think the boss ain't smart. It takes brains to figure out that idea. Drag this dumb cluck to the house and we'll find out who he is."

SILK WAS awakened by being dragged over the rough ground. He didn't betray the fact that he was conscious, for the conversation of his captors might be revealing.

"Maybe this bozo is just some pier cop. He musta seen the boss go out to that plane and followed him. Say, I never told you guys before because I thought you'd turn yellow. The boss told me over the radio that the clothes on the guy in that launch made him think it was the Black Bat. Ain't that a howl?"

A thug shivered.

"Yeah, it's a howl now, but suppose we had tackled the Black Bat instead of this funny-lookin' punk. They'd be holding a inquest over what was left of us in the mornin' and they wouldn't wonder who killed us, either. Right between our eyes they'd find a little seal in the shape of a black bat. If he's mixed up in this business, I'm gettin' out. His lead carries too much poison."

"Shut up!" the spokesman of the men growled. "Let the wrong guys heard you talk like that and you'll be shoved down an old well or somethin'. The Black Bat ain't no ghost. He can be brought down with a piece of steel any day. Hell, you don't think he's as smart as the boss, do you? Did the Black Bat ever swipe five million bucks' worth of rocks and make dummies outa the cops? Ease him up these steps and don't bust his head yet. We want to hear what he's got to say. There's the other boys waitin' for us at the place."

Silk was thrown on a soiled, rickety old settee, and someone slapped him stingingly across the mouth. He opened his eyes and stared foggily at the seven men who stood around him. "Wh-what happened?" he mumbled. "I was driving along and then all of a sudden something hit me. Where am I? Who are you?"

"Suppose you answer some questions first."

One of the men stepped forward. He was a rangy, loose-jointed man.

"Let me handle him, Stringy," a thug said.

"I'll take care of it," Stringy grunted. "How come you followed our car up this road? It's private and you musta saw the sign."

Silk thought rapidly. "Well, it's like this. I was heading toward town when I saw a small car start going all over the road. Then it dived into a country road and a bigger car followed. So I just parked and waited. Then I saw this big car come out alone. I figured something was wrong, so I just followed."

"Who told you to follow us?" Stringy demanded. "Talk, you funny-lookin' hayseed, or I'll blast your ears off."

Silk hung his head, thankful for the disguise that typed him as a small town youth with funny ideas as to how the modern man dresses. He had to have a logical excuse and it must sound authentic.

"I'll tell you the truth," he admitted. "After your car came out of that lane, a man crawled from the bushes. He was hurt pretty bad—lots of blood on his shirt and it looked to me like a bullet had smacked him across the forehead. Anyhow, he said he was a cop and I was to follow you. That's what I did. I should have minded my own business."

"Search him," Stringy ordered.

TWO OF the men obeyed, obviously enjoying the way they tossed Silk around. Stringy had taken two others aside and was talking swiftly in a low voice. By the malicious grins on the faces of the listeners, Silk knew they were arranging some sort of good-by party for him.

Silk was worried, too, although his bland, rather stupid countenance showed nothing but bewilderment. The Black Bat must have leaped out of his coupé after it turned into the lane. Undoubtedly he had heard and witnessed what had happened and had watched Silk take up the pursuit. But the Black Bat himself was stymied. Butch might have lifted the coupé out of that ditch, but not even the Black Bat could have done it without help. Therefore he was probably miles away, without a possibility of trailing the murder brigade to their hideout.

"Nothin' on him," one of the thugs reported. "What'll I do—bury a chunk of lead in his bean?"

Stringy came back with the other killers.

"Of course not. Look, rube, you butted into something that's very unhealthy. The guy who told you he was a cop wasn't. We're G-men after a gang of smugglers. This is their hideout and the guy you saw was one of them. He shot it out with us and lost. Say, he wasn't wearing a mask, was he?"

"Gosh, thanks for not thinking I meant to gum up your detecting," Silk said. "Nope, he didn't have no mask. Just a gray suit and a white shirt that was pretty bloody. Don't rightly think he's alive now, judgin' by the way he looked."

"Well, you're willin' to coöperate," Stringy said, "so we're gonna give you a break. Ordinarily we'd stick you right in the can, but we're pretty good guys. A couple of my men will escort you to a path that leads to the road. Your bus is smashed up, so you'd better start walkin'. Next time don't butt into what don't have nothin' to do with hay and seeds. Get it?"

Silk let out a gasp of gratitude and made solemn promises, but inwardly he knew this was just a game. They really intended to take him into the night and blast him. But there was more of a chance dealing with two men than seven, so Silk was pathetically willing to oblige them.

Two men got on either side of him and gripped his arms, yanking him roughly out of the house. They reached the driveway, but turned away from the direction of the main road. Straight ahead Silk could see a starry sky, with no sign of trees.

The whole landscape suddenly seemed to be cut off. As they progressed, he knew why, for pieces of quarried slate lay all over the ground. He was being led to a precipice. In all probability, he would simply be shoved over the edge to crash down on the rocks far below. Then at some future time, when his body was discovered, there would be no evidence of murder.

The pair of guards each kept a hand in a coat pocket. Silk knew they gripped guns, taking no chances that their victim might suddenly realize his danger and try to battle his way out. Actually Silk felt helpless. By seizing one crook, he would expose himself to the attack of the other. For the first time, Silk wished he were Butch. Then he could have tackled both thugs at once.

But he wasn't, and he was powerless in the face of inexorable death, grim doom that might strike any moment.

CHAPTER VI

PICTURE OF A DEAD MAN

A **PPROACHING THE** edge of the old quarry, the darkness prevented Silk from seeing all the details of his doom. But he knew his hunch was right, for they were headed straight toward the brink. Silk determined not to betray the fact that he understood their intentions until they were fairly close to the edge, when the killers would naturally be a little afraid of a rough and tumble fight that might also carry them over. He tensed his muscles and got ready.

Like some great bird that had been startled, a weird object suddenly arose from the tall grass and swooped down on the trio. The thugs gave yelps of terror and started to draw their guns. Silk expertly stuck a foot between the legs of one man and sent him crashing down. He lunged for the other, but the gun held by the gangster slapped Silk across the face. It sent him reeling backward.

The thug, thick-witted and none too brave, decided to get rid of Silk first. He pointed his gun downward. His finger tightened against the trigger. At that moment he heard the rush of sound which announced the arrival of the Black Bat. Torn between the urge to exterminate his helpless victim and at the same time defend himself from an attack by the Black Bat, he lost a precious instant trying to make up his mind.

The Black Bat's gloved fist swept in a terrific blow at the gunman's neck. It was a nerve-paralyzing punch. The thug's gun went off as his finger flexed instinctively, but Silk had hastily rolled out of the path of the bullet.

The first thug was getting up, his gun aiming at the Black Bat. Silk lunged for him, and two men tumbled furiously in the tall grass. Silk hammered home a dozen punches. At such close quarters he couldn't put much steam into them, though he did keep the thug from using his pistol again.

The Black Bat bent over. Suddenly the thug relaxed, for the muzzle of an automatic was pressed against his head. The threat was bad enough, but not nearly as terrifying as the eerie creature behind the gun.

"The Black Bat!" the thug yapped. "I give up! Don't shoot! See, I dropped my gun."

Silk picked up the weapon. At the house, hundreds of yards to the rear, there was a confusion of activity. The crooks were running toward parked cars. Before the Black Bat could make a move to stop them, they were off. He eyed his two prisoners doubtfully.

"I really don't know what to do with these gentlemen," he said.

"I know," Silk declared. "They were going to toss me off the cliff, so why not hand them some of their own brand of medicine?"

"You—you wouldn't do that! We—we were just gonna scare you, pal. We were—"

"See how they lie?" Silk said disgustedly. "What good are they to us? I say let's get rid of them."

"Unless they coöperate a bit," the Black Bat amended. "How about it, boys? Who leads your mob and what's back of it all? Don't lie, because I know enough about the case to catch you."

THE THUGS stared at each other, shrugged defeatedly.

"It's Jules Andrus and—and Stringy. They pay us off. We been collecting a lot of rocks—diamonds. I dunno what happened to the stuff. We ain't seen none of it and there hasn't been a cut, either, except a century apiece a couple of times. That's all we know. Honest!"

"And where were the diamonds kept?" the Black Bat insisted. "And from whom do Stringy and Jules take their orders? Who provides the cash to finance this business? Not your so-called bosses, because cash would stop all their activities until after they lost it at some race-track or card-game."

"We don't know. That's the truth. Nobody ever said anything about there bein' some big shot, but I guess maybe there is. Jules and Stringy were busted flat when they organized the mob. Right after that, they had dough to pay us that first century note apiece. The rocks are kept in a safe in that house back of us. We just moved in while the guy who owns it is away some place. Stringy opened the box with one of them things a doctor uses to listen to your heart."

"See that they don't try to get away," the Black Bat told Silk. "If they move, you have the right to plug them. I'm going into that house. Bring them inside after I have a few moments alone."

Keeping his gun ready, he approached the wide-open front door. There was no opposition. The crooks—like all their breed—had fled the moment one of them had spotted the Black Bat charging to attack. He looked the house over and noticed the gaping door of a wall safe. It had been cleaned out.

Silk herded the prisoners inside and the Black Bat coldly faced them again.

"These diamonds you've told me about—where did they come from? What kind of places did you rob to get them?"

"Little joints," one of the crooks answered. "Some places we got a couple of grand' worth. One joint gave up twenty grand. The cops are goin' nuts tryin' to bust the robberies. Give us a break and we'll spill everythin' we know, and we promise not to join the mob again. If we do, they'll knock us off anyhow for talkin'. We didn't know you was in on this case. Plenty of the boys will cut loose from the mob now, after they hear you're workin' against them."

"I think you'll be safer in jail," the Black Bat said judiciously. "Lead them to the car. We'll tie them up. There's a fair-sized baggage compartment in the coupé. It ought to take care of them. If their legs hang out, we'll cover them with a blanket. Riding in a baggage compartment isn't so bad. That's how I got here. I turned into that lane, jumped and let the coupé have her head.

"When the mugs were busy closing in on the coupé, I took their keys out of the ignition, opened the trunk and then put the keys back. I just curled up, let the trunk lid down and stayed there. That was an excellent act you put on for them, my friend and aide. When Stringy plotted your finish, I was just outside the window and I heard what he said. That's how I happened to be conveniently near the edge of that cliff."

The thugs were herded back to where Silk's coupé had been thrown by the impact of that heavy chain. One tire was flat, but Silk enjoyed watching the pair of work-avoiders sweat as they put on the spare. There was other damage but not serious enough to prevent the car from being operated. The Black Bat tied up his prisoners, stuffed them into the fairly commodious rear compartment and fastened them there with more rope. Then he and Silk headed back to town.

"You can roll right up to McGrath's garage," he ordered. "He won't hear you, unless that shot of whiskey I gave him doesn't work as it should. We'll leave our friends as a sort of payment for the headache he'll have in the morning."

QUIETLY THEIR task was accomplished, with the prisoners so tied up that they could not possibly get away nor shout for help. Then

Silk and the Black Bat left McGrath's driveway and headed toward Tony Quinn's home, where they used the secret tunnel to enter.

Silk went to the phone immediately and called Carol. By the time the Black Bat had divested himself of his bullet-perforated regalia and freshened up a bit, she arrived.

Quinn put on his smoking jacket, clamped a pipe between his teeth and nodded unemotionally to her. They had worked together for a long time, but he rarely showed the actual affection he held for her. That could not be while the Black Bat fought crime and exposed himself to the bullets of gangsters. Some day he hoped to retire and let the Black Bat and Tony Quinn disappear. Then with no further reason to pretend blindness he and Carol could enjoy life as they wished. That time seemed more distant than ever just now.

Silk had drawn the window shades and Carol sat down on a foot-stool near the fireplace. She looked up at Quinn.

"Tony, what's it all about? Silk said I was to bring over all the clippings and information on two crooks named Jules Andrus and Stringy. I've brought what I had. The rest is in your own files. Silk is getting the papers now. Are those two hoodlums connected with a five-million-dollar diamond robbery? Tony, I don't think they possess enough brains, even jointly, to plan a big job like that."

Quinn laughed wryly. "They don't. That's what makes this case so difficult. There is a genius directing their movements. He seems to be concentrating on diamonds—to get all there are, apparently. Why, I can't say. The fact that he resorted to the murder of seven people indicates the stakes are extremely big. Now let's see what we have on our two pals."

They studied the batch of clippings and notations. Jules was the cleverer of the two, with a record of some rather daring jewel robberies. But Stringy was only a hood who used brass knuckles, whose idea of fun was slipping up on a victim to surprise him with a knife in the back. But Stringy was also an organizer and a leader, pushing his men by ruthlessly playing on their fears.

"Well," Quinn mused, "Jules was taken into the fold because he probably knows diamonds pretty thoroughly and wouldn't be tempted by anything that just glitters. Stringy controls the gang needed in these raids. A good working combination, but what I need is the identity of the man who tells them when and where to commit their robberies. Carol, will you take a look in my files and bring me all the recent data on jewelry store breaks?"

Carol returned with the necessary papers. They studied them together.

"Twenty jewelry store breaks in five weeks," Quinn said thoughtfully. "Enough to make the police sit up and take notice, but not to suspect that some gang is specializing in diamonds. I notice other types of gems were taken, too, but only when they simply required picking up without loss of time or energy. Stringy carried a stethoscope around, so he probably has mastered the art of opening the average safe.

"You notice the gang hasn't tackled any of the big firms yet, where guards are employed all night and time locks and burglar alarms are in use. But if this is a concerted effort to grab all the diamonds possible, they'll invade those bigger places in due time. I wonder why they concentrate so single-mindedly on diamonds?"

CAROL SMILED and shrugged her capable shoulders.

"Maybe they like the way diamonds sparkle. Or maybe it's because they're so valuable and so easily disposed of. Tony, I agree with you that there is something behind the surface—something much greater than we can estimate now. Yet how are you going to start tracking down this mystery man who heads the outfit?"

"From what those records say about Jules and Stringy, they aren't the type to open up and confess all. According to those men you and Silk captured, Jules and Stringy are the only ones who know the identity of this mystery man, and they aren't even sure about that."

Tony Quinn closed his eyes slowly.

"I know, Carol. The only suspects we have so far are Paul Hawley, who was Van der Veer's American manager, and that butler in the Van der Veer house. I'm going to question them. We don't even know what killed those seven men. Someone—a funny-looking duck with a Vandyke beard and black hair—tried to gun me out. He also threw something big into the sea. He was risking a lot to dispose of that object, so identifying it would go a long way toward solving the case."

"How about divers?" Carol asked.

Quinn shook his head. "Much too deep at that point, and the object has probably been shifted around considerably by the tides. We'd better get some rest now. Head for home, beautiful. I don't want overwork and lack of sleep to give you crow's-feet." He grinned bitterly. "I have all we'll need in this family, and I'm afraid this case is going to add a few more to my unlovely countenance."

CHAPTER VII

THE DEATH DOUBLE

EARLY THE next day, Captain McGrath stopped his car in front of the morgue. He had gone there to learn the results of the autopsy on Van der Veer. Those odd burns still puzzled him and he wanted another look at the dead man's hands. The morgue's chief clerk looked up and nodded a cheery greeting that somehow seemed out of place in this home of the newly dead.

"That stiff I sent in last night—Van der Veer," McGrath said. "I want a look at him if the body is still here." "Certainly." The clerk arose to lead the way. "I've heard that the pathologist who did the initial examination says there is no evidence to show why the man died."

McGrath followed the clerk. He didn't like morgues, even this big one, which had the latest equipment.

The clerk seized the handle of a sliding slab in a refrigeration compartment. After checking the number of it with the card in his hand, he pulled the slab out. The instant he raised the sheet, McGrath gave a startled cry.

The face revealed to him had no red beard! It was the face of a rather old man. Instead of having a head of coal-black hair, this man was bald as an egg!

"That's not him," McGrath stated. "That's not Van der Veer. Mister, you'd better do some fast checking to make sure there hasn't been a mistake."

"But that's the man who was brought in from Van der Veer's house," the clerk insisted. "I was on duty when the boys checked it in. I tied a tag on the dead man's ankle. It's there now. Nobody could get in here without being seen. What more proof do you want?"

They hurried back to the office. At McGrath's suggestion, the two attendants who had come for the body were sent in.

"Sure, the guy we put in the basket had a red beard," one said. "I remember because his hair was the blackest I've ever seen, and I never saw anybody with black hair and a red beard."

"Now listen carefully," McGrath pleaded. "You put the body of the real Van der Veer in the morgue wagon. That's a proven fact. Then you started for the morgue. Did you stop anywhere for even just a minute or two?"

The attendants looked at one another speculatively. Finally one shrugged.

"That call came after hours, Captain. We hadn't eaten since noon. We stopped at a lunch cart and had a cup of coffee."

"And lost one corpse and got another," McGrath growled. "Somebody switched bodies, you dopes! The truck you used isn't to be touched. Understand? I'm sending men over to check it for prints, even though I know we won't find any. The guy who is pulling this fancy stuff wears gloves. Meantime look that corpse over again and see if there are any identifying marks. The real Van der Veer had a bad burn on his right hand."

"Wait a minute," the chief clerk interrupted thoughtfully. "So has the corpse back there. At least I think it's the right hand. Maybe you're wrong, Captain."

McGrath marched wearily back into the refrigerator room. This time the sheet was half-removed from the body. McGrath's jaw dropped. The dead man did have a burned right hand, and the burn was exactly like the one Van der Veer had suffered.

"Holy smokes!" McGrath breathed. "Do you think that black hair could have been a wig and the red beard a fake? Maybe instead of switching bodies, those mugs just yanked off the whiskers. Listen, no matter who comes to claim Van der Veer, or even this guy who we don't know, hold him. Phone me. If necessary, wrap a chair around the guy's head. And you might put a man on guard, too, before somebody swipes the whole morgue."

McGrath reported directly to Commissioner Warner, describing in detail exactly what had happened.

"Maybe the Black Bat can figure it out," he concluded hopefully. "You know, Commissioner, I think I've been all wrong about him. He's okay, and what's more, I don't think he is Tony Quinn."

Warner smiled. He had his own opinions about that although, like McGrath, he wasn't absolutely certain. There were times when he was sure Tony Quinn and the Black Bat were the same man, but something always happened to make that supposition impossible.

Warner fished a thick file out of his drawer.

"There were two more jewelry store robberies last night, Captain. They now add up to twenty-two. The newspapers are getting big stories out of it, trying to link these with the theft of Van der Veer's five million dollars' worth of stones. I want some action on this. We can't cover every jewelry store in town, of course, but I want you to select about thirty fairly small stores, the kind that can be robbed easily. Post men to watch them twenty-four hours a day. An Edmund Clive of the International Diamond Syndicate was here to see me last night, and he's prepared to raise the roof if we don't do something."

McGRATH MADE a sour face.

"Oh, sure, one of those guys who thinks all a cop has to do is consult a ouija board and go out and collect the burglars. Let him bark, sir. We're doing the best we can."

"His bite," Warner said, "happens to be worse than his bark. The man is extremely important and he wields a lot of influence. Therefore, Captain, you will put yourself and your squad on a twenty-four-hour working basis until this case has been cracked. Don't wait for the Black Bat to do it, either. That's all."

McGrath returned to his office, angry but hopeful, for the Black Bat was sure to contact him again. He was a little annoyed at Commissioner Warner's attitude, but he didn't stop to realize that Warner was also being hounded.

McGrath did what he could during the day. Examining the places that had been robbed, he marveled at the slick manner in which the crimes had been performed. The total value of the gems that had been stolen from the twenty-two establishments reached a fairly high sum, and it seemed that the game was just beginning.

McGrath went home at seven o'clock, worried because the Black Bat had not called yet. He was getting ready to prepare a meal for himself when his phone rang. He sped into the living room and answered it eagerly. The Black Bat's voice spoke softly to him.

"Things are beginning to develop, according to the latest papers, eh, Captain? We'd better have a conference—a private one. Be careful. The men behind this plot may be having you watched. Drive to the intersection of Blake Road and Sexton Lane. Watch your speedometer. When you are exactly three-tenths of a mile beyond, you will see a side road. Take it. I'll be there waiting for you. Make certain you are not followed. Captain, the truce still goes. Remember?"

"If you were hog-tied, I wouldn't look under that doggone hood of yours," McGrath promised. "I'll be there at seven forty-five on the dot."

He hung up and felt a little better about the whole business. Perhaps the Black Bat could figure out why a substitution of bodies had taken place. McGrath had tried until his head ached. He lit the gas under a pan of water and prepared to boil four eggs—his one specialty in the culinary arts.

Whistling quietly, he walked over to the refrigerator, bent slightly to peer inside and started to open the door. It closed again with a thud. His sagging body had pushed it shut, but he didn't know that. Captain McGrath didn't know much of anything at that moment.

Two scowling men, one of whom held a blackjack, stepped back and let his unconscious body slump to the floor. The thin man with the sap jerked a thumb toward the back door.

"Get the car as close to the house as you can. Then bring another guy in and haul this side of beef out. Snap it up. He ain't the only bozo we're goin' to smear tonight."

TONY QUINN gave Silk last-minute instructions as he donned his somber clothing and tucked the silken hood and cape into a specially prepared pocket in his coat. He slipped two automatics into their holsters and then raised the trap door that led from the laboratory to the tunnel.

"Butch is waiting for me," he said. "I intend to make a few calls tonight, so I may need him for a fast getaway. McGrath has given his word not to trap me, but he's only one bluecoat. There are eighteen thousand others. Your job is to stall anyone who comes to see me. Carol is on deck beside her phone. If I need you, she'll call."

"Yes, sir," Silk answered, "and good luck."

Quinn drew down the brim of his hat and descended into the tunnel. Two minutes later he darted out of the gate at the rear of his estate and jumped aboard Butch's new second-hand car. Quinn gave the necessary directions and then leaned back so it would be difficult to see him. They arrived at the rendezvous ten minutes ahead of time.

"This will be a private little talk, Butch." Quinn drew on his robe and hood. "Also it wouldn't be a good idea if McGrath spotted you, so be a good fellow and drift out somewhere among those trees. I won't be long."

The Black Bat wriggled behind the wheel and settled back to wait. Once he thought he heard tires scrape against the dirt somewhere near the main road, but McGrath would be coming with his headlights on, making no attempt to keep hidden. The Black Bat, however, rolled down both windows and kept listening.

He didn't underestimate the prowess of the man who headed this mob, nor of the men who formed it. On impulse he drew one automatic and snapped off the safety. Then he opened the door quietly.

The moment he put one foot on the running board, there were two quick shots. They missed, for the Black Bat had moved a second before they reached him. They hit the side of the coupé and ricocheted off into the night. He took a single leap that carried him off the road and into the brush. The headlights of the coupé were doused, so darkness held sway for everyone but the Black Bat.

His keen eyes spotted six men moving toward him, coming from all directions. Apparently they had formed a complete circle to prevent their victim from escaping. Each held a gun ready.

The Black Bat quickly estimated his chances. By shooting his way through one segment of that circle, he might get clear, but the risk was great. Staying put and shooting it out, though, was even more dangerous.

He knelt on one knee like a track runner and waited. As the ring closed, so did the distance between each man, Believing he was still inside the car, they were converging on it. Suddenly the Black Bat fired point-blank. One of the killers let out a screech as his leg buckled under him. The Black Bat's bullet had not been meant to kill.

When the eerie figure came streaking through the brush, bedlam burst loose. The five men who were still on their feet raced after him. The wounded thug began shooting at close range but the pain from his injury made his hand unsteady.

With his head down and his feet covering the ground fast, the Black Bat had a fair chance. He wasn't accustomed to running away from trouble, but there was more than his own welfare to be considered. The fact that these thugs had known of the rendezvous indicated that they had overheard his phone conversation with McGrath. The detective-captain was either in their hands as a prisoner or dead.

CHAPTER VIII

DANGEROUS RESCUE

BECAUSE HE could distinguish objects in the dark, the Black Bat's flight was really remarkable. The bullets were less frequent now and wide of their mark. Abruptly two men rose up before him, holding their guns aimed and ready. At no more than a hundred feet, they couldn't miss.

The Black Bat fired from the hip and hurled himself aside. He went down with a crash. The other crooks, far to the rear, heard the commotion and doubled their speed. The two newcomers were cursing and zigzagging to get closer. They remained huddled together, though, for they knew the reputation of the man they hunted.

Both guns were in the Black Bat's hands now, ready for action now that his only recourse was to shoot his way out. The guns blazed. Instantly both advancing thugs flopped on their bellies. The Black Bat retreated a dozen feet, veered to the left and streaked away. But the crooks were at his heels.

Suddenly his nostrils quivered. There was a swamp nearby—he could smell the characteristic odor. He kept on going until the brush thinned out to the lower shrubs that flourish near the damp ground of a marsh. Butch was somewhere about, too, probably floundering around in the darkness. Once or twice one of the crooks showed a flashlight and the Black Bat promptly fired a bullet dangerously close to the beam.

He saw the swamp, a wide area of marshland, deadly with bogs and extremely dark. He took a leap that carried him from firm ground, across the black swamp and onto a tiny island. Instantly discarding unsafe islands with his uncanny eyes, he jumped from one to another, each time landing on dry ground.

The thugs, unable to see much of anything and not daring to use flashlights, stumbled headlong into the marsh. The muck came up past their knees. They yelled curses and gave vent to their rage by firing bullets in the direction of the slight noises he made.

Deep in the marsh, the Black Bat grinned and started back. He was far more anxious to get clear of the killers and find McGrath than to fight it out with them. They were merely tools in the hands of a dangerous individual.

Before the crooks extricated themselves from the swamp, the Black Bat was nearing the lane again. He emitted a piercing whistle that was answered by the blink of his coupé's headlights. He streaked toward the car. Butch had it rolling already. He had found that swamp, too, and countless barbed branches that had torn his clothes and flesh.

"Gosh, Boss," the giant grumbled, "when the shootin' started, I ran back, but them mugs seemed to be comin' from everywhere. I figured you knew what to do, so I just laid low. Then I saw you scrammin' and I started after you, but I got lost. Next thing I was back here, so I got in the car and waited."

"The best thing you could have done," the Black Bat said. "Let's get started."

Near the outlet of the lane he saw two big cars half-hidden in the brush. He snapped an order and Butch jammed on his brakes. The Black Bat got out and spent five precious minutes disabling the two cars. Then with Butch at the wheel, they streaked for town and Captain McGrath's house.

"I hope them mugs stumble and bust their necks," Butch growled. "I had a swell chance to smash a few heads and I muffed it. Next time—"

The Black Bat hardly heard his gigantic aide, for he was trying to figure things out. It was clear that McGrath was in trouble. His first move was to clean up that angle, then search out the logical suspects and put them through their paces. If much more time elapsed, the gang would accomplish whatever purpose they were organized for.

BUTCH BRAKED the car to a stop near McGrath's house. The Black Bat jumped out, ran to the back of the house and drew one of his freshly loaded guns. The rear door was ajar. He entered the house cautiously.

The kitchen light still burned and a table lamp was lit in the living room near the telephone table. Detecting the odor of scorched metal, he turned toward the gas stove. A pot was glowing red-hot.

"McGrath was cooking," he mused. "He was slugged and hauled away. They took care not to leave any traces, but they forgot that the gas was on."

The Black Bat went into the darkened dining room. The only way those crooks could have known of that rendezvous was by tapping the phone wire. But they could not tap the phone which the Black Bat had used, so they had tapped McGrath's.

The Black Bat found the cellar door and went down the dark steps quickly. He located the phone wire. When he traced it, he saw that his theory had been correct. The wire had been tapped and each conversation recorded on a small disk. He bent over the instrument. The recording needle was poised at the outer edge of the disk, indicating that the eavesdroppers had removed the one on which his conversation was impressed.

"They'll be back for this," he muttered stonily. "All I can do is wait and pray that they arrive before McGrath is murdered."

Instead of remaining in the cellar, he returned to the street, where Butch was waiting. He gave the giant orders to move well up the street. Then the Black Bat selected a dark spot behind the house from which he could watch both entrances.

Each minute seemed as long as an entire day. Time was the most important element now. Once the gang leaders knew they had failed to trap the Black Bat, they would wreak their vengeance on McGrath, yet the Black Bat could do nothing but wait.

An hour passed before he saw a car slow up. One man dropped off the running board and for a moment was out of sight. He reappeared from behind a hedge that skirted the limits of McGrath's yard and proceeded directly to the back door. After staying inside for a few moments, he carried out the recording and wire-tapping apparatus. The car had already turned around and slid to the curb as the killer ran toward the street.

The Black Bat vaulted the hedge, raced behind the houses and found Butch ready for a quick getaway.

"That sedan!" The Black Bat pointed to the dwindling tail-light. "Don't lose it, Butch. A man's life depends on you!"

The trail led back to the city. Butch had his hands full in the heavy traffic, but he clung to the tail of the sedan as though his own life hung in the balance. The Black Bat had stripped off his hood and cape when they reached the city limits, and put on his wide-brimmed hat. He gave a grunt of surprise when the sedan pulled up before one of the biggest office buildings in town. Two men got out, one still cradling the wire-tapping apparatus in his arms. They disappeared into the lobby.

"Stick around," the Black Bat ordered Butch. "This is a risk that I'll have to take alone."

HE DARTED into the lobby. Only two elevators are in use and one of these, according to the indicator, was traveling express toward the roof. It stopped at the thirty-first floor. The Black Bat entered the other car and got out at the twenty-ninth floor, making certain that the operator had not noticed him.

He ran up the two flights of stairs to the thirty-first floor and moved silently along the deserted corridors. Most of the offices were unoccupied, but halfway down one of the halls he saw yellow light gleaming from beneath a door. He moved forward silently till he could read the letters printed in gold on the metal surface.

NORTH GERMAN RAILROADS

The Black Bat's eyes narrowed. His hunch that Nazi agents were mixed up in the five-million-dollar theft seemed to be verified. He approached the door cautiously, one hand on his gun.

The door was thick and fitted well. Ordinary ears would have detected nothing but a muffled mumble, but the Black Bat had no difficulty in hearing through the heavy panel. McGrath was there. His name was mentioned in a threatening manner more than once, and the Black Bat heard the thud of a fist against human flesh.

To burst open that door and shoot it out would have been as foolish as it was useless. McGrath would promptly die and there was no telling how many armed men were inside.

The Black Bat moved away from the door and began looking around. He saw a porter's closet, went to work on the lock and soon had the door open. Inside he discovered a window-washer's life-belt. Taking it, he went back toward the office and used that slender keylike bit of metal on another office two doors away.

Sheltered from possible guards, he removed his hat and put on the hood and cape. Then he buckled the window-washer's belt around his middle, opened the window and sprang to the sill. He looked down and grimaced. The street seemed miles below, but height also offered a degree of safety, for no one would be able to spot him.

He attached one strap of the belt to the window hook, gently eased himself out and thrust a foot toward the next sill. He made it with even greater litheness and ease than the men who earned their livings in this dangerous, uncomfortable way. He opened that window as far as it would go. Then he hooked the right ring of the belt, unhooked the left and swung out to gain the window of the lighted room. His foot reached the sill, but he could not swing over to it. The men inside the office would be certain to see him.

The Black Bat had to trust his life to that belt. Letting go, he dangled in free space for a moment. His heart almost stopped, until he realized the belt would hold. He reached up, took a grip on the window sill and gradually hauled himself up. Supported by his own powerful muscles and the strength of the belt, he was able to peer into the office.

McGrath was seated in a chair. Four men hovered around him menacingly. One was Stringy, the tall, thin murder lieutenant whom the Black Bat had already observed. Two others were run-of-the-mill gangsters, but nonetheless dangerous. The fourth was the Vandyke-bearded killer whose voice reached beyond the window.

"So you are a stubborn *Dummkopf,* eh? Perhaps more of the same treatment will bring oudt the truth, *ja?* Who is the Black Bat? Do you prefer to die rather than give us his name?"

McGRATH'S LIPS were swollen, his face bloody, but his eyes were clear and defiant.

"Go to hell and get it over with," he muttered. "If I knew who the Black Bat was, I still wouldn't tell. You're going to murder me, anyhow. Go ahead."

The Vandyke-bearded man stepped back. One of the thugs was standing beside a desk and fingering a letter-basket. The bearded leader whirled on him and ejected a string of oaths.

"Stop it! Did I not say we leave no traces that we have been here? Now we waste no more time. Take the stupid pig out. Find an office which is not used. Put him in there and shoot him. Do it quietly. Use his coat to stop the sound."

The Black Bat slowly raised himself a little more. The window was not closed all the way. He eased it up an inch, shoved his fingers under it and waited. Everything depended on getting McGrath's eye now. What the Black Bat intended to do was one of the riskiest tricks he had ever attempted, but McGrath was doomed anyhow and should be willing to take a desperate chance.

When his hooded head was framed in the window, the Black Bat saw McGrath make an almost visible start of amazement. The other men were getting ready to perform their mission of murder. The Black Bat drew himself up even more. Supporting his weight with one hand and the aid of the life-belt, he signaled McGrath.

The detective-captain gulped when he realized what the Black Bat meant, but he was game. The Black Bat worked the window open wider, using such careful pressure that he made no noise at all. Fortunately there was no wind to cause a draft that the killers might notice.

When he was ready, the Black Bat drew his automatic with his free hand, aimed at the wall switch. He nodded abruptly, at the same instant that his gun blasted.

The office plunged into darkness. McGrath violently shoved a killer out of his way and ducked silently to the window. The Black Bat whispered an order. McGrath felt an arm of steel around him and allowed himself to be pulled through the window.

"Steady," the Black Bat whispered. "They don't know what happened yet, but they'll turn on flashlights in a second. Keep your nerve and don't yell when I swing into space. Grab the sill of the next office as soon as we reach the end of our swing."

The Black Bat planted his feet to one side against the brick wall. He gave himself a terrific shove. The life-belt creaked in protest and for a moment he thought he had been cut in half. Desperately McGrath grabbed the other window and pulled himself through it. He stuck his head out an instant later, reached for the Black Bat's hand.

"Come on!" he whispered urgently.

"Not yet," the Black Bat replied in a low, unhurried voice.

CHAPTER IX

THE BLACK BAT VISITS

IN THE offices of the North German Railroads, flashlights were cutting swaths through the darkness. When the Black Bat heard someone yell that the window was open, he shifted his gun. Dangling from the life-belt, he tossed the weapon straight toward McGrath. It sailed through the air and directly into McGrath's hands. Swiftly the captain nodded understandingly.

Two thugs thrust their heads out of the other window. One of them yelled the Black Bat's name and snapped a shot. It went wild, for McGrath had sent a slug through his hand. Howling, the killer pulled back. McGrath kept them inside by a barrage that covered the Black Bat's retreat. The Black Bat was hauling himself up on the strap that was still attached.

"They're coming for you," he said to McGrath. "Never mind me. Cover your door."

McGrath spun around. The door leading into that office was opening, but a well placed shot closed it again promptly. Meanwhile the Black Bat had hoisted himself to the sill and swung across space to reach the German railroad office window again. It was empty now. He hooked the other belt strap, released the one at McGrath's window and pulled himself into the office.

He raced for the door, opened it a crack and saw that the Vandyke-bearded man was gone. Stringy and his two fellow-rats were cautiously edging their way toward the room in which McGrath was besieged. The Black Bat's reserve gun blasted twice. Stringy howled an oath and like three puffs of smoke in a high wind, the trio of thugs vanished.

The Black Bat was swift in pursuit, but he heard an elevator door slam shut and the whine of the motor as the cage dropped. It was a service elevator. The passenger cars were all downstairs.

McGrath stuck his head out. He was still shaky and white.

"D-did they get away?" he stammered.

"Unfortunately. We'd better get out of here, too. Those shots are certain to have attracted attention."

"Sure," McGrath said unsteadily. "I—I'd prefer the cellar. I want to get as close to the ground as possible. That dive out the window—*Whew!* I'm ten years older right now."

The Black Bat slapped him encouragingly on the shoulder.

"Nonsense. Cops go through things like that every day. After the tenth time you don't mind it at all. But we can't stand here chattering like a couple of old ladies over a pot of tea. There's work to be done. Our bearded friend—"

"Did you see him, too?" McGrath gulped. "That's the guy who heads this outfit. He's the real big shot."

McGrath took a firmer grip on his nerves as they approached the elevators. He squared his shoulders and bravely marched ahead of the Black Bat.

"I'm all right now, but I think I'd rather let those mugs gun me out than take a dive through a window again. Did you realize we were thirty-one stories above the hard sidewalk?"

There was no answer and McGrath turned his head. He stopped and gaped. The Black Bat was gone! There hadn't been a sound, yet the corridor was empty. McGrath shrugged and punched the elevator button.

In the lobby, he met four radio car patrolmen who were answering a call to investigate shots fired near the top of the building. McGrath sent them away. He took a taxi home, wondering why the Black Bat had vanished.

HE FOUND out a couple of minutes later. As soon as he stepped into his house, the Black Bat's voice startled him.

"Sorry I couldn't accompany you home, Captain, but it would have seemed odd if you had been walking beside a man whose hood and cape identified him as the Black Bat. So I just slipped away by myself. Now we can have that delayed chat. By the way, I removed a telephone-tapping apparatus from your cellar. I don't think they'll try that stunt again, but one never knows. I advise you to check the line now and then."

McGrath poured out two drinks.

"I'll do the honors this time," he said with a reminiscent grin. "When that mug socked me on the head, I thought at first it was another bang from that drink you fixed for me last night. You ought to know about Van der Veer. His body is missing. On the way to the morgue, the boys got hungry and stopped for a bite to eat. Somebody thought it was a good chance to switch bodies. But Van der Veer had a serious burn on his right hand and the corpse in the morgue has the same kind of burn on his right hand. Only Van der Veer had a lot of black hair and this guy was bald."

"Highly interesting, Captain, but the solution of the case as a whole will also solve that problem. So far, this gang has held the upper hand and we must get off the defensive. When you gave orders that the strato-liner was to be left unguarded, who could have overheard the conversation you had with Headquarters?"

"I talked to Commissioner Warner," McGrath explained. "This afternoon he told me that he had some visitors about the time I called. There was a man named Reicher, a diamond wholesaler who has lost a lot of stock that was on consignment to some of the robbed jewelry stores. Then another man named Edmund Clive came and howled bloody murder about the robberies. I think the commissioner said Clive had something to do with a diamond syndicate."

"The International Diamond Syndicate." The Black Bat nodded. "I've heard of Mr. Clive. Was your friend Hawley also where he might have known what was going on?"

"He was right in the office," McGrath grumbled. "Warner had him brought there so Clive and Reicher could have a look at him. Neither one knew him at all."

"Then we have three possibilities—Hawley, Reicher and Clive. Yet we must also consider the idea that your phone may have been tapped yesterday and your orders to Headquarters overheard. Although we may be going off on a wrong tangent, I still think those three men should be considered as logical suspects. Don't bother them yet. Hawley is being held for—"

"No, he's free," McGrath groaned. "He got himself a smart lawyer and Warner had to let him go. We didn't have a single thing on the guy, anyhow. There was no question in my mind but that Van der Veer—or whoever it was that died—was alive when Hawley was with me in the hallway. I wish I could figure out why the corpse was ice-cold one minute and warm the next. It doesn't make sense."

"It will," the Black Bat said calmly. "Everything will make sense when we put the finishing touches on this mob. I'm getting ideas, so I'll be on my way. Thanks for keeping your promise not to try to find out who I am! It must be rather difficult, having me at your elbow like this and not giving in to an impulse to yank this hood off my face."

"Difficult?" McGrath put down the rest of his drink and closed his weary eyes. "That's a mild word, but I keep my promises. I know Warner is laughing at me for actually working with you. I notice he doesn't give me orders not to."

McGrath sighed and opened his eyes. He was talking to himself again. That Black Bat had spread his wings and apparently soared away.

IT HAD not been quite as easy as that for the Black Bat to vanish. He had the ability to move noiselessly, and McGrath had given him a momentary opportunity.

He met Butch well up the street.

"We are going to visit a man named Edmund Clive," he said. "He lives on Teneyke Road in one of those places that are easy to slip into."

"Do I get some action, Boss?" Butch asked hopefully. "I ain't forgettin' how I missed up back there in the woods. Let's stick around the city, huh? I ain't so good with a lot of trees and bushes around me, on account of I don't see like you do in the dark."

"No action right now, Butch. Clive represents the diamond interests and I can't see him bucking a combine like that, when he makes an excellent living out of them. That's why I'm going to call on him. He may have ideas about what this mob is up to."

The Black Bat easily entered Clive's pretentious home. The underworld had lost a crack burglar when the Black Bat had chosen to fight instead of joining them. By dint of some quiet prowling, he located Clive's bedroom, closed the door softly behind him and drew a gun. Then he switched on a small table lamp near the bed.

Clive awoke with a startled cry. He saw the gun first and then the weird figure behind it. Clive was no fool. He understood the situation and recognized his visitor.

"So you are the Black Bat." He blinked in awe. "I've got a gun under my pillow if you'd like to get it."

"Thanks." The Black Bat pressed the muzzle of his automatic against Clive's chest and whisked the weapon from beneath the pillow. "It doesn't pay to take chances even with men who allow their fangs to be drawn. You probably know why I am here. I think it will be to your advantage if you do some talking."

Clive swung his legs off the bed.

"I'm more than willing to. People—even high police officials—don't quite grasp the full significance of what is going on. Since the war began, diamond markets and stone-cutting establishments have been driven to all corners of the earth. In Amsterdam and Rotterdam, the enemy took over whatever gems they could find. There was a lot of loot, naturally.

"The diamond dealers, like everyone else, didn't believe a blitzkrieg really moved like lightning. So diamonds which would normally have been placed on the market are now being used either on machinist's tools for getting out war supplies, or the Nazis are holding them for use in international trade. They are as good as gold, you know."

"I know," the Black Bat answered. "Then you believe that the loss of Van der Veer's five million dollars' worth of gems and the subsequent theft of other stones will affect the diamond market?"

"It already has." Clive started to get up, but a glance at the gun decided him to relax again. "You see, there is also war in Africa, where almost all the best gems are mined. The operators of the mines are taking no chances on continuing work and then having the stones pass into the hands of an enemy. The worldwide diamond market is deliberately limited to keep prices where they belong. The loss of several million dollars' worth of stones will raise the general price per carat."

"DID YOU know Mr. Van der Veer?" The Black Bat asked abruptly.

"Of course. Van der Veer was a shrewd buyer and seller. His business went to pot in Amsterdam, but he saw the end coming and hid his stones before he fled the country. I helped him come to the United States. He confided that he would have his fortune in diamonds shipped here by a chartered plane, just as he did do."

"Then you are positive that it was the real Van der Veer who came to New York?"

"As sure as I am of my own identity. In fact, I called on him only a couple of hours before he was murdered. Why, you couldn't mistake the man. He had an absolutely singular appearance and personality. Besides, there isn't another one voice like his in the world. The man didn't speak. He roared."

"One more thing, Mr. Clive. Yesterday evening you visited Commissioner Warner. While you were in his office, he received a phone call. He gave certain orders that Van der Veer's chartered plane was to be unguarded. Did you hear those orders?"

"Yes. I had heard that something happened at the plane. I'm aware that I was in a position to realize what a great opportunity there was to visit the plane secretly. However, I did not do so. Have you considered Mr. Reicher as a possible suspect? He really is a diamond merchant, but he is also a Nazi secret agent. He is connected with the offices of the

North German Railroads, which is nothing more than a spy organization. Who would want to travel in Germany today?"

"Then my work in stopping these thieves also acts to your advantage, and the interests you serve," the Black Bat said. "Therefore you should have no objection to keeping my visit a strict secret. You've been very helpful. I'll find out about Mr. Reicher."

"I hope you will be even more helpful," Clive declared. "It's not exaggeration to say that if a few more large shipments of stones vanish and the number of domestic diamond thefts increase, there will be an actual panic in the diamond market. It doesn't take much to upset the equilibrium of our type of business. If you need my help, I'll be glad to have you—er—drop in like this any time, even though it's not benefiting my heart much."

The Black Bat stepped back and extinguished the bed lamp by the simple expedient of pulling the cord out of the wall socket. In the darkness he silently faded away.

Edmund Clive remained seated on the edge of the bed, slowly counting the seconds. When he was positive that the Black Bat had disappeared, he reached for his telephone and dialed a number. His voice was a whisper when the connection was completed.

"Mankensen? Listen carefully. The Black Bat was just here. He may know more than he indicated and we must watch our step. What we intend doing happens to be our personal affair and we want no interference. Is that quite clear?"

"Quite, sir," Mankensen replied.

He was just as respectful as when his master, Van der Veer, had been alive. Mankensen was, above all else, a good butler.

CHAPTER X

NO WAY OUT

FRITZ REICHER was a shrewd man. Only those gifted with a high degree of slyness are chosen for work as Nazi agents. He was worried, too. Things were definitely not going the way he had prophesied. If he failed to accomplish his purpose— He shuddered at the consequences. The regime he served tolerated no failures.

Reicher's florid face was suffused in wrath as he crumpled a message into a tight ball and dropped it into his ash tray. He applied the flame of his lighter to the thin paper and watched it burn. Then he put out the light and stamped off to bed.

As he disappeared from the room, another figure came out of the darkness. The gently blowing curtains before one window indicated how entrance had been effected.

The Black Bat sat down behind Reicher's desk and quietly opened the drawers. They held nothing of any consequence. Reicher was too clever to leave incriminating papers about. But the ashes of that message intrigued the Black Bat. He carefully slid a piece of paper over the ash tray, held it there with his fingers and picked up ash tray and all.

Five minutes later he was in the car beside Butch.

"Careful now," he warned. "I'm carrying something so fragile that a breath would destroy it. We'll go back later and see what Van der Veer's house has to offer in the way of clues."

Silk and Carol were eagerly waiting for word from the Black Bat. Carol came over immediately to find him out of his robe and hood and engaged in setting up an infra-red apparatus and a high-speed camera.

"These ashes," he explained, "are what is left of a message which the estimable *Herr* Reicher burned. I couldn't stop him from doing it, but I did notice that the contents of the message displeased him. In fact, he nearly had a tantrum. I'd like to find out what upset him so much. Ink, pencil or typewriter-ribbon marks can be distinguished with infra-red because they absorb the ray varyingly."

As Carol handled the shutter of the camera, Tony Quinn kept rotating the ash tray slowly, so every portion of the charred paper would be photographed. He left the developing of the prints to Silk and ate a hasty lunch with Carol.

Before they got up. Silk's work was finished. They all bent over the photographs, examining the faint tracery of handwriting.

"From what I gather," Tony Quinn said, "this message reached the United States by short-wave radio from Amsterdam. It was then written and passed on to Reicher. It seems to be concerned with the departure of Van der Veer's chartered strato-liner for the United States. See those three words? They are in German and they mean 'diamonds definitely aboard.'"

"That proves Reicher has been checking up, which seems to eliminate him as a suspect to the actual robbery and murders done in the plane. You note I say 'seem,' because we haven't got the entire message. It's enough to involve Reicher, though."

"The nerve of them!" Carol cried. "Following those diamonds halfway around the world. Tony, do you think that Reicher is after those stones and their theft prevented him from carrying out certain plans?"

"Possibly." Quinn nodded slowly. "If he had the gems, he wouldn't be worried about them any longer. Carol, in the morning I want you to investigate a person named Edmund Clive. On the surface he appears to be above board in all his affairs, but it would be a man with his specialized knowledge to head this diamond stealing outfit. Check on his friends, his financial affairs and how he spends his spare time. You'll find facts about him in the files.

"Silk, you stay here. Butch and I are going out to visit Van der Veer's house. Maybe we'll run into his ghost. Oh, yes. Butch, take that camera along. Perhaps we can set a little trap for our ghost."

GETTING INTO Van der Veer's home would be a more difficult task for the Black Bat than entering Clive's house. Two men were inside and both were bound to be highly nervous after what had happened. The house was in darkness, which the Black Bat fully appreciated. He went to work on a window, succeeded in moving the latch away and raising the frame silently.

As he slipped into the house, he realized that he was in the same room where Van der Veer had been murdered. He placed the camera on the floor behind a chair and looked around. Fingerprint powder covered everything. Apparently Van der Veer's butler was slipping a bit.

The Black Bat moved out into the hallway and mentally visualized Captain McGrath's actions just before the body was found. Suddenly he drew back into the shadows of a far corner. His keen ears had caught the sound of several feet descending the stairs.

Before the hall lights were snapped on, he retreated to a window. He stepped behind the thick drapes, making sure they reached the floor so his feet would not be exposed. His hand darted toward the gun on his left hip. Jules Andrus, the squat jewelry thief, walked into the murder room. At his side strode the Vandyke-bearded, tousle-haired leader of the killers.

The Black Bat edged out of his hiding place, reached the door and took a quick look inside the room. The murder leader had moved the ornamental fireplace mantel aside. It seemed to work on hidden runners. When the gleaming surface of a wall safe was exposed, he casually manipulated the dial, as though he had done it quite often in the past. He removed something from his pocket, unwrapped it and let the paper fall to the floor. Putting the object in the safe, he closed the door and slid the mantel back in place.

"Nice work," he said in a thick, restrained voice. "A pleasant evening all around. Now see that matters in the closet are working right."

Jules nodded. He walked through the hall without noticing a deeper shadow in the corner of the dark corridor. He stepped up to a closet door, put his ear against the panel and grinned with satisfaction. There was a medium-sized table against the wall just opposite that door. A long cloth was draped over it, reaching almost to the floor. Jules opened a cigarette box that stood on the table, took out a cigarette and lit it. Then he returned to the room where the bearded man waited.

The Black Bat followed soundlessly almost at his heels. Here was a chance to find out the identity of the ringleader, an opportunity that might never come again. But he changed his mind abruptly. A car had pulled into the driveway beside the house. At the same moment, someone upstairs called down a warning.

"I think it's the boys, Boss. Want me to come down and let them in?"

The Black Bat darted toward the cellar door, opened it quietly and stood motionless on the stairway landing. The arrival of Jules Andrus' gang changed his plans. Now if he tried to corner the bearded man, he might not succeed. It was better to lie low and wait for developments.

HE HEARD Stringy's rasping voice and the pounding of many feet in the hallway. The bearded man's thick voice gave instructions.

"Jules, you will have one of your men stay by the door. The Black Bat is abroad tonight and it would not be well if he came at this time. The rest of you come with me. Not in the study. The stupid police have left fingerprint powder over everything and we must not leave clues."

The voice was muffled a bit after that, indicating that the leader of the gang had led them to some room farther down the hall. Yet a few words were still audible to the Black Bat's superhumanly sensitive ears.

"The Continental Gem Shop—good, very good. Thirty thousand dollars—best haul yet. Now I have plans—easy to get. Mark Freiber and Company next—later on—big job— More gems than you ever saw."

The Black Bat fought down an impulse to take a chance of slipping into the hallway despite the guard who had been posted at the front door. But the risk was too great. Stringy's men were nervous and ready to shoot. Reluctantly the Black Bat stayed where he was, until he heard them shuffling out into the hall. Then the leader spoke again.

"Never mind what is in the closet now. I will see to it later. We have no time to lose. I—"

A sudden bellow from the study made the Black Bat start. There was a concerted rush of feet toward the room. He held his breath, hoping though he knew there was no hope.

"It's a camera hidden back of a chair!" Jules shouted. "How could anybody take pictures—"

"Fool!" the bearded man howled. "It was placed there in a hurry. Take care of the one upstairs quickly. The rest of you search the house, shoot anyone you find. Jules, your men take the second floor. Stringy, the first floor and the cellar."

Swiftly the Black Bat slipped down the stairs. Any one of the cellar windows or the door would offer a ready exit if things got too hot. But he did not intend to leave so soon. Something might break that would let him lay hands on the cunning supervisor of theft and murder.

As his eyes penetrated the gloom of the cellar, he groaned. Van der Veer had apparently used the cellar as a workshop for cutting diamonds. The small windows were heavily barred and the door was fashioned of steel and securely locked. Given time, the Black Bat could have opened that lock.

But even before he could examine it, he heard the killers running to search the cellar.

He raced toward the farther and darker end of the basement. There was a long workbench set against the wall, with several vises attached to it. The Black Bat realized that he was trapped, that one of the searchers would be certain to spot him and shout an alarm to the others. They would turn on the lights first of all, which would rob the Black Bat of the advantage of darkness.

DRAWING HIS reserve automatic, he hastily clamped it in the vise near a corner of the bench. Then he picked up the spool of fine wire he had seen while examining the place. He fastened one end of the wire around the trigger of the gun, unrolled the rest of it, passing the wire around a metal supporting post until he was just behind the cellar stairway.

He dropped the spool. Rushing over to the meter and fuse-box, he grabbed the insulated cable that led in from the street. Just as the door opened upstairs, he yanked the cable, pulling it free.

Instantly every light in the house went out.

"We heard a noise!" one of the thugs at the head of the cellar stairs yelled. "It came from down here. Somebody give me a flashlight!"

"Nuts," Stringy growled. "We ain't got no lights with us. Go on down. What are you scared of? It ain't no army of cops waiting."

UNSTEADY FOOTSTEPS announced the fact that a couple of thugs were warily entering the blackness of the cellar. One of them scraped a match and held it high. Then his hand was afflicted with sudden palsy and the light went out.

"It's the Black Bat!" he yowled. "He's in a corner and he's got a gun. Lemme outa here!"

"Stay where you are," Stringy called back. "If he's down there, we've got him. Shoot at any sound—"

A terrific explosion in the cellar interrupted him just as he was calling the rest of the men for help. Stringy shouted encouragement.

"That's the stuff, boys! Blast him out!"

"That—that wasn't our guns," one of the thugs quavered. "A bullet just kissed my ear. I gotta get outa here."

But Jules and all the rest of the thugs were coming down the cellar stairs. From the vicinity of the workbench, an automatic blazed flame and death.

One crook yelped in pain and clapped a hand to his side.

The shot drew a fusillade from the gangsters. Jules and Stringy were trying to take command at the same time.

"Rush him!" Jules yelled.

"And be knocked off?" Stringy argued. "That guy ducks bullets. Empty your guns at him, boys. Blast every inch of the cellar."

Though they disagreed on tactics, Jules and Stringy both realized the advisability of keeping well behind their men.

CHAPTER XI

PICTURE OF A GHOST

WHILE THE gunmen knew they were facing only one man, they were far from eager to engage in battle. More than anyone else, they feared the Black Bat. All they could do was shoot fast and furiously. No less than fifty slugs smashed against the further wall of the basement.

"Okay!" Jules shouted. "See what's left of him."

The group moved forward cautiously. There was a jet of flame, a deafening explosion in the close air, and they flopped hastily. Even Jules was astonished by this proof of the Black Bat's charmed life. The horrified men pumped more lead in the direction of the shot. When Jules shouted for silence, they stopped shooting. This time no defiant blaze of lead answered. Yelling triumphantly everyone surged forward. The Black Bat ran up the staircase to the first floor.

Two thoughts were predominant in his mind. All this gunfire was bound to draw the police in droves. The bearded man had not been among those in the basement. Therefore he was probably upstairs.

The Black Bat took the steps three at a time, veered left at the second floor landing and slowed down. There were six or seven rooms and all the doors were shut. He could not afford to waste time. If the police surrounded the place, he would be in a bad fix. His truce was only with Captain McGrath.

He heard a window suddenly being shoved open. The sound came from one of the rooms down the hall. He sprinted toward it, found the door locked from inside and threw himself against it with all his weight and muscle. It required a full minute before the strong panels splintered.

Gun poised, he rushed in. There was a rope made of blankets and sheets hanging over the sill. He looked out and saw a man running frenziedly toward the rear of the house. The Black Bat aimed and yanked the trigger. The fleeing man threw up both hands, tripped and fell. But he sprang up almost instantly. Though his mad run became a slow limp, he was soon out of sight.

The Black Bat started to turn away from the window, but dodged back again. From the cellar stairs at the rear of the house came Jules, Stringy and the rest of the men. They had all had enough and probably knew the police would descend on the place promptly. Somehow one of them had a key to that steel door.

The Black Bat left the room without trying to pick off any of the men. Vandyke was legitimate prey, but the others were only plain and fancy gangsters. They would keep.

He raced back into the hallway. The closet door downstairs intrigued him. Vandyke had said he was going to attend to it himself, so it must contain something of vital importance. The Black Bat did take time to open bedroom doors on his way along the upper floor, though. He flung one open, darted into the room and stepped up to a bed.

There was a man lying beneath the sheets. The Black Bat shook him without getting a response. He whipped off the covers, exposed a dead man dressed in the livery of a butler. The right hand, lying across his stomach, was swollen and seared. The Black Bat picked it up by the wrist. The flesh was ice-cold. The left hand showed more burns.

How could a man be burned so severely and still be as cold as that? His limbs were flexible, too, indicating that the chill of the skin had not yet penetrated the entire body.

The Black Bat went back to his task of searching the various rooms, keeping his ears cocked for the first whine of a police siren. The last room before the staircase revealed another man, lying on the floor. His arms and legs were so tightly bound that the skin was beginning to swell around the ropes. His forehead was smeared with blood and he was unconscious. His pulse was good, however.

The Black Bat knelt beside him. He had never seen Paul Hawley, but he had a reasonably good idea that this was Van der Veer's American manager.

ABRUPTLY A siren howled. The Black Bat raced out, dashed swiftly down the steps and paused in front of the closet which interested him so much. The door was slightly ajar. He flung it wide. Despite the darkness, even the Black Bat's eyes could not penetrate its mystery. A few clothes hung on hangers, several pair of shoes were on the floor and that was all. If this closet contained a secret, it was a well hidden one.

Brakes squealed out in front to the accompaniment of a dying siren. The Black Bat fled to the back of the house, went through the exit like a shot and disappeared in the gloom. He selected a good spot from which he could observe the house without being seen.

Flashlights slashed the darkness. Other police cars howled up. He heard excited shouts when the dead man and the trussed-up manager were found. Then a larger car came to a stop and a man got out. As he ran across the path of the headlights, the Black Bat recognized him. It was Captain McGrath.

He could hear the captain giving orders a few minutes later. Men were dispatched to search the grounds. The Black Bat retired until he saw that McGrath was going to take part in the search himself.

The doughty detective-captain had trembled in fear when he heard there was a dead man in the house. His relief was so obvious when he identified the corpse that two or three patrolmen looked at him suspiciously.

McGrath headed to the left and the Black Bat went to meet him. As McGrath passed by a lilac bush, he felt a tap on his shoulder. He whirled, gun ready. Then he lowered the weapon and expelled a deep breath.

"I thought we'd find what was left of you some place out here. What happened in there? Hawley is a mess. I've sent for an ambulance already. Can't wake him up. Mankensen, the butler, is dead. Stone-cold, too. Must have been dead a long time."

"Van der Veer was also cold," the Black Bat reminded him. "I don't know how or why they killed him. There was no time to make an examination except to see that his hand was burned. Did you notice it? Was that burn similar to the one on the corpse you identified as Van der Veer and the other you noticed on the substituted body?"

McGrath nodded. "Exactly the same. They roast 'em and freeze 'em at the same time. By the looks of the cellar, they must have rubbed out about a hundred guys. The wall looks like an execution squad had used it for a year or more."

The Black Bat laughed softly.

"Those bullets were meant for me, only I was the little man who wasn't there. I simply fastened one of my guns in a vise, hooked a long wire to the trigger and fired it from a safe distance. Elementary but efficient, Captain. Now do this for me. In the living room, your men may find a camera behind one of the chairs. Don't touch it. There's a clothes-closet in the hall, also. Leave it strictly alone. Don't ask me why. Just do it.

"Now I'll be on my way. Oh, yes. You might conclude your investigation as soon as possible and lock the place up. Don't leave a guard. Our Vandyke-bearded pal plans to return, and when he does, there will be a reception committee of one. So long, Captain."

McGrath saw the Black Bat step away and then vanish as the night closed around him.

THE BLACK BAT knew that Butch had shifted the car to a spot where the police would not be apt to notice it. Therefore he headed toward a street that was parallel with the one that Van der Veer's house faced.

Just as he had expected, Butch was parked at the curb halfway up the block. The giant opened the door for him.

"Say, there was more shootin' in there than they have in gangster movies, Boss. You sure you don't have no bullet holes in you?"

"Not a one," the Black Bat stated. "We'd better get away from here. Not too far, though. We're coming back here soon, and this time I want you along with me. Too bad I couldn't take you. There would have been some rare sport. I— Wait! I just heard a moan."

"Yeah," Butch said, trying not to look proud. "I forgot to tell you. When all them buzzards come flyin' outa that cellar, I picked off one of them. I wanted to grab another guy, but he pushed this one right into my arms. I stuck him in the back of the bus, like we did with them other two. Don't worry, Boss. I didn't hit him hard enough to kill him outright. He'll live for a while."

"Turn down that side street," the Black Bat ordered, after looking at the limp figure on the back seat. "Follow the road until I stop you."

He nudged Butch when he heard gasping and groaning behind him. They were a few miles from Van der Veer's house, on a dark road that had only one building three blocks away. Butch stopped the car.

"Get out here and wait behind the car," the Black Bat instructed. "I can't expose my aides."

Butch did himself just as the gangster shuddered awake. As the Black Bat looked down at his captive, he saw the stupidly crafty eyes go wide with fright and superstitious dread.

"Your jaw has not been broken—yet, so you can still talk," the Black Bat said ominously. "Can't you, my murderous friend?"

The thug's mouth quivered open, but no sound came out. Everything had happened too quickly for his weak little brain to follow. Now he was face to face with the most terrifying personality he had ever encountered, and the hard object prodding him was a gun that he knew would not hesitate to go off.

"D-don't shoot!" he yammered in a sudden rush of words. "I ain't heeled. I ain't got no gun!"

"That's your good luck," the Black Bat retorted. "What was in the closet on the first floor of Van der Veer's house? I want the truth, weasel."

"I don't know. Honest! Nobody said nothin' about the closet. I come in with the mob, and before we get set, there was the Black Bat—" His voice trailed off and he amended in horror: "There was you."

"What about the plans to rob jewelry stores? You can't tell me you don't know anything about that."

"But I don't," the killer chattered. "We was gonna get our orders, only you didn't give us no time. I wouldn't be here, either, if it wasn't for them wise guys Stringy hired. I belong to Jules' mob, see? We don't work much with Stringy's boys. They're a bunch of saps, see! Somebody made a grab for Dodo, one of the boys in Stringy's mob. Dodo shoved me and I flopped right into somebody's arms. But Dodo and the rest of Stringy's mob is gonna get theirs. Our boys ain't gonna keep takin' all that guff, see?"

"Mutiny, eh?" the Black Bat muttered. "That certainly makes it easier for me." He spoke aloud to the trembling thug. "You look tired, my white-livered friend. I think it's time for you to go back to sleep."

Almost gently he tapped the killer on the skull with the butt of his gun. So expert was he that he knew within three minutes either way how long the thug would remain unconscious. At the muffled sound, Butch reappeared. "He's sleepin' like a baby, ain't he, Boss? Want me to drop him in the gutter?"

"No," the Black Bat said. "Put him in your lap. I'll take the wheel. We can't let Captain McGrath rush out here for nothing. I'll drive by Van der Veer's house. If there are no police in sight, stuff this object into McGrath's car."

SILENTLY McGRATH watched the medical examiner replace his instruments in a kit and followed the morgue men as they completed their grim task. Then he cleared the place, made sure the camera was still behind the chair and locked the house. Everything was just as the Black Bat had asked.

McGrath hurried out to his car, opened the door. His Christmas present almost fell out at his feet. McGrath shoved the unconscious man back into the car, spotted a white card fastened to a button of the coat and read it.

LOOK WHAT I FOUND

That was the message, but the signature was a small sticker in the form of a bat with its wings outspread.

"Another punk," McGrath growled. "All he'll know is he's innocent. They're all innocent. We send hundreds of innocent guys to prison and to the chair every year. It's sad."

"You say something, Cap?" a sergeant queried. "Hey, where'd that rat come from?"

"He's a gift from the Black Bat," McGrath snapped. "Eleven of you dumb clucks here and one man gets us a prisoner when none of you even see a shadow. Beat it!"

CHAPTER XII

THE BLIND CAN ONLY LISTEN

PARKED IN a safe place, the Black Bat waited. Soon he saw the police cars leave the vicinity of the house. When he was sure all had left, he drove back. This time he left the coupé two blocks away. The Black Bat proceeded to the house through neighboring yards. When Butch sauntered onto the front porch, the door was open. He looked around and entered.

"We'll set up our camera and then wait," the Black Bat said. "If our friend comes back himself, or sends someone else, we'll at least get a picture of him."

He placed the camera on a low shelf of the small table directly in front of the closet door. By cutting a tiny slit in the cloth which was draped far enough down to conceal the camera, he created an excellent little trap. The lens of the camera could catch anything that approached the door. He opened the shutter. In the inky darkness of the hall, the film would catch nothing until someone moved in front of it.

From his pocket the Black Bat removed several small devices. He hooked these up. Now if that closet door were opened more than two inches, there would be an electrical connection between two small dry-cell batteries and a tiny mound of flashlight powder. It would snap the picture of any intruder and at the same time warn the Black Bat of the prowler's presence.

"We'll go into another room and wait," he told Butch. "Follow me. I know the layout."

Butch sank into an easy chair and sighed luxuriously.

"This is the life, Boss. If we gotta wait for somebody, it's nice to have a soft chair."

"Isn't it," the Black Bat agreed. "That's the chair Van der Veer was found dead in. See that nothing like that happens to you."

Butch came out of it in one jump. He stumbled against the desk and sat down more carefully in a straight-backed chair. Comfort was comfort, but he wasn't flirting with any kind of death that first froze a man and then burned him.

Butch dozed the time away, but the Black Bat was alert every second. Finally he looked at his watch. In half an hour it would be dawn, an unhealthy time for bats. He shook Butch.

"Nothing doing, I'm afraid. Vandyke either is too wary to return or I winged him better than I thought. Bring the car around while I gather up our apparatus."

The Black Bat closed the shutter. As he turned to pick up the flashlight apparatus, he suddenly frowned. The closet door was open a fraction of an inch—not enough to set off the trap, but open just the same. He looked inside. Everything was just as he had seen it after the battle. He shrugged. Perhaps the door had not been closed tightly.

They reached the gate of Tony Quinn's estate just as the sky became gray. Butch parked the car near his boarding house and went to bed. When the Black Bat entered the house via the tunnel, Silk was almost a nervous wreck.

"There was a late news bulletin, about two A.M. It said the police were answering an alarm at Van der Veer's house. There was shooting there. I thought maybe, when you didn't come back, that you had found yourself at the wrong end of a gun at last. The station went off the air right after that broadcast, so all I could do was sit up and hope."

The black clothing came off and Tony Quinn smiled at Silk.

"When anything happens to me, you won't have to wait four hours to find out. Put away the camera and the other stuff."

"Didn't you get a picture, sir? Isn't there anything for me to develop?"

Quinn thought of that partially open door.

"You can try. It's probably a waste of time, but you never can tell. I'll be getting a little rest while you do it."

TWENTY MINUTES later Silk entered the kitchen, holding a dripping print in his hand.

"You did get something, sir! Darned if I know what it is, though. Looks almost like a ghost."

Quinn gazed at the print and gasped. In the darkness, something *had* materialized. A wraithlike object seemed to be climbing toward the ceiling. If a ghost had ever been photographed, this was it. Quinn felt an odd, prickling sensation at the nape of his neck. Van der Veer was dead. The butler had been murdered. The house was a veritable domicile of death and now it had produced a ghost.

He looked closer. That wraith seemed to be coming from beneath the closet door. Did ghosts open doors when they wished their freedom? Nothing in the closet had been disturbed. Nothing which could have formed this weird apparition was there. Where had it come from? Was this what Vandyke intended to return to the house to get?

"Scramble about five eggs for me," Quinn said slowly. "Ghosts give me an appetite. And coffee, Silk. Lots of it. I'll be double damned if I know what this thing is or where it came from. But thinking about it can't seem to ruin my appetite."

In the middle of the afternoon that same day, Tony Quinn tapped his cane inquisitively along the paths that led through his estate. His eyes were dead-looking, his step faltering. Once he almost slipped and fell, and only Silk's quick rush to the rescue saved him. Quinn didn't have to act this part. He knew exactly how it felt to stumble that way. Those many months of blindness would never be forgotten.

A car pulled up in front of his house. Silk whispered a word of warning and hurried to receive the visitor. It was Commissioner Warner. Quinn turned as he heard him approach and extended one hand a little to Warner's left.

"I'm glad to see you, Commissioner," he said warmly. "Always glad when you drop in. Silk and I have been planning the way our garden will look next year. I can't see the flowers, but I can smell them."

Warner shook Quinn's hand, took his arm and piloted him to a bench in one of the garden arbors.

"You're an amazing man, Tony. Nobody mentioned a word about my identity and yet you called me by name. Sometimes I wonder if McGrath's hunch isn't right."

Quinn smiled and fumbled in his pocket for a pipe. When he had it going well, he said:

"There are certain recompenses for the loss of one's sight, Commissioner. I've learned to recognize steps. I could identify yours anywhere. You walk lightly and fast. McGrath, though, advertises his career. Did you know he paid me a visit the other day? He insisted that I was the Black Bat and even went so far as to describe an interesting case which had him stumped. I never heard him quite so worried."

"He found the Black Bat," Warner said. "Oddly enough, while he was here trying to convince you that you were the Black Bat, that friendly enemy of the police was in McGrath's own house, waiting for him. The case has progressed, Tony, though we're nowhere near the solution of it. On the contrary, we're in deeper than before. There has been another killing. Van der Veer's butler was found dead last night."

QUINN PUFFED in silence for a few moments.

"Sounds almost like one of those old stories in which a house is cursed and ghosts lurk in every nook and cranny."

"It's got me down," Warner groaned. "Doctors worked for hours over the six people who were found dead in the strato-liner. They just got finished examining the corpse which was substituted for Van der Veer's body."

"Corpse? Substituted?"

Quinn removed the pipe from his mouth and looked puzzled. Warner flushed slightly. That had been a deliberate lead, for no word had leaked out about the substitution of bodies. If Tony Quinn had fallen for it, he would have given away the fact that he was the Black Bat. Warner hated to try these little tricks, but they slipped out almost as soon as he thought of them.

"Oh, I'm sorry," he said. "Of course you couldn't know. The fact is that somebody stole Van der Veer's corpse and put another one in the morgue wagon. What makes it so difficult is that Van der Veer and this new body both had serious burns on the palms of their right hands. Now the butler also had a similar burn. Eight perfectly good specimens for autopsy, and the doctors found no trace of poison, no clues which indicated violence. All they've discovered is that the blood seems to lack oxygen.

"One doctor reported it must be a case of strangulation, but how can a man be choked to death without a mark on his throat? Smothered, perhaps, but doubtful. Men struggle when they die that way and inflict bruises upon themselves. Not one of the learned doctors, pathologists or toxicologists can offer a single theory. Examinations of the burned hands show nothing significant."

"How I wish I could get my sight back, my former position as district attorney, and wade into a case like that!" Quinn said fervently. "But then a man must be satisfied with his lot, I suppose. Aren't there any suspects at all, Commissioner?"

"Well, yes. We've had Hawley—Van der Veer's manager—in for questioning. But he seems to have no reason for the murders, except of course to profit from the sale of the diamonds. I think there is something even bigger behind it. Then there's a man named Edmund Clive, who is an official of a diamond syndicate. He'd certainly know what it was all about, but the man is surprisingly reticent.

"He even resents our questioning him, although he shows up often enough and asks plenty of questions on his own account. Another person—a Fritz Reicher, who wholesales diamonds—claims to have lost many of the stones he sent to various stores on consignment. These stores were robbed and Reicher's gems apparently were not covered by insurance."

A thought flashed into the Black Bat's mind. Stores which dealt with Reicher had suffered robberies, but not only the stones that belonged to Reicher had been taken. There would have been others, too. Reicher or his salesmen might easily have examined these stores and planned the breaks.

"I'VE BEEN following the newspapers closely," Tony Quinn said. "Silk reads them to me every evening and morning. Crime news fascinates me, as it always has. I noticed this morning that there was a small item concerning Van der Veer's secretary or manager. Seems he was nearly killed."

"He was attacked," Warner said. "Darned near had a bad skull fracture. McGrath and I talked to him after he regained consciousness, which wasn't until early this morning. We learned nothing at all. Hawley was the American manager for Van der Veer. He simply insisted that he was in the house with the butler. Someone slipped up behind him and struck him on the head. Later he regained consciousness and heard the butler moaning. Two men he couldn't see struck him again. The next thing he knew, there were nurses and doctors bending over him looking anxious."

"The killer's mob certainly works well," Quinn said thoughtfully. "They seemed to make no slips at all. You know, I'm very grateful for your visits, Commissioner. When you come calling and tell me about these cases, it gives me something to think about. The days and nights are pretty long and dull for a blind man."

Warner put a comforting hand on Quinn's knee.

"Perhaps there is a reason why I tell you these things, Tony. Often in the past you've mulled over details of various cases and reached some astonishing deductions. The newspapers have been fairly explicit and I've told you everything else we know. See if you can determine why these men concentrate on diamonds. They're raiding jewelry store after jewelry store, robbing diamond-cutting establishments. I've tried to find out and can't.

"Reicher, for instance, is well up on the diamond market, yet he can offer no suggestion. Neither can Clive. Above all people, he should know, being a member of the international gem combine. Think it all over, Tony. I'll drop around in a couple of days and find out if that keen mind of yours has accomplished anything. I hope to heaven it has. Well, there's always work for the police commissioner. Have to run along. Can I help you back to the house?"

Quinn smiled and shook his head.

"I'm inside too much. I like sitting out here. There are more sounds and the air is nicer. Drop in again just as soon as you're able. Sometimes I even enjoy having McGrath call and accuse me of being the Black Bat. Anything is welcome if it can break the monotony."

Quinn remained in the garden house, staring straight ahead and slowly tapping his cane between his feet. He stayed there for ten minutes after Warner's car pulled away. Then he hesitantly walked back along the path in the direction of the house.

Silk came out to meet him.

"Carol and Butch are coming over, sir. I notified them as you instructed. I hope you'll have something for me to do—something with a little excitement. But no quarries, if you don't mind."

"I've called this meeting to arrange the details of our attack against Vandyke, Jules, Stringy and the rest of this vicious mob. They've had the upper hand too long. It's about time we struck a few blows. Pull down the shades in the study so I can enter the lab. Be sure all the door are locked and then join me there."

CHAPTER XIII

PLAN OF ATTACK

QUINN KEPT the point of his cane probing around as he threaded his way between furniture. But after the window shades were drawn, he dropped the pose of a blind man, walked quickly over to the wall. Quickly he opened the narrow, hidden door which led into the laboratory meeting place of the Black Bat's little clique. He smiled warmly at Carol, nodded to Butch and they sat down for Silk to put in an appearance.

"There are a number of peculiar things about this case," Quinn told them. "The greatest mystery is the identity of the man with the beard. He knows Van der Veer's house like a book. I saw him open a wall safe as if he had done it before very often. The murder of Van der Veer's butler is a complete puzzle. I can see no reason for it. If he knew a secret, Hawley must also have been aware of the same thing.

"Why wasn't Hawley murdered immediately instead of being tied up and hit on the head? Perhaps they intended to try making him talk later on and then planned to kill him with whatever ghastly method they use. But we must not lose sight of the fact that Hawley is a suspect."

"McGrath swears that Van der Veer was alive when he was talking to Hawley," Carol objected. "Doesn't that seem to eliminate him?"

"Yes," Quinn answered slowly. "It is a good alibi and McGrath is satisfied with it. However, we also have *Herr* Reicher to contend with. We know he was interested in the shipment of gems from Holland, that he knew they'd been actually sent on the strato-liner. Reicher is likewise believed to be in the pay of Nazi authorities. Perhaps he is the man with the Vandyke, masking his dirty work so the Nazi regime will not be suspected of stooping so low as to kill and rob for the sake of those diamonds.

"Edmund Clive acts mysteriously, too. The night I saw him, I wasn't perfectly satisfied with what he told me nor with his actions. He deliberately went out of his way to show he trusted me, even going so far as to hand over his gun. He gave me interesting information about how these continued robberies would finally affect the diamond market, yet he has made no such statements to Commissioner Warner. Why not? If he trusts the Black Bat, he must also rely on the police."

Quinn opened a drawer in the lab bench and removed the weird picture which Silk had developed the night before.

"This—whatever it is—was present in Van der Veer's home last night, while Butch and I were waiting in another room. It seems to have an indefinite shape and yet it does look like someone who has wrapped a sheet around himself to resemble the popular conception of a ghost. This picture was taken over a long period of time on an exposed film.

"I left the camera shutter open. In the darkness I don't believe anyone's form would have registered clearly on the film. It would have seemed to start at one end of the picture and pass over to the other. This visitation appears to rise from the floor and go straight up."

BUTCH PEERED over Quinn's shoulder and his big body gave a jerk.

"Hey, that does look like a ghost."

"It does," Quinn admitted. "If there is such a thing. Do you believe in them, Butch?"

Butch licked his lips nervously.

"Well, no, I don't. Just the same, I'm scared stiff of 'em."

Butch wondered what his three friends were laughing at. Then a slow grin stole over his big face. He still didn't know, but he enjoyed amusing his more sophisticated colleagues.

"It's time to get to work," Quinn said seriously. "Butch, you will look up Fritz Reicher. Carol will give you his address and all the details we have, including his picture. Get onto his trail and stay there. Make notes about where he goes and whom he sees. Pay strict attention to the time element also."

"Don't you have a job for me, sir?" Silk queried anxiously.

"Edmund Clive is your man," Quinn said. "Like Butch, hang onto his trail. Clive is a slippery sort and I'm certain he is very clever. Be on your toes, Silk."

Quinn walked over to a huge steel cabinet and took out a detailed map of the city when Butch and Silk left through the secret tunnel. He pulled a chair over beside his own and motioned for Carol to help him.

"With the use of directories and phone books," he said, "we'll try to indicate where diamond-cutting firms and jewelry stores of more than minor importance are located. As soon as it's dark, you can get your car. Both of us will make a tour of the city to watch these places. The gang intends to strike at a place operated by Mark Freiber and Company, but that may not be on tonight's schedule. Freiber's is one of the biggest diamond-cutting establishments on this side of the Atlantic."

Carol nodded and they went to work. They were a splendid team, these two. Both were in love, but neither spoke of the fact. They were fighting death and pillage, preparing to risk their lives so that killers and ruthless crooks might not accomplish their aims.

It was well after dark when their work was done.

Carol's sedan was a low-slung, fast job. A radio under the dash was tuned to the police frequency band. Carol drove. Beside her sat a man dressed entirely in black, his features obscured by a turned-down hat.

"We'll cover all the places," the Black Bat told Carol, "or as many as we can before the excitement breaks. Don't worry. They'll tackle a couple of places tonight. There's a mighty big reason why they want to corral as many diamonds as possible in a very short space of time. Let's have a look at the Freiber place first."

Freiber's gem-cutting establishment was on the second floor of a big downtown building. It looked complacently safe behind its barred windows. Not a light shone in any of the offices.

"Shall I keep on driving?"

The Black Bat nodded. "Cover the northwest part of town first. Most of the bigger places are located there."

They cruised around for an hour. Carol stopped across the street from the Continental Jewelry Company—a lavish store with huge plate-glass windows protected by steel bars. The Black Bat peered carefully into the store.

"Everything seems okay there. Thanks to the eyesight you and your father provided me with, I'm able to see even into the darkest corners of the front part of the store. No one is hiding there. We'll try the other places."

ALMOST A mile had been put between them and the Continental Jewelry Company when the police emergency signal came over the radio.

"Continental Jewelry Store. Burglars now inside building. Signal thirty-two. Signal thirty-two. All cars of precincts below Andover Avenue answer this alarm."

"But I thought—" Carol looked at the Black Bat.

"You thought correctly. The Continental Jewelry Company isn't being robbed. That's a false alarm to draw cars away from another section. Let's see."

The Black Bat spread his map across his knees and studied it. There was no dashlight, but he could read the map as perfectly as though a spotlight were shining on the paper.

"Look, if the cars assigned to this job go to the scene, the entire area around the Gem Import Galleries will be unprotected except by patrolmen. Step on it, Carol. That place auctions diamonds as a specialty and keeps thousands of dollars' worth on hand all the time. The gang is going in for the big stuff now, just as I expected they would."

Carol turned the next corner on two wheels, and her foot gradually depressed the accelerator until they were traveling at high speed. She was a cool and capable driver. She ducked in between trucks and buses as she cut through the business center. They reached an avenue and streaked north along it. Two more sharp turns and the Black Bat reached for his gun. Two shots had come plainly to his ears.

Carol stopped. The Black Bat doffed the hat and replaced it with his hood. Enveloped in that eerie cape, he ducked out of the car and raced into a dark alley. The fence at the end of it was no impediment for the Black Bat's muscles were always in excellent condition. He vaulted over this barrier and kept on going.

Soon he was near the delivery entrance of the jewelry auctioning firm. A blaze of gunfire gave him the direction. One man seemed to be shooting desperately and his fire was answered by at least three guns.

The Black Bat went into a crouch and continued running. The lone defender was lying prone behind a big packing case. He fired one more shot and through the darkness the Black Bat saw him hurriedly trying to reload. The crooks realized this, too, probably had been counting his shots. Stringy's voice shouted a command.

"Go get the flatfoot! Rub him out. One of his bullets almost creased my skull!"

Four men started forward boldly. Their kind was always bold when there was no opposition. The Black Bat realized the patrolman could never get his gun reloaded in time to ward off the attack. His two automatics came up and blasted simultaneously. One thug went down without uttering a sound, nor did he move after he hit the ground. The others, stunned by this unexpected barrage, retreated. They snapped a couple of shots in the Black Bat's direction, but suddenly fear had made them lose their marksmanship.

The patrolman methodically kept stuffing cartridges into the cylinder of his pistol. He had no time to wonder about the two shots which had saved his life. Then he gave a visible start and glanced aside again. A figure, all in black, crouched beside him.

"Yes, I'm the Black Bat," his eerie protector said calmly. "Are you willing to attack those rats?"

"I'm aching to. Let's go!"

They ran forward, their guns blasting. The thugs shouted in alarm and scurried away. The Black Bat, in the lead, was swiftly approaching the loading platform. He saw that the delivery door was open. Jules and his men were probably inside, engaged in looting the place while Stringy was to keep a clear exit when the job was done.

THE PATROLMAN mowed down one of Stringy's less cowardly men with a well-placed shot. He grunted in elation and looked for another target. The Black Bat had suddenly vanished, but the patrolman had no doubt but that he was somewhere nearby.

Jules and four of his thugs came rushing out of the door, scampered down the steps. The patrolman heard a low, insistent order.

"Shoot!"

He opened up. The shots scattered the five men. Jules, clinging to a heavy sack, wheeled and snapped a couple of blind shots. Then a black form came out of nowhere, apparently flying with outspread wings. It came down on Jules' back with terrific force.

The thug gave a scream of terror and alarm. He tried to maneuver his gun around, but his attacker was too agile. A blow thumped against his neck, almost snapping his head off. Another smashed into the pit of his stomach, doubled him up. Then he went careening backward from a well-placed punch on the chin.

But Jules was sturdy and tough. His jaw was made of steel, not glass like those of most of his followers. When he hit the ground, he bounded up again, but he didn't rush back into the fight. Unarmed now, facing the Black Bat and well aware of his prowess, Jules took to his heels. The patrolman blasted a bullet after him. It served only to increase Jules' speed.

Stringy's lanky shape had also disappeared and his men were covering the retreat. The Black Bat's guns joined in the rout of the gangsters, barking above the boom of the service pistol in the patrolman's hand.

Police whistles were shrilly sounding an alarm. The Black Bat appeared out of the gloom. The patrolman faced him, gun in hand, then slowly lowered the weapon.

"Orders are that you're to be brought in on sight and shot if you resist," he stated. "The day they were delivered, I was a little deaf. Anyway, I don't even think you're the Black Bat. He's supposed to be dressed all in black, and that suit you got on is certainly the white of an angel's robe to my eyes."

A black-gloved hand reached forward, holding out the sack of gems that had been taken from the store.

"It must be difficult, going through life with such bad hearing and color-blindness," the Black Bat said. "Here is the swag. See that it is put away safely. There is no reason to say anything about my being here. I hope you win your sergeant's chevrons. You deserve them. Any man who will shoot it out with a whole gang of murderers doesn't belong in the ranks. Your friends are coming, so I'll slip off the bandwagon here. Stand just as you are. Good night."

The Black Bat streaked out of the alley and darted into Carol's sedan.

"The weather was a little warm back there for a few minutes," he said. "I had Jules, but he must be made of rubber: He got away. Two or three of the boys won't be robbing places any more, though. Carol, we've given them their first real defeat, and I don't think Vandyke is going to like it. It seems a bit odd to me. That was the biggest haul they've tried so far, yet the man with the beard wasn't there. Maybe he realizes he is being trailed."

"You mean by Butch and Silk?" Carol asked.

"That's right. If Reicher or Clive happens to be Vandyke and has even a hunch that he's being watched, he'll maintain a very simple life for a while. Silk and Butch can solve that problem. They are to report at midnight, so we'll go back and meet them. The gang won't try any more breaks tonight—not in the shape they must be in."

RETURNING TO the house, he and Carol waited patiently. Silk returned first. They did not ask for a report till Butch came in twenty minutes later. The giant was highly disgusted with his results.

"I follows the guy like you said, Boss. I never seen a mug who likes to walk so much. My dogs are dead-tired. He trotted over to some meeting where everybody blabbed in German. Then he hiked uptown about thirty blocks and went into a little delicatessen. Imagine a dope who'd walk that far for baloney! But that ain't all. He went to three other places—a tobacco store, a newspaper stand and a drugstore. When he walked in, them guys stood up like he was a general. The names and addresses is in my book."

"And you, Silk?" Quinn asked.

Silk smiled. "Clive wasn't quite so ambitious, sir. He went calling on a party named Norden—a refugee who owns a lot of Swedish and Norwegian freighters. Clive stayed there about an hour and a half. Then he went straight home. He's there yet, as far as I know."

"Reicher's movements are highly suspicious," Quinn said, examining the addresses in Butch's notebook. "All German places. I wonder if he's laying the groundwork for a coup. This mystery is coming to a head pretty soon. Perhaps Reicher is the man with the beard and doesn't trust Jules and Stringy any longer. After tonight he'll have less confidence in them, so we'll wait and see. I wish I could talk to Hawley. He may have some interesting information, but I can't risk visiting him at the hospital. He's probably guarded, anyhow."

CHAPTER XIV

ANONYMOUS TIP

HAWLEY WAS being watched. Husky patrolmen sat at his bedside twenty-four hours a day. Hawley's head was still bandaged, but he was rapidly regaining his strength. McGrath had come to question him twice, but he could offer no additional information.

At eleven-thirty that night, McGrath called and said he could go home, after accompanying his guard to Police Headquarters. He was to study the prisoners assembled there and try to identify them.

Hawley put on his clothes. On the way out he clung to the patrolman's arm, for he was still weak from the terrific blow on the head. A cab was waiting at the door. The patrolman stepped back to let Hawley get in first. As he did so, two men appeared suddenly and a pair of guns were poked into the patrolman's side.

In the act of entering the cab, Hawley was seized and pulled inside. The patrolman was shoved in after him and the taxi pulled away. All this took no more than a few seconds. The slight fracas was unnoticed even by a group of people less than a hundred feet up the street.

The taxi threaded through a park. Hawley said nothing, but he was white as paper. The patrolman lay huddled on the floor. When he moved, a foot kicked him under the chin.

In one of the darkest sections of the park, the cab stopped. Two of the kidnapers pushed the patrolman out. Hawley heard gun butts crack against the officer's skull and saw him crumple to the grass. Then the taxi darted away again.

"What is this?" he blurted. "Who are you?"

"Be quiet or we shall treat you like the policeman," one of the kidnapers warned. "You will soon find out what this is about."

Hawley was not prevented from watching the route taken by the driver. He realized that these men certainly had no intention of his living to talk again. He shivered. Once he made a grab for the door handle and a hard hand slapped him across the mouth with savage ferocity. He sank back against the seat and tried to resign himself to death. He was not successful.

Finally the taxi, far out of the city, turned off the main highway and followed a well paved side road for about a mile. It stopped in front of a small building that was completely dark. A nudge with the muzzle of a gun forced him to get out.

He raised his arms shoulder-high as he was escorted to the building. One of the men used a key to open the door. Hawley took a quick look around and recognized his surroundings. He was being marched into the caddy-house of some golf club.

They shoved him along a narrow corridor and stopped him when a door barred the way. One of the kidnapers rapped on the panels in a quick signal. A key turned in the lock and the door opened. At the same moment a weak light was turned on. Hawley's eyes grew wide and round with terror. He balked a little and one of the men at his rear gave him a hard shove that sent him stumbling into the room.

"So," a low voice snarled, "you have come at last, *ja?* That is good, my friend. We have much to talk about. It will be very wise if you do not force me to use persuasive methods. I know several good ones. Tie him up tightly. I have been waiting for this day for a long, long time."

CAPTAIN McGRATH went home at three A.M. after a fruitless search for Hawley. He opened the door of his bungalow, hoping he would hear the Black Bat's voice greet him. There was nothing but silence, though McGrath needed the Black Bat far more than at any other time.

He flung his hat on the chair, thought of what his wife might say about that if she were home, and picked it up again. As he hung it on a clothes-tree, he distended his nostrils. If that wasn't ham he smelled cooking, his wife had been fooling him for years.

McGrath drew his service pistol and tiptoed in the direction of the kitchen. Now he could hear the meat hissing in the pan.

"Come in, Captain," the Black Bat's voice called from behind the kitchen door. "You're just in time for a snack."

McGrath shoved the gun back into its holster and pushed the door open. He gasped, for the kitchen was in utter darkness except for the gas flame under a frying pan. Yet the Black Bat moved around without stumbling against any of the furniture. He glanced at McGrath and chuckled.

"I forgot you need light. Turn it on."

McGrath snapped the switch. The kitchen table was set for one. As he watched, the Black Bat slid a thick slice of ham and three eggs on a plate.

"There you are, Captain. Now while you're stowing that ammunition away, let's have all the details about Hawley's kidnaping."

"Is there anything you don't know?" McGrath demanded as he buttered a slice of hot toast. He bit into the ham and a slow smile relaxed his face. "Say, this is good!"

"It ought to be. It came right out of your refrigerator. Don't ask me to dine with you. It's very difficult to eat without removing my mask and you wouldn't want me to do that, would you, Captain?"

"No," McGrath said. "Honestly I wouldn't. When I land you myself—fairly, too—I'll take care of that item. But listen to this. The cop I placed to guard Hawley was found in Sunset Park. He'd been pretty badly messed up, but he could talk. At least three mugs grabbed Hawley. Why? Because maybe he knew something and they were afraid he'd tell me. I've put every available man at work searching for him, but they won't succeed. This guy with the beard is too smart.

"Oh, yes. Thanks for giving one of the boys a hand. Patrolman Cassidy reported to me a couple of hours ago and handed over a sack of jewels. He said you had a hand in it, but of course I couldn't report that or he'd be in a jam. So I just patted him on the back. Now I'll have to slate him for a quick promotion. Maybe he deserves it."

"He's a good man, Captain. Anything else happen tonight?"

"It's been a lovely evening," McGrath said disgustedly. "The only good news I have—besides the fact that you saved those gems—is that the body substituted for Van der Veer's has been identified. Seems the guy had once been picked up in some town out West as a bindlestiff and they printed him. He was a nobody, so it seems that the murderer used him as easy pickings. We still don't know what killed him."

THE BLACK BAT straddled a chair.

"There's egg all over your face, Captain. What else happened? I can tell by the gleam in your eye that you're saving a surprise."

McGrath wiped his chin, reached into his pocket and dropped an envelope on the table.

"That came by special delivery tonight. Read it."

The message inside that envelope was terse, neatly typed on expensive paper.

> May interest you to know that five million in diamonds secretly shipped aboard Swedish freighter *S. S. Sundsvall* due New York tomorrow night.

"Well!" The Black Bat laid the letter down. "That's interesting information. We seem to have a secret ally. Maybe Vandyke's mob is beginning to split up. Have you tried to verify this, Captain?"

McGrath nodded. "There is such a ship and she is due in tomorrow night, but I couldn't find out anything about the diamonds. I cabled. You can't get information anywhere in Europe these days. The answer just said that freighter was carrying general merchandise. I don't like the set-up."

"You think it may be a trap? Of course Vandyke must know you and I are working side by side in this game, so it would be an excellent opportunity to get both of us together. Just the same, Captain, we'll meet that freighter. Five million more in diamonds will just about satisfy Vandyke, I imagine. There may even be a chance of turning this into a trap for him.

"Keep trying to find Hawley. He seems to be a very important cog in this machine. Also see to it that a police launch is left unattended at the same pier where that strato-liner docked. Find out the position of the ship by radio, broadcast the time she'll be twenty miles from port over the police hookup at exactly three o'clock tomorrow afternoon. I'll be listening. We'll need about an hour and a half to intercept that ship, so all you have to do is board the police launch an hour and a half before she is twenty miles from port. I'll be there."

"You mean we'll go out alone?" McGrath gasped.

"Exactly. I always play a lone hand, Captain. This time you'll be just a means to an end. I'll tell you all about it when we meet."

IT WAS raining and foggy when the Black Bat slipped aboard the empty police launch the following night. He already knew that all attempts to find Hawley had failed and the man was about given up for dead. Butch was trailing Reicher with the dogged persistence he brought to every job, while Silk clung to the trail of Edmund Clive. Carol remained at home in case things went wrong and the Black Bat needed help. Butch and Silk were to phone in and report every hour.

There had been no more robberies, but the Black Bat had a feeling that this was just a lull before the real storm broke out in all its fury. The mysterious Vandyke was sitting pretty right now. If he managed to land five million in gems from the freighter, plus his loot from a score of diamond-cutting establishments and jewelry stores, he would possess a huge fortune in gems.

None of the stones could be traced, for he seemed to care little for famous big diamonds. News of the loss of all the gems would spread like wildfire. With no more coming in from abroad, the market was bound to rise fast. Any deficiency in supply always raised prices.

McGrath came aboard at nine-twenty. He carried a sub-machine gun cradled in his arms, and two extra drums of cartridges hung from one shoulder.

"So this is war," the Black Bat said.

"If I have anything to do with it, yes. I'm taking it on the chin. The newspapers are beginning to ride me, and the commissioner put me on the carpet. But I held out on all of them. Nobody knows about that tip. Just let me see those crooks try to board the freighter. I'll massacre 'em!"

The Black Bat started the motor and piloted the craft out to sea. McGrath stood beside him, shivering with the rawness of the air. They proceeded slowly because of the thick fog.

"A bad break for us," the Black Bat said. "They can slip up to that freighter and be protected by the fog. Here is the plan. You hail the ship and board her. Warn the captain that he may expect trouble. Then leave, get back into the launch and head for shore. Stand by the marine radio."

"But how about this?" McGrath patted the machine gun. "And, hell, man, I'm not going to let you take all the risk!"

"Sorry, I insist. It's my belief that there are traitors in the crew. They'll have ways to contact Vandyke. If you remain on board, they'll smell a rat and perhaps stage the robbery after the stuff is ashore. No, you've got to do what I ask."

McGrath agreed reluctantly.

The Black Bat remained silent as he piloted the speedy launch on a course that would cut across the bow of the incoming freighter.

CHAPTER XV

SHIP OF DESPAIR

NOT LONG after eleven o'clock, they saw the ship's lights through the fog. The Black Bat pulled for the siren cord and held it taut. The freighter answered with a hoarse bellow from her own whistle. A blinker light signaled that she was heaving to.

"Do your stuff," the Bat ordered. "Give me a chance to slip on board."

McGrath nodded. They came alongside and a ladder was dropped. McGrath tied up the launch, climbed the ladder and returned the salute of the big, blond skipper.

"I have a message of great importance to you and your crew," he told the captain. "Just come over here and I'll give you the details."

He deliberately stood against the starboard rail as he faced the men and held their attention. He made sure none of them glanced toward the port side, where the Black Bat would be slipping aboard.

"We have reliable information that a gang of pirates is ready to board you somewhere near shore. I want you to hold a steady course. Patrol boats will meet you very soon and convoy you to port. If anything happens, defend yourselves. Remember that these crooks won't hesitate to shoot, so it's up to you to shoot first. That's all. I'll see you ashore."

"We take good care of ourselves," the captain growled. "I have good crew. We come through mine fields, sail without lights and think any minute submarine shell us or send torpedo into our hull. Pirates do not scare us."

McGrath went down the ladder to his launch. The Black Bat was gone. He turned the bow of his craft shoreward and wished the Black Bat had been more open to suggestion.

There were hostile eyes watching his departure. Two men slowly turned away from the rail and went below. In a cabin, they found another pair of scowling men engaged in playing rummy. One of the men closed the door.

"The cops," he said. "I think it was that lunk-head McGrath, the guy who's in charge of the case. He warned the skipper, so we gotta watch our step. Stop playing cards, will you? Joe, get the flash and put on the green lens. We're about ready to get goin'. Signal Jules we're set, but tell him about the cop comin' aboard, too. If he signals back okay, we start things rollin'. I fixed the radio so nobody can yell for help."

Joe dug into a sea-chest and hauled out a big flashlight. He slipped a green filter over the lens, opened a porthole and looked out. He cursed the fog and glanced back at the man who was studying maps and charting their position. When Joe received a nod, he blinked the flashlight in a signal.

Like a tiny speck in the fog, an answer came. All four men remained silent while the messages were being exchanged. Finally Joe closed the porthole.

"He says to go ahead. We grab the skipper and make him open the safe right after Jules shows up. The boys will take care of the rest. There's five million in that box, boys."

"Yeah," one of the others grumbled discontentedly. "And they got a habit of stringin' up guys for mutiny on the high seas. I don't like it, five million or only a dime."

Joe raised a fist in a threatening gesture.

"You're cooked, anyhow if we're caught, we squeal, see? Now get on deck, all of you. I'll stick around the cabin, so when Jules shows, I can signal all clear."

The three left the cabin.

UP ON deck, the captain drew his heavy coat closer about him and paced the bridge nervously. Then he heard the unmistakable sound of another ship's engines. A moment later there was a bellow from a siren.

"Cutter to port, sir!" the lookout yelled.

A powerful searchlight slashed through the fog. The captain, peering through the fog, saw huge numbers painted on the bow of the approaching craft. It looked like a Coast Guard cutter. It came alongside and a man in an officer's uniform leaned over the rail with a megaphone to his lips.

"Follow us. Area ahead is mined. We're the escort you expect. Do you know this coast?"

"No," the captain shouted back. "Give us a stern light to follow."

The cutter veered away and the searchlight switched its position so the freighter could easily follow. Below deck, Joe put his flashlight away and grinned savagely. He removed a heavy-caliber pistol from the sea-chest and started toward the door.

"I wouldn't," a voice said quietly.

As he whirled around, the lights in the cabin went out. He did not dare to fire, that would start the ball rolling and he was not ready yet. Suddenly a hand closed over his gun-wrist and twisted it brutally, Joe cried out in pain. The gun dropped to the floor. He stooped to fumble for it, but a foot kicked it into a corner.

Snarling with helpless rage, Joe straightened and lashed out blindly with both fists. They hit nothing but air. Abruptly steel fingers fastened around his throat, cut off his breath. He kicked backward, struck out with his fists, and he touched nothing. Those mighty fingers seemed to have no body attached to them.

When the darkness of the cabin went from blood-red to intense black, the fingers relaxed. Joe stumbled away to what he thought was safety and drew in a shuddering breath for a yell. But a hard fist shot out of the blackness and crumpled him to the floor.

The Black Bat picked him up and carried him to a chair. He ripped the sheets off the twin bunks, tore them into strips and quickly bound the crook. Then he rolled the man onto a bunk, shoved a chair into the middle of the cabin and sat down to wait.

In a few moments he heard someone open the door. As the light entered the cabin from the corridor outside, the man who stepped in gave a yelp of fear. He saw a huge figure in black that looked like a big bird of prey about to swoop down on him. He backed away, trying to muster a scream. Before he succeeded, the bird's wing sprouted a fist that smacked him unconscious.

The other two killers arrived shortly after. The Black Bat rammed a punch at the chin of the nearest, but the agile killer ducked and caught it on the shoulder. Terrified and desperate, they battled like cornered rats.

THE BLACK BAT hooked one on the cheek and took a staggering blow over the heart in return. But the advantage was on his side, for he could see in the darkness and the crooks could not. He dropped one with a solid blow, whirled and tackled the other. Too scared to give up, the lithe killer, who had ducked the Black Bat's first punch, retreated with swinging fists till his back was against the wall. The

Black Bat let him duck a slow, obvious left, caught him on the chin with a murderous haymaker of a right.

Turning, swiftly, he saw that the third crook had recovered and was scurrying to the door. He leaped, brought the killer down in a heap. Scissoring him to his back, the Black Bat disposed of him with a short jab to the chin.

Panting, the Black Bat wasted no time. He searched the men and deftly bound them up. The assortment of weapons he took from them went out the porthole.

From the adjoining lavoratory he picked up McGrath's sub-machine gun and slipped out of the cabin, locking the door after him. He reached the companionway and crept up it cautiously.

He knew the freighter carried a crew of no more than twelve or fourteen men, including the skipper. Four were already accounted for, and the Black Bat hoped to get the rest on his side.

At any moment now Jules would strike. The Coast Guard uniform had deceived the skipper, but not the Black Bat. Jules looked just as much the criminal with a gold-braided cap as when he prowled the night, looking for loot.

The deck seemed clear, and the Black Bat ran lightly across it, heading for the captain's quarters. Now the fog aided him, for none of the sailors, alert though they were, spotted him. The skipper's cabin door was closed and the Black Bat slowly turned the knob. Then he flung the door wide and held his rifle ready.

The captain was seated before his desk. He tipped over the chair as he jumped up.

"Don't move or make a sound," the Black Bat warned. "I'm sorry to show force, but until I'm sure where I stand, that will be necessary. You have a valuable cargo of diamonds in your safe. There are some dangerous crooks after it. I doubt that you've ever heard of me, so I won't go into detail. I'm the Black Bat, fighting on the side of law and order."

"With a mask on?" the skipper said scornfully. "You try to get the jewels. I do not give them to you."

"I know it sounds unreasonable," the Black Bat said persuasively. "I know I look and act like a crook, but listen to this. I came aboard from the police launch. I work with Captain McGrath. He warned you to be careful and you've just sailed into a sweet trap. The cutter that hailed you is a fake. The man in uniform is Jules Andrus, a killer. His men will outnumber your crew and they won't stop at murder. Open your safe, give me the jewels and I'll get them ashore somehow."

The skipper folded his arms calmly, unfrightened, not even deigning to reply. The Black Bat groaned. Because of the stubborn nature of the captain, his plans were being delayed. He stepped forward and raised the rifle of his gun slightly.

Suddenly there was a terrific grating sound and alarmed shouts from on deck.

"We're aground—rocks," someone yelled.

"Now do you see I'm right?" the Black Bat asked. "Open the safe before it's too late."

The ship gave a bad roll and heeled over at a dangerous angle. The captain and the Black Bat were both sent crashing against the farther wall, but the Black Bat sustained the impact. The captain, though, lay sprawled out on the floor, unconscious.

CHAPTER XVI

THE BLACK BAT'S CLAWS

O N DECK there were shouts and screams of pain. The Black Bat whirled, raced up the tilted companionway and saw four of Jules' murder crew swarming over the rail. Two of the sailors lay prone on the deck. The others held their arms high.

The sub-machine gun at the Black Bat's shoulder bucked and chattered. The men boarding the freighter disappeared like magic. There were angry shouts overside as the Black Bat raced to the rail.

Jules' fake Coast Guard cutter was trying to tie up to the freighter. He swept the decks with a burst from the machine gun. The fake cutter began to drift away.

"Go below and get your skipper!" the Black Bat shouted to the freighter crew. "He was hurt when we ran aground. Put him in a boat and shove off with everyone else. Quick! Those men will try again and they'll shoot you down."

The authority in the Black Bat's voice compelled the sailors to obey him. They carried the captain on deck, eased him into a lifeboat. The Black Bat peered through the fog. The cutter was nosing back. Her slim hull could maneuver through the rocks onto which she had so treacherously led the freighter. Half a dozen guns began to spit fire. The Black Bat heard slugs hammer into the hull.

"Lower away and head for shore!" he called out to the sailors.

The davits creaked as the lifeboat lowered to the sea. The Black Bat masked this betraying sound by another burst from his gun. The cutter veered off, but this time she did not retreat as far as before.

The Black Bat was now alone. Below were five million dollars in jewels, for which these killers were willing to sacrifice any number of lives. It was a desperate situation. They numbered probably as high as a score, augmented by the crew who manned the fake cutter.

Sweat poured down the Black Bat's face, under his mask. The chill dankness of the air no longer made him shiver. He stood like some weird gargoyle on the sloping deck and knew the probability was that he would be dead before dawn.

The attack came with lethal ferocity. The fake cutter dropped a dory, which circled the freighter and came at it from the starboard side, while the cutter itself covered the port.

The Black Bat went racing across the deck, through the concealing veil of fog. The dory was almost alongside. One of its crew was trying to grab the rope ladder. The Black Bat's sub-machine gun pointed downward and he sent a hail of death into the bow of that boat. It shipped water. The men yelled and scurried around in helpless terror. The hull was riddled and the sea began to pour in.

Someone shouted an order and the oars were hastily manned again. The Black Bat smiled grimly, but when he turned away, his smile died. A swarm of Jules' choice killers was coming over the side. The Black Bat leveled his gun, yanked the trigger. The burst died midway, for the drum was empty and the other ammunition was below.

He sprinted across the deck toward the bridge, sprang and seized the railing to pull himself up and over it. Bullets smacked the deck. One ripped a hole in the flowing cape he wore. From the cutter, Jules barked commands and Stringy's strident voice added venomous encouragement.

The Black Bat saw a group of the killers racing toward the bridge. He wrenched open a locker door, reached inside and snatched out a rocket pistol. He crouched, waited until the killers were close by. Then he emptied the gun squarely into their startled faces. The red fire routed them. They fled, screeching in pain from dozens of burns.

THE BLACK BAT located two more of the signal guns, thrust one into a hip pocket and held the other ready. He jumped to the main deck, scooped up his sub-machine gun on the way and went down the companionway ladder in two leaps.

As he unlocked the cabin door, he heard his four prisoners curse him luridly. Swiftly he began inserting a fresh drum of bullets. The other drum he tucked under his arm and hurried back on deck.

When he reached the rail, overlooking the smaller craft almost alongside, he heard voices.

"I tell you we ain't wrong. It is the Black Bat. He flung down offa that stage. We saw him. Honest!"

"You guys are crazy," Jules rasped. "The Black Bat nor nobody else knows about this ship. That's maybe the skipper and you crazy lugs got bats on the brain. Get back there and drill that guy. Snap into it before I lose my temper and do a little shootin' on my own."

"Hey, wait a minute!" Stringy cut in. "You can talk to your own mob like that, but not to my boys. We'll take that guy, all right, but we won't take no guff from you. Come on, boys."

The Black Bat drove the killers from the rail.

They slung two ladders from the freighter's deck and started clambering up them. Stringy prudently dropped back and permitted his men to go first. He was always polite when it came to facing death.

"Back!" the Black Bat ordered. "Back or I'll blast everyone of you into the sea."

"The Black Bat!" Jules yapped, while Stringy's men fell all over themselves in their attempts to get clear. "L-look, I got a p-proposition."

"So have I," the Black Bat replied. "Come aboard alone and without guns."

"Listen," Jules countered, "there ain't no use tryin' to kid you. That stuff on board the ship—we'll split it three ways. Two! Is it a deal or do we come up and cut you to pieces?"

"Come on," the Black Bat invited. "That's what I'm waiting for."

"Go get him!" Jules snapped.

"None of his men moved to obey. He ground out curses, seized a rifle and clapped it to his shoulder. The bullet whistled over the Black Bat's head as he aimed his sub-machine gun at the wheel-house of the fake cutter and released a long burst of slugs. He heard glass shatter and the cutter began moving rapidly away. Jules and his men were tough, but the pilot of their craft had had plenty. He was anxious to get out into the fog. Jules started for the wheel-house with murder written on his cruel face.

The Black Bat realized that he had no more than a few moments to spare. He sent another warning fusillade at the craft. Then he raced for the captain's quarters, where he eyed the old-fashioned iron safe.

Its combination dial was a huge device. With the right tools the Black Bat could have opened it in half an hour, but he had no tools and no half hour to spend. Gently touching the dial, he turned it. The sensitiveness of his touch, developed during his blindness, served him well. A more modern safe would not have responded to his coaxing, but this one did. The tumblers began falling into place.

Five million dollars in an old box like this! The Black Bat knew that only the war made such flimsy protection possible. There were no modern ships to venture on a daring trip across the Atlantic any more.

HE KEPT looking at his watch. At any moment Jules would have his craft alongside. If the Black Bat were not on deck to repel boarders, they would swarm all over the ship.

Then the handle of the safe turned and he swung the door wide. Inside were two big tin boxes. He opened one and saw that it was packed with small boxes, all labeled with the name of Van der Veer. He inspected only only, found it jammed with cotton and jewels.

He seized both boxes and hurried back to deck. Jules' craft hit the freighter with a loud crash, for expert hands were no longer at the wheel. The pilot lay crumpled in a heap, bullet-riddled.

A face appeared cautiously above the deck. The Black Bat pounded a few slugs into the killer's hide. With a yelp, he disappeared. Then a wad of oil-soaked blazing rags was flung onto the after-deck. The Black Bat started back to squelch the blaze and a dozen more of the flaming wads was hurled onto the freighter. They were getting desperate.

Leeward, the Black Bat could see lights ashore. All this excitement was bound to be noticed. Real Coast Guard cutters would be shoving off at any moment. The Black Bat judged their position at about ten miles south of New York harbor.

Suddenly he saw four men coming toward him. They were the phony sailors he had attacked in the cabin. Somehow they had gained their freedom. They were armed with guns stolen from the ship's arsenal. The Black Bat sent a burst of fire in their direction, but other shots roared behind him. Jules' men were coming aboard.

The deck was slowly catching fire. The old weather-beaten tub would make a grand blaze and certainly the killers had no intention of putting it out.

Hemmed in, the Black Bat resorted to daring measures. He charged straight toward the rail, shooting as he went. When the crooks disappeared, he changed his course and headed toward the crow's-nest. He still held the gems securely under one arm. They impeded his movements, but nothing could have induced him to leave them for the killers to find.

Ships were no mystery to the Black Bat. Before he became blind, they had been his hobby. Knowing freighters like this one, he realized that there was a circular ladder inside the hollow mast, by which he could climb to the crow's-nest. There he would be able to fight off the men and have a chance for his life. By holding them back long enough, sufficient time might elapse for help to come. McGrath would undoubtedly have every police boat available scouring the sea already. The Black Bat remembered the rocket pistol in his pocket.

He started to squirm through the narrow door in the mast, then suddenly dropped flat on deck. Two of the fake sailors were approaching. In the fog they had not spotted the Black Bat. He could have shot them down with one burst, but he held his fire. They divided, one coming directly toward him.

When the sailor saw those outspread wings nothing else mattered for him. The Black Bat had almost bent the gun barrel on the crook's skull.

HE HOISTED his captive over one shoulder, entered the mast and began climbing to the crow's-nest. Encumbered by the boxes of gems, he shoved them into a dark spot. From the noise on deck he knew that Jules and Stringy's full complements of killers were aboard and searching for him. The three sailor-crooks were aiding in that search. Soon they hit upon the only place left on deck for him to hide.

He dropped his prisoner on the deck of the crow's-nest and then went down the ladder for the jewels. Getting them, he started up again. But he had to cling to the rungs of the ladder with one hand and fire a warning blast that smashed into the hollow mast far above the head of a man who held a flashlight. But that was enough. The flash winked out.

Then the Black Bat reached the crow's-nest. The tiny circular platform did not give him much room, hampered as he was by the crook who was slowly regaining consciousness.

"Up there!" Jules' voice sounded a mile away. "Either you come down with those rocks or we set this mast on fire!"

CHAPTER XVII

BUTCH COMES THROUGH

DRAWING HIS rocket pistol, the Black Bat pointed it skyward and sent two red flares into the heavens. Peering over the side, he saw preparations being made to burn down the hollow mast. Guns roared below and bullets hit the deck beneath his feet. He was grateful that it was steel and offered good protection.

But he was unable to drive away the men below, who were piling everything combustible around the mast. Every time he tried to peer over the rail of the crow's-nest, guns blazed away on deck and he had to draw back. His prisoner was still unconscious.

The Black Bat raised his hood and mopped his sweaty face. He had been in tough spots before, but this one made the others seem pale. It would not take long before the mast began to topple.

Jules, intent on murder, did not figure that the Black Bat would be thrown far away from the freighter and that if he had those precious diamonds, they would go to the bottom. His one-track mind could think only that the Bat was going to die this time, that Jules would accomplish what no other crook had ever succeeded in doing, what he would do.

The Black Bat tried to penetrate the fog for signs of approaching help. There was none. He did not know whether to feel relieved or grow more worried. No matter what happened, it seemed that he was finished now. If help came, he would be taken and the result would be catastrophic. Unless—

He glanced down at the groaning crook near his feet. Quickly he hoisted his prisoner up and pinned him against the mast.

"Come out of it!" he snapped. "Your pals down below are trying to kill you as much as they are me. They don't care if you die just so long as I die with you. There is one way out, if you've got the nerve."

"Wh-what?" the thug gasped in bleary terror.

"Can you swim?" the Black Bat asked. He received a dazed nod. "Good. I have no more use for you than you have for me, but we're facing the same kind of death. Here is your one chance for life. If Jules or Stringy picks you up, tell them you were unconscious when you rolled off here. Put on my robe, climb over the rail of the crow's-nest and jump."

"J-jump?" The thug opened his mouth wide in horror. "But—but I'll be killed."

"No you won't. The ship has heeled over badly. The starboard rail is almost awash. If you simply fell out of this crow's-nest, you'd clear the rail. Which is it—a chance to live or do you want to be burned alive?"

The crook looked over the rail and saw the fire rapidly eating at the base of the mast. Jules was using oil and the thick column of smoke that arose made both of them cough. Abruptly the guns opened up again.

"I—I'll do it," the thug yapped.

The Black Bat stripped off his billowy cape and fastened it around his captive's trembling shoulders.

"I'm giving you a chance to live, so you've got to help me. They don't know you're up here and wouldn't care if they did. They'll think you are the Black Bat leaping into the sea. Don't worry, they'll save you because they know I've got the loot on me. If I don't get away, I promise not to tell them what you did."

THE THUG stood erect, nervously thrust one leg over the rail of the crow's-nest and the wind billowed out the cloak. The guns below went silent as the crooks waited to see what the Black Bat was up to.

The thug gave one last despairing look at the Black Bat and then jumped. The cloak spread out and he seemed to soar down. Yells went up from below. The diving man cleared the rail with several feet to spare. In a flash Jules shouted orders.

One of the freighter's lifeboats was lowered, and as many men as it would hold crammed into it. They were all eager to fish the Black Bat out of the sea and learn his identity. The few who were left on deck crowded the rail, despite the water surging at their feet.

The Black Bat was already down the hollow shaft inside the mast. Smoke made his eyes water and dried his throat, but he securely held the two metal containers of gems. Discarding his sub-machine gun, he opened the mast door. A tongue of flame licked in at him. He held his breath, covered his eyes and dived through the wall of fire.

His soft crepe-soled shoes made no noise as he sprinted across the deck. The fake cutter was tied up on the opposite side from which the crooks were working and watching. The Black Bat drew one of his automatics, climbed over the rail and jumped aboard the cutter. A startled member of the crew promptly elevated his hands when the Black Bat motioned with his gun.

"Man the wheel," the Black Bat ordered in a tense whisper. "We're getting out of here."

"Yes, sir." The sailor saluted alertly. "And damned glad I'll be to do it, too!"

The first inkling that Jules had of the Black Bat's escape was the sudden movement of the cutter that had taken him out. Then some of his thugs hauled up the man who had dived from the mast and recognized him as one of their own gang.

Jules emptied his gun at the cutter, now showing her heels at a great clip. The Black Bat, inside the wheel-house, laughed. He had won again, but it had been the most difficult battle of his entire career. He knew just how dangerous Jules and Stringy were now. They had to be disposed of promptly or capturing the man with the beard would still remain a perilous task.

"Where the devil is Vandyke?" the Black Bat muttered anxiously. "He never sends both gangs out on a job without supervising them, so they won't fight among themselves."

BUTCH O'LEARY was engaged in following Fritz Reicher. His quarry had remained indoor most of the evening, but now he sallied out. By the grim look on his face, someone was going to suffer. Butch trailed him with his coupé and did a neat, careful job of shadowing.

When Reicher turned into the road which led to a golf course that had been closed for the season weeks ago, Butch slowed up. Finally he parked the coupé and proceeded on foot. All of the buildings on the course were dark except the caddy-house, and only a faint glimmer of light came from beneath a black curtain there. Reicher was nowhere in sight, but his car was standing in the shadowy darkness of the clubhouse.

Butch crept forward, slowly clenching and unclenching his great fists. He felt he had been altogether too idle during this case, and he longed for a chance to sail into a fight with some real opposition.

Peering carefully beneath the black curtain of the caddy-house, he grinned with anticipation. Four men were in the room, gathered around the table, smoking and obviously waiting for someone important. He drew his gun, though he hated to rely on anything but his fists. But the

The thugs leaped in, grabbed Butch's arms from behind.

killers were armed, as he could see by the ominous bulges under their armpits.

Butch was huge, but he was also fast. When he sprang into the room, the men were shocked motionless. Unfortunately he also had big feet, and they stumbled over a chair when a hood sprang up and tipped it over in his path.

"Get 'em up!" the giant yelled, undismayed as he regained his balance.

Instead of obeying, the thugs leaped, grabbed his mighty arms from behind. Butch growled, inflated his gigantic chest and his arms flung his assailants away like a dog shaking water from his coat. The killers gaped in awe. Butch closed two dangling jaws with punches that rattled every tooth in the thugs' heads. The other two saw their partners folding up like leaky accordions and wisely decided that this was not a healthy spot. They started to run.

Butch followed them out of the caddy-house and across the green. They made the mistake of running together for moral support. When they looked back over their shoulders, they began to blubber, for with each stride Butch was gaining two feet. The hindmost thug gave a piercing yell just before a great fist came down squarely on the top of his skull. He dropped flat and did not move. An instant later the other killer was smacked to one side and sprawled motionless on his face.

The giant grinned and rubbed his knuckles. Then he began running toward the caddy-house, which suddenly erupted the two recovered hoods, both with drawn guns. Butch changed his tactics. He jumped behind the protection of bushes and waited. When they were almost upon him, he sprang out and grabbed them both at once.

He held one of his struggling captives in each hand and then practiced his most delightful stunt. He lifted them off their feet and banged their heads together.

A motor roared behind him. Reicher's car spurted forward, turned into the road and disappeared. Butch dropped his two unconscious victims and hurried into the caddy-house. He heard a faint groan, went into the locker room.

Paul Hawley was strapped to one of the long benches! A cord had been twisted around his neck, like a garrote. He was turning blue.

Butch yanked wide the strangling knot, cut Hawley free and raised him into a sitting position. He had standing orders that whenever he was forced to expose himself to anyone connected with a case on which the Black Bat worked, he was never to give any indication that he was the Black Bat's aide.

"Gosh, what happened?" he asked with an innocent expression in his huge face. "I was just takin' a shortcut home when all of a sudden two guys jumped on me. Then a couple of more came out."

"They—they kidnaped—me," Hawley choked out. "They were going to—kill me. Take me home. I—I just got out of a hospital yesterday—I'm sick."

THE GIANT didn't doubt that. Carrying Hawley in his powerful arms, he glanced at the four men lying on the green. He grinned contentedly as he put Hawley into the coupé and drove him home. Hawley was able to navigate under his own steam when they reached Van der Veer's house.

"If you will call on me in a few days," he told Butch, "I'll reward you."

"Aw, that was nothin'," Butch said modestly. "Just a little exercise. I oughta thank you for givin' me the chance to get it. So long."

He didn't try to reason anything out. That was for the Black Bat to do. He returned to Tony Quinn's house. Silk was there and came immediately into the lab.

"Oh, it's you," he said despondently. "I thought it was the Black Bat. I'm worried, Butch. He should have been here long ago. Carol has been phoning every ten minutes. I hate to keep disappointing her."

"Well, I got news," Butch said, "but it'll keep until the boss gets here. You got any idea where he is? I'll go see if he needs help."

Silk shook his head and sat down. Butch smoked a cigarette, enjoying the memory of his brief but effective scrap at the golf course.

It was almost four in the morning when a tiny green bulb glowed over the lab bench. Silk jumped to his feet and Butch opened his eyes sleepily.

It was a signal that someone was using the garden house to enter the tunnel.

The Black Bat came up through the trap door. He was tired, smeared with soot even under the hood, and his cape was gone. He sank wearily into a chair. The two metal boxes under his arm he held out to Silk.

"Heft five million dollars' worth of diamonds, and don't think I didn't sweat five million dollars' worth getting them. Anything happen while I was away?"

"Yeah." Butch sat erect. "I beaned four guys—Heinies, I think they were. I followed Reicher way outa town to some golf course. He had Hawley there, all tied up and chokin' to death. Reicher got away, blast him, but Hawley is okay."

The Black Bat nodded. "I've been to Van der Veer's house and Hawley was sleeping the sleep of the innocent. So Reicher snatched him, eh? That puts our Nazi friend in a very bad light. However, he'll keep until morning. Silk, fix me a drink and then draw a hot bath. I feel as though I've been through hell's fires."

"Five million dollars—" Silk looked into one of the small boxes, and his long, sensitive fingers twitched with eagerness to fondle them. "Boy, what I would have done with this swag ten years ago!"

"Both of you get as much rest as possible." The Black Bat stripped off his hood and climbed out of his soiled, ripped clothes. "Tomorrow night, with luck, we put the finishing touches on this mess."

"Can I punch Reicher's puss in?" Butch asked hopefully.

The Black Bat grinned. "You may have the chance. Now clear out, both of you. I'm going to call Carol."

Butch stepped over beside the trap door and made an odd face.

"Love," he opined, "makes me sick."

Tony Quinn's shoe missed him by a deliberate half an inch. The big man casually dropped into the tunnel, yet his head still poked above the floor level.

"You missed, *Boss*. You used to be better than that."

He ducked, but he was a fraction of a second too late.

CHAPTER XVIII

DOG EAT DOG

JULES AND Stringy were back in business on the following night. Their forces were somewhat depleted, but they still had enough men to raid the diamond-cutting offices of Mark Freiber and Company. One of Jules' men and one of Stringy's were stationed as lookouts. Each gang leader took another three of his own men with him.

The entrance to the plant was a steel door that gave Jules little trouble. He knelt, placed a sharp-pointed instrument against the steel panel and pounded with a padded wooden hammer until he had punched a fairly good-sized hole in the door. Then he inserted a slender, extremely sharp saw and began to cut. It required ten minutes to saw away enough of the steel to get at the lock inside. A moment later they silently filed into the place.

"Stay near the door," Jules told Stringy. "Keep those dopes of yours away from me—you included. You mugs are saps. We'd have got the Black Bat last night if it wasn't for you. We didn't, and he got our five million bucks' worth of rocks. Wait till the boss hears about that."

"It wasn't my fault," Stringy rasped. His hand significantly dropped into his coat pocket. "You wanta make somethin' outa it?"

"Pipe down!" Jules whispered. "You get dumber by the minute. We're on a job, or didn't you know? Cops have good ears and if we slip on this job, the boss will skin us alive. I asked you to stay by the door while I get the stuff. You don't know a diamond from a chunk of glass, so just shut up."

Jules tackled the safe next. It was a modern affair, but Jules was prepared for that. One of his men hauled out a small bottle of nitro-glycerine, handling it with extreme politeness. Jules' men set to work while Stringy kept muttering about the effectiveness of his own stethoscope and how he could open any can with it.

Jules worked methodically, not too fast, and always making certain each step was completed before he tackled the next phase. Of the two, Jules was the far more deadly. He had more brains and was utterly ruthless.

His men hurriedly spread out and searched the various offices until they acquired a good supply of clothing and even a couple of blankets from a cot in one room. Jules carefully piled all this around the safe and then touched off the fuse. The explosion shook the building, but it was fairly well muffled. Even if it drew the police now, Jules did not care. His forces, augmented by Stringy's men, could handle the first batch to show up.

He pried the shattered door away, reached into the big safe and began emptying trays of finished and partially cut diamonds into a leather sack. There were even a few stones which were completely in the rough. They all went indiscriminately into his sack.

"Hey!" Jules called cut to Stringy. "Take the rocks. I'll go out first in case there's trouble. If you hear shootin', use the back way and meet me at the hideout. Got that?"

Stringy accepted the sack of gems. Jules signaled his men and they hurried downstairs. Just then Stringy decided he ought to get going, too. He took half a dozen steps across the middle of the office and suddenly plunged flat on his face. The sack of gems flew from his hand and slid across the floor until they struck the wall.

STRINGY, HALF-DAZED by the sudden fall, clambered to his feet and blinked dizzily. Then he heard Jules calling up an all clear signal. He hastily fumbled around in the gloom, found his precious sack of gems and rushed out.

"You crazy stumble-bum," Jules grated. "Fell on your face, huh? You'd make a swell burglar, you would. All feet, that's you. Got them rocks?"

Stringy reddened and held out the sack. Two cars pulled up and the crooks hastily piled into them. Stringy was in the second car, while Jules and his men occupied the first. Their course took them far downtown.

Jules tried to figure out why the blast had not aroused at least one bluecoat. He had expected to shoot his way clear, yet he had not even glimpsed a single uniform. He didn't like it, nor did he like Stringy. He made up his mind on the spot that they were going to part. He and his men could handle the bearded leader's tasks. Stringy was only in the way.

The hideout was a two-story frame dwelling, not far from the river front. A rickety staircase led up the outside of the house. Stringy was already inside when Jules arrived.

"We're through!" Jules snarled. "You and your dopes can get outa here. I'll fix things so the boss pays you off okay. Don't worry about that. You didn't earn the dough, but I don't like to hear anybody squawk. Now don't start arguin'. Hand me them rocks so I see what kind of a haul we made."

Stringy glanced at Jules' three aides. Each one stood perfectly quiet, hands dug far down in their coat pockets. Stringy knew what the bulges meant—guns. He knew because he gripped his own weapon in a similar manner and he had four of his own men parked on the other side of the room.

Jules unwound the string from the mouth of the sack and started to throw it away. Then he checked that impulse and looked keenly at the cord.

"How come?" he muttered. "I coulda sworn I used a piece of leather and not string."

He opened the sack and dumped its contents onto the table. Instantly the room sparkled with livid light. Jules' eyes popped wide open. Then they narrowed and he made a covert movement with his left hand. His men saw it and grew tense. He picked up one stone at random and held it in front of the light.

"Stringy, you double-crossing rat!" he gritted between his teeth. "So you pulled a fast one at last, huh? Where are the real stones? These are zircons—the nearest thing to a diamond, maybe, but they ain't diamonds. A smarter guy than me might have passed on them, but you forgot that some of the rocks I dumped into that sack weren't all cut. These are, every last one of 'em. You got an explanation?"

Stringy's lanky form seemed to droop, but Jules knew what that meant. The thin killer was ready to shoot at the blink of an eyelash.

"YOU AIN'T pullin' nuthin' like that on me," Stringy growled. "Them are the rocks you handed me, and the same sack. If they're fakes, you fixed it and hid the real stuff yourself. Holdin' out on the boss, huh?"

"This ain't the same sack," Jules said murderously. "I tied mine with a strip of leather. This one had a green cord around it. You switched them, you heel. You hid the diamonds. Where are they, or do I have to blast it outa you?"

Stringy had four men to Jules' three, and downstairs were more members of both mobs. They had been long on the verge of fighting among themselves. Stringy's cunning mind figured the odds and decided they were with him.

"Blast away, damn you!" he shouted.

At the same instant he pulled the trigger of the gun concealed in his pocket. Jules sprang away from the table with a bound, but a thirty-eight slug sent him back against it. His three men blasted revenge. Stringy took a pair of slugs through the shoulder before his men began shooting. Excited yells came from downstairs and Stringy shouted orders for his men to tackle Jules' mob. In half a minute the house was a bedlam of noise, swearing, shots and blood.

Jules painfully raised the pistol in his hand. Stringy, badly wounded, was backing away toward the door. All of Jules' men were down. Only one of Stringy's remained on his feet, and he was incapable of help, for he was trying to stop the flow of blood from a wound high in his chest.

"Here it comes!" Jules snarled.

His gun exploded a fraction of a second before Stringy fired. At the same instant Jules flung himself from the table. Stringy missed. Jules didn't. The lanky thug leaned back against the wall and slowly began sliding down. Jules got up, bared his teeth in a snarl, and took careful aim. Stringy died with a slug through the head.

Jules looked around, scooped up the sack of zircons, for they were worth enough to salvage, and ran to the door.

As he stepped out on the rickety old porch, his blood froze.

Below were cops—dozens of them! All the shooting had not been done by the mob.

They had only shot one another, while the police had sailed in to capture those left alive.

A curse ripped from Jules' lips. He leveled his gun threateningly. Captain McGrath, a sub-machine rifle in his arms, shouted a warning.

"Hold it, Jules! Hold it, or I'll drop you!"

Jules had one solitary chance. If he jumped off the back of the porch, he might land on a low slanting roof. His wounded side ached miserably, but he had to take the chance. A bullet from his gun was lodged in Stringy's body, and that alone would whisk him to the electric chair. So Jules took a chance.

With a wild scream he jumped over the railing, but he was not quite fast enough. His foot caught on the rail and for a second or two he hung head down while McGrath opened fire. Other officers cut loose.

When Jules finally hit the sloping roof of the building over which he had hoped to escape, he did not know it. His body rolled down and plumped onto the ground.

McGRATH LOWERED his gun and heaved a long sigh. Then he walked slowly over to where an official car was just pulling up. Commissioner Warner climbed out.

"I got your message," the commissioner said. "What on earth happened?"

"A couple of mobs started fighting among themselves," McGrath explained. "It just happened that Stringy controlled one faction and Jules Andrus the other. They've been working for the bearded killer we're after. From the shouts we heard when we got here, there was an argument about some loot. We've got them all."

Warner shook his head. "They lived as they died—by the gun. It's the justice of retribution, Captain."

"You're wrong," McGrath answered softly. "It's the Black Bat's justice, or I miss my guess. He warned me that there might be trouble tonight, but he didn't say where. Maybe he didn't know at the time. But he phoned and we came right down. We were too late, or we'd have got them alive. I guess Stringy is dead, and I know Jules is finished. They were the only two people who might have identified our bearded killer. Looks like the Black Bat slipped a little."

"Yes, it does seem that way, Captain. He would scarcely have planned that the only two persons who might solve the case would die."

A detective-lieutenant stepped up and saluted.

"Stringy is dead, sir. The rest of the mob shoot like they live—crooked. Only fatalities are the leaders, and none of the other men got away. We'll need a flock of ambulances though."

CHAPTER XIX

THE MURDER THAT FAILED

GRUMBLING, **McGRATH** turned his sub-machine gun over to a member of the riot squad and walked slowly back to his departmental sedan. He slid behind the wheel and drove off.

"Poor, stupid fools," a voice said.

"Yeah," McGrath agreed absently.

When he realized he was supposed to be alone, his car started to zigzag until he finally got it under control again. The Black Bat climbed from the rear seat and sat down beside him.

"They're like a lot of people abroad these days," the Black Bat went on. "They rely on the power of a gun to win their battles, and in the end they all die. They won't listen to reason. They see only their own side of questions. You know what always happens to them."

"I know." McGrath was almost getting used to the Black Bat's sudden appearances. "It looks as if you had a thumb in it."

"I did. The deaths of Jules and Stringy will never make the world bow in sorrow, nor were they any longer useful to me to identify our mysterious Vandyke. But I'm glad those satellites of theirs survived. Some of them may have an ounce of goodness in their hearts."

"Not a gram," McGrath grunted. "They got what was coming to them and they punished themselves. Just how did it all happen, anyway?"

"I knew they were set to raid the Freiber gem-cutting place, so I got there ahead of them. They were fighting among themselves as they came in. Stringy happened to fall over a piece of cord that I happened to pull taut as he was passing by. When he fell, the sack of jewels scooted across the floor. Stringy picked up a sack, but it was a different one. He didn't know that.

"If he had possessed enough brains to know the difference, he'd never have been a crook. Anyway, the real diamonds are back in Freiber's safe. Oh, yes—better send a couple of men over to guard them. I called Freiber and told him what had occurred, but if anything delays him, it would be best to have a guard."

"I left two men in front of the place," McGrath said. "How come they didn't spot you?"

"You've missed me a few times, too, Captain. Don't be hard on them. Would you mind stopping here? I have a little business which needs attention."

"Sure," McGrath grumbled. "Just as soon as you put five million bucks' worth of diamonds in my lap. You got them off that boat last night and they don't belong to you. I— Hey, is that a gun in my ribs?"

"It is, Captain. The diamonds will keep for the moment. I asked you to stop."

"But what's the idea?" McGrath argued as he braked the car. "Say, you're not turning crooked, are you? You don't intend to keep those diamonds, even though they're five million dollars' worth?"

"It is an attractive nest egg," the Black Bat chuckled. "Well, good night for the time being, Captain. If you are at leisure in about two hours, drop over to Van der Veer's house. You might meet some friends there. Come alone."

"Wait a minute!" McGrath almost shouted. "I forgot to tell you. Hawley got clear last night. Reicher is the guy we're after. He snatched Hawley and tortured him to make him tell where Van der Veer's stuff is hidden. We can't find Reicher. Just before this broke, I got word from the two detectives I assigned to guard Hawley. He's gone again! Reicher's got him. We'll iron out the diamond angle later on, but you've got to help me find Hawley."

"In due time," the Black Bat agreed. "As I said, be at Van der Veer's home in two hours. A pleasant journey to you, Captain, though you can't have your five million dollars' worth of gems."

McGrath's face was purple as he drove away. How could he explain five million into obscurity? The Black Bat had double-crossed him! He had always thought the Black Bat was not hunting crime just for the sake of excitement. But a five-million-dollar cut! McGrath groaned and did not even hear the angry yells of a truck driver whose vehicle he missed by an inch or two.

THE BLACK BAT stepped into the darkness of the quiet street and waited. In a moment a coupé drove up with Butch at the wheel. The Black Bat got in.

"Reicher's place," he ordered. "Go as fast as you can without putting a policeman on our rear fender."

Butch let the Black Bat out and then drove to a better spot to park.

The Black Bat approached Reicher's place warily. Stringy and Jules were gone, but Vandyke might not have had all his cards in those two crooked decks. Then, too, McGrath was already suspicious and angry. He might show up too soon. The Black Bat wanted no interference now.

Entrance to Reicher's house was a simple matter for the Black Bat. Gun in hand, he walked directly upstairs, turned left and headed toward the ladder which led to the attic. He went up this cautiously. The intense darkness meant nothing, for his eyes penetrated it easily. He saw a big wardrobe far toward the end of the dusty attic.

He approached it quickly, found the door tightly closed and locked. There was no key, so the Black Bat resorted to the clever little methods which had taken him so long to master. The door opened and Fritz Reicher fell out!

The Black Bat knelt beside him. The man was unconscious but alive, his flesh ice-cold, his pulse low. The Black Bat picked him up. As he turned away, he saw a pale wisp of gray substance gently wafting out of the wardrobe. If he watched it long enough, he knew, it would assume the shape of a ghost, or what was supposed to look like a spectre. He didn't wait, though. Reicher needed attention.

On the second floor, he removed the man's clothes and put him to bed. He forced brandy between the cold lips, packed a couple of hot-water bottles under the covers and massaged the Nazi agent's hands. Soon Reicher opened his eyes. He shuddered like a man with a violent attack of chills as he stared at the weird figure.

"You're safe," the Black Bat said. "You came very close to dying this time. Luck was on your side, though. There were too many chinks in that old wardrobe."

"Cold—I am cold." Reicher chattered miserably. "Listen to me. In my safe is thirty thousand dollars in cash. If you let me go, you take it, *ja?* I promise to go far away."

"Sorry." The Black Bat rejected the proposal. "Your shirt tails aren't exactly clean, and your methods border on the ruthless side. Bribes don't work much in this country, *Herr* Reicher. I have already notified the F.B.I. that they will find you here."

REICHER TRIED to get up, but he was too weak. The Black Bat eased him back and covered him again. Then he took a pair of handcuffs from his pocket and calmly chained Reicher to the bed.

"Just to make sure you'll be here when they arrive. That reminds me. If I want to stay out of their way, I'll have to leave. You won't get out of this mess. Incidentally, most of your agents are under arrest right now. You should have realized that the whole world isn't composed of trusting fools. The United States is inhabited by people who have learned to suspect your regime, so your schemes and plots won't work too well here. Good-by, *Herr* Reicher."

The light in the room winked out and Reicher knew he was alone. The chills soon left him and he began to sweat. When he heard someone enter the house through the front door, he shivered again. The F.B.I. agents would not appreciate the fact that Reicher had been up against the toughest adversary in the world—the Black Bat. He knew now that he had fought a losing battle from the very beginning.

The Black Bat watched three F.B.I. men enter the house. Then he hurried to where Carol had the car parked. He got in and for a moment he held her hand tightly.

"The case is nearly over. We've accomplished a great deal of good this time, Carol, and you have done your share. I'm grateful. Now we're off again. I'll have to drop you, for I must work solo now. I'm driving to the Old Well Country Club. I've got to rescue a man named Hawley. The poor chap has suffered a lot during the last couple of days."

"Can you make the rescue alone?" Carol changed places with the Black Bat. "Don't you need help?"

The Black Bat smiled and shook his head.

"Not this time. Hawley's captors are too sure of themselves. A little surprise and— Well, you'll see."

Carol got out near Quinn's home. The Black Bat drove out of the city, parked and approached the same caddy-house where Hawley had been kept a prisoner before. Suddenly a man appeared in the doorway, whipped out a gun and fired two quick shots. The Black Bat's gun answered and the man turned and raced away into the night. Gun still ready, the Black Bat walked into the caddy-house.

"Help me," a weak voice called from the locker room. "Help me!"

The Black Bat followed the direction of the voice. Hawley was once more strapped to one of the long benches, though not quite as painfully as before. He saw the Black Bat's weird form and for a moment he could only stare.

"I'll have you loose in no time," the Black Bat said as he began to work on the bonds. "From what I've heard, they've been treating you pretty roughly."

"It's Reicher—he's a Nazi spy," Hawley croaked. "Those diamonds that Mr. Van der Veer sent over—Reicher wanted them and others, too—others that I've never heard of— He tortured me—I spent almost two days strapped to the bench—and Reicher had his men watching. Last night someone happened to pass by. He was a big chap. He routed

Reicher's men and got me free—took me home. But in the middle of the night, even with a police guard outside the house, Reicher sent more of his men. I was taken again. He means to kill me. You're the Black Bat! You fight for what is right. Get Reicher—get him before he kills me!"

"Just take it easy," the Black Bat soothed. "We'll go back to your place—Van der Veer's, rather. I have a car outside. Can you walk without help?"

Hawley nodded and followed him out to the car. Hawley rubbed his chin, apparently thinking of something. He hesitated for a moment before getting in beside the Black Bat. Then he shrugged and maintained silence until they were near the city limits.

The Black Bat chose the darkest, quietest streets possible, for he was still wearing his hood and cape. He had not had the slightest opportunity to remove them.

"I don't know how to thank you," Hawley blurted at last. "Seems that's all I'm doing these days—being grateful to people who rescue me."

"Forget it," the Black Bat said. "If it makes you feel any better, take my word for it that Reicher won't bother you again. Here we are. There's someone on the front porch. Well, it's Captain McGrath."

"A fine cop he is," Hawley grumbled. "Watches the place after I'm kidnaped. Why isn't he out looking for me? Oh, I guess I'm being unjust. The police are only human after all. How did you happen to locate me?"

The Black Bat pulled into the driveway and stopped. McGrath started over belligerently.

"I have my own methods, Mr. Hawley," the Black Bat said quickly. "Clues are left, men talk when they're afraid. Just be satisfied that you are safe. Oh, hello, Captain. I've brought back the twice-missing witness."

"Hawley!" McGrath gasped. "Every one of my men is out looking for you. Are you all right? Who did it?"

"I'm no worse than I was before," Hawley said bitterly. "It was Reicher and a gang of German agents. They think Van der Veer had a lot of other jewels and they were trying to make me tell where they were hidden. All you have to do is grab him. He's responsible for all of it."

Hawley marched up on the front porch and unlocked the door. He turned on the lights and then stepped back in surprise. There was a man sitting in one of the hall chairs, and not of his own volition.

Stout, capable-looking ropes held him there.

Edmund Clive's mouth was gagged, but his eyes revealed the mute fury in his heart.

CHAPTER XX

THE MYSTERIOUS
VANDYKE

R**ELEASING CLIVE** and taking the gag from the captured man's mouth, McGrath groaned in helpless bewilderment.

"How did you get here?" he demanded.

"I was brought here!" Clive shouted. "Somebody dropped a cloth bag over my head. When it was removed, I was tied the way you found me. Aren't these crimes ever going to stop? Hawley, I didn't see you. Why weren't you here? You live in this house, don't you?"

The Black Bat stepped forward.

"He was in a difficulty similar to yours, Mr. Clive. Now that we're here, all but Reicher, I think there should be a few explanations."

"Just a minute. Pardon me, gentlemen."

McGrath took the Black Bat's arm and led him into the next room.

"Listen, you're not going to keep those gems, are you? The commissioner wanted to know where they were, so I told him. You'll be a crook if you don't turn them over. Every cop in town will be looking for you."

The Black Bat laughed. "Haven't they been trying to nab me for months, Captain? Haven't I always been labeled as a crook? We'll discuss the diamonds later. There are more important matters just now."

"What could be more important than five million dollars' worth of diamonds?" McGrath protested. "Get this. You turn them over soon, or this truce of ours is busted. I don't play ball with crooks."

The Black Bat gravely stepped past the captain and went back to the other men. Clive was massaging his wrists and glaring at everyone in general. Hawley sat on the steps, apparently still weak. McGrath took up a position close to the door, as if to prevent the Black Bat's escape. But the Black Bat pulled over a chair and put one foot on it.

"We'll begin by clearing up the method the killer used to dispatch his victims," he said. "In the first place, the first five million dollars' worth of diamonds never left Europe. The guards who were chained to a valise that was apparently stuffed with gems were protecting a lot of dry ice. During the trip over, the ice evaporated, leaving the boxes which were supposed to contain diamonds mysteriously empty.

"The murders of the plane crew and the two guards are clear enough. Our murderer was very fond of dry ice as a method of getting rid of people who were in his way. We may never prove this, but it is my opinion that there was a great deal of dry ice in that plane. You will remember that it flew in the sub-stratosphere and its cabins were supplied with oxygen.

"If that oxygen were cut off at a certain moment—which could easily be done by regulating the pressure gage on the tanks—then the carbon dioxide from the dry ice would naturally fill the cabin. The passengers and crew simply became sleepy, much as victims of carbon monoxide from automobile exhausts are affected.

"The pilot, however, sensed something wrong and put an emergency oxygen tube in his mouth. That enable him to land the ship successfully, even though he died immediately afterward."

"Hey, wait a minute!" McGrath forgot everything except the flaws he was sure he saw in the Black Bat's analysis of the murders. "If the diamonds never left Europe, then why did the killer ride that plane? Somebody was aboard, because the pilot's oxygen tube was cut. There was a parachute missing and we had the oxygen apparatus gone over. All okay."

"Certainly it was," the Black Bat said quietly. "When I first visited the plane, our bearded killer was aboard. He took advantage of the withdrawal of the guard, which was made for my benefit. He adjusted the oxygen tanks so there would be no clue. He removed a parachute from the plane and dropped it into the sea. When you checked up, there was a 'chute missing. That would naturally serve to confirm your suspicion that someone had dived out of the cabin before the plane landed.

"The pilot's rubber oxygen tube was not purposely cut. He wanted to see how the passengers were, after the copilot collapsed. He got out of his seat, opened the rather heavy door and looked into the main cabin, constantly keeping the oxygen tube in his mouth. But when the door closed, it severed the tube. There are traces of the tubing still on the bottom of the door."

Edmund Clive was openly skeptical.

"I suppose, since you were able to reason all this out, that you can also tell us what become of Van der Veer. I'll even go so far as to wager you'll say he is alive."

"Of course he's alive," the Black Bat answered. "The man McGrath found in the study of this house was not Van der Veer, but a double for him. Van der Veer has always been a crook. You see, I've been in touch with certain authorities in Europe, using your name to get my information, Captain McGrath. I hope you won't mind. Anyway, Van der Veer operated a huge diamond-cutting business, but many of his stones were stolen.

"When his country was overrun by Nazis, Van der Veer fled to the United States. He came incognito and allowed his double to enter publicly. That double was always useful to Van der Veer. When he traveled around Europe, supervising the theft of diamonds, his double alibied him. Hadn't that occurred to you, Mr. Clive?"

Clive was staring open-mouthed. The Black Bat continued.

"Van der Veer had no use for his double in this country, so he disposed of him by simply placing him in a closet with a quantity of dry ice and sealing it up. The victim, trying to escape the chunks of dry ice, touched them and was burned. He'd just been removed from the closet when you came, Captain. That was why his body was cold on the surface. The internal heat returned before the doctor examined him.

"But the real Van der Veer happened to recall that his double was also a crook and had an international police record. The corpse would be fingerprinted and this secret was certain to leak out. So he stole the corpse and substituted that of a vagrant whom he had picked up several days before. He had used the tramp in an experiment to see if dry ice fumes would really kill."

Captain McGrath headed for the door. "I'm going after Fritz Reicher. He's the man we want."

"But the Black Bat!" Hawley interrupted. "He said that Reicher would no longer bother us. I thought he was dead."

"Let Reicher wait," the Black Bat suggested. "Hear me out first. The body of the false Van der Veer will probably never be found. He was nothing but a stooge, anyway. The real Van der Veer killed him for one big reason, besides the fact that he was now a nuisance. If anything went wrong on the plane, Van der Veer would naturally be suspected. The real Van der Veer, using a short-wave radio, picked up the broadcast stating that the pilot was coming in.

"He became frightened, believing that the passengers were alive and would talk. That was a bad mistake, although it kept me puzzled for a long time. However, once the fake bearded man was accepted as Van der Veer, the real diamond thief went ahead with his plans. He wanted to gather together all the diamonds he could. Two huge robberies and a great number of smaller ones would be big news. Diamond dealers all over the country would believe that there was about to be a shortage and begin to buy.

"There is a shortage already because of war conditions, so that belief was easy to encourage. With the market high, Van der Veer could then sell fast and reap a huge profit. Not, however, with the original five million dollars' worth that he professed to be sending over by plane. They didn't exist to send over. Van der Veer had them at one time, but he sold out, reaping a nice profit. They were not his property but stones he was supposed to be hiding for his clients so the Nazis wouldn't get them."

"I told you about the market inflation from the shortage of stones," Clive put in glumly. "I also sent Captain McGrath an anonymous tip about the new shipment of stones."

"For which I'm grateful." The Black Bat bowed slightly in Clive's direction. "You are a very good actor, Mr. Clive. All I have told you seems to make no impression on you. Oh, by the way, you want to know who your kidnaper was. I confess unashamedly. It was the one way I could be sure you'd be present."

Clive started forward belligerently, but McGrath checked him.

"As a British agent of the International Diamond Buyer's Syndicate, you now realize how Van der Veer fooled you," the Black Bat said. "You don't like to be told what a real mutton-head you are. Mankensen, who was the butler in this house, was also one of your agents. Something you or he did gave his identity away to the killer, and Mankensen died.

"Now Van der Veer—the real one—was distinguished by his strange red beard and his coal-black hair. His beard really was red. Mr. Hawley, you haven't shaved lately, have you? Too many interruptions. Do I really notice that your whiskers are red?"

Hawley leaped to his feet. He looked around, his eyes flaming madly. Then he took a wild dive for the door. The Black Bat's foot sent a straight-backed chair directly into Hawley's path. The killer stumbled and fell heavily. McGrath seized him and handcuffs clicked on his wrists.

"Stop protesting your innocence," the Black Bat snapped. "Reicher isn't dead. You tried to kill him with dry ice, but you failed. When you escaped last night, you went directly to Reicher's house and surprised him. He's talking to F.B.I. agents. Reicher was after those diamonds, but like everyone else, he thought they were in the United States. He also knew that you were the real Van der Veer.

"Some of your allies in Amsterdam were apprehended by the Gestapo and persuaded to talk. I hate to think what that persuasion was. Reicher was ordered to get the gems and he tried to, in the only way he knew how—by forcing you to tell the hiding place. Even your friends in Amsterdam thought you still had the diamonds.

"You wore a false Vandyke beard and hired Jules Andrus, Stringy and their mobs directing every move they made. When you were trapped in this house, you took off your disguise and had one of Jules' men—whom you were forced to take into your confidence—rap you on the head. But he was excited and did too good a job of it. That man escaped through the window, with one of my bullets in him.

"Then you went to the hospital, were kidnaped by Reicher and, before you could shave off that telltale red fuzz, snatched again by me. I wanted to make sure you wouldn't shave. During that time your hired crooks carried out your plans, but you were never around. If the man with the beard had been Clive or Reicher, he would have been in evidence. You weren't there because you couldn't be, physically.

"The dry ice puzzled me, especially when I got a picture of it fuming out of that closet. You meant to dispose of the stuff that was cleverly hidden there, but you had no chance. You fooled McGrath into giving you an alibi. You were the only living man in the room where the supposed Van der Veer was dead. You merely used the voice which you always used as the real Van der Veer, and answered yourself in the voice you had adopted to fit Hawley."

McGrath looked grim.

"I'll take him away, but you're coming, too. The case is over and so is the truce. You've got five million dollars' worth of rocks. You're holding out, so I'm not giving you a chance to get away with them."

"But, Captain," the Black Bat chided, "if you'll just look down at my right hand, you'll see a gun. You know, I'd hate to shoot you—"

McGrath advanced a step or two.

"I—I always said you were a crook. Now you've proven it. I'll get you, if I'm ninety-five years old when the time finally comes. Oh, I realize you've helped me, but that isn't worth five million...."

The light in the hall suddenly winked out. McGrath lunged forward, but the spot which the Black Bat had occupied was empty now. McGrath thought of Hawley. He darted to the wall, found the light switch and flooded the hallway with light again. Hawley lay on the floor, unconscious.

From the rear of the house a taunting voice made McGrath turn livid.

"Sorry to run out on you, Captain. Hawley tried to get away, so I slugged him. I've been wanting to, ever since the case began. Five million dollars in diamonds. Aren't you envious?"

McGRATH HAULED Hawley to his feet. He looked at Clive. "The dirty crook! Yes, I mean the Black Bat. Help me lug this side of beef out to my car. I'll jug Hawley and then start a hunt for the Black Bat. I trusted him, like a fool." Clive was still a little dazed by the rapid events of the last, few moments.

"Captain, it's almost worth five million to have Hawley—or Van der Veer—in your custody. The Black Bat was right. I am an agent for the diamond association, which has been trying to pin something on Van der Veer for years. I really thought he was dead this time. He's a vicious, clever fellow. Watch him closely."

Clive opened the door of McGrath's car and helped to stow Hawley inside. McGrath ran around the car and tried to slide behind the wheel. There were two metal boxes on the seat. He picked them up. A small piece of paper was pasted to one. It said:

Merry Christmas. Now do you believe in Santa Claus?

Below the message was the sticker of the Black Bat. McGrath placed the tin boxes on Hawley's lap. Hawley did not know it, though. He was still unconscious. McGrath stepped on the starter and growled an oath.

"The crust of that guy," he said.

Hawley stirred and groaned.

"Aw, shut up!" McGrath bellowed. "The nerve of that guy."

Two pair of eyes watched the car disappear. The Black Bat chuckled.

"Poor McGrath, he didn't know whether to be sore or happy. Now let's get back to the house and explain things to Carol and Butch. You acted like a real disciple of mine at the caddy-house, Silk."

Silk looked proud. "Hawley certainly thought I was one of Reicher's men. The car is over this way, sir. Shall we go?"

THE BLACK BAT AND THE RED MENACE

CHAPTER I

MURDER SAILS THE SEA

THE SEVEN-THOUSAND-TON freighter, *Amber Cross,* her holds loaded with ore from South America, steamed serenely along. Things on board were not as calm as the weather, though. Intrigue, rumors of murder, and hate were running rampant.

More than half the crew went about their tasks sullenly. The captain, saltwater-born and bred, paced the bridge, fully conscious of the volcano that rumbled below decks. Three men were in the brig, men who demanded to eat with the officers, even though the food served officers and men was the same. This troubled the captain.

Husky, cool-eyed Frank Adams, able-bodied seaman, knew it all. He was not particularly worried about himself, but he was about his kid brother, Joey, who was aboard as an assistant radio operator. Frank Adams went up the companionway ladder slowly, heading for the radio room. His hand touched something moist, and he saw blood smearing his palm. He frowned and went on, his mind centered on Joey.

Radio had always been Joey's greatest interest, and for months before he had finally landed this job, he had tried to find work on a ship. Now he had it, but Frank Adams was deeply concerned about his young brother in this cauldron of hate. Joey scarcely had the physical stamina to hold his own, should the expected man-explosion blow them all sky-high. Joey was about five-feet-six, and weighed not quite a hundred and twenty-eight pounds, and though the sea air had darkened his skin, still he was no picture of health.

Reaching the radio room, Frank Adams closed the door and the port.

"Joey," he said, "plenty is due to break loose on this tub. The first mate hasn't shown up for the last hour. I just found blood on the companionway ladder. The mate has been 'taken care of,' all right. Now listen to me. You and I have had our arguments about the union I joined, and in some ways maybe you were right. I should have asked more questions, probably, should have learned more about what I know now—that there is an alien group who have insinuated themselves into our union, and are using any means whatever to dominate it.

"But the main point now is, that you and I *are* on this tub that's practically being run by that bunch of aliens—and we're in danger. Just as every good union man is coming to be when he refuses to be bossed by those devils. What's worse, when the hellish foreigners are in the majority—as they are aboard this freighter—too often the union men who won't play along with them never have a chance. I've seen that happen plenty of times, Joey—men who sail on a voyage never coming back because the freighter they sailed on has been sunk. A lot of freighters have disappeared lately."

JOEY LAID his earphones on the table and turned around in the swivel chair.

"That's the principal reason I refused to join your union, Frank," he said seriously. "I've had good reason to know about those men who are trying to take it over. Communists, redder than a matador's cape, started it all. And now the Nazis and Fascists have joined up with them, and unless the American union men get wise and toss them out, they *will* be running the whole maritime union before anybody knows what's happened.

"I know more now than I did before about those guys who want to push the good Americans right into the sea. I know from my boss. He's beet-red. All he reads is Lenin's theories and the pamphlets put out by those crack-potted dopes who want to run the world according to a plan crazier than they are themselves."

Frank went to the door and peered out quickly. Spying on board, he knew, was more common than sleeping.

"Well," he said quickly, "I've got my union card. And these rats who plan to raise the merry devil with this ship—just as they have with other tubs—don't know whether I stand with or against them. At least I've been that wise, not knowing until after we sailed whether we were sailing with a bunch of Commys, Nazis and Fascists, or with Americans. That was just self-protection, because…. Why, I know of at least five freighters that have gone down in the last six months. In each case, a third of the crew went down with the ship. Those who were saved—belonged to this radical bunch. To me, that means they plain murdered the American union men who might squeal."

Joey closed his eyes. "I suppose I'm elected to go, then," he said, quietly resigned. "I don't even belong to the union. I'll probably be the first to get it in the neck. Frank—when do you think the blow-off's due to happen?"

"Tonight. We're sailing the regular routes, so a rescue ship won't be far away. Those rats always see to that. But Joey—they won't get you. Leave that to me."

Joey sighed. "And I thought there was nothing in the world I'd like better than to be a radio operator and go to sea. Ships aren't fit for real Americans any more, Frank. They're being filled with scum and rabble—foreigners who have infiltrated and want to run everything their way, even if they have to commit murder, mutiny, and scuttle their ships to do it.

"I can't figure out what's behind it. Sure, maybe those dopes think they want to create a new era in the world and operate everything with their nutty ideas, as they say, but if they keep on killing people and sinking ships, there won't be enough left to prove their golden theories."

Frank Adams was tight-lipped when he answered. "Okay, kid. I didn't tell you this before, but it's a show-down now. If I don't get clear and you do, sing it out from the housetops. They're trying to stop the United States from re-arming. They're helping Hitler and his satellites—because if he wins, the world will go to pot and make it that much easier for Communism and the Axis powers to take over. The orders come right from Moscow and Berlin. So does the money to finance this devil's own work. The sea isn't fit for decent men so long as those vultures hover over it. Younger brothers never listen to their older brothers as we should have listened to Mark. He was right about the whole business, telling us to watch out for those birds. Now you watch yourself, kid. I'm going on deck to see how the wind blows."

As Frank left the radio cabin, a burly, bow-legged sailor swaggered toward him.

"I'm checkin' up," he said. "I'm hearin' you're one of us, pal. That right?"

Frank nodded and the sailor lowered his voice.

"Tonight—right after dark. Lifeboat Three—and keep your lip buttoned."

FRANK WENT below. He inspected several cabins and the second mate's looked as though a furious fight had taken place there. He saw a locked trunk in one corner, and hastily pried it open. Inside he found what he was looking for—a heavy automatic, fully loaded. He stuffed this into his belt and pulled his sweater over it....

The moon was coming up when Frank heard a scream and several shots. He raced on deck. The captain was slumped against the rail, eyes already glazing. Two sneering men stood before him, both with smoking guns. Others were nearby. Frank reached for his own weapon, but quickly realized he could not fight three quarters of the crew. Already he had discovered that the alien element was in that majority.

Reluctantly he backed away, but during the next swift minutes he saw similar scenes being enacted. Men were ruthlessly shot down or knocked out with skull-fracturing blows.

Frank managed to sheer away from the men assigned to that dirty work, dodging into shadows as again he hastened toward the radio cabin.

Even before he reached the ladder, Frank was flung against the rail as suddenly the ship listed. He could hear the crackle of the wireless sounding an S.O.S., but that wasn't Joey sending. Joey was faster than that. Where *was* Joey?

Almost in answer to the question, the radio room door opened and Joey lurched out. Blood streamed down his face, and his shirt was soaked with it.

The regular radio operator left his instrument board for a moment, stepped onto the deck, and gazed at Joey, staggering away. He lifted a gun, started to aim it.

Frank Adams fired from the hip—twice. The radio operator crumpled, without a sound. Frank knew he'd been seen, knew what the consequences would be, but he also knew that the ship was sinking fast. Holding Joey protectively, he ran along the slanted deck to Lifeboat Three, lifted his brother, limp and half conscious, into it, and scrambled in himself. Dragging Joey to the stern, he squatted beside the young radio operator, his gun trained on the crew members who were lowering the boat.

"Lower away!" Frank shouted defiantly. "Or would you rather stay aboard and go down with those poor devils you slugged or shot?"

"Now listen, Frank," one of the men protested whiningly. "You're one of us. You know what we've done is for the Cause. There ain't no reason for you to get all riled up. Anyway we only got three lifeboats. The others been wrecked, just in case some of them guys ain't dead. Eight of us got to get into the boat with you."

"Get in then," Frank snarled. "Though I don't know why I should bother about saving rats who scuttle their own ship. Get in—but drop your guns first. If one man carries a gun into this boat, I'll blast all of you, so help me!"

The freighter was listing dangerously, going down at her prow. It was no time to argue. The other two lifeboats had already pulled away. The men assigned to this one threw guns into the sea and hurriedly slid down the ropes.

FRANK DIDN'T row. He left that for the killers. In his anxiety for his brother he had little time even to show his utter contempt for them. Joey was badly hurt. Unless they found help quickly, he might die. Frank's eyes were narrow, his jaw out-thrust, his voice brittle when he spoke.

"I know well enough we'll find a rescue ship soon. The S.O.S. was sent before the ship started to list. But once we're aboard the rescue ship—you hear me?—leave us alone! Pass the word to the others. I know you'd like to finish this job on my brother because he's a real American who'd tell the whole world what you seagoing wolves have done. Well, you made one bad mistake. I'm registered as a member of the Independent Maritime Alliance—but I don't belong to your bunch who want to scuttle it, too. I'm not one of you Communists who play along with Nazi spies! I know what you're up to, though—trying to destroy all mercantile shipping of the United States! Hoping to break the backs of all passenger lines. Material necessary for defense of the United States is being sunk—like that ore aboard our ship.

"Those red tentacles reached out into France—into Spain—into China! What's the result? Chaos! Ruin and starvation! Now you're trying to strangle the greatest nation on the earth today. Well—you can't do it, do you get that? Nobody can! You can kill me and my brother, but we're only two out of millions upon millions!"

"Fine speech," one of the men said, scowling. "Very fine, my bucko, but it's also your death warrant. Nobody who's in on what our bunch are up to walks away from us—and lives."

Frank laughed coldly. "No? Well, take a good look at two who will. I'm going to, and so is my brother. As I've got this gun you won't dare tackle me. After we're ashore, I'll fix things so I'll never be bothered. The union will be glad to know a few things the bosses can get their teeth into, where you're concerned. I'm not quite as much of a sap as you birds think I am. Now start rowing—and don't get within pistol range of the other lifeboats either."

CHAPTER II

VACATION CRUISE

E N ROUTE from Bermuda to New York, the liner sailed a calm, moonlight-swept sea. The captain's only acknowledgment of the war in Europe consisted of American flags painted on the sides of the ship and searchlights playing on them.

It was shortly after dinner, A dance orchestra going at swing music full blast, and the bar was busy.

At this hour few were on the decks. One man walked slowly along the after-deck, hugging the rail closely. He carried a cane which was thrust out as if he expected to meet some invisible barrier. He was tall, sturdy-looking and had, at one time, been a handsome man. Now deep, glistening scars marred his features. He wore dark glasses, and most of the scars were near the eyes.

He grasped the rail and turned slowly to face the foaming wake of the ship, apparently staring out into the darkness. Another strolling man suddenly stepped beside him at the rail, a man of about forty-five, carefully dressed, and a little on the pompous side.

Slowly puffing his expensive cigar, he studied the man with the dark glasses, with an odd expression on his face. Usually shipboard acquaintances are easily made, but this man with the scarred face seemed none too eager to make friends.

"I—ah—hope you are enjoying the trip," the pompous one said presently.

The other man jerked as if startled. Then he smiled slightly.

"I am, of course. Peaceful here, isn't it? You'd never think the same moon shining down on us also lights death and destruction over Europe."

The man with the cigar stuck out his hand. "My name is Gibbons— Brad Gibbons. You may have heard of me. I make armaments—shells, guns, grenades. The war hasn't hurt my business, of course, but I'd much rather be making bicycles, as I used to do years ago."

The man with the dark glasses paid no attention to the proffered hand. Gibbons flushed.

"I—I'm sorry," he said. "I know a lot of people detest a Merchant of Death, as I'm called. Still I thought—"

The other man turned to face Gibbons. "You offered me your hand, didn't you? It's I who should be apologizing. You see—I didn't know. I'm blind."

Gibbons' lips pursed, and he spoke impulsively. "Terribly sorry. But you being here alone.... Is there anything I can do?"

"No." The blind man smiled. "And don't be sorry. My secretary is due here at any moment. He'll take care of everything. Thanks, anyway... I'm Tony Quinn of New York."

Gibbons said a hurried word, turned away, and disappeared down a companionway.

Almost at once "Silk" Kirby, Tony Quinn's valet, secretary and friend, came on deck.

"I had a little company while you were below," Quinn said softly. "An armament manufacturer named Gibbons. One of the big fellows. What I'm wondering is how he ever found time, with present day conditions, to take a vacation. I think we'll take a turn around the deck, Silk. Better hold my arm."

THEY STROLLED slowly, and as they neared the radio room the door opened and a steward came bolting out. He raced down the deck clutching an envelope in one hand.

"Something's happened, Silk," Tony Quinn commented. "When you see a steward move that fast, bank on it—the matter is urgent. He came from the radio room which may bear out my idea that trouble is impending. Let's go aft again. Something may happen to break the monotony of the trip after all."

Silk glanced curiously at Quinn. He spoke in a low voice.

"If you don't mind, sir, it seems to me you're almost too sure something is about to happen. It has also struck me that we left on this trip quite unexpectedly. Do you *know* that something is due to pop, sir?"

Quinn chuckled. "No, Silk, I'm not sure at all. However I did happen to notice that several ships have been sunk recently, and all of them were engaged in hauling materials needed for defense work. They all were sunk close to our present course. Just on a hunch I thought we'd take this little trip because at this moment several freighters owned by the line which has suffered all the losses so far, are in our vicinity. And if the reason for the sinkings *should* happen to be sabotage—then we'll do our share toward breaking up any combination of spies working to scuttle our merchant marine."

They were approaching the rear of the radio cabin when a bare-headed young man in tuxedo barged around it and plowed straight into

Tony Quinn. Both went down in a tangle of arms and legs. The young man scrambled up, brushed back his sleek blond hair and scowled at Quinn. Suddenly a firm hand gripped him by the collar and jerked him around. Silk's eyes were narrow and his temper mounting.

"It's dangerous to pop around corners like that, you nit-wit!" Silk exploded. "This man you knocked down is blind—and you stand there cursing at him."

The blond young man wrenched himself free of Silk's grasp, put the heel of his hand against Silk's chest and shoved. Silk tripped over Quinn's legs and went down himself. The young man sprinted away toward the bridge.

Tony Quinn's chuckle interrupted Silk's bellow of rage.

"Ten times in the last few hours you've said if something didn't happen, you'd go crazy, Silk," Quinn remarked. "Now it's starting, and so far—you haven't done so well. Help me up. You know"—Quinn got

"This man you knocked down is blind, you nit-wit!"

to his feet with Silk's aid—" it strikes me odd that our blond-headed young friend should be in such a rush to overtake that speedy steward. If he hoped to, we settled that. Let's go aft."

As they proceeded along the deck, Tony Quinn brushed his sleeve and then, certain that no one observed him, picked off a blond hair. There was hardly enough light on deck to examine anything the thickness of a hair closely, yet Tony Quinn raised the colored glasses for a second, then carefully stowed the single strand of hair in an envelope in his pocket. One swift glance had interested him in that hair, for Tony Quinn was not blind, though his pretense of being a blind man was without a flaw. There was good reason for this deception though, and in fact Tony Quinn had had plenty of training, for once he had been blind for months.

"Our hasty young friend, Silk," Quinn said in a low voice, "has blondined hair. I discovered that when one of his hairs clung to my coat in the mêlée. Ordinarily he is quite dark and he'll need another application of bleach soon. Women often bleach their hair, but men—the only time a man does that is when he wants to disguise his real appearance. Perhaps there is some nice big plot brewing aboard."

Quinn glanced upward and nudged Silk.

"Look at the funnels. We've changed our course. The direction of the smoke has shifted from south to direct west. We're traveling full speed too. Something *is* going to break, Silk!"

FOR A full hour the ship headed in the general direction of Europe, instead of following the coastline. And for some reason best known to themselves the ships' officers had not notified the passengers that they were off the course.

Then a huge searchlight went into action, sweeping the water for a mile ahead. Sailors manned three lifeboats. Others stood by with life-preservers and ropes ready. The purser hurried into the saloon and posted a bulletin that informed the passengers that an American freighter had radioed for help. Immediately everybody streamed out on deck.

"We've answered an S.O.S.," Quinn said softly. "And, yes—to starboard there. I can see a boat—a freighter, I think. Her stern is coming up for the final plunge! I only hope her crew is off. Yes—they're in lifeboats!"

Silk, however, could see nothing until the searchlight's beam held on the sinking ship. Tony Quinn's eyes, once blind, had gained a remarkable proficiency with the return of his sight. He could see as well in darkness as the average person can see in full daylight. He could even distinguish colors, which accounted for his noticing the difference in the shades of that strand of hair.

The crew of the freighter were pulling madly toward the liner. Ladders went overside. Sailors stood ready. The first boatload came over the rail and the men were quickly wrapped in warm blankets and given brandy.

The last boat was unloaded slowly. Quinn and Silk, leaning over the rail, caught the flash of a gun. A tall, husky young man stood erect in the lifeboat, cupped his hands to his mouth and yelled for a rope. One came down and he fastened it around the limp form of another passenger in the lifeboat. That passenger was hauled up fast and the armed man came after it via a sea ladder. On deck he hurried to the injured man, stood there glaring.

"I want it understood," he shouted hoarsely, "that I'm taking care of my kid brother and nobody except the doctor is going to see or talk to him. He's badly hurt, and believe me it wasn't any accident. If anything happens to Joey, I'll squawk like a parrot!"

"That's telling 'em, Silk," Tony Quinn said, surprised. "And he meant those words for the members of his own crew. Look—over on your left. There's Brad Gibbons, the armament manufacturer, taking it all in and looking a bit seedy. Our phony blond-headed friend over there looks as if he'd just had a shot of vinegar—straight. Silk, there's plenty more here than meets the eye. Move about and keep your ears and eyes open. I'll see you right here in half an hour."

Tapping his cane, Quinn walked slowly toward the group of rescued sailors who were talking in low voices and looking around furtively. Quinn's hearing, made doubly acute during his period of blindness, served him well. He could distinguish words not meant for a stranger's ears.

"Big Hans got it while he knocked out the last sea cock. Cargo shifted and pinned him down."

Another man spoke in a hoarse whisper. "Stop talkin' about things like that. You want somebody to get wise? We got rid of them as were meant to be got rid of. All except them two brothers and they'll get theirs. You pipe down."

SILK UNCOVERED a little information also.

"I'd say, sir," he informed on his return to Tony Quinn, "that the freighter was scuttled. An American ship—carrying ore from South America to New York. Part of the North Freighting Line fleet. The crew is the most sullen bunch of foreign bums I've ever seen. I did manage to pick up that the ship's captain sent a radio to the owners, saying the ship foundered and that eleven members of the crew were lost and twenty-one saved. But none of the lifeboats were crowded, sir, and foundering craft doesn't fall apart and kill the crew—not eleven of them. Seems to me that chap whose brother was hurt knows something, and is holding it over the heads of the others of the crew so they'll leave his brother alone. Perhaps we ought to watch the cabin to which he was assigned."

Quinn was staring straight ahead, his head erect and unmoving, in the way of the blind.

"You'll have to do it, Silk," he said. "There isn't enough room on this ship for me to work properly. And—if the Black Bat should suddenly appear on the same ship where Tony Quinn is a passenger, there might be questions. Especially from Captain McGrath, back in New York, who is more than half certain now that I'm the Black Bat.... Take over, Silk. I'll be in our cabin."

CHAPTER III

MURDER
HAS LONG ARMS

Q **UINN WALKED** away, asked directions of a passenger who bumped against him, and in a moment was provided with a steward who led him to his cabin.

"Horrible accident, sir," the steward said. "Lots of 'em lately too. I guess they don't make freighters as seaworthy as they used to be. And the crews. They're a bad lot. Met 'em in port, I have. Lot of Rooshians, Heinies and the like. Here we are, sir. If you'll give me your key."

Quinn ordered a drink, locked the door after the steward had brought it, and sat back sipping the drink while he tried to puzzle out the meaning of what had so far happened.

Once a district attorney, Quinn's keen mind was trained to combat criminals. It had been in the line of duty that he had been blinded. Crooks, trying to destroy evidence with acid, had hurled some of the corrosive stuff into Tony Quinn's eyes. The lights had gone out for him instantly, and had stayed out for a long, long time.

Specialists had given him no hope. As wealthy as Quinn was, he had been assured that no amount of money could get him back his sight. Then, when he had reached the lowest depths of despair, hope had come—through a girl. A pretty girl with a mission in life. Through her, Quinn had met a doctor in a small midwestern town. The girl's father, a police sergeant dying from a gangster's bullet, had donated his eyes to Tony Quinn. The operation was successful—in fact it gave Quinn's eyes that power to see in the dark that was far beyond ordinary man's optic capacity.

The girl, Carol Baldwin, whose policeman-father's eyes were now in Tony Quinn's head, had become an essential part of Quinn's forces organized to combat crime. Tony Quinn had fallen in love with her, not only for her soft beauty, but for her level-headedness, though they rarely spoke of love.

Of the other two of the three who formed Quinn's private crime-fighting organization, Norton Kirby, better known as Silk, was a slim, almost bald individual who had once been a confidence man who had won encomiums from others in that questionable field. He came to rob Tony Quinn, and had remained to become his servant, friend and confidante. The third of the trio was Butch O'Leary, a hulking, two hundred and fifty pounds of bone and brawn. He was not too quick-witted, but his enormous strength served Tony Quinn well.

With these as his helpers, Tony Quinn fought crime under the mantle of the Black Bat. Clad in a hood that covered his scarred features and a cape which was ribbed to resemble a great bat's wings, he prowled the night and tackled crime with a directness no police officer could afford to attempt. He did break the law—frequently—and when it became necessary, he even killed—in self-defense. But he always branded his victims, or his deeds, with a sticker fashioned in the shape of a black bat so that no one else would get the blame.

Secretly the police respected the Black Bat and would work with him even though they had orders to arrest him on sight. All but Captain McGrath who had, paradoxically enough, risen to his present rank because of cases which the Bat had solved and for which he had allowed McGrath to take credit. But McGrath had sworn to land the Bat behind bars, and since McGrath was a tenacious individual, nothing could make him modify that oath, even though he sometimes worked with the Bat under a flag of truce. Other times, though, McGrath made things a little embarrassing, because he had a deep-seated belief that Tony Quinn was not as blind as he pretended and that he was the Black Bat.

TONY QUINN was brought up sharp from thoughts of all this as a soft tap on his cabin door indicated that Silk had returned.

"Things are going to pop, sir!" the little ex-confidence man said breathlessly. "I've learned that the injured man was probably slugged with a big wrench and was going to be left on the sinking boat to die. His brother—the big boy—saved him and guarded him with a drawn gun until this ship arrived to rescue the survivors of the crew of that freighter. The big fellow's beside his brother's bed now with a gun in his lap. No one but the doctor can come in."

Quinn arose and took a small jar from his steamer trunk. It was labelled shaving cream, but was in reality a soft clay which he used to fill in and erase the deep, acid-burned scars around his eyes. He also changed into a dark suit and put on a wide-brimmed hat that came well over his eyes. A topcoat, collar turned up and a big muffler finished this effort to conceal his features.

"Take up a post where you can watch the cabin where those brothers are," he told Silk. "I'll keep my eyes on it too, but if anything happens to occupy me, you stay there anyhow."

In three minutes Quinn was on deck, leaning against the rail, apparently looking out to sea. But his eyes flicked around continually, and his remarkable sight penetrated even the darkest corners.

As a man slipped around the corner of a cabin, Quinn tensed. It was late now, and the decks were rather well cleared. The shadowy figure drew closer to the cabin. So did Tony Quinn—and saw that the man was one of the rescued members of the freighter's crew. The sailor had to cross an open space before he could reach the cabin and, concealed by darkness, Tony Quinn waited in that space, standing to one side of a companionway hatch. As the sailor sprinted by Quinn's foot shot out. The sailor tripped, started to yell, but a big hand closed over his mouth. He was dragged back into the inky darkness and shoved up against a wall.

"All right," Quinn snapped. "Don't make a move."

Quinn discovered a wicked-looking dagger thrust into the man's belt. He hurled this overboard. He was quite well aware that questioning this man would likely elicit no more information than if he talked to a dummy. Outfits that ran to murder and scuttling ships held their members in check by fear. Quinn decided to try subterfuge.

"You fool!" he grated. "Orders were for you not to show yourself. Don't you know you would have been caught in another few moments?"

"Then you—belong?" the sailor choked.

"If I didn't you would be dead or a prisoner," rapped Quinn. "Orders regarding the ship were well carried out except for the presence of the two men in this cabin who know more than is good for them—or us. Who bungled it? Why were they not killed?"

"I—I don't know. All I know is I heard Frank got the drop on the fellows in his lifeboat and made 'em row him and his brother here. I was just coming up to take a look around for a certain person you know, and see if there was a chance of getting at those two squealers."

"Well things have changed," Quinn said. "I'll take care of those two myself. Go below again and stay there."

THE SAILOR touched a finger to his forehead. "Yes, sir. But don't you want me to draw any guards away from the cabin so you can get in? I was supposed to do that if anybody was around."

Quinn shivered. Perhaps the real killer was even now taking advantage of this interlude to invade the cabin. Quinn whispered orders for the sailor to hurry away, then walked swiftly toward the cabin which murder haunted.

A yellow ray of light spread over the deck as that cabin door was opened. A man stepped out. He was in uniform, and carried a physician's bag. He closed the door, his back toward Quinn. Tony Quinn felt relieved. The ship's doctor making a routine call. The presence of the doctor meant that both those boys were still safe.

Quinn looked for Silk and saw him, blended with the shadows, and practically invisible. Then Quinn saw something else about fifty feet down the deck. Someone sitting in a deck chair, well covered with a blanket. One arm hung down.

In the darkness normal eyes would never have noticed the thin stream of blood that flowed along the wrist. Quinn saw it.

He made sure he was unobserved, went swiftly to the chair, and raised the blanket. The man beneath it wore no coat—only a shirt, which was blood smeared. He had been stabbed through the heart!

Quinn took in the watch on the dead man's wrist. Its second hand was larger than the other two hands, and the dial was spaced off in seconds. A doctor's watch! The kind used to check a patient's pulse, and Quinn looked sharply at the dead man's hands. The nails were scrupulously clean and pared far down—like a surgeon's.

Quinn let the blanket drop back, moved away and stood against the rail. His thick finger ring tapped it sharply. The hidden Silk instantly decoded those taps. An oath rasped in his throat as he realized that Quinn was telling him the ship's doctor was dead. Therefore the man in the doctor's uniform had been an impostor.

Silk raced for the cabin door and pounded on it. There was no answer. He tried the knob, found the door unlocked, and pushed it wide. His face became bleak at what he saw. The wounded young sailor lay back against the pillow with the pallor of death already graying his face. The brother sat in a chair beside the bed. A knife had been driven through the back of his neck with such a ferocious force that death had come before he'd had a chance to call for help.

The killer had searched the dead man's clothing. The pockets were turned inside out.

Silk knew that every second he stood there might also mean death for himself, but he waited long enough to pick something up from the floor, and wipe the knob to remove his own prints. Then he walked hurriedly in the direction which Quinn had taken.

"Dead," he whispered to Tony Quinn. "Both of 'em. The killer must have fooled the big brother with the doctor's uniform all right. He fooled me too, sir. I didn't suspect anything, even when the fake doctor came out two minutes after he had entered. I thought he was just going for some medicine."

Tony Quinn shook his head.

"There's going to be the devil to pay when those bodies are found, Silk. We can't afford to be connected with it—not even as innocent bystanders. Once ashore, though, things will be different. Hurry back to our cabin now. Silk, this mess may be discovered at any moment."

CHAPTER IV

THE TRAIL BEGINS

TONY QUINN was in bed, with Silk seated close by, reading to him when a knock sounded on their door. Silk unlocked the door, and two ship's officers entered.

"Sorry," one of them said. "But we find it necessary to ask each passenger to account for himself during the past thirty minutes. You gentlemen will coöperate of course. I assure you the matter is serious."

Silk jerked his head in Quinn's direction. "The gentleman is blind, sir," he said softly, then raised his voice to say: "I accompanied the master for a turn around the deck an hour ago, sir. We returned to the cabin about thirty minutes ago and have been here ever since."

"What's wrong?" Quinn asked testily. "Who is here?"

"A couple of ship's officers, sir. They want to know where we have been the past half hour."

"Yes—yes, I know that," Quinn snapped. "I can hear, even if I can't see. What's it all about? Why are we forced to alibi ourselves?"

"Sorry, sir," one of the officers said. "We're not permitted to talk. The ship is quite safe, however. We'll dock in the morning on schedule. Sorry to have bothered you."

Silk locked the door after them and sat down again.

"There must have been an urgent reason to shut that injured youngster's lips for good, sir," he said. "Even going so far as to murder the doctor for his uniform."

Quinn removed the dark glasses, but his eyes were pale and stony. To all appearances they were the eyes of a blind man, yet within a split second Quinn could change all that by the movement of muscles, and have the use of eyes that had few, if any equals, for strength and keenness.

"It had something to do with the sinking of that freighter, Silk," he said. "If she was loaded with ore—metals necessary to the United States defense program—then it was sabotage, and in all likelihood treacherous crew members murdered those who would not have stood for the scuttling. This youngster undoubtedly was marked for death, but his brother apparently rescued him and used a gun to guard him. Both of them knew something that made them dangerous to others, so had to be forever quieted. It shouldn't be difficult for us to get the names and address of those two murdered sailors."

Silk grinned a little as he dug into his pocket and produced a wallet.

"That comes from the big brother's body, sir. I—copped it. He was Frank Adams, able seaman. Union card shows he belonged to the Independent Maritime Alliance. His address is on it too, sir. Waterfront section. And—er—here's a picture of three men. Two of them are the murdered sailors. No way of telling who the third one is."

"I'll take that stuff," Quinn said. "They won't search a blind man. All right, Silk. Let's go on deck again and see what we can see. The whole ship will soon be aroused, if it isn't already."

AS THEY slowly paced the deck, Tony Quinn kept his eyes straight ahead, and Silk seemed to be guiding him. At one spot Quinn gave a faint tug at Silk's arm and veered off to the left slightly as Brad Gibbons, puffing one of his huge cigars, came strolling their way. He started to nod to Quinn, then shrugged. How could a blind man see him? He kept going.

Silk frowned. "I don't like his looks, sir. If you don't mind my recalling it, I used to be a confidence man, with a knack for picking the real ones from the fakes. And this Gibbons looks like a phony to me. If I were roping, I'd never put the mark on him, sir. Which is to say, he'd be a poor specimen for a confidence man to take over for all his money and big position."

Quinn was well aware that Silk's inherent ability to judge a man was to be respected. Confidence men are always good judges of character, and Silk had once been near the top in that smooth game....

It was well after midnight before the gayety of the last night aboard ship got under way. But Quinn and Silk sat in deck chairs, with other things in mind. Both were certain that the murders of the Adams brothers was but a small episode in the progress of some gigantic crime machine. The death of the ship's doctor indicated clearly just how badly the killers needed to silence those two brothers.

Quinn also was sure that the actual killer had been a stranger to Frank Adams. Never would he have permitted a known enemy to enter that cabin, for Frank Adams had given plain notice that he meant to protect his injured brother at gun's point.

What lay behind it all? Why had a ship, loaded with ore, been scuttled? Why had so many members of her crew gone down with the craft? Tony Quinn didn't know, but was grimly determined to find out. Which meant the Black Bat was preparing to spread his wings again....

About noon the next day, when the ship docked in the Hudson River, Silk led blind Tony Quinn down the gangplank. As they stepped off it, a stocky, firm-jawed man with a neat mustache and granite-hard eyes touched Quinn's shoulder. Silk scowled.

"It's the estimable Captain McGrath, sir. Seems he can't leave us alone one second after we land."

"But Silk"—Quinn laughed and extended his hand slightly to one side of the captain—"McGrath is merely welcoming us home. We've had a very pleasant trip, Captain. Marred only by—ah—some unfortunate incidents last night."

McGrath nodded. "Yeah—I know all about that. Listen, Mr. Quinn, you've been away for two weeks, and not once has the Black Bat put in an appearance. What I was wondering was whether or not the Bat happened to be seen flitting around the deck of this ship last night. That wouldn't tie him up with you—much. I'm going to find out." He started to turn away, saw Quinn's hand still outstretched, and reddened. He accepted the hand and shook it. "Anyway, I'm glad you're back."

As McGrath hurried away, Quinn's laugh died in his throat. His eyes, shielded by dark glasses, had seen a parked sedan and a girl waving a greeting. Silk hastened to the car.

CAROL BALDWIN, restful to the eyes at any time, had never seemed quite so beautiful to Quinn. He thumped the driver on the back as he got in the back seat beside Carol, and Butch O'Leary's wide face broke into a broad grin. Silk got in beside Butch and the car pulled away.

"We saw McGrath waiting for you," Carol told Tony Quinn, "so we stayed in the background.... Tony, we heard something dreadful happened on board your ship. It was a shame to spoil your trip like that."

"Spoil?" Silk turned around. "Quite the contrary, Miss Carol."

"Silk means the trip bored him stiff." Quinn chuckled. "But seriously, we may have run head-on into something big. At any rate we'll soon find out. Butch, you're due to stick your thick neck into a hornet's nest before nightfall. That is, if you crave excitement."

Butch turned into a side street and eased the car to the curb.

"You just tell me whose head you want busted, Boss, and I'll take care of it."

Quinn and Silk got out of the car.

"We'll take a cab the rest of the way," Quinn said. "Wouldn't do for you and Carol to deliver me to my house, Butch—not if McGrath happens to have someone hanging around. Put the car up, and you and Carol report to the lab immediately."

Half an hour later Tony Quinn, comfortable in smoking jacket and tweeds, puffed on his pipe and strolled idly through the gardens of his estate. His cane tapped a path before him.

When he returned to the house, Silk was drawing the shades in the spacious library.

Quinn proceeded straight to the west wall of the room, opened a door, and stepped into a large, perfectly equipped laboratory. Here were all the scientific devices necessary for the tracking down of criminals. Here were reference books, chemicals, mementos of past cases—and Carol. Tony Quinn's eyes, blank and blind-looking, came to life. Even his scars seemed to soften. He sat down beside her.

Butch was there also, waiting for orders.

"Butch," Quinn said at once, "you're exactly the type for this particular job. I want you to pose as a dock worker. I'll give you an address on the waterfront. The two men who were murdered aboard ship lived there. Find out all you can about them and their connections. Perhaps you can say you loaned them something, and since they're dead, you'd like to get it back. They belonged to the Independent Maritime Alliance. I want what information you can get about that, too, particularly if the union has been troubled with infiltration of undesirables, who may have had an idea of getting control. I've heard considerable about that lately."

Butch blinked several times. "Boss, that union must be in kind of a tough spot, because of some of them Heinies and Commys and dirty Fascisti. Because a lot of guys I know that used to work on the docks have quit their jobs so's they wouldn't have to mix in with them phonies that think this Rooshian guy, Stalin, and this here Hitler and Moosolini is pretty swell. My pals say the guys that want to run things their own way down there, no matter what the union says, plain smell bad."

Quinn whistled in surprise. "Communists! So that's the angle. And Nazis and Fascists, too, of course. That places a different slant on things.... Go ahead with your job, Butch. Silk, get our newspaper files on all recent criminal activities on the waterfront. Also any listings of freighter sinkings during the last several months."

CHAPTER V

ON THE
WATERFRONT

BUTCH WALKED over to the farther end of the lab. A section of the floor slid aside and revealed a ladder which led into a tunnel. This, in turn, took Butch far behind Tony Quinn's house, where it ended in a small garden house. Only a few yards separated the garden house from a gate. Butch was soon on the street and hurrying in the direction of his boarding house, not far away. There he got into a battered old coupé and drove straight to the waterfront. He stopped the car a block away from the address Quinn had given him and a few moments later punched the doorbell of a cheap rooming house.

The woman who admitted him was thin to the point of emaciation. She had bright, deep-set eyes, and a thin slash for a mouth. Butch took a newspaper from his pocket. It was folded to the story about the murders at sea.

"I'm a pal o' Joey and Frank," he said. "Before they sailed, I lent Frank my suitcase. I paid eight bucks for it and—well, I want it back. If you let me go up to Frank's room, I could find it easy."

The woman stepped aside and pointed up the stairs.

"His room is the last one on the left—way down the hall. The door is open. I was just cleaning up in there. Dead men don't pay rent, so I'm getting the room ready for somebody else. Mind you—don't steal things that don't belong to you."

Butch plodded up the stairs. A man not quite as trusting as Butch would have thought it peculiar that the landlady was so willing for him to go to the room of the dead sailors, unaccompanied. But Butch simply congratulated himself on the fact that things were going along so smoothly.

Downstairs, the landlady hurried into the kitchen and dialed a number on a wall phone there.

"You know who this is," she cackled when she got an answer. "Some big gorilla just walked in and gave me a flimsy excuse to look over the Adams boys' rooms. Said he loaned Frank a suitcase. Well, if he did, Frank took it with him."

"Keep him there for at least ten minutes," a man at the other end of the wire said. "No matter what you have to do—stall. By that time we'll have your place covered. When he comes out, come to the door with him so we will know he is the right man. Leave the rest of it to us."

"It'll cost you twenty-five dollars," the woman said. "That gorilla may be a G-man. But I'll finger him for you."

She hung up, hurried into the front hall and went directly to the room which had been occupied by the murdered brothers. Butch heard her coming and stepped lightly to the closet.

"Maybe he took the suitcase with him, huh?" Butch asked the woman. "It was a brown one with one strap almost busted. You remember if he carried one like that away?"

He was hoping she wouldn't notice the bulge several periodicals and pamphlets made in his pocket. They had looked interesting to him. Perhaps they'd be even more interesting to Tony Quinn.

Butch headed for the door. The landlady moved to intercept him.

"You were a good friend of the boys, eh? How is it you never came to visit 'em here?"

"Well y'see, lady," Butch said haltingly, "I go to sea a lot. Me, I'm a sailor.... Now I gotta travel. Guess maybe my suitcase went down with the ship."

The landlady put her hands on her hips and eyed him belligerently.

"I don't think you even knew the Adams boys!" she declared, "I think you come to rob 'em. Maybe I should call the cops. Robbing dead men! What did you take?"

BUTCH SHRUGGED, and picked her up as though she were a piece of furniture in his way. He set her down in the middle of the room and walked out. She flew after him, howling at him.

On a small table near the front door were several letters. In a frantic effort to stall Butch, the landlady swept one of them up, grabbed Butch's arm and pulled him away from the door.

"Wait a minute!" she shouted. "If you're a friend of the Adams boys, maybe you can return this letter which came for Frank this morning. It's from his folks back home. Maybe you know them, eh?"

Butch took the envelope and the landlady gulped. Perhaps this was a mistake. Her orders were to hold all mail addressed to the Adams boys. She had to get it back, yet she also must stall Butch another minute or two. The next minute, as she took a quick look out the small window beside the door and saw a burly, hard-faced man across the street she was so eager to get rid of Butch that in her excitement she forgot about the letter.

She practically pushed Butch out of the house. As he walked down the steps, she nodded her head vigorously. The man across the street turned to follow Butch.

In a moment two other men in dark clothes also took up his trail. Several blocks up the street a fourth joined in.

Butch, heading for the docks, stuck his big hand in his pocket for a pack of chewing gum. He unwrapped a stick, turned to throw the paper into a rubbish can and, out of the corner of his eye, spotted the four men trailing him. The had stopped almost so abruptly they had given themselves away.

Butch knew crooks of the average breed, but these men seemed different. More sinister if anything. Butch turned a corner and stepped into the first doorway. All four men breezed down the street, but only one kept on going while the other three dissolved in the gloom of approaching night. Butch was trapped and knew it. He had not fooled them.

He tried to figure out if it would be easier to lure those men close, grab them and put them out of commission, or to give them the slip. He decided to phone Tony Quinn about that, from the busy drugstore a block away. As he came out of his hiding place he saw that two of the men were searching every doorway, but they didn't spot him until he had almost reached the corner.

Butch stepped into the drugstore, saw a vacant phone booth between two others that were in use, and entered it. He dialed Quinn's home and heard Silk's smooth voice answer.

"Tell the boss," Butch said, as softly as he could, "that I got me some trouble. Three or four mugs are on my tail. Should I bust 'em on the snoot or take 'em for a nice long walk some place?"

"Walk them," Silk said. "Pass the corner of Whiting and Main Boulevard in exactly—"

"Hold it," Butch broke in. "One of the guys is gettin' into the booth next to me. Can't get where you say—too far. I'll write another address and pin the paper under the shelf in the fifth phone booth from the door of the Elite Drugstore. Get here fast."

Butch didn't hang up. He pretended to be talking to a casual friend as he scrawled a rendezvous on the back of the letter the landlady had given him. He pasted it to the under side of the small shelf with the chewing gum he'd been munching. Then he hung up, stepped out of the booth and wondered if those mugs were going to cut him down with revolver fire, or if they would follow him for proof of his identity and connections.

TWO OF the men pretended to be examining a display of books. Butch barged hurriedly out of the drugstore and led those men on one of the most zigzag courses he'd ever taken. It wound around city blocks and every now and then Butch paused, as if about to change his mind about where he was going. Finally he headed for the rendezvous he had selected, though he believed it was a toss-up whether Silk or Quinn had found that letter he had left in the phone booth or whether it had been found by one of the mysterious men trailing him. He was certain of only one thing—his temper was mounting steadily. And his big paws kept clenching into mighty fists, wanting to land on those trailing men.

Butch was about a block and a half away from the spot to which he had left word he would lead these men when it happened. As he passed an alley, two men darted out of the darkness. Butch turned to meet the onslaught more than willingly. But he could not battle the blackjack that sailed toward his skull. Then three of his trailers leaped. More vicious blows of the blackjack followed, and Butch dropped.

A car pulled up. Butch was dragged over and dumped into the rear seat. The sedan drove away as Butch's attackers melted into the darkness....

In the meantime Silk delivered Butch's phone message to Tony Quinn in the laboratory. Quinn gave quick orders.

"Silk, disguise yourself to play the role of a member of a ship's crew. A union steward or waiter out of work, possibly. Hurry! We'll leave in ten minutes. Carol, you'll go to that drugstore and find that written message Butch left there."

"And what will Tony Quinn be doing while all this goes on?" Carol asked, with a smile.

"Tony Quinn is very tired after a long trip. He's going to bed and the house will be locked up, and the Black Bat, Carol, is wide awake and more than eager for a battle. The hood, cape and my guns are going to feel good. Slip through the tunnel and bring your car around to the side gate. I'll meet you there."

After Carol had departed, Tony Quinn quickly removed his clothes and donned black trousers, black crepe-soled shoes, and a black shirt. The cape, ribbed to look like the wings of a bat, fitted about his shoulders neatly. He drew on the enveloping hood, then examined a pair of automatics and slid these into their holsters.

Silk was still busy at the slower task of disguising his features. He was good at that, and improving daily. Silk had learned makeup when he had used disguises to elude "suckers" who had taken his bait and then refused, in the lingo of the con men, "to be cooled out like a good mark."

The Bat sat down at the lab bench with the union card which had once belonged to Frank Adams in front of him. He prepared a colorless solution of two chemicals, dipped a small brush into the liquid and carefully wiped it across the name of Frank Adams that had been written in ink on the card. The name slowly vanished and yet the coloring of the card was unaffected. The Bat wrote in another name for Silk to adopt in his work.

Five minutes later Silk Kirby slipped out of the garden gate, looked around and gave a low whistle. The Bat flitted through the darkness, almost invisible. They reached Carol's car and got in. The Bat drew a wide-brimmed hat over his head after removing the hood, in order to attract no attention.

Carol sent the car rolling toward the drugstore from which Butch had phoned. She parked on a side street, and hurried into the store. In the proper booth, she pretended to phone, while her fingers located the letter on the under side of the tiny shelf. She thrust it into her purse and returned to the car.

The Black Bat glanced at the words written on the back of the envelope.

"Butch is to lead his trailers to the corner of White and Beecher Streets at exactly eight-ten o'clock," he said. "Carol, once there, park near the corner. When Butch comes by, tell him, without letting his trailers know it, that he is to walk two blocks, turn the corner, and start running. You are to meet him. Drive him away. His pursuers will then return to whoever put them up to this. Silk will trail them, and I won't be far away."

CHAPTER VI

MEETING PLACE

A **S CAROL** headed for the rendezvous corner, the Black Bat turned the envelope over and, despite the darkness in the back of the car, read the address on it easily. He grunted in surprise, wondering how Butch had ever come into possession of a letter addressed to Frank Adams.

He slit the flap, extracted a folded piece of paper, and as he read the contents, slow rage began burning in his soul. The letter was from the mother of the murdered boys. It appeared that they had often written her of their experiences, and she was giving them some parental advice. The letter read:

Dear Frank:

Your father and I have talked it all over. You and Joe are to come home at once. I hope this letter reaches you as soon as you return from your voyage.

I have a feeling that some of the men with whom you are now associated are not true Americans, Frank. I've read how a Senate committee has been learning that subversive elements have crept into unions, so maybe yours cannot protect you as it once did. If you listen to those dissatisfied foreigners, they may lead you along a path that will take both of you into acts you may be sorry for all your lives.

Don't fail me, because I have a mother's intuition that all is not well with you and Joe. I won't sleep soundly until you return.

The Black Bat slowly refolded the letter.

"Silk," he said quietly, "we were right. Those two young sea-faring young men were in danger because they may somehow have managed to get mixed up with a bunch who are trying to get control of their maritime union—men who have un-American interests. The Adams boys even wrote home about it. A review of the clippings you dug out for me reveals a curious thing, too. All the freighters that have been sinking far too rapidly of late carried cargoes helpful to the United States defense.

"Other clips indicate that the Independent Maritime Alliance has been having plenty of labor difficulties during the past year, all caused by men within their ranks who have Communistic interests. The Nazis and Fascists who have infiltrated into the union are not as well established as the Communists, but they are insidious, thorough, and dangerous. This time we're fighting something big, Silk. I only hope it isn't too big."

Carol suddenly applied the brakes. "Tony—straight up the street!" she said breathlessly. "See those men? They've attacked someone. Look— it's Butch!"

"Stop!" the Black Bat ordered. "Shut off your parking lights. They've got Butch all right! When their car starts off, follow it at a distance, Carol. Silk, watch out for a taxi and grab it. Trail that car, too, in case they get wise to us and we have to drop back. There they go! Easy now,

Carol. Butch's life may depend on how we handle this! They won't kill him before trying to make him do some talking."

Carol's hands were steady on the wheel. She had learned to steel her nerves when the going became rough. Silk hopped out a couple of blocks farther on, and Carol clung to the trail without apparently arousing any suspicion on the part of her quarry. The Bat sat in the shadows of the car, alert and ready for anything.

THEIR COURSE took them toward the waterfront and the big sedan finally turned into a driveway beside a two-story brick building which was well illuminated. Carol stopped a block away and Silk soon joined them, though he didn't look like Silk Kirby. His face seemed thinner, his eyes smaller, and he seemed well tanned, as if by ocean breezes.

"I had a look at the sign over the door of that building where they took Butch," Silk said. "It's a branch of the Independent Maritime Alliance. Are there any orders, sir?"

"Yes. You can make yourself at home in there by showing this union card." The Black Bat handed over the prepared card. "Don't forget that's your name on it. Once inside, look around. Try your best to unlock all doors which lead into the alley. Most important, take note of the men who act as if they were important—probably in spite of the regular union. Remember their faces. That's all get going."

Silk walked briskly up to the building and entered it. He ambled down a corridor, and discovered a spacious meeting hall he walked into was half filled with men. On a platform, half a dozen men who were huddled in a group, seemed to be talking over the soon-to-start meeting. One man, with a shock of white hair, seemed to predominate the others. Even at a distance Silk saw that he wore expensive, tailored clothes, and that a big diamond sparkled on his hand.

That man stood out in Silk's mind, though he noted other members of what seemed to be an executive committee who were the earnest type of men to be found at any regular union meeting. There were some frowsy-looking foreigners among them also, however, who didn't look so good to Silk. His all-encompassing glance covered each man and his brain tucked away descriptions of them.

Certainly there was nothing here that would particularly interest the Black Bat, so Silk decided to look further. Strolling unnoticed into the hall again, he walked to the end of the long corridor, then spotted a stairway leading downward. He followed it. Apparently it led to a basement of some kind.

Reaching the bottom of the stairs, Silk looked around. The floor was of cement and cleared, just as a meeting hall would be cleared. In one corner folded chairs were stacked. He saw a door, too—perhaps the door through which Butch had been brought into the building. If he had been brought here.

Silk slid back the heavy latch, unhooked a burglar chain, and turned the key. He opened the door a crack to see if the Black Bat now had a ready means of entrance. If there was anything to be found here, especially anything of which most of those union men upstairs, holding an orderly meeting, were unaware, the Black Bat would find it.

As Silk closed the door again, he thought he heard a scraping sound, and beat a hasty retreat to the other side of the basement. The scraping sound came again, yet no one was prowling about and there certainly was few places for a man to hide.

Silk had started for the stairs when suddenly he stopped. Beads of sweat broke out on his forehead. An oblong shadow was outlined on the further wall—the shadow of someone holding a gun.

Silk spun around, ready to attack. No one was to be seen. He glanced back at the wall. The shadow was gone too, but whoever had cast that shadow must be between Silk and the single electric light bulb in the middle of the ceiling.

Yet where could a man be hiding? There were only the bare walls. Somehow Silk had a feeling that he was being watched. It gave him an eerie sensation. He didn't know what to do about it, either. A man can't fight something he can't see.

MOVING CLOSER to the north wall, Silk began examining it. He had both palms pressed against the wall when he felt, rather than heard, that scraping sound again. Silk turned fast. A man was coming out of a narrow, secret door, holding a gun, raised high to crack Silk's skull.

Silk ducked under the swing of the gun and came up too close to the thug for the weapon to be used effectively. Silk was not a big man, nor especially strong, but he knew how to use his fists and he used them now to good advantage. He doubled that gunman up with short jabs to the midriff, broke the thug's weakened embrace and stepped back to get set for the haymaker. He wound up the swing, but it never landed. Silk had not heard another man come out of that secret door, knew nothing about it until a gun butt landed squarely on his head and he felt an explosion within his skull. He toppled forward and was quickly seized.

He was rapidly searched, then dragged through the secret door, which closed softly and so effectively that there was no trace of its existence.

Butch had been unconscious when he had been thrown into the car, and he didn't awaken for more than an hour. When he opened his eyes, he thought the whole world had become a mass of searing flame and heat. He closed his eyes quickly, but that light penetrated the lids as if they did not exist.

Suddenly he felt a cooling sensation, and tried opening his eyes again. This time the light was not so intense. A man with a stethoscope at his ears was examining him. The man wore a long black robe, something like a monk's, tied around the waist with a rope—but this could be no monk's robe, with its scarlet hammer and sickle blazoned on the chest.

"He is a peasant," this man said scornfully. "Nothing can hurt them. They are built like oxen and have the same amount of brains. But try the lights and the noise machine again. If he does not answer our questions then, we may as well kill him. He probably hasn't the intelligence to know he is being scientifically treated to loosen his tongue."

Butch tried to speak, but his tongue seemed ten times as thick as normal. He made an attempt to raise himself, and found he was strapped to a cot.

Two men bent over him, unstrapped and lifted him from the cot, and iron-linked handcuffs were snapped on his wrists before he was dragged to a table and slammed into a chair opposite a mustached man in a strange uniform with the red hammer and sickle on one sleeve, and the same insignia on his uniform cap on the table. In the man's hand was a gun which was steadily leveled on Butch.

Again Butch tried to speak, but at that instant a pair of earphones were clamped to his head, and instead of speaking, Butch's mouth opened wide and he emitted a crazy yell. He was certain his eardrums had burst. A sound, unlike anything he had ever heard before, had come from those phones.

It came again and again until Butch thought his skull would break open under the terrific impact.

Then the lights that had been in his face while he lay on the cot came again—the ghastly heat and searing light. Sweat poured down from his face. The noise, combined with the hot lights, was enough to drive away a man's senses.

Every few moments the earphones would be removed and the deadly, monotonous voice of the man in the robe would ask questions.

"Who sent you to the Adams brothers' room? What government agency are you connected with? Who pays you? What is your right name? Speak, you fool, or the sound machine will deafen you for life and the lights will blind you."

But Butch O'Leary only shook his head weakly, even when the robed man emphasized his words with a prod in the neck from the long, sharp dagger he held. Once more the hideous noise would begin then, and the lights flash on. The robed man seized Butch's head and held him so that he received the full benefit of the light. From that horrible din in his ears there was never the slightest escape.

Then Butch became aware of a sudden change of interest in the room. The next minute a slender man was shoved toward him and permitted to look at Butch. Though Butch could not guess it, the man was Silk who, realizing the utter helplessness of this giant, knew that his own slight body would have no chance under that torture.

The man in the robe gave some curt orders. He seemed to be in charge, and every now and then someone addressed him as Dr. Vanin. Silk stowed that name away in his mind, but wondered if he'd have a mind after they had finished with him. Help might have come from the Black Bat, but two armed men had been assigned to watch the basement outside in case Silk had not been alone. They were hidden behind the secret door.

What chance would the Black Bat have? If Silk didn't die by their guns, he would crack under this ghoulish torture.

CHAPTER VII

TORTURE LIGHTS

VANIN'S ORDERS were quickly carried out. Butch was unstrapped, the handcuffs removed—probably for use on this latest victim—and he was dragged over to a corner where he was dropped. The coolness of the cement floor, the comparative gloom of a room lit with ordinary light, were like soothing balm. And there was no more of that ear-splitting din from earphones.

Butch's tremendous vitality served him well. As his wits returned, so did his strength. No one paid much attention to him and he lay like a man dead, aware that someone else was to be subjected to the torture of light and sound. But Butch had not recognized Silk in this particular disguise. If he had, weak or not, Butch would have managed to get to his feet, somehow, and give as good an account of himself as possible.

Silk, strapped to the cot, and with no use for the handcuffs as yet, kept telling himself that no matter what happened, he must not talk. Then a clap of thunder resounded in his ears and he groaned. Lights seared his eyes and the sound came again and again until Silk's groans changed to pleadings.

Butch recognized that voice then. He curled his legs under him so he could drive with a spring and leap straight into the fight, centering his attentions on this leader called Vanin. Butch might not find a chance like this again. The seven men in the room were gathered around the cot, watching Silk being reduced to a state wherein his brain would refuse to work and his lips would unwillingly blurt out the truth.

Suddenly Butch relaxed with a soundless grunt of despair. The secret door had opened and someone was coming in. Those cursed guards probably. Yes, it was the bulkier of the two who had been torturing Butch until Vanin ordered them to watch the cellar.

But this guard moved strangely—as if he were a mannikin and some strong hand guided every movement. Then Butch restrained a shout of triumph, for a shadowy form came from behind the guard and sprinted toward the darkest corner of the room. The guard toppled forward like a felled tree. He dropped with a crash that whirled everyone in the room around.

"Up with your hands!" a voice snapped.

A gun cracked and the battery of powerful lights winked out, for that bullet had been aimed at the fuse box. Another gun banged—from the direction of the door. The gunman was shooting wild, but when the Black Bat's automatic answered, it wasn't shooting in the dark. He had the gunman covered and his shot took effect.

The man called Vanin gave a strident yell of terror and howled orders in Russian. The Black Bat saw him lower his head and do a nose dive through his guards. He reached the door just as bullets from the Black Bat's guns smacked the panels all around him. The Black Bat was trying to cripple, not kill, and therein lay Vanin's single chance of escape. One of the slugs did crease his shoulder, but he managed to slip through the door. It was quickly blocked by his followers.

Butch got quickly to his feet, towering like some immense avenging angel. With a roar, he charged. A glimmer of light from the main cellar let the torturers see Butch coming. With bleats of alarm they tried to escape, but Butch grabbed one man by the neck, thrust him toward the wall and dented it with the victim's skull.

He seized a second man, raised him high, and hurled him at the others who were trying to get through the narrow doorway all at once.

His human missile knocked down two more. Two of the three left managed to get clear. The third, pop-eyed, watched Butch's huge hamlike fist start a bone-shattering journey toward his jaw.

BUTCH CHECKED the blow at a quiet word of command from the Black Bat.

"Leave one the use of his tongue. Get our friend off that cot."

Butch grabbed the last man, searched him, and then the Black Bat took over the custody of the prisoner. Butch unbuckled the straps that held Silk down and helped the nerve-shaken, sweat-covered man to stand into an erect position.

"D-did I talk?" Silk asked. "Did I mention that we worked—"

Butch's big hand clapped across Silk's mouth. He ripped the silenced earphones from Silk's head and spoke in a whisper.

"The boss is here and we got a bird who maybe will sing. Don't start talkin' names."

Silk indicated that he understood, and managed to walk a few steps before he sank into a chair. Butch strode over to where the Black Bat had his prisoner covered. When Butch grabbed him, the Black Bat flitted through the gloom and into the main cellar. He could hear the sound of dozens of feet on the floor above, yet no one seemed to be coming down to help. Hadn't those men who escaped called upon their friends for aid? It seemed not.

Returning to the secret room, the Black Bat found that Butch had hurled the prisoner onto the cot and was clamping the earphones on him.

"He gets some of his own stuff." Butch growled. "I know what it'll do to a guy's head—nearly bust it open. Don't worry, you pasty-faced tramp, you'll be glad to talk."

"D-don't use th-the sound machine—nor the lights," the prisoner gasped. "I—I've seen men go mad. Stark, raving mad. You're the only person who ever stood up under them. Please don't use them on me!"

The Black Bat stepped closer. "We don't use such methods in this civilization," he said quietly. "Torture of this kind originated in the minds of certain tyrannical overlords in Europe. But—the weapons used against us certainly cannot be considered unfair if we, in turn, use them. Therefore, it might be best if you talked promptly. Just who are you? Who are these men who pretend to be good union men and use the organization for such a purpose as this? Who is the leader, and what do they think they're trying to do?"

"I am Max Reiber," the man mumbled, though he seemed willing enough to talk freely. "They made me jump ship and—and since then I have been forced to help here. If I refuse, they threaten,to have me deported, and that would mean—the headsman's axe. I do not know who is the real leader of this Cause. There may be none in this country. I know orders come from Moscow, from Berlin, and are obeyed by the men who have been told they must take over the Independent Maritime Alliance at all costs.

"Yet I have heard there is one—a man who bosses us in this country. The idea is to get control of all American shipping through maritime workers who are to be forced to act under threats and punishment by the men who want control—and are not Americans. They hold secret meetings and decide what to do—in secret places they have fixed up in regular meeting halls such as this, without the real union leader having the slightest idea of it. Even now a meeting is in progress at another place. An important meeting of the high-ups."

He hesitated, then his voice took on a whining, pleading note.

"If you promise I will not be sent back to Europe, I'll tell you where they are holding this meeting. Promise me! Everybody has heard of the Black Bat—knows he can be trusted if he gives his word!"

THE BLACK BAT shook his head.

"I make no promises," he said sternly, "but I will do what I can. By helping us round up these men you will be protecting your own hide, Max Reiber. They can't harm you if they are in jail."

Reiber nodded glumly. "I know. I have thought this over many times. I lived in the United States for years and then, like a fool, I returned to Germany. But it was no longer the Germany I knew. It was a land ruled by uniforms and laws and restrictions. I tried to escape into Poland before it was taken over and did reach Russia, and was accepted by them. I came back to the United States under Russian protection and—well, I have told you the rest Except that I do not wish anything more to do with this business. It leads straight to the grave."

The Black Bat was sure this man told the truth. "You'd better find some quiet hotel," be advised. "Register under another name and stay there until we've broken down this organization. Then give yourself up to the authorities. I'll have things arranged. You'll find fair treatment on this side of the Atlantic."

Reiber nodded sadly. "I know that very well. Yet I worked to aid in the downfall of the only decent free government left on earth. They almost had me convinced that their Cause was the right one. You cannot possibly believe all they have in mind. Those men are mad. They speak of comradeship and sharing of wealth, but they do not share what they now have.

"They filter into all the unions and take over before the leaders know what's happened. Part of the money sent to them is used to finance sabotage, and to help the work of the Communistic International and Axis spies here. Also, men in their power are forced to subscribe to their newspapers. Pamphlets are printed in big lots and distributed where they do the most good. Those who hold out against them too long, or know too much about their intentions, usually wind up by being 'accidentally' killed. Heavy wrenches fall from the hands of workmen when someone dangerous to the Cause 'happens' to be standing below."

"Such matters have long been rumored, but never strike home with all their force until someone like you tells about them," the Black Bat said soberly. "Now—another thing. Your colleagues, who escaped, made no attempt to get help from anyone upstairs. Why?"

Reiber shrugged. "The last thing in the world they want any of those American union men to know—until they can persuade, or force them to line up on the side of the Cause—is what is actually going on. Such as things that happened down here. And it might ruin everything for them if those union men and their real American leaders should find out there is such a secret torture room as this right in their own meeting place. They'll do anything to keep from having a show-down with loyal union men—until they're ready to take over."

Reiber laughed, a ghost of a wry laugh.

"Anyhow, Vanin was satisfied to save his own skin. He's always been that way. In Russia, he was a veterinary, but with the rise to power of those now in control, they made him a regular doctor. Then he was so sly in reporting rebellious peasants that he was made an agent. He's a dangerous man, without a spark of mercy. I'm more afraid of him than of all the rest."

The Black Bat delegated Silk to accompany Reiber to a hiding place. Then, with Butch at his side, he headed for the outside and Carol's waiting car.

"How'd you get by them guards?" Butch wanted to know. "Boy, when I knew Silk was caught, I figured it was all over."

THE BLACK BAT'S face beneath his wide-brimmed hat, which had again replaced the hood, was grim.

"Silk had unlocked a door before they got him," he said. "When I slipped into the basement I had an idea things were not quite as peaceful as they seemed. Then I noticed a faint ray of light near the floor, and since there were no signs of a door, I knew some secret entrance must exist. As I crossed the cellar, another slit of light came from the blank wall—a narrow slot the guards pulled back so they could watch me. I don't believe ordinary eyes would have noticed it because the cellar itself was illuminated, but I'm fortunate in the way my eyes serve me, and I noticed the difference in the light intensity from those banks of torture lights behind the panel. So I took up a position close to the secret door where the guards couldn't see me. They were bound to come out, because they knew I must be somewhere around. When they did—I acted."

Butch rubbed his hands. "And when I meet those mugs again, I'm gonna act too. That guy Vanin ain't got no heart, so I'll take him apart and see what *is* tickin' inside him."

CHAPTER VIII

LEAGUE OF HATE

U NDER THE Bat's direction, Carol sent the car rolling toward the address which Reiber had given. Union Hall on Forest Avenue. It proved to be much like the building they had just left. Yet, despite Reiber's certainty that a meeting was in progress, the place was dark.

The Black Bat slipped into the night, his hood in place again, his guns reloaded and ready. He had reached the rear of the building and was trying to determine the easiest method of entrance when a coupé pulled into the alley and one man got out. He shut off the lights of his car, fumbled in his pocket and extracted a key. With this he unlocked the door which led into the same type of basement as that which the Black Bat had just left.

As the man stepped through the doorway, he heard a rushing sound and then, to his startled amazement, saw something that resembled a huge bird descending on him. Two powerful hands encircled his throat and stopped his yell of fear that rose up. The man pounded fists against a body that seemed to be made of steel, but the blows grew weaker and weaker until finally the man dropped, totally unconscious.

The Black Bat draped his victim over one shoulder, carried him into the basement and examined the farther wall. The same sort of secret door must be there. The Black Bat found it quickly, dropped his prisoner inside, returned to the alley and drove the car out of sight. Returning, he locked the door and entered the hidden room.

Reiber had been wrong about one thing—the private meeting had not started yet. Twenty minutes later, using the lookout panel, the Black Bat saw a dozen men enter the basement. It was plain to the Black Bat why they had selected this basement for their meeting. If anything happened, the foreign members of this subversive group would use the hidden room until danger was past.

Soon at least thirty men were seated in folding chairs and the door leading upstairs was tightly locked and guarded. Banners, bearing the. emblems of the hammer and sickle and of the swastika were brought out and hung on the walls, as were also portraits of Hitler, Stalin, and Mussolini.

Finally every man arose, raised a clenched fist or gave the Nazi or Fascist hand salute and stood at rigid attention. Two men mounted the dais. One was Vanin, still bleeding slightly from the wound the Black Bat's bullet had made. The other man was tall, beetle-browed and wore a mustache resembling that of his mentor and master as closely as possible. Instead he looked more like some comedy Western sheriff, for the ends of the mustache dropped well below his mouth.

Yet the Bat did not underestimate this man. His eyes, close-set, were alive and intelligent. Here was a man much more dangerous than he seemed to be. Could he be the leader of this ambitious revolutionary group?

Vanin and this man responded to the salutes and the men before them sat down.

Vanin spoke first.

"LOOK AT me, comrades. You will see that it is only through courage that I am here at all. Just a short time ago, with my men hopelessly outnumbered, I put up a terrific fight. Counterspies tried to liquidate us, but they failed—miserably. Most of them are dead or badly wounded. We won, of course, so I now stand before you, though with a serious wound in my shoulder. I have not taken the time to dress the wound, even though I am a surgeon. I have had to come here to warn all of you of the inner circle that the Black Bat is working against us. He and his forces raided our other meeting place. He is alive, for he fled like a coward, but the man is sly. He will return to plague us. Therefore, we must devote all our energies to locating this man and disposing of him.... Now, we shall listen to B. Blinov, member of the secretariat of the Communist International. He has returned from Moscow, by way of Siberia, with news and orders."

The tall, heavily mustached B. Blinov arose. He had a harsh, rasping voice, but he spoke rather good English.

"The orders are clear," he said. "We work toward the prevention of further manufacture and transportation of munitions and the materials necessary for war. We must break the imperialistic forces behind this war. Break them without mercy. Our mother country has never been anything but anti-war. All our plans are to this end. I repeat, Russia is anti-war."

From the rear of the room came the sound of a struggle.

"What about Finland?" a man's voice shouted. "That was no game of tiddly-winks, was it?"

Held by four of the audience, a poorly clad man was hustled forward. He drew himself erect and looked steadily at the platform.

"No, I'm not one of your rotten breed!" he shouted. "But I managed to get in here! You and your kind are so dumb you never even noticed there was one more present than there should have been. I was after a story. I got one too! It'll be printed on the front page—in red ink!"

"Silence the fool," the mustached man snapped. "Later I shall look into this matter of carelessness. Watch him closely. He must not get away."

The intruder put up a spirited, but useless fight. One man slugged him while three others held his arms. The Black Bat's lips were a thin line as he witnessed this cowardly punishment. Yet he did nothing. The rash youngster was in no great danger yet, and the Black Bat was determined to save him if it meant his own life. Right now the Black Bat's first duty was to pay attention to that meeting that had started again, to hear the theories propounded by this emissary from Communism's stronghold.

"The workers of Finland did not fight," he said, with a note of sarcasm. "It was the cursed imperialists. But we have no time to discuss that now. It is here that our present great interests lay. Until recently we have had a free hand in this country. Now certain forces are watching us closely. We must be doubly careful, for our plans are now ready for fulfillment. The orders I have are brief and plain. Go out and crusade. American workers, if called upon to go into this war, must turn toward the same goal as Russian workers. The equality, the peace, the prosperity we all enjoy in Russia. American workers must turn against their real enemies— the capitalists.

"But until that time comes, we must be anti-war, and our campaign to paralyze all war plans of those who do not believe in our goal must be followed in factories, munition works, on piers and ships. You here are the chosen ones to lead the stupid union members along the right paths. Preach the theory of the brotherhood of equal men. Speak of the day when all shall have wealth in proportion to his neighbor. In that Utopia, my fellow workers, we shall find ourselves the leaders. All the wealth we desire shall be ours, all the power. But"—he shrugged carelessly—" it is not meant that others should know of this."

EVERYONE IN the room, except the intruder who sat groggily in a chair, arose to his feet and cheered. A slow smile curled around the Black Bat's lips. He stepped into the secret room, found exposed cellar wiring near the ceiling and pulled it down. All the lights winked out.

The Black Bat slipped into the darkened meeting room. The radicals milled around like frightened sheep while Blinov tried to restore order. The Black Bat jumped up on the platform, stepped close to Blinov and suddenly clapped a hand across the man's mouth. At the same time he raised a knee to the small of the Communist's back and bent him over until the pain indicated what would happen if he tried to get free.

The Black Bat was moderately good at imitating voices and in the confusion he was sure he could get away with it. He shouted orders in what sounded like Blinov's raspy voice.

Something resembling a huge bird descended on him.

"Stand away from the door and our traitor prisoner! I shall take him away and attend to him myself! Let no one else leave here!"

The Black Bat thrust Blinov away, and moved before the man could countermand those orders. His fists lanced through the darkness, pounding men unmercifully. Unerringly the Black Bat raced to where the outspoken young man was slumped, and picked him up. In the gloom where men were only shadows, the Communists believed Blinov was taking his prisoner away, and hastily moved aside for the Black Bat to get through the door.

Fully six or seven minutes went by before it was possible for the meeting room to be flooded with light again. It presented a strange picture. Comrade B. Blinov, on the floor of the dais, directly below the huge picture of his leader, had two rapidly swelling eyes and a bluish bruise near the point of his chin. But what made the astonished ambitious foreign group who were posing as good union men cry out in earnest fright was the black bat sticker pasted on Blinov's forehead.

Moreover, the unconscious interloper, who had dared to challenge the word of Moscow was gone.

Panic seized the group. They bolted for the door, pouring out of the building like rats leaving a burning ship. Only two had presence of mind enough to carry Blinov out. One was Vanin—and the man who helped him had a healthy respect for Vanin's gun.

Those men moved much faster than the Black Bat had hoped they would. Two minutes after they had vanished, several cars loaded with Federal operatives pulled up. When they rushed into the building all they found were several surprised American union men playing billiards. These men denied any knowledge of trouble—with good reason. They knew nothing of it.

One of the agents rubbed his chin. "I wonder if the Black Bat gave us a wrong steer for some reason of his own. I've heard he's to be trusted, but after all, a man who hides his identity is— Sure he's helped us in the past, but this is plainly phony. All I can think is that maybe it wasn't the Black Bat who called."

MEANWHILE, GOING through the pockets of the unconscious man he had rescued, the Black Bat had learned that the rash young man's name was Ted Jordan, and that he was a reporter for the *Morning News-Globe*, a tabloid noted for its exposés.

Carol drove into a park, stopped and the Black Bat deposited Ted Jordan on a bench. The reporter was beginning to snap out of it as the car rolled away.

The Black Bat rubbed his hands in satisfaction.

"One thing," he said, "this mess will be aired properly. Exposure is almost as bad as bullets to undercover outfits like this who are trying to take over a whole union. I hope young Jordan's story gets them lambasted all over every front page in the country. He's certainly got a swell beat, and he's plenty, nervy too. The way he yelled about Russia's attack on Finland when that speaker told of Russia's great peace aspirations, was something I'll remember a long time. Well—he's safe now, and we're on our way back for a night's rest. I hope."

Carol let him out near the garden entrance to Quinn's estate. Then she drove the car to a garage, and walked slowly home. She passed by a small store, run by a blind man named Higgins.

Carol bought everything she could there, knowing exactly what handicaps Higgins was under to make a living any other way.

"It's Miss Carol, isn't it?" Higgins asked from behind the counter, eyes blankly staring. "I've grown to recognize your step."

"Yes, it's I," she replied.

Carol made her purchases, leaned against the counter and spent a few minutes chatting.

"Did you ever go for your eye examination?" she asked.

Higgins shrugged. "What's the use? They say I'll never see again. I suppose that's so, but I'll have the examination some day. Costs a lot of money, though, and gives little satisfaction. Thanks for your business, Miss Carol. Good night."

CHAPTER IX

THE PEACE LEAGUE

IN THE morning, when the newspapers were delivered, Silk looked in vain for some mention of the secret meeting which the Black Bat had smashed. There was none. Tony Quinn, eating the toast, scrambled eggs and bacon which Silk had prepared, said nothing for a moment or two.

"It is odd," he admitted finally. "Jordan should have got that story printed in spite of the devil, and high water—unless someone higher up killed it. If that's the case, somebody would have had to kill Jordan as well, because that boy wouldn't take having a story like that passed up. Silk, phone Carol and have her prowl around the *News-Globe*. Find out if Ted Jordan is still on the staff, and if he has been seen this morning, or even last night. Get all the dope possible about him."

Silk hurried to phone while Tony Quinn's utterly blank eyes stared into space unwinkingly. Behind them a shrewd, smoothly functioning brain went over the case. The reason for the murder of the two sailor brothers was now obvious to him. They had known too much. Perhaps Frank, the elder, had half-heartedly agreed to join the forces of destruction within his union. Joey, the younger boy, probably had refused. They had tried to kill Joey, so Frank had protected him until both died by violence. Neither of them could have provided much information. Underlings were permitted to know little of what actually went on.

After the meeting which the Black Bat had secretly attended, he knew what the motives of those people were. While they preached equality and division of wealth, they privately were ambitious to be rich and powerful themselves, raised far above the average person. They worked for their own benefit, using the masses to that end.

The Black Bat had given much study to the subject, and was assured that the Russian peasant today is no better off than when he lived under the rule of the Czar. The same starvation, the same ignorance, the same high-handed authority. The only difference lay in the fact that under Communist supervision punishment comes faster and harder. Naturally that goes for their allies who are helping things along—the Nazi and Fascist spies.

Silk returned and refilled Quinn's coffee cup. Quinn sipped the fragrant beverage and shook his head.

"They are up to something big in this country, Silk," he said slowly. "And the painful part is that the American union leaders—the actual ones—haven't the faintest inkling what it really is. They work cleverly—their agents obey orders without asking or knowing why. Then, when everything is ready, they spring their coup, and it's usually too late to stop them. One thing to remember, Silk—Russia has a pact with the Axis powers. The pact isn't worth a cancelled one-cent stamp, but they'll abide by its terms until one or the other sees a chance to do some knife sticking. Russia's organizations, in this country, have been at work longer than have the Nazi and Fascist organizations, but they're all equally snaky, and must be stopped before they can do real damage to us."

Silk sighed and cleared the table. "Yes, sir. Butch had some literature which he picked up in the rooms of those murdered sailors. I read a couple of the pamphlets—as much as I could without becoming ill, anyway. They certainly have aspirations, sir. Do you think they've a chance of taking over the maritime unions—the regularly recognized labor groups?"

Tony Quinn lit a cigarette and took a long puff on it.

"They have gone far enough now, Silk, to suit their ulterior purposes. And we must discover the identity of their head man in this country. Quite likely he's someone who stays in the background and professes to be something so radically different from these termites that he'd never be suspected. And he may have a motive of his own—other than helping Moscow or the Axis powers."

THE DOORBELL buzzed. Quinn didn't move. Silk admitted Police Commissioner Warner and a stranger. Warner was a lean, active type who supervised the police department with an efficiency that surpassed that of all his predecessors. He and Tony Quinn had become fast friends when Quinn had had his eyesight and been district attorney.

Warner's companion was equally slender, and taller than the commissioner by half a head. He wore gold-rimmed glasses and continually squinted over the top of them which made him cock his head oddly. He was pleasant-looking, suave and wore expensive clothing—all of which details Silk quickly took in.

Quinn started to arise, his features wrinkled in an unspoken question.

"I know it's you, Commissioner, but there is someone with you. Someone whose step I have never heard before. Would you and your friend join me in a cup of coffee?"

They would, and Warner introduced his companion.

"I want you to know Samuel Barnett, Tony. You've heard of him as an international banker, but he has resigned to head the League for Worldwide Peace. He's looking for contributions, and I told him you were an easy mark."

Quinn fumbled around, and Barnett hastily moved the sugar bowl toward him.

"Thank you," Quinn said. "Warner is right too—I am a pushover for things of that sort. Peace movements don't seem to get far these days, but they are worthy in their objectives. I'll be glad to donate."

Warner lit a cigar and leaned back comfortably.

"Looks as though we need some kind of a peace movement of our own around town, Tony. The whole city is filled with talk of impending strikes. Business men are frantic, but hardly more so than the union leaders who are bewildered, declaring they know nothing about the trouble. The whole affair is so general that I've been wondering who the guiding genius behind it all can be. I've had to cancel all police leaves and order my men to stand ready for riot duty."

Sam Barnett was more cheerful.

"Nonsense, Commissioner. Why, in a country like ours there will always be strikes. I doubt if there can be any hidden reasons behind the recent ones. Or hidden people either."

Silk brought a checkbook, filled in a check, and guided Tony's hand to the pen. Barnett was volubly grateful. Warner stepped close to Quinn as Silk escorted the Peace League official to the door.

"Heard the Bat handed out a bad steer last night. The Federals are a little hot about it, and McGrath looks like the cat who just ate the canary." He smiled. "Of course you know nothing of the Black Bat's activities—I thought you'd be interested."

Warner grinned and bent over Quinn. He spoke in a voice, too low for Barnett to hear.

"What I told you about strikes was more or less vague. However, there is the very devil to pay among the maritime workers. I've heard rumors about a strike on the Merchant Line. That would be a serious blow to the country's defense, Tony. The line hauls much of the ore we need, and handles a great deal of the raw material business with South America.... Good-by, Tony. Perhaps I'll drop by soon to talk over old times—and maybe the present."

SILK'S EYES were narrowed as he closed the door.

"What did he mean by that, sir?"

Quinn laughed. "You know Warner thinks I might be the Black Bat, and comes here on all kinds of excuses—by the way, this one cost me money—so he can talk. The mention he just made of a rumored maritime strike gives me a direct lead. Warner isn't sure whether or not I'm the Bat, but he doesn't like to overlook any possibilities. He knows his department can't start investigating strike rumors, but that the Black Bat goes to work in his own cute little manner.... Study our files, will you, Silk, on what we have about the Merchant Lines. I think a man named Freuling owns it. If I'm not mistaken, he used to be a German subject. But he would be serving his Fatherland in a weird capacity wouldn't he, by destroying his own business?" He sighed heavily. "Oh, well! Some Nazis would do anything for a couple of *heils*.... Silk, it looks as if we might be busy tonight. I'd better clean my artillery."

Carol came in the middle of the afternoon. She had little to report.

"Ted Jordan has worked for the *News-Globe* more than three years," she told Tony Quinn, "and is one of their nerviest reporters. He came to work this morning, went on some assignment covering the fraudulent sale of chickens in retail markets. I've followed him around until I've got chicken feathers in my teeth. He wrote nothing about that meeting last night. In fact, he casually informed a talkative telephone operator in the office that he went to bed early and slept like a log."

"But why?" Quinn frowned. "A reporter, with a great yarn, doesn't stop at anything. And now Jordan, known to be nervy, drops something sensationally red hot. That young man will bear a nice little investigation. The pressure has been put on him somehow, and if the press can be muzzled, the power of those rats is greater than we think. I wonder why Butch hasn't appeared?"

"He called me early this morning and said he was headed for the waterfront," Carol said. "He thought perhaps he might pick up some scraps of information from his pals down there, but my belief is that he's hoping he'll spot one of the men who kidnaped him last night. If we read about the police finding a man apparently crushed by a steam-roller—then Butch has been working."

Butch didn't appear until a few moments before the Black Bat was ready to merge with the darkness outside. Butch looked grim and somewhat disgusted.

"Trouble's ready to bust around the waterfront," he said. "I dunno when it'll start, but it's stewin' up, and about ready to boil over. It won't be no picnic either. I heard the company won't give in an inch and some of the union guys talkin' about wreckin' their docks and warehouses and ships. Foreigners mostly, Boss. They figure it'll happen maybe sometime tomorrow mornin'. Say, Boss, if there ain't anythin' special for me to do, I'd like to be down there. You know—just to sort of look around and maybe get in a sock or two at some of them lugs."

"Get back there right away," Quinn ordered. "Eat there, sleep there. Keep your eyes open every second. As soon as things look ready to pop, call Silk or Carol. If this thing is to be nipped, it must be done promptly."

QUINN DONNED his regalia. He was well aware that a strike of the proportions Butch had suggested might stir up a bloody riot. It had to be stopped before it started, and the logical thing to do was to visit Hans Freuling and convince him of that. The group inside the union with which he battled might be working in direct opposition to their own actual bosses, but that would make no difference in the eventual bloody outcome. If Freuling was no fool, he should be willing to give in until a careful check could be made.

Quinn left the house through the tunnel, and hurried to the coupé that was always parked on a street not far away, waiting for him. He drove straight to the vicinity of Freuling's home, left the coupé around the corner, and quietly invaded an estate adjoining that of the ship owner's.

The intense darkness didn't impede the Black Bat. He stepped over objects which would have tripped a person with normal sight. Reaching the back of Freuling's home he saw that an expensive roadster was parked in the driveway. A glance at Freuling's garages showed they were full, which meant that he probably had a guest.

Two minutes later the Black Bat saw that guest. Brad Gibbons—the armaments manufacturer who had struck up a brief acquaintance with Tony Quinn on shipboard! Freuling was accompanying him to a small side porch where Gibbons said good night, then got behind the wheel of the roadster.

"I'll meet you at noon then," Gibbons called. "We'll arrange things satisfactorily—don't worry."

Freuling stepped off the porch and for a moment talked to Gibbons in a low voice. Neither man noticed the black spectre that filtered past and vanished into the house. Freuling returned to his study after Gibbons drove away, sat down with a sigh, and began tapping the surface of his desk.

"You're nervous, Mr. Freuling," a voice said softly. "Can it be that you expect trouble?"

Freuling's impassive face turned a shade whiter. He arose slowly and turned around. Typically Prussian, he had to fight the urge to call for help. This black-hooded, wing-caped figure he saw would have been eerie even in full light, but in this room illuminated only by a small desk lamp, the shadowed figure was even more sinister and weird.

"You are the Black Bat," Freuling said, "What do you want with me?"

"Sit down," the Black Bat answered, and moved around directly opposite the ship owner. One of the hooded man's big guns rested on the desk and his gloved hand never strayed far from the butt.

"I'm here to help you—if I can," the Black Bat said. "It depends upon you. There are evil forces at work, Mr. Freuling. Forces about which the average person knows little. Until a short time ago, for instance, your firm dealt with the leaders of a union with whom you could negotiate properly. Suddenly you discovered that other so-called 'leaders' had cropped up right within the union itself, and they were disregarding the commands of the real leaders, and making demands on you—impossible demands. Am I right?"

"Yes—yes, that is the truth. If I paid the wages and permitted the laxity of discipline those men demand, I would be forced to give up my business."

"Exactly. So now you've learned they plan a campaign of terror which will tie your vessels up and scare the owners of other lines. Now—just what are your intentions regarding the strike?"

FREULING DID not seem to welcome the idea of confiding in the Black Bat. "That hardly seems to be any of your business," he declared. "I do not deal with men who hide behind masks. How do I know you are not an emissary from that blasted bunch of Communist and Nazi rats?"

"You don't." The Black Bat shrugged. "Yet I have a reputation for fair dealing. My motives are only to see justice done. I need coöperation and you can give it. Will you fight any strike by so-called members of the Independent Maritime Alliance that you are in nowise sure has been called by the real leaders? In fact, for which they flatly deny responsibility?"

Freuling looked at those eyes, gleaming from behind the mask.

"A strike will be a serious blow," he said. "I might lose my contracts to haul ore from South America and war supplies from the United States. Tomorrow an arms manufacturer and I are to close one of the biggest deals of my career. I am afraid of the strike—but if it comes I will not grant their impossible demands. I'll simply close up until all the men agree to return under present conditions—which happen to be at least equal to those of any other firm."

The Black Bat slid his gun into its holster. "To learn that was the sole purpose of my coming," he said. "Thank you for confiding in me."

Stepping over to a window, the Black Bat raised it, and it looked to Freuling as though he melted into thin air.

Less than twenty seconds later one whole section of Freuling's house was blasted into ruins.

CHAPTER X

McGRATH MAKES A PINCH

RUNNING LIGHTLY away, the Black Bat was hurled forward by the force of the terrific blast. Debris fell all around him and automatically he covered the back of his head with his hands until the deadly rain stopped.

Then he leaped to his feet and sprinted back to the house. He felt his nerves go numb with horror. The entire side of the building was beginning to blaze up. That bomb had been a combination incendiary and explosive.

Smashing a window, the Black Bat crawled through, and coughed as acrid smoke assailed his lungs. There was one solitary hope for Freuling. If he had walked to the window through which the Black Bat had exited, there was a chance that he still lived, for that particular portion of the room had not been leveled.

Fighting his way through the quickly mounting flames, the clouds of smoke and the debris, the Black Bat reached what was left of the room in which he had interviewed Freuling. The ceiling was down, two walls had been blown out, the floor caved in toward the front of the house and furniture had been blasted to bits. That bomb had not been the work of an amateur. Hitler's *Luftwaffe* could not have been much more thorough.

The Black Bat knew he had only seconds, for once an alarm went in, he would be forced to leave, and fire fighters and police would concentrate on putting out the flames before determining if any victim was imprisoned beneath the debris.

A groan reached the Black Bat's ears. Freuling *had* gone to the window. With all speed the Black Bat clambered over wreckage of the shattered room until he saw an arm protruding from the debris of the ceiling. He pulled at the wreckage until he had uncovered half of Freuling's body. The man was unconscious, bleeding from several bad wounds.

The fire was all around as the Black Bat labored. Flames licked at his cloak and he beat them out. He could feel his flesh become hot and dry under the intense heat, yet he kept on until Freuling was freed. The Black Bat picked the man up, turned to face a wall of living fire that seemed to leap at him. Covering Freuling's face with a portion of his cloak, the Black Bat surged ahead. Once he almost fell over a piece of wrecked furniture. In spite of his uncanny sight in darkness, smoke formed a barrier through which even he could not see.

He heard the distant wail of the first siren just as he reached what was left of the front of the house, raced to the sidewalk and gently laid his burden down. Freuling would be promptly discovered here.

A police emergency truck and a fire department hose wagon rolled up. Powerful searchlights swept over the scene. The man behind the light on the police truck thought he had seen a will-o'-the-wisp for a moment. Something that moved as fast as the eye could follow streaked across the path of the searchlight, then vanished completely.

The Black Bat whipped off his hood and replaced it with his hat when he reached his parked car. He started the motor, endured a cold sweat as two radio cars whizzed by him, then he quickly headed for the vicinity of his home.

AS HE maneuvered the car through the less busy streets, taking a roundabout route, he was thinking. Gibbons had been the last visitor at Freuling's home. Could a man in Gibbons' position stoop so low as to plant a deadly bomb? Would he do that anyway on the eve of a contract with Freuling to haul his armaments to South America? Of course the bomb might have been planted days before. Timing was perfect enough for that, but the Black Bat had his doubts. In a private home like Freuling's, servants knew every nook and cranny. Anything out of the ordinary would attract their attention.

The Black Bat stopped the coupé, made sure he was unobserved, and got out. He ran lightly toward the garden gate leading into his estate. As he passed through it, a dark form arose, and the Black Bat's hand darted toward his holstered guns. But it was Silk.

"What in the world has happened?" Silk demanded anxiously. "Your clothes—they're burned!"

"And you've brought me fresh ones out here?" The Bat frowned. "What's the idea. Silk?"

"It's McGrath! He showed up less than two minutes ago. He rang the bell, kicked the door and even banged on a window, but I didn't let him in. He's thoroughly mad this time, and he sat down on the porch as if he's ready to stay there all night if necessary."

The Black Bat whistled, stepped into the garden house and peeled off his regalia. He donned the suit Silk had brought, put on topcoat, muffler and dark glasses, and picked up his cane.

"I see you're prepared as if we were taking a walk," he said to Silk. "Good! We'll circle the block quickly. We have been out for air—have been gone about half an hour. And no matter what happens, don't show any surprise. Unless I'm wrong, McGrath is going to pull a fast one tonight. I had some trouble. McGrath must have reached the scene, talked to someone I left there, and then come rushing here. When he found us gone, he jumped to conclusions. We've got to change those ideas of his, Silk."

They ambled slowly down the street. Silk held Tony Quinn's arm and the apparent blind man tapped his cane occasionally. McGrath muttered a curse as he saw them coming. He drew back into the deeper shadows of the porch. McGrath's face had never been more grim.

Quinn and Silk mounted the steps. Silk unlocked the door. Quinn sighed deeply.

"We must do that every night, Silk. I used to like darkness until it became so permanent. There's something about night air. Refreshing and clean. Well—help me over the doorstep, and some day remind me to have it removed."

Suddenly Silk gave a start of surprise and grabbed Quinn's arm.

"What is it?" Quinn's voice rose shrilly.

"Just relax, smart guy." Captain McGrath stepped up, a gun in his hand. "Silk, lift 'em! You too, Quinn. This is a pinch. The Black Bat has always been a pretty decent sort of guy. Sometimes I admired him; even though I didn't want to. But tonight he planted a bomb in a man's home—the most vicious thing any rat could do. And there's no mistake about it either. By some miracle his victim didn't die. He was blown out of the house and clear of the wreckage. When he recovered consciousness he told who must have done the trick. *You,* Tony Quinn, alias the Black Bat! When I came here, I'll admit I hoped you'd be home, but you weren't. Now even Commissioner Warner can't stop me. I'm going to have two of the best eye doctors in the city come down here as fast as they can travel. They'll look you over and we'll settle this once and for all."

QUINN'S FACE showed none of the anxiety he felt. This was the one thing he had always prayed would not happen—that McGrath wouldn't get steamed up enough to insist upon an examination. There was a chance that Quinn might fool specialists, but he could not be sure.

McGrath searched both men, above Silk's strident protests. He forced them into the house, ordered them to sit down in Quinn's library while he checked the phone numbers of two specialists, and insisted on their coming here, at once, in the name of the law. When he hung up, he faced Quinn.

"We been playing cat and mouse too long," he snapped. "I believe you're the Black Bat and if you can see, I'll be sure of it. That means a pinch for attempted murder. Of course if you want to come clean, I'll use my influence—"

Quinn laughed dryly. "In a way I'm glad you decided to go through with this, McGrath. You realize, of course, that if you're wrong, I can sue. I can demand your shield, and probably get it. You're pretty sure of yourself or you'd never go this far." McGrath crossed his legs and looked complacent.

"I'll say I'm sure. A guy can't be suspicious twenty-four hours a day for a couple of years with nothing to back it up. Oh, no, Tony Quinn, this has been coming for a long time. I just never had a good enough reason to do it, but now an important man makes the accusations about the Black Bat, and to me that's the same as putting the finger on Tony Quinn. The docs will be here in half an hour or so. Then we'll see."

Silk let one hand touch Quinn's thigh. His finger tapped a message. "What'll we do?"

Quinn, cane between his knees, began tapping it nervously. Silk read the signals. "Don't know. Follow my lead."

"Captain," Tony Quinn said, "if there is that much time, do you mind if I clean up a bit? With Silk's help, of course. Whether you believe it or not, I am blind,"

"Go ahead." McGrath arose. "I'll trail along to see you don't clean yourself right out of the house and the town too." Then McGrath had an attack of uneasiness. "Boy, will Commissioner Warner be sore if I'm wrong!"

"What he'll feel will be nothing compared to me," Silk roared. "Your only chance is to change your mind—now—before those doctors get here!"

McGrath licked his lips. "Nope. I'll see it through to the finish whether I'm wrong, or not."

As they left the study, there was a faint click. Quinn heard it because his ears were super-sensitive. It sounded as though the secret door of the laboratory had been open a crack, and had been closed softly.

Now he had another worry. Who could have discovered that hidden room? Tony Quinn's nightmares had all been filled with such moments as this, when everything went wrong. McGrath could not prove, beyond reasonable doubt, that Quinn was the Black Bat, but if he could prove that Tony Quinn was not blind, that his life as a helpless man was just a sham, then steps might be taken to make a complete inspection.

The tunnel, the lab, everything would be found—and cell doors would yawn. This would mean the finish of the Black Bat.

CHAPTER XI

COLD-DECKED

SOMEONE RANG the doorbell thirty-odd minutes later. McGrath looked out the upstairs window.

"Let's go," he snapped. "The doctors are here. How does it feel, Quinn, to reach the end of your rope, eh? Remember all those times when you kidded the life out of me—you with those Black Bat stickers you pasted all over everything?"

Quinn walked slowly toward the head of the stairs and calmly waited until Silk appeared to help him down. Before McGrath reached the door, the phone rang. Silk answered it, and led Quinn over to the instrument. McGrath hesitated. He wanted to admit the doctors, but he also wanted to keep Quinn constantly in sight.

The telephone conversation was short. Quinn merely grunted a couple of times, then said:

"At the moment I'm not particularly interested in cars. Yes, I know I promised to take a ride in one but later, man. I'm occupied just now."

Quinn hung up, turned, and looked vaguely about three feet to the left of where McGrath stood.

"Captain, I'll wait for your doctors in the study, if you don't mind. The shades there can completely darken the room. Your specialists will insist upon that. I ought to know—having seen enough of them during the past few years."

"Go ahead." McGrath moved toward the door. "But Silk stays with me. This is one time he won't pull any of his smooth tricks."

Silk lowered the shades in the study and returned to the living room where McGrath was giving instructions to the specialists. They were eminent men and would do a proper job. Silk knew this, and suddenly knew how a condemned man felt when the procession marched up to his cell door.

"The examination will require about thirty minutes," one doctor said. "You will please see that we are not disturbed, Captain."

They marched into the darkened study. The door closed and Silk's heartbreak vigil began. It was no serene half hour for McGrath either. He kept pacing the floor and scowling at Silk. Both could hear the low hum of voices in the study.

Silk had never been in prison, but he was visualizing how a cell must become after about ten years. He tried to figure out some means of warning Carol and Butch. The moment McGrath knew that Quinn was not blind, he would go to town. If the Bat's other two aides blundered into the house, then they would be taken, too. His utter helplessness made Silk writhe.

Lights flashed beneath the door where the examination was going on. McGrath peeled cellophane from a cigar and bit the tip so hard his teeth came together with a click. He lit it, took half a dozen puffs, then waved the cigar to emphasize his words.

"This is on the level, Silk—you understand that. Those doctors don't know Quinn. They have never examined him before. He can't influence them as he might doctors he chose himself. But they won't say he can see when he can't either. I'm trying to be fair."

Silk coughed. "If you have to wave your cigar under my nose, I wish you'd buy good ones. And, Captain, you talk as though I'm worried. Take a look at me, then face the mirror behind you. See who looks the most agitated. You're practically on the verge of a breakdown now, so what'll you be like when Commissioner Warner calls you into his office? I understand there's a plenty worn carpet in front of his desk from saps like you being on it."

BEFORE McGRATH could growl an answer, the door of the study opened. Both doctors emerged. They drew on gloves and one of them spoke to McGrath.

"We can't quite understand how you even suspected this man is not blind. We gave him every test. He cannot see now—he will never be able to see again. No treatment, no surgery could help him, and that's final. To whom do we send the bill?"

"The bill?" Silk gloated. "Oh, send it to Captain McGrath at Police Headquarters. I don't think the city will pay it. In fact, I doubt the city will ever get it, but McGrath isn't a poor man. He can pay nicely too. Good evening, gentlemen."

As Silk hurriedly escorted the doctors to the door, McGrath slumped in a chair, bent over, holding his head between his hands.

"I just can't understand it," he kept muttering. "I—wait a minute!" He jumped up and headed for the study. "Maybe this was a fast play and I been cold-decked. Maybe Quinn wasn't examined at all."

He skidded to a halt as he entered the room. Quinn sat in a straight-backed chair, staring straight ahead. His features were grim. McGrath gulped.

"I—guess maybe I was wrong. I—don't know what to say, Quinn, but you can't blame me too much. I was so sure. I.... Well, what are you going to do about it? Warner will cut my heart out for this and by the look on your face.... Oh, what's the use? I slipped, and I'll pay for it."

"Wait, Captain," Quinn said in a steady voice. "The look on my face isn't that of anger. You see, I had possessed some faint glimmers of hope that one day my eyes might be healed. I wanted to be examined, but I was afraid I'd blast that hope. Well, those two doctors blasted it all right. To put it mildly, they were rather blunt."

McGrath's color began to mount.

"I—I'm sorry. That's all I can say. Anyhow, if you had been the Black Bat, I'm not sure I could have made the pinch. So I'll get out of your house, Quinn. You won't have to report me to Warner. I'll look him up right now and take my medicine."

"But why?" Quinn asked, and arose slowly. Silk instantly was at his side. "I—feel a trifle weak. Captain, would you mind—my other arm? I think I'd better go upstairs and lie down."

McGrath jumped to help lead Quinn to his bedroom. Inside the room, Tony Quinn stuck his hand out in McGrath's general direction.

"We'll just call the whole thing a total loss," he said, with a queer smile. "You're disappointed, and so am I. In a way, you've done me a favor—forced an examination upon me so I'd know the truth once and for all. I will make no mention of this to Commissioner Warner, and I hold no grudge in your behalf, Captain."

McGrath half stumbled down the stairs. His own sight was a little foggy when he left Quinn's house and sent the department cruiser rolling toward his own home in the suburbs. The bungalow was dark, for his wife was away. McGrath stopped in front of the garage doors and blew his nose violently.

"The trouble with me," he said half aloud, "is my suspicions. And maybe I've been wrong about the Black Bat. He has helped me plenty of times and I owe him something for that. If only he wouldn't tantalize me with those blamed stickers—"

McGRATH STARTED to open the garage door. Something impeded the passage of the key into the lock. He squinted, then his face turned beet-red. A Black Bat sticker was pasted over the lock. That was just the beginning. Inside the house, McGrath found the stickers everywhere—pasted on mirrors, on doorknobs, on dishes and furniture. Even the pillows on his bed had a couple pasted there....

Back at Tony Quinn's house, Silk had raced back upstairs the moment he had closed the door behind McGrath, and tried to find his voice. Quinn grinned at him.

"So you wonder how it was done. Simple, Silk. McGrath was right—he was cold-decked. You see, Carol happened to be in the lab. She heard McGrath make his accusations, heard his telephone call to the doctors—and Carol used her head. I'm not certain of all details yet, or how she managed it, but when I entered the study, I simply stepped into a closet where Carol was hidden with a man who was really blind. She put him in the chair to wait for the doctors, and I hid in the closet. After the doctors went out, I changed places with the blind man, and got McGrath to help me upstairs so Carol would have a chance to whisk her blind man out the back door. She'll be here soon."

Silk collapsed on the edge of the bed.

"What a girl!" he said fervently. "No kidding—I'm ten years older. With all due respect to your judgment, sir, why did you let McGrath get away with it?"

Quinn laughed softly. "After all, put yourself in his place. I am the Black Bat, and he has suspected that up until now. That's his job. And, Silk, it gives the game just a little more spice, don't you think? We'd probably have had a dull evening if Mac hadn't shown up."

"Maybe." Silk was still mopping his face. "But give me the dull evenings."

Quinn looked serious. "To change the subject now, Silk, I've had little time to tell you what happened to me." Hastily, and briefly, he recounted what had occurred at the Freuling house. "Brad Gibbons, whom we met on the boat from Bermuda, visited Freuling about some contract or other," he added. "He could have planted a bomb—a small, but powerful one which might be carried in a pocket. It certainly was powerful whatever its size. You should have seen what it did to Freuling's house.

"Freuling accuses the Black Bat of the bombing. Naturally he would be suspicious of a masked man who had just interviewed him, but the fact is, I saved his life. I put him on the walk in front of his house, and he thinks he was blown there by the explosion. We have problems, Silk. I haven't forgotten our blondined friend on board ship, either, nor the murder of those Adams boys and the ship's doctor. Ted Jordan, that reporter on the *News-Globe*, is another mystery. He risked his life to get a story, and hasn't kicked up a row because it wasn't printed."

THERE WERE light footsteps on the staircase. Carol Baldwin, radiant because she had won a battle against McGrath's attempted coup, came in. Quinn made no pretense of being blind now. He held her closely for tense moments while Silk looked at the ceiling, the floor, the walls, and finally closed his eyes.

"Now tell me how you worked it," Quinn insisted to Carol.

Carol sat down. "I heard McGrath phone the doctors and of course I knew what it might mean. I remembered a blind storekeeper, named Higgins, whom I know fairly well. He has often spoken to me about having his eyes examined again, even though he has been told he would never see. I went down to his store—not far from here—and told him if he came with me at once, I could have two of the best specialists in the city make the examination and that I'd pay for it. He was more than eager to oblige. I dialed the phone number of this house and had my blind friend talk until you got on the wire, Tony. Just in case McGrath answered. Then I told you what I was about to try. You lured McGrath upstairs and I brought the blind man into the study through the back door."

"But your blind friend—didn't he become suspicious?" Silk asked.

"He accepted my word that he was being taken into the home of a doctor and that he would be examined there," Carol said. "I warned him to say little, and to answer only questions about his eyes. Tony hid in the closet with me. After the examination I had a moment or two in which to hurry Higgins into the lab. Tony took his place in the study and McGrath was completely deceived. After Tony got McGrath upstairs again, I led my friend out the back door and took him to his store. He doesn't feel bad about what the doctors told him. He knew there was no chance of his seeing again, but welcomed a free examination just the same. He hasn't the vaguest idea that he substituted for someone else."

"That McGrath," Silk grumbled. "I still think he should have been taught a lesson. He'll stop suspecting you, sir—but not for long. Next time he might be luckier."

Carol's silvery laugh rang out.

"I thought myself that McGrath should be punished some way, so I beat him to his home. I pasted so many stickers around that McGrath must have nothing but black bats before his eyes right now!"

CHAPTER XII

LEADER UNKNOWN

WHILE **TONY QUINN** and Silk were engaged with their own problems, events moved fast in other quarters. Not far from the waterfront was a fairly large book store specializing in second-hand volumes. Its shelves extended deep into the store and they were none too well lighted. A woman wearing shell-rimmed glasses sat behind a cashier's cage. Two other women served as clerks. All three were middle-aged and serious-looking.

A man entered, nodded to the woman at the cashier's desk, then began studying the shelves of books. Finally he walked over to one of the clerks.

"Have you a copy of *The New Civilization?*" he asked.

The woman shrugged. "You might find one far down the store—at the very rear."

The man headed in that direction. Within five minutes another customer entered and made the same request. He also vanished down that long corridor lined with books. More than an hour went by. Both clerks walked up to the cashier.

"We have counted eighteen, which is the total for tonight."

The cashier slowly closed a drawer and gave a sigh of relief. There had been a loaded automatic at her fingertips in that drawer.

"It checks," she said. "The meeting will take hardly more than an hour, so we must wait and keep the store open. They have much work to accomplish tonight. The time is not far off now. We, who have sacrificed so much, will come into our own."

Each of the men who had requested that book had passed through a faded, dusty velvet drape at the end of the corridor. Each had walked along a narrow hall and down a flight of rickety steps. At the bottom each had been stopped by two armed men who had thrown a flashlight beam into his face before waving him on.

Now, in a small room, ceilinged with pipes for water and gas, were the eighteen chosen men. Commissar B. Blinov was there, his eyes swollen shut except for small slits. Vanin, who had risen from a horse doctor to a physician in his own land, toyed with his ever present stethoscope. When the last man appeared, Blinov, standing behind a cheap, splinter-edged desk, raised his hand for attention.

"Tonight," he said, "we are in executive session. You will hear the voice of the man who has been appointed to lead us. The usual procedure will be followed, and any who disobeys shall be instantly shot. We are now ready."

Someone turned out all lights, except a dim one above the desk. Blinov and Vanin joined the others as all turned and faced the rear wall of the room. Blinov clapped his hands smartly. Someone walked across the room with brisk, firm steps, but none could see him. A voice, bitter and stern addressed them.

"The strike has been fully prepared. Demands have been made on that fool Freuling by our own selected leaders, even though he is in a hospital. The man is more obstinate than ever—which is in full accordance with our hopes and plans. In spite of the protests of the leaders of the Independent Maritime Alliance we are now strong to take matters in our own hands, so have ignored them and ordered a general strike to begin in the morning with a walkout. The workers will be instructed to leave quietly and return just before the beginning of the afternoon shift to form picket lines.

"During that time they will be properly exhorted to resent the presence of scabs or finks. Meanwhile, you of the executive council will have done your work. The men selected by you will act according to your instructions—that is, if you have told them fluently enough what the consequences of refusal may mean. Are there any questions?"

VANIN SPOKE without moving a muscle.

"The returning strikers will find the scabs we have chosen taking their places. There is bound to be bloodshed—much of it."

"And what do you think I have spent my time perfecting this scheme for?" the Unknown shouted angrily. "Of course there will be bloodshed. I hope at least a dozen men are killed. From this battle will grow the nucleus of strikes all over the waterfront. The fools of workers will fight because they are told to. It isn't necessary to tell them any reason except that Freuling's company hired strike breakers, armed them with guns and knives and ordered the murder of union members. It always works—such a plan.

"Within forty-eight hours we shall have the waterfront paralyzed in a strike which no negotiation can break, because as the government gets its conciliators here, we shall stage more violence. You all know our aims. Those below you in rank have been informed we work only for their good. Let them keep thinking this. It is not a sign of strength to allow riff-raff to know what we intend. Now remain as you are, for five minutes. Then Blinov and Vanin will give the detailed orders."

Blinov took command after the unknown and unseen director of death had made his exit. Blinov was no less deadly.

"All of you have the proper photographs," he said. "You know the names of those who will become our scab workers in the morning. Many have already been told what will happen if they disobey. The others must be informed tonight—and shown plainly by those pictures. Arrangements have been already made to plant some of our trusted men among these stupid fools. They will be armed with loaded clubs, knives and a few guns. Others, with identical orders, will be a part of the picket line. At the proper moment a small fight will start. It will grow into a pitched battle. If the police interfere, knives are to be used.

"And one thing further. We can now be certain that the Black Bat knows nothing about our plans. We have taken extreme precautions. However, should he be seen anywhere, at any time, he is to be promptly killed, unless there is a chance to break his skull. Should we be able to take him alive, then I promise you we will all hear some amusing cries for mercy. That is all. You will leave as you came—singly—through the book store. Remember that tomorrow is our day, that success means we'll soon control this gold mine of a country—and use it as we see fit."

The eighteen members of this inner circle filed out. One of them, Sorokin by name, followed his orders exactly as did the others. He visited a shabby tenement house, climbed dark stairs to a fourth floor cold-water flat and banged on the door. A woman, carrying a baby in her arms, let him in. She said nothing, but in her eyes was sullen hatred.

Her husband, sitting woodenly in a rickety chair, listened without protest to Sorokin until he was told to smash the head of at least one man on the picket line. This he stubbornly refused to do. Sorokin took an envelope from his pocket, and extracted a snapshot which he laid on the table. It showed an old man crumbling, after being riddled with the bullets of a firing squad. The wall behind him was bloodstained and pock-marked from the almost constant hail of bullets it had checked. There was no mistaking the features of the victim either.

THE OBSTINATE tenement dweller moaned and covered his eyes as Sorokin put the picture back into his pocket.

"Yes—it was your father. He refused to obey those who know what is best. And, in case you grow forgetful, there is still your mother, your three brothers and two sisters. But of course you do not wish to be responsible for the death of your own people. Go then, and obey me. The police will not touch you, for we will see to it that they have no proof.

Then—perhaps—we may let you send a letter home, eh? And receive one too."

Sorokin smiled benignly, and left, for like the others, he had many visits to make. In fact he had been so busy the past ten days, doing just this kind of work that it became routine. Even women's tears were routine, and Sorokin took a sadistic delight in showing those pictures.

One of his last calls was made at a tenement house sandwiched between two towering warehouses. He marched up the dark stairs and when someone came down, Sorokin didn't move out of the way. His ego had been too greatly inflated by the kowtowing people he had intimidated for that. He thought everyone would bow, but the hulk of a man coming down these steps was not in the habit of bowing.

Sorokin bumped shoulders with Butch O'Leary.

"Lout," Sorokin snarled, glaring, "get out of my way."

Suddenly Sorokin discovered that it was not the house that had collapsed and left him standing in midair, but that a giant hand held him suspended. Blinking into the wide face of his captor, Sorokin decided he had been a little too hasty.

"I dunno what lout means," Butch said, "but it sounds an awful lot like somethin' else that ain't me or maybe you'd like to argue about it, huh?"

"No—oh, no!" Sorokin managed to say. "Let me down! I am choking to death. Let me down!"

"Sure," Butch agreed. "Why didn't you say so before?"

He let go of the man's collar and Sorokin went tumbling down the steps. At the bottom he arose, his face contorted in a mask of hatred. Butch was ambling down the steps. Sorokin definitely did not use his wits now, for he reached into his pocket, removed a knife and pressed a button on the handle. The blade snapped into place, a long, sleek, razor-edged weapon of destruction.

Before he could get the knife into position for use, Butch came sailing through the air. Naked steel roused an animal instinct in Butch. He possessed a hatred that bordered on an insane rage for any man who tried to use a knife.

Sorokin went down. The knife flew into a corner, and Sorokin passed out cold. Butch arose, brushing his hands as though he had touched something contaminating. In the mêlée, the contents of Sorokin's pockets had been strewn on the floor. Butch picked up several of those blood-curdling pictures. He studied them in the weak light, thrust them into his pocket and picked Sorokin up by the vest. He held him erect and slapped the man back to consciousness. Then he knocked him cold once more with a smashing punch to the jaw.

"Now," Butch said, "I feel better."

Doors opened on the floors above and necks were craned over the stairwell. One man on the third floor came running down.

"What happened, Butch?" he asked. "Did somebody try to stick you up?"

"Slit me up makes more sense," Butch responded. "See that shiv in the corner? He musta thought I was a side of beef.... Say, you acted funny upstairs, Benny. Not like the old pal I used to know. How come you kicked me out on my ear? In a nice way o' course, but it sure was the bum's rush."

THE MAN called Benny had worked with Butch years before and they had been fast friends before Benny married and settled down. Butch, in the course of a careful investigation of conditions at the waterfront, was contacting all his former friends and pumping them for information when he could. Benny, once as voluble as a phonograph, had shut his lips tightly at the first mention of the word "union."

Benny looked over at the huddled form of Butch's victim. His sudden cry held more of fear than surprise. He raised Sorokin's head from the floor and looked up at Butch.

"You big ape!" he howled. "This man is a—a friend of mine. Help me carry him upstairs. Why did you have to break this man's face?"

Butch pushed his friend aside, picked Sorokin up and carried him three flights to Benny's tenement. If Benny had looked worried, his wife was frantic when she recognized Sorokin. Instantly she broke down and vanished into one of the bedrooms. Butch gaped, put Sorokin into a chair, and looked puzzled.

Benny glared at him. "Now get out. You've done enough harm. Did he know you just came from visiting me? Did he ask you about me? Answer! I've got to know!"

"He just called me a name I didn't like," Butch explained. "So I socked him after he pulled the shiv. He musta got sore because I threw him down the steps. The guy never even mentioned your name."

Benny ran to the door and held it open.

"Butch, you got to beat it! If he wakes up and finds out I know you.... Please, will you scram out of here?"

Sorokin groaned and moved. Benny ran to him as Butch kicked the door shut from inside, and then squeezed his bulk into the small pantry.

Benny, believing Butch outside, ran over and locked the door. Sorokin came out of it fast. He didn't talk as much as usual, but what he said went a long way. Sorokin had never been treated like that before in his life, and he was sore at the whole world.

"Who was he—the hulking peasant who kicked me when I fell?" he demanded. "Who was he?"

"I don't know," Benny lied. "I heard a noise, and I found you at the bottom of the steps."

"Get me a drink," commanded Sorokin. "Whiskey—brandy. Hurry! I do not feel good."

Benny had some cheap whiskey and Sorokin swallowed half the bottle in a couple of gulps. He started to wipe his mouth with the back of his hand, but stopped abruptly. The pressure didn't feel good either.

"Listen carefully," he snarled. "Tomorrow morning you will report outside the warehouse of the shipping line owned by Hans Freuling. There will be others—perhaps three or four hundred. Take with you a thick club. When the strike pickets come, break their heads, do you understand? Unless you obey—well, your brother's family is in grave danger. You may see more pictures like this one of your brother. Now help me out of here and do not forget—shortly after noon tomorrow."

Benny didn't answer. When Sorokin left, he went into the bedroom to console his wife. Butch slipped out, and when he got outside the tenement he saw, with considerable regret, that Sorokin had gone bourgeois enough to have hired a taxi. Butch would have enjoyed another encounter with him. Instead he started back for Tony Quinn's house.

He had some news now, even though it didn't make much sense so far as he was concerned.

CHAPTER XIII

STRIKE!

E **IGHT O'CLOCK** the next morning saw a police car pulled up in front of Tony Quinn's house and a uniformed sergeant got out. Silk admitted him and delivered a letter to Quinn. It was from Commissioner Warner and much to the point.

"Get my hat and coat," Quinn said, as he slid out of his smoking jacket. "Warner wants me at his office immediately. Looks like McGrath's conscience got the best of him."

Silk laughed gleefully. "Maybe Carol planted so many stickers, McGrath went soft in the head. I'll stay around in case anything develops."

Quinn put on his dark glasses. "I hope Warner doesn't keep me long. Butch's news last night means a small war is ready to pop at noontime, and we've got to do something about it."

The sergeant driving the police car took Quinn's arm after they reached Headquarters, and piloted him into Warner's private office. Warner closed and locked the door.

"McGrath talked to me as soon as I arrived this morning, Tony," he said. "He told me what happened at your home last night. I've got him cooling his heels in an anteroom and frankly, I don't know what to do about it all. That was a gross insult. Naming you as the Black Bat was serious enough, but accusing you of bombing Freuling's home—well, that's going too far."

Quinn chuckled. "So has this whole affair, Commissioner. I told McGrath not to report the matter. He's an honest man—a good policeman too. I'd say let him alone. It takes courage to admit a mistake, and anyway McGrath is satisfied now."

Warner sighed. "Yes, and so am I—I suppose. You know Tony, I really had hoped that you were…. Oh, well, let's forget it."

Warner's phone rang, he answered with a grunt, and then hung up. He unlocked the door.

"It's Sam Barnett, the Peace League advocate who put the touch on you, Tony. Sometimes he gets on the verge of becoming a pest."

Barnett came in with a flourish. He grasped Quinn's hand and wrung' it until Quinn felt limp. Then Tony Quinn even forgot to listen as Barnett started talking to Warner. A young man had discreetly followed Barnett into the room. He carried a brief-case and he sat down meekly. It was the young man who had collided so violently with Tony Quinn on shipboard! The young man whose dark hair that had been bleached! It was still blond.

Quinn's eyes, masked by his colored glasses watched the young man narrowly, yet the most intent observer would not have suspected this. For Quinn's head was partly turned away from the young man.

Barnett suddenly raised his voice.

"Mark, bring the brief-case.... Commissioner, this young man is Mark Minor, my secretary. Worked for me almost a year now. Good lad—when I can find him. Has a habit of running off."

Apparently Mark Minor had not had a good look at Tony Quinn until he arose. He gave a violent start of amazement. The brief-case dropped from his hand. He recovered quickly, picked up the brief-case and joined his employer. Barnett's mission seemed to be getting more names of possible subscribers to his cause and Commissioner Warner had to restrain his annoyance. Finally Barnett thrust sheafs of papers at his secretary and left.

The secretary had said only a few words, the formal acknowledgement of his introduction to Warner. Yet that voice was registered in Tony Quinn's mind as deeply as the young man's deceptive appearance.

MARK MINOR could have murdered the Adams boys and the ship's doctor. Yet, if he had done the killing, was it for reasons of his own, or had Sam Barnett, exponent of peace, ordered him to do the job? The possibility was there, but Quinn also realized that almost anyone aboard could have committed the murders—even members of the sunken freighter's crew though they had apparently all been put to bed.

"I'm glad he's gone," Warner growled. "Enough is enough, and Barnett has gone beyond the borderline of friendship. Well, you and I were talking about McGrath. As you wish, Tony, I will file no charges against him. It's magnanimous of you. Some people would have instituted a civil action by now, with good chances of collecting a settlement. Accept my thanks for both myself and the department."

"Wait a moment," Quinn said slowly. "It may do McGrath good to stew in his own juice. Suppose we do this—order him to drive me about wherever I wish to go. Tell him that if he remains in close contact with me for a few hours, then he'll be certain I'm blind."

Warner laughed. "That's one way of convincing him—if he needs any more convincing. All right. I'll have him meet you out front, eh? Wait until I ring for someone to escort you."

A patrolman led Quinn into the front office. He asked to use one of the phone booths and was helped into one. Quinn dialed his home and spoke to Silk in a low voice. When he stepped out, McGrath was waiting.

"Maybe you think I'm a fool," the captain said, "but I had to tell the Commissioner. He says I'm to drive you around, stick by your side until I'm certain you can't be the Black Bat, and that you are blind. Good Lord—don't I know that now? But orders are orders, and where do you want to go first?"

Quinn's eyes rested on a wall clock for a second. It was eleven o'clock.

"We'll try the waterfront section first," he said. "A blind man must depend on sound and smell, instead of sight, for his amusement."

"Humph! There's plenty of sound and plenty of smell down there. You're the boss, Quinn. The car is waiting out front. Here—just a minute, while I help you down those stairs."

McGrath sent the police car rolling slowly down the avenue fronting the busy harbor. Suddenly Quinn touched his arm.

"Captain, there is river traffic moving at this point. Lots of activity. Please stop and let me listen for a while."

"Sure," McGrath said, and laughed. "I'm getting paid for this."

He nosed in to the curb, shut off the motor, and set the emergency. Then McGrath leaned back and closed his eyes. He hadn't had much sleep the night before. But as suddenly, McGrath's eyes shot open and he sat rigid. So did Tony Quinn.

Two men, lounging against a light post about a yard from where the car was parked, were talking fast. Apparently they had just walked to the spot and had not realized anyone was in the car. They were an oddly assorted pair. One was big as a horse and the other a slim, gray-haired man. Both wore work clothes.

"YEAH, THAT'S it," the big man said. "Freuling's help has struck. They're all around the warehouse and docks right now, but pretty soon they'll go away. Guys gotta eat even if they are on strike. When they get back, Freuling's got a bunch of scabs who're gonna try to slip in and bust the strike. What a surprise they'll get, huh?"

"You said it," the smaller man declared. "Me, I'm gettin' as far away from here as I can travel between now and one o'clock. If you so much as look like a scab, them tough monkeys will bust your skull wide open.

You better come along with me. This ain't goin' to be no healthy place in about an hour or so."

Both men ambled off.

"Did you bear that, Quinn?" McGrath said. "Look—I've got to leave you. Those guys are right. There'll be the devil to pay around here if Freuling is crazy enough to drag in strike breakers. It won't stop at bloody noses or black eyes either. Those boys will use clubs and that may mean murder. I know what waterfront strikes can be. I've been hearing that trouble was brewing, but nobody has been able to lay a finger on what it was. Just one of those vague things that don't seem to develop until it busts you one right between the eyes."

Quinn seemed worried. "I know, Captain. But I—well, I can't stay here sitting in the car. They—they'll congregate not far from here and sometimes such strikers and strike breakers tip over cars and hit anyone they meet. Is there time enough for you to drive me to some safer spot?"

"I know just the place," McGrath said. "I hate to leave you, but you see how things are. I'll contact Headquarters, have an augmented riot squad standing ready, then I'll keep my eyes open."

McGrath drove the car about four blocks north, turned sharply and went down a murky alley between the big warehouses. There was a small shed behind an idle warehouse. McGrath opened the doors, drove the car inside and got out.

"You're safe now," he told Quinn. "You and the car are both in a small building where you'll never be seen. Here, let me take your hand. Feel that little button on the drive shaft? That controls the siren. If anybody comes snooping, you just press the button and if there are any cops within ten blocks, they'll come running."

McGrath headed for the big doors and vanished. After several minutes Quinn got out himself. His eyes were the staring orbs of a blind man. He felt his way along and used his cane. Reaching the doorway he stood there, every sense alert. Finally he gave a long, low-pitched whistle. Soon the gray-haired, slender man who had been instrumental in tipping McGrath off, darted from behind the warehouse, streaked across the cleared space and joined Quinn. The bigger man appeared then, and Quinn closed the doors of the shed.

"That was well done, boys. McGrath fell for it, as I knew he would. It was the only way I could get down here in time. How are things going at Freuling's place?"

"Bad," said Silk, who of course was the gray-haired man. Another of Silk's disguises. "About eight hundred men walked out this morning. They're sure the pay is too low and the work too hard. The world's come to be a funny place when a stevedore complains about hard work. They used to eat it up. At any rate, sir, the Communist agents who are doing the influencing, have been plenty active. They have the men primed to commit criminal acts to gain their ends."

"Yeah," the big man grumbled, "And what's just as bad, a bunch of scabs are on the way. I been watchin''em. Soon as the strikers go away at noon for some kind of a pep meetin' and food from a soup kitchen the union furnishes, the scabs go in and leave enough of their strong men to stop the strikers if they get ideas. I've smelled trouble before, but never as ripe as this, Boss."

"You're right, Butch," Quinn said, half angrily. "Those men are filled with the poison of Communism, and they don't even know it. Silk, you brought my regalia?"

"It's hidden close by, sir. I'll get it at once."

SILK RETURNED with a bundle. Quinn hastily removed his coat and placed it under an old box in a corner. He drew black silk trousers over his own pants. He changed his shoes for the black crepe-soled ones. The cape covered his shirt and the hood came down over his eyes.

Silk, with hands as steady as iron, pumped bullets into the firing chambers of both automatics. The Black Bat slid them into his holsters.

This time the Black Bat was coming out of his usual element. Prowling by night was his safest course, but this impending violence would not wait until darkness set in. The Black Bat now would fly in the full light of the sun.

CHAPTER XIV

MURDER PLANS

HANDING SILK several of the blood-chilling photographs which Butch had appropriated the night before, the Black Bat gave Silk instructions.

"You can work this easily in your disguise," he said. "As soon as the scabs show up, mingle with them quietly. They'll come in small groups. Tell these men they must assemble immediately in this unused warehouse in front of where we are now standing. If they protest, or seem a little uncertain of your authority, flash some of these pictures and warn them sternly that you are to be obeyed. They'll follow like sheep because they think that by doing so they'll save the lives of people they love."

Silk took the photographs. Butch frowned.

"How about me, Boss? Ain't I gettin' in on this party?"

"With both fists. Listen carefully now. When Silk begins his work, you'll notice some of the Communists, planted in the ranks of the so-called scabs, try to intercept him. You are to see that no one bothers Silk. Use your own gentle methods, Butch. This is one time I'll not ask you to pull punches. Get going, both of you. Work as fast as you can, because we have little time and much to accomplish.

After his aides were gone, the Black Bat removed his hood, drew on the wide-brimmed hat and folded his cape so that it resembled a coat. He eased out of the shed, saw only a few dock workers on their way to lunch, and made for the empty warehouse.

So far the quiet was almost ominous. Freuling's workers had gone out peacefully enough and the Black Bat doubted that even the persuasive Communist agents who had been responsible for the strike could get them to join a wave of destruction and death. Yet they could fill these men with venomous stories of how Freuling would try to break the strike, lock them out and even hold out their pay.

When the men saw strike breakers taking their places, the agents planted in their ranks, armed with knives and guns and clubs, could whisper suggestions which might be adopted. They could open the hostilities with a violence not planned by the strikers, yet those men would follow up until a full-sized riot would be in full swing.

The Black Bat saw a small door that led to what had once been an office of the warehouse, and he had it open in two minutes with one of several master keys he always carried. He made his way to the front of the place. Although he was reasonably certain that the building was vacant, still he took no chances and moved with the stealth of a cat.

This vacant warehouse was only two doors away from Freuling's docks and buildings. Probably a part of the impending riot would be staged in front of it—if he failed to nip the plan before it got started.

The Black Bat was prepared to encounter almost anything, but hardly what he saw a moment later. On the fifth floor of the big building, he paused, and his nostrils quivered. There was a distinct odor of cigarette smoke. Then his exceptionally sensitive ears heard hoarse whispers.

He crept toward the front of the building and the narrow, steel-shuttered windows. Then he saw what these sly radicals were up to. Three men lounged beside three windows. Each held a sub-machine gun in his arms and each wore a policeman's uniform. The Black Bat did not have to wonder if they might not in fact be police officers, for the uniform coats were open, revealing work shirts. Their speech also gave them away.

"BOY, AIN'T this gonna be somethin'," one gloated. "Soon as the scrap gets goin' good, we just mow 'em down. Swell practice for the days to come maybe, huh? Don't none of you guys forget now—we send a couple of bursts into the mob. Then we show ourselves for a couple of minutes. After that we beat it. The regular cops will come plenty fast, and when they do those tough eggs will expect more machine guns, and will them cops run into a mess!"

"Yeah." Another spiraled a cigarette butt into the middle of the floor. "Only what if some of them strike breaker babies spot us and recognize us? We done a lot of work telling 'em what to do, and they'll know we ain't cops."

"Listen, Nick," a third man grumbled, "this is all set, ain't it? We take our orders, and they always work out. If any of them suckers recognize us, they won't talk. Because we'll show 'em some more pictures. That always gags 'em. Now shut up and make sure the guns.... Hey, what's happenin'? The scabs are showing up, but instead of getting in front of Freuling's place to put up a fight, they're headin' for this warehouse. I don't get it."

The man called Nick peered out of the window.

"Maybe there was a shift in plans—or is goin' to be. Those lunkheads mighta been told to come here. A final meeting or somethin'. We'd better lay low."

The Black Bat had heard enough. He crept back to the stairway and ran down the steps softly. On the first floor, in the huge empty room, the intimidated strike breakers were silently lining up against the wall. Silk appeared in the doorway and shouted orders.

"Stay just where you are—all of you!"

Silk began closing the big doors. There were few windows on the first floor and these faced the blank walls of other buildings so that little light came in. Silk peered through the door, saw two men lying in a heap at the mouth of an alley, and saw Butch looking around for more prey. Silk called him and Butch came in a great hurry. Both made their way through the crowd of sullen men and entered the small office. The Black Bat was there.

"Fifth floor," he said. "Three killers with machine guns to mow down men during the riot. One is named Nick. They think the bosses have called a meeting here. Go up and get those men, one by one. Don't knock them cold—unless it's necessary. There must be no shooting. Silk, you call to the one named Nick. You grab him, Butch. Then get the other two the same way."

The men standing around the warehouse floor were becoming impatient. Scared, too, because they expected further orders and were apprehensive as to what they might be. Yet each man knew he would follow orders, for unless he did someone would die a ghastly death.

They gaped at the man who finally appeared; gaped at the hood that covered his head and the cape around his shoulders. The Black Bat held up both hands and spoke in ringing tones.

"I am not one of those who forced you to come here. I am called the Black Bat. My mission is to fight crime and treason, to help those who are oppressed, and of all that I have so far met, you are the most downtrodden. Will you listen to me? Will you be assured that I can protect you?"

ONE OF the bolder of the men moved forward.

"How do we know that?" he demanded. "And what of our people in Europe? You haven't seen the pictures they have shown us."

"I have. The man who persuaded you to come here is one of my men. I gave him the pictures so that you would not dare to refuse to come. How can I protect you? By putting your oppressors where they belong—behind bars. Most of you men are not United States citizens. You all have relatives in Europe. Perhaps you have been promised all kinds of rewards for helping this gang of human vultures. Your only reward will be more work, more blood-letting, and more of those pictures that drive you into this.

"In just a few moments you are expected to draw up before the entrance to a ship line's warehouse and offices. When the regular workers return, you are expected to stop them from entering the buildings. But did you know that these other men—who are on strike through the machinations of a subversive group within your union ranks—will believe you are scabs come to take their jobs away? They'll fight. Some of them will use guns and knives. Some of you will die. Can you help your people in Europe by dying here?

"Before you entered this building, there were men among you who have not been forced into this as you have. They simply pretend to be of your numbers. They also have guns and knives with which to kill the strikers. They want a deadly battle to result. Why? To get more and better jobs for men like you, or men like those strikers!

"That's far from their minds. What they do want is to put the Freuling ship lines out of business, to stop them from hauling ore and other vital materials to the United States. Then they will go after the other maritime firms. They'll build up an era of hate and bloodshed all over the waterfront and soon all of you will be out of work—those who are not in prison."

"How can we believe this?" Another man stepped forward. "Perhaps they tell the truth and you lie. Prove it!"

The Black Bat walked swiftly over to the steps. He disappeared for a moment and when he returned, three men with hangdog expressions were walking ahead of him. They still wore the policemen's uniforms, but they no longer had guns.

"These three men"—the Black Bat waved one of their own sub-machine guns at them—"were planted upstairs. They were to use these guns on you and on the strikers. You would believe police officers did the shooting and that would make the riot worse. Some of you will recognize these men, because they came to you with orders. Isn't that so?"

Several men shouted affirmative replies. The Black Bat's voice became brittle and deadly as he spoke to the three prospective killers.

"Tell these men that what I have just said is the truth. Tell them—do you hear me? Or are you afraid of what they might do to you? If that's it, stop worrying, because that is only problematical, and what this gun I have will do is definite. I have yet to feel sorry over the death of poisonous serpents, tarantulas, spiders, rats or skunks. You fall well within the classification of each—so talk."

NICK GULPED. The Bat's verbal threats were bad enough, but those piercing eyes that gleamed from behind the mask made him shudder.

"I—I…. Well, that's right. We were supposed to mow 'em down—but not these boys. It was the others. Anyhow, we had to do it. They'd kill us if we refused."

The low murmur that arose from the men who were moving closer and closer, rose to a steady roar of wrath. They knew now that they had been duped, that it made little difference whether or not they followed orders. Those whom they wished to save from death and torture in Europe would receive that treatment anyhow. The Black Bat's calm, reassuring voice had influenced them greatly, but this confession, of one whom they knew to be close to the leaders, settled it all.

Nick and his two companions were backing up as the mob approached. They looked for the Black Bat, to beg protection. The Bat was no longer there. He had vanished completely.

Those three expected death. They didn't die—not that day. They were hemmed in, but not by murderers. Much later, police found them and called ambulances.

CHAPTER XV

WITHOUT VIOLENCE

MEANWHILE, THE strikers were returning from a meeting and a lunch that had not quite come up to their expectations. Some men carried placards, some wore signs over their shoulders. Others just whopped it up.

Among them were a dozen highly puzzled men. Those scabs should have been in front of the building. By this time shots should have been fired and the riot started.

Vanin and Blinov were among those stunned by the absence of those men they were positive would be on deck. "Something is wrong," Vanin whispered. "Now these fools will only parade up and down. How has this gone wrong?"

"How can we tell that now?" Blinov grated. "But those fools who have failed to obey will pay—pay by knowing their relatives have been hurled into graves of quicklime after the firing squad is finished with them. As for ourselves—we cannot afford to remain. This may be a trap. Leave only those who have been accepted by the strikers as fellow employees. Pass the word along that there will be a meeting at the usual place tonight—at eight-thirty. Until then everyone is to look out for himself."

Blinov gave a pretty good example of that by quietly dropping out of the ranks and hurrying a block away to a taxi. He did not see a slender, gray-haired man take up his trail, because the Communist leader was much too intent on getting far away from this area. His features were frozen into a mask of hatred as he wished he had the power his superiors in Europe had so that he might inflict the supreme penalty on the whole group of traitors who had failed him.

Something had slipped, but Blinov was far from discouraged. True, the whole strike which he had so painstakingly arranged and spent so much money on, was a fizzle. Yet, there were other methods. A shipping firm could not carry freight without ships and crews. Blinov had an ace in the hole and he was ready to lay it face down on the table—at once.

The crafty Red organizer had a suspicion that the Black Bat might have been behind this failure. That galled Blinov, because in this case all the money in Moscow and Berlin would be of no avail. The Black Bat was bribe-proof and without the slightest fear. Blinov did not like this at all.

He would have been much less sure of the success of his future plans, too, if he could have observed the Black Bat at that moment. All employees of the Freuling firm who were not on strike had been sent home. Freuling was seated behind his desk in a big office. The walls were covered with maps and pictures of the company's ships, the furniture expensive and comfortable.

Brad Gibbons, munitions tycoon, occupied one chair and puffed complacently on one of his ever-present cigars. Captain McGrath stood beside a window overlooking the area in front of the firm's property where the strikers were parading up and down. On Freuling's desk a telephone was off its cradle to maintain an open wire direct to the riot squad which remained out of sight so as not to interfere with the strikers until things really happened.

"I CAN'T understand it," McGrath grumbled. "The tip was okay. And when we saw those foreign-looking men swarming over this way, I was sure it was about to happen. But they've disappeared. The strikers came back and are carrying on a peaceful demonstration."

"You believe idle chatter and rumor, Captain," Gibbons declared. "Of course it is best to be prepared, but—well, where are all the broken heads you prophesied?"

McGrath opened his mouth to answer, but no words came. He stared at the entrance to the office. The Black Bat, a gun in his fist, stood there.

Freuling and Gibbons, sensing something wrong, turned hastily.

"Please don't move," the Black Bat said. "McGrath was quite right. There was a plot hatched which would have been extremely serious. The men whom McGrath saw swarming this way were to take up positions in front of your gates, Mr. Freuling. When the strikers returned, they would think those men were scabs and the war would be on."

"Then why did not those men keep their positions?" Freuling demanded hotly. "I don't believe one word you say. You came to me before, and I trusted you. In return, you tried to murder me! Only a kind Providence saved my life."

Freuling's head was bandaged, and one hand was covered with surgical gauze. He grew more and more excited, half rising from his chair.

Then he saw the gun in the Black Bat's hand and subsided, muttering under his breath.

"Whether you believe me or not," the Black Bat said, "I did not plant that bomb in your home. I had the opportunity, yes—but so did Mr. Gibbons here, and you don't suspect him, do you?"

Gibbons' jaw sagged, and the cigar almost fell into his lap.

"I resent that implication!" he objected. "But in a way this masked man is right. What's more, I have never heard anything detrimental to the Black Bat's character. Freuling, you're a fool if you don't believe him. I assure you that I do."

McGrath's mind was a jumble of ideas. He tried to concentrate on what was going on here, but could not keep from wondering if Tony Quinn was in the car parked within that old shed. McGrath had been sure Quinn was totally blind. Yet how had the Black Bat learned of this trouble, and how had he arrived in such good time to nip the whole plot?

McGrath moved toward the disconnected telephone. The Black Bat's gun suddenly jabbed him in the ribs.

"I'm no mind reader," the Black Bat said, "but if you expect to use that phone to call your men and have this area surrounded so I can't get clear, you are greatly mistaken, Captain. The wiring of that instrument is connected with the switchboard downstairs. I disconnected this phone, but left the main trunk line open so that your men will not know they are cut off. Now shall we proceed?"

"I want to know about those strange men!" Freuling snapped. "Who were they? What right did they have to block my gates?"

"None. You didn't hire them to break the strike, did you, Mr. Freuling?"

"I did not. Such a thing would only have led to violence and I would rather close my business up than have one man injured. Let them strike—they only lose their pay. Even though it brings me to the verge of bankruptcy, still I do not give in. What became of those men?"

"They were intimidated by Communists and other subversive elements and forced into this business," the Black Bat explained. "The regular union officers did not call the strike, but the men took over and did call it—illegally, but surely—wanting it to appear as if the men you saw were scabs hired by you. A fight was bound to result. The police would have been dragged in as killers, and within twenty-four hours the whole waterfront would have been chaos. You ask where those men are now? You will find them inside the old warehouse two doors away. They will not cause any trouble."

"Can I send somebody to be sure of that?" McGrath demanded. "Those men may have evidence which will help us to clean up this whole rotten business."

"OPEN THAT window," the Black Bat said. "Two of your men are posted just below. Tell them to handle those men gently. They've been subjected to some harsh treatment and a little kindness will go a long way toward making them willing witnesses and, later on, good and useful citizens."

McGrath gave the orders, careful not to say anything which the Black Bat might misconstrue as a signal. Then he closed the window. Freuling toyed with a paper weight and stared down at the desk as he spoke.

"The motives of these devils who are trying to run the Maritime Alliance themselves is clear," he said slowly. "They wish to break my back because I have refused to listen to them or condone their principles. I am Austrian by birth, but American by choice for many years. What those men represent has no place in this country of ours. My employees have been fooled by their promises and their actions. You here cannot realize what these foreigners who have infiltrated into the Independent Maritime Alliance have done to me and those in a similar business."

"I think I can," Gibbons said, "because I have had experience with freighters and passenger liners in my business. It's a ghastly state of affairs."

Freuling nodded without looking up. "They sign as crew members. They refuse to adhere to the traditional discipline of the sea even though they must realize how necessary it is. The captains of my ships have had sitdown strikes in mid-ocean. Passenger liners have experienced the novelty of dirty stokers coming into the saloons and defying anyone to put them out. Now they are enlisting my warehouse laborers and stevedores in their 'Cause.' If this keeps on, I shall no longer have a business. No other single man will have one. The Communists, the Nazis and the Fascists will have slyly taken over, and then what?"

"Mr. Freuling," Gibbons broke in. "Your case sounds like a good one to me. Unions in themselves are essential, helpful, but when their real leaders no longer have a say, and they are controlled by radical elements taking orders from another nation, then we must do something. I'll furnish cash with which to fight them. I'll get your ships if yours are sunk. I'll provide cargo enough to keep your line busy every moment. Just as long as you keep fighting those treacherous rats, depend on me for all aid."

McGrath stepped closer to Freuling's desk.

"I can't give that much help, but I can furnish protection. I'll even work with the Black Bat if necessary—because I know he doesn't stop at much to finish off problems like this. I'm… listen! Isn't that a phone ringing some place?"

Freuling pulled open a drawer which had been slightly ajar. He picked out a French type phone.

"This instrument can cut in on any call in the place," he explained. "Just a moment."

Freuling got his party and with a queer expression on his face, he handed the instrument to Gibbons.

"It is for you. A woman, and she sounds as though she is crying."

Gibbons grabbed the phone.

"Yes—yes, this is Brad. What's wrong?"

They saw Brad Gibbons close his eyes as though he were suddenly very tired. He hung up, and covered his face with both hands.

"All deals are off," he said in a muffled voice. "That was my wife. She was allowed to identify herself and then a man's voice came on—told me if I wanted her to live, I must stop coöperating with you. I must break my contracts. I—don't know what to do. It was my wife, do you hear? We've been married for twenty-four years. I can't let anything happen to her."

McGrath swore softly. This was a matter which the Black Bat could handle far better than any law agency. He looked around. The Black Bat was gone. McGrath headed for the door.

"I'll be back in a few minutes," he called. "Don't spread this news around whatever you do."

CHAPTER XVI

HUNTING EXPEDITION

POLICE CAPTAIN McGRATH raced away, heading for the old shed, his car and Tony Quinn, blind and helpless.

He burst into the shed. He yanked open the door of his car and his face grew grim. The car was empty. Certain before, beyond the slightest doubt that Quinn was totally blind, McGrath now began wondering

Freuling, with his head bandaged, subsided when he saw the Black Bat's gun.

just how Tony Quinn had tricked those two eye specialists. He had caught him cold anyway. How would Quinn take this?

Then McGrath heard a clear, melodic whistle. He ran to the doors and looked out. There, at the end of the dock, sat Tony Quinn, legs swinging above the water, sightless eyes staring out to sea just as though he could distinguish the blue water and the sun which was now definitely in the west.

McGrath started toward him, but before he reached the end of the pier, Quinn spoke without turning around.

"I recognize your footsteps, Captain. Were you startled at not finding me in the car? I sat there for what seemed to be hours, then decided to take a walk. Foolish of me, I suppose, because I almost fell off the pier. So I sat down. A blind man is always sure of being safe so long as he doesn't move around. Will you help me up now?"

A moment or so later, with Tony Quinn seated beside him, McGrath drove the car around to the front of the old warehouse. His men were carrying out three badly battered men. A sergeant saluted crisply.

"We followed your orders, sir, and proceeded at once to this warehouse. There were only three men here—all beaten up badly and all unconscious. There were no signs of any crowd and several hundred of 'em couldn't hide on us."

"I wonder," McGrath said, as he shifted gears and drove off, "why the Black Bat told me I'd find all the supposed scab workmen in that warehouse?"

Tony Quinn was wondering the same thing. Where had they gone? His orders had been for every man to remain there until they could be questioned and their statements taken to create evidence that would break down this Independent Maritime Alliance. How had so many men vanished?

McGrath said little more before he pulled up in front of Quinn's residence.

"I don't think you enjoyed your little trip much, Quinn," he said apologetically, "but after all I am a cop, and when trouble breaks, I've got to help. Maybe some other day we can take that ride again."

Quinn smiled. "It wasn't your fault, Captain, though I did expect to hear fireworks. Good-by—and thanks."

Quinn's cane tapped his way across the sidewalk. He fumbled with the gate, opened it and then tapped some more until he reached the porch. Silk came hurrying out, took Quinn's arm and helped him inside.

"You must have put one over on our sourpuss, or he'd never have let you come back," Silk observed. "However, I'll bet you've got him wondering again—if you are the Black Bat."

"I'm afraid so."

Tony Quinn sat down in a deep leather chair in front of the fireplace. He filled a pipe, tamped the tobacco down.

"I have news, sir," Silk said, as he applied flame. "Looks good, too. I followed our friend Blinov when he left so abruptly. He went straight to a certain book store. He walked in and was in such a hurry he didn't make much pretense of looking for a book. He just walked through the store and disappeared. I waited around about an hour and he never came out, but several other rather crummy-looking persons went in and vanished in just the same manner as Blinov had done."

TONY QUINN'S forehead was wrinkled in thought.

"We'll look into that store tonight. It may give us the one lead we so desperately need. They snatched Brad Gibbons' wife this afternoon and are holding her as a hostage to make Gibbons toe the mark. If he helps Freuling with contracts or money, his wife will probably return to him in small pieces.

"Without Gibbons' help Freuling is apt to go broke. If he does, his ships, warehouses and docks may pass into the hands of a Communist-controlled firm. At any rate Freuling's failure will harm the United States defense system tremendously. That mustn't happen, and the only way to prevent it is to restore Gibbons' wife to him. He's just sore enough to fight those subversive elements with all he's got, once he knows his wife is safe. I would like to know what happened to those men I left in the warehouse, though."

"Maybe Butch knows," Silk suggested. "He's at home. So is Carol, but both should be here soon."

Twenty minutes later Quinn walked over to the secret door. He entered the lab and Silk followed. Butch gave them a broad grin of welcome. Carol smiled at Quinn as he sat down beside her.

"Butch and I both have news," she said. "It's important, too. Let Butch tell his story first."

"It's about them guys you talked outa fightin' this afternoon," Butch said. "A couple of minutes after you left, somebody musta told 'em somethin' awful important because they just filed out the back door, walked up the alley and split up. Not one of 'em said a word, but they were plenty worried. I tailed a couple of the guys and they went straight home."

"Which settles one thing on my mind," Quinn said. "And you, Carol?"

"I spent the afternoon checking up on the crew of that sunken freighter who were picked up by your vacation ship. I have a list of the survivors and their addresses. Got 'em from the steamship line and a funny thing happened. I posed as a reporter after a feature story, so they let me prowl. Tony, the Cameron Line—you sailed from Bermuda on one of their ships—is owned by Freuling. Under a phony corporation name, but he backs the outfit and they're doing all right, too, since European travel has practically ceased."

Quinn whistled in surprise.

"And that isn't all," said Carol. "I've been quite the detective today. I looked over the passenger list of the ship you came in on and discovered that our good and peaceful friend Mr. Sam Barnett was aboard. Did you run across him on board, Tony?"

"If he was sailing with us," Quinn said, "he kept to his cabin. That may explain the presence of his straw-haired secretary though that young man still has one or two things to account for. It likewise places Barnett high on our list of suspects. Which gives us Barnett, Gibbons and Mark Minor, the secretary, as possible instigators of three murders at sea.

"Of course that could have been carried out by someone ashore giving orders to treacherous members of the crew and from what Freuling says, there must have been plenty of them. As I told Silk a few moments ago, Gibbons' wife has been kidnaped and it's up to us to get her back. If the police try it, the snatchers may murder the woman."

SILK LOOKED thoughtful for a moment.

"How can we handle it?" he asked. "They may have shipped her almost anywhere—even out to sea."

"There is a way," Quinn answered softly. "Each group of this kind who are working against the organization of which they are members always has a weak spot. One man is more frightened than the rest—or more treacherous. We'll find that man and I'll do a little snatching on my own. It works both ways, although crooks and traitors never seem to think so. We'll all go on this hunting expedition. Arm yourselves.

"You too, Carol. There's a ladylike pearl-handled automatic in the drawer near you. Put it in your purse and don't have too many qualms about using it in a tight spot. We're fighting men who aim to destroy our entire civilization and replace it with a mad regime of Communism or Nazism or Fascism."

"Yeah," Butch broke in. "Y'know, I been thinking a lot about how things are in Moscow, for instance. Seems they hold big parades every time some big shot feels like seein' a few guns. Now take me. I got bad feet. I couldn't do all that marchin', not even with a bayonet stickin' in my back."

Quinn grinned and began to get ready. It had become dark outside, the time when the Black Bat was in his element.

"Silk," he said, "see if you can do anything with Butch's face. Change his appearance a little anyway. Disguise yourself, too. The three of you will have to work more or less openly."

When they left the house, Carol had the car near the garden gate. She drove straight to the vicinity of the book shop where Silk had observed Blinov seeking sanctuary. They drove past it while Quinn observed the place.

"Park about a hundred feet north of the entrance," he told Carol. "We've a dangerous job ahead of us tonight, and a woman's life depends upon the way we handle things. Obviously the police cannot be called in because Gibbons knows those kidnapers will know it. I've a rather firmly fixed idea that someone well up in the financial and social world is directing this move to cripple American shipping—someone with plenty of contacts who knows what's going on. Now here are the plans, so listen carefully...."

Silk was first to enter the book store. He had a package under one arm and the wrapper was torn slightly so that any casual observer would see that Silk carried several dog-eared volumes in the bundle. He also wore big glasses that gave him a droopish appearance and he moved about with short, almost nervous steps.

Silk tipped his hat politely at the narrow-eyed woman in the cashier's cage, then started to browse, killing at least ten minutes. He heard the door open and bang shut again, admitting Butch. This huge, ungainly gorilla didn't look nor act much at home in a book store. He removed his cap and held it in his hand.

"I gotta get me some books on English," he told one of the middle-aged women clerks. "My boss says if I don't learn somethin' pretty fast, I'll get fired. You got some nice easy books—cheap?"

"This way," the clerk said disgustedly, and then she gulped.

A third customer had entered—a pretty girl who immediately found the shelf of light, romantic books. Three customers at one time was something of an event, because this store discouraged trade. Particularly none were wanted tonight, because there was an important meeting downstairs.

THE PRETTY girl moved a small stepladder over to the shelves, climbed up to reach the top shelf, and her eyes darted to the right. She could look down at the cashier now, and see the gun in the open drawer, right at her fingertips.

Carol stepped down. She carried three books over to the cage, shoved them through, and the cashier had to use both hands to stop them from falling into her lap. She looked up with an angry glance that changed to one of dismay and fear. At that moment Carol's small pearl-handled automatic looked to that cashier like a howitzer.

At precisely the same instant Silk seized the arms of the clerk hovering near him and clapped a hand over her mouth. Butch acted, too—perhaps a little less strenuously, for the clerk accompanying him was frightened of his size even before he tucked her under one arm. By prearranged plan, they carried or led their prisoners into a small side room where books were repaired. Carol passed her gun to Silk, stepped out and closed the door.

She hurried to the cashier's cage, hastily destroyed a fingerwave by combing her hair straight down like a Dutch cut, and when she glanced in a mirror she wondered why feminine Communists always try to look their worst. She donned a red sweater which hung on the back of a chair and sat down at the cage. Anyone passing would have thought her the regular cashier. Nevertheless Carol was glad that an efficient-looking automatic lay at her fingertips.

A dark figure flitted past the window, entered swiftly and kept on going. The Black Bat headed for the rear of the store and the meeting of the executive council for murder, sabotage and any other kind of violence that would blast United States plans for becoming strong in weapons of war.

CHAPTER XVII

THE BAT'S PRISONER

JUST AS soon as he reached the rear of the premises the Black Bat adjusted his hood. By the weak lights he spotted three closed doors. One led to a small delivery platform outside and was securely locked and bolted. Another must have led to a supply room, for the last person to sweep up had carelessly pushed debris against it. The third might lead anywhere—upstairs, downstairs or even into another room.

The Black Bat turned the knob slowly and opened the door a crack. The coolness of a cellar reached him. He slipped through and found himself at the head of a long flight of narrow stairs. Looking straight down, he saw two men with drawn guns. Possibly they were deceived by the poor light, for both did a peculiar thing. They deliberately turned around and faced a wall.

The Black Bat walked slowly down the stairs, guns ready. Neither of the guards moved. He stepped up to the nearest and without much hesitation his gun butt slugged the guard into unconsciousness.

The second man whirled, amazement in his face. Before he could raise that gun, a fist smacked him full on the chin and a hand with fingers that felt like steel closed around his gun wrist and turned it slowly so that muscles and nerves were paralyzed. Another blow finished the job.

The Black Bat disarmed both unconscious men, then tiptoed toward the only door he could see.

What he would meet now was highly problematical. He had noticed a partially hidden button close by where the guards had been standing. This might have been used to give a warning signal.

Boldly, knowing he risked everything, the Black Bat opened that door. For a moment he was stunned. For the twenty or more men in that room were all turned squarely around so that he could not see their faces nor could they see him.

It came to the Black Bat then that these men expected someone—a man who refused to allow even his own followers to see his face. That accounted for the way the guards outside had acted. They had probably mistaken the Black Bat's black outfit for that of their leader. Quite probably he appeared here masked.

The Black Bat had about five seconds in which to make a momentous decision. Should he withdraw, take a chance that the men inside would respectfully keep on waiting, and seize the leader when he appeared? Or should he carry out his original plan of getting Sorokin, the weak link in this mob?

If he waited, the Unknown might not appear for some time—long enough for his men to grow impatient and start an investigation. Mrs. Gibbons' life hung in the balance, and catching the unknown leader of the mob might possibly result in her instant death.

The Bat's lips barely moved as he spoke one word.

"Sorokin!"

The agent whom Butch had almost shattered the night before, began turning his head. Blinov, beside him, growled a warning that he was to obey orders, but not look at the leader. Sorokin began walking backward and the men parted to let him through.

He approached the Black Bat that way, and this prowler of the night had to restrain his laughter. He could not have wished for anything better. Suddenly the Black Bat wound an arm around Sorokin's throat and lifted him high so he couldn't scuffle with his feet. He backed out, closed the door, and stopped only long enough to turn Sorokin from a struggling man into one who was limp and easily handled. The Black Bat's fist was an effective weapon of magic.

UPSTAIRS HE found Silk in the store. Carol came from the cashier's cage and Butch pounded across the floor after he had locked the three women in the anteroom. When they reached the car the Black Bat threw Sorokin into the rear seat, hopped aboard himself, and Carol pulled away. The Black Bat had invaded the sacred privacy of a Communist's Inner Circle and had stolen one of their members from beneath their noses, yet not a shot had been fired and it was highly probable that the men inside the small meeting room were still standing with their backs toward the door.

Silk leaned over from the front seat and glanced at Sorokin.

"Is he out, sir?" he asked. "You're certain of it?"

The Black Bat opened one of Sorokin's eyelids, nodded to Silk, and pushed the unconscious Communist back to the floor.

"I didn't want him to hear this," Silk went on. "I was in the store when it happened. A man came by, walking rather fast. He returned in a minute, walking slower, and I had a look at him. He was that bleach-haired chap who works for Sam Barnett. I couldn't mistake him, sir. I saw him aboard ship often enough."

The Black Bat leaned back and seemed plainly puzzled. Had Mark Minor, secretary to Sam Barnett, been the man those Communists expected? Was he the man whose face must not be seen even by his closest lieutenants? The Black Bat decided that before morning Mark Minor's private life was not going to be quite so exclusive.

For the moment, he had Sorokin. Carol, acting on instructions, drove out of the city to a small farmhouse which belonged to Tony Quinn, but which he rarely used. There was nothing unusual about the place which was listed as a summer home on the town tax records.

Yet, hidden away between those four walls were rooms where prisoners might be kept for weeks if necessary. Emergency weapons were well concealed, and disguises for Silk's use. The Black Bat had acquired title to this place for just such an emergency as this which was now presented.

Sorokin recovered his wits, groaned, and sat up slowly. He blinked, for the light in the farmhouse room to which he had been taken was fairly strong. When his eyes became accustomed to the light, they grew and widened until they seemed in danger of popping from their sockets.

Only one man was in that room with Sorokin, but the Communist would rather have been facing a hungry tiger. Butch O'Leary, slowly massaging the knuckles of his left hand, looked ferocious.

"You and me," Butch said in preamble, "are gonna have a little talk. Your jaw is still lopsided from where I conked you last night, pal, but that's nothin'. Absolutely nothin'. We're about ten miles from no place, so if you holler it'll just be to amuse yourself. Now suppose we start off with this question. You and that phony mob of yours were expectin' somebody to show up tonight. The big shot, huh? Who is he, weasel?"

Sorokin was truly the organization's weak link. So long as he dealt out the violence, he reveled in it. But when it came time for him to take punishment, he turned yellow.

"I—I don't know who the leader is. No one knows, not even Blinov nor Vanin, and they're pretty high themselves.... Yes, the leader was coming tonight. When you or somebody called me, I thought he was already there, asking me to a special conference, We are not allowed to face him, on penalty of death. You must believe me."

Butch showed he did not, but passed on to the next question.

"Sometime today your mob snatched a woman," he said. "A lady named Mrs. Gibbons. Where is she now, rat? You'll answer this one or I'll bust somethin' in you."

Sorokin gulped and drew back a little.

"I swear I know of no kidnaping. There has not even been any talk of one, and the woman—I have never heard of her. You are wrong! But you cannot hurt me if I do not tell what I do now know. I cannot lie."

Butch bared his teeth in a snarl and grabbed Sorokin's wrist. He squeezed it gently, and made no attempt to twist the limb, but Sorokin gave vent to a series of wild yells intermingled with pleas that his wrist was being broken. But Butch's persistent questioning brought no answer from Sorokin. It was clear that he really did not know who guided his murder and sabotage plans, nor where Mrs. Gibbons had been taken.

Butch let go of him and walked into the next room. The Black Bat shook his head slowly.

"He's telling the truth, Butch. If you wrung his neck, that story wouldn't change—unless he started to lie, and that would be of no use to us. Describe Mark Minor to him—average height and weight, straw-colored hair and dark eyes. Dark eyebrows, too, and a dimpled chin. See if he happens to know him."

Butch returned and Sorokin began yelling again, this time in anticipation of pain.

"Shut up," Butch snapped, "or I'll give you something to yowl about. Now listen—I know the name of your leader. It's a guy with the moniker of Mark Minor. He's about your size, blond hair—"

"I tell you there is no way of telling what he looks like!" Sorokin insisted. "I have never laid eyes on him. I know only this—that if anything else happened in the book store tonight, except seizing me, then the leader did not appear. Upstairs, in the store window, a certain sign is set out when everyone is ready in the meeting room. Unless that sign appears, the leader will not come inside, but simply pass on by. If I have lied, you may kill me."

"Don't hand out such swell invitations," Butch rumbled. "Okay—relax. Maybe I'll be back."

"That certainly is the way Mark Minor acted," Silk whispered to the Black Bat, in the other room. "He came by twice, and must have been sure the sign wasn't there. He looked sharply at Miss Carol too, sir, but she did resemble the real cashier from a distance. Minor didn't see the sign, knew it wasn't safe, so went on. That must be it, sir. Perhaps Minor isn't the actual big man behind the scenes, but he works for Sam Barnett who easily could be. It would be like those devils to masquerade under the cloak of a Peace Mission."

The Bat's mind clicked smoothly.

"It is possible and quite probable that Sorokin has never seen his leader, but I'll bet ten to one the unknown boss of the outfit has seen Sorokin and knows him. He would have to, to operate safely. Therefore we'll try to attract him, like a moth to the flame. Sorokin will furnish the flame. I want him tied, gagged and blindfolded. You'd better block his ears also. That's your job, Butch, but leave enough of him for his lord and master to recognize."

CHAPTER XVIII

PROLOGUE TO MURDER

O THER THINGS, however, and just as important, had to be done before the Black Bat was ready to exhibit Sorokin as a lure. He had little doubt but that the Communist, Nazi and Fascist spies who were infesting the Maritime Alliance were planning for greater things than strikes, which would only tie up industry for a limited time. The sinking of the freighter was a good indication that their plot would also take in ships and the men who sailed them as well as those who loaded them.

The Black Bat had made his plans for the night, and though Ted Jordan, reporter on the *News-Globe*, had no idea of it as yet, he was slated to take an important part in the night's events. Jordan hadn't slept well during the last few nights. His food hadn't tasted right, and he even found his job growing monotonous. He came out of the newspaper

The sailor made a savage sweep with his bar—and missed.

building, pulled up his coat collar and kept his head down. As he passed a doorway, a figure stepped out.

"Jordan," the man said, "there's a car at the next corner—you can see it from here. Get in, if you know what's good for you."

Jordan shivered. "Don't you fellows ever leave me alone? Can't you see a man can take just so much and then…. Oh, all right. I'll do it."

The rear door of the car opened as Jordan approached. He climbed in, sat down glumly, then turned to glance at his companion. For a moment Jordan just gaped. Then he edged away slowly.

"You're the Black Bat," he said, and there was a mixture of hope and despair in his voice. "You—want me for—something?"

"Just for a little talk," the Black Bat replied. "Jordan, why did you obey a total stranger who ordered you to get into this car?"

Jordan flushed. "I can't answer that. Believe me, I can't. Perhaps you know a lot about me. I'm not proud of what I've done, but I couldn't help myself."

"You believed the man who stopped you was an agent of that Communistic gang which has been threatening you," accused the Black Bat "That's why you neglected to turn in one of the greatest yarns a newspaperman ever came across. I was present the night you lost your temper and denounced the speaker at that meeting. The way you acted showed the roots of patriotism and love of your country are planted in you deeply. You're an American right through, Jordan. You'd have turned in that story to be blazoned on the front page, even if you'd known it meant bodily harm to you. It must be that they silenced you by threats of injury to someone else. You're American-born. Your parents are Americans, therefore I haven't been able to figure out who—"

"So you guessed it," Jordan said. "All right. I'm with you. I'll risk everything, because nobody knows better than a newspaperman that the Black Bat has never failed to come through. Listen—they almost killed me that night. Then they did a little fast checking up and discovered my mother is in Belgium. She can't get out. She's an artist, and was caught in the war.

"You ask me how can Communists carry out threats in Nazi-held territory? You don't know Communists. They are one of the reasons half of Europe is in ruins. They are everywhere. Sometimes they even have Nazi coöperation. So I obeyed them. Now they've gone even further. They're forcing me to write stories sympathetic to themselves. A little quiet propaganda by an American. I thought they had something else up their sleeves when that man told me to get in this car, even though I already had orders about what to do tonight."

"One of my men spoke to you," the Black Bat said. "Now, listen to me. I want your mother's full name and her present address. She's an American citizen, and even if she is more or less held a prisoner by Communist-Nazis powers, we can free her. In return I ask your help. You just said you had been given instructions what to do tonight. Is there a meeting—or what?"

JORDAN LIT a cigarette with hands that shook slightly.

"I'm with you wherever the road leads. Nothing could be worse than what I've been through lately. Every night there is something different. I'm so sick of listening to their silly speeches, promising themselves the whole world with everybody free, equal and rich—on what they will dole out to them. They're running the biggest racket ever foisted on an unsuspecting world. Tonight I'm to meet two of them in some dump near the river. The poor saps wouldn't know how to act in a place with a tablecloth."

"Hear what they have to say," the Black Bat said. "Consent to their plans, but find out when their next executive meeting is to take place and where. I must know that."

Jordan nodded. "I'll do my best. A half-baked slob named Vanin is meeting me tonight. He's fairly high up in the ratty crowd and perhaps he'll know. I'll hand him a line and hope for the best. You'd better let me out now. Sometimes I'm met by representatives of the mob. They trust me implicitly, you see—just as far as they can reach with a dagger."

Jordan ambled down the street. Half a block behind him was Silk, doing his usually careful job of shadowing. The Black Bat, with Butch driving, headed for Jordan's rendezvous. It turned out to be a poorly lit place with dirty curtains, and a couple of frowsy waiters standing in the doorway. Butch parked up the street.

"Are you positive Sorokin is all right?" the Black Bat asked.

"Him?" Butch snorted. "I got him tied up with so much rope he looks like a wicker basket. Anyway, the guy is so scared of what his gang will do to him that he wouldn't run for it if he did get free. Don't worry. And he has no idea where he is, either. I got him in my room, but he's blindfolded. When are you going to use him, Boss?"

"I don't know. Depends on what happens tonight. Here comes Jordan. Slump down behind the wheel a bit, Butch. We don't want to attract any attention."

Jordan was inside the restaurant about five minutes and when he emerged, Vanin was on one side of him and a burly, scowling man on the other. Jordan's face was white. His eyes flashed around as they waited for a car to pull up. Then Jordan's shoulders drooped in despair. He couldn't see the Black Bat's car.

But Butch followed, well to the rear and so expertly that Vanin had no hint he was being trailed. Silk was in the front seat with Butch now, watching carefully.

Vanin's car pulled up before a cheap boarding house. He got out and so did the driver, but Jordan and the burly man remained in the back seat. Vanin rang the bell, spoke to the woman who answered it then both men entered. They were gone about ten minutes, and two other men accompanied them when they emerged. This was a dark street, but the Black Bat's remarkable eyesight easily distinguished the features of the men who were with Vanin.

"Those are members of the sunken freighter crew," he said. "I saw them after they were rescued. I see something else too. Neither sailor wants to go on this trip, but they are being urged by guns hidden in Vanin's pockets. This looks promising."

NOW THE trail led them straight is across town to the river. Vanin's car stopped again, and Jordan got out first. He lit a cigarette, cupping the flame in his curled hands so that his face was illuminated. Jordan wanted to be sure the Black Bat, if he were anywhere near, would see him.

The prisoners got out next. One of them seemed to realize that he might as well die fighting, for he swerved around and started to uncork a haymaker. Vanin's companion raised his right hand. A blackjack slid out of his sleeve and the fighting sailor slumped onto the running board of the car. He was half carried, half dragged along.

They seemed to be heading for a garbage scow moored at the end of a pier. The Black Bat, moving stealthily toward the same spot, drew a gun just before he reached the end of the pier. He leaped and his cape spread out to closely resemble the wings of a bat. He landed lightly on the after-deck of the scow, crouched, and ran along the narrow catwalk which surrounded the giant bins that were partly filled with refuse to be dumped at sea.

Well forward, he heard the sound of a struggle, then a curse. He sped to that point. One forward bin was equipped with a sliding hatch cover. This was partly open, and he could look down at a prologue to murder.

The two members of the sunken freighter crew had been knocked down. Both were covered with blood from the savage beatings they had taken. Jordan stood against the wall, grim horror written on his face.

Vanin and the burly aide were busy with heavy iron chains. They clamped these around the wrists and ankles of their victims. Some rusted pieces of scrap metal were attached to the chains. Vanin kicked one of the victims, then stepped back.

"You see, Jordan, what happens to traitors. We dump them—with the other garbage. The scow goes well out to sea. Fish follow it. These two fools will die quickly, and soon there will be little left of them."

"But why bring me here to witness it?" Jordan gulped. "I don't need any object lessons."

Vanin shrugged. "Who knows? Of course, being here makes you an accessory to murder, so if from now on anything happens to me, I could drag you into it. We'll leave now, because the scow will sail soon."

Grim-lipped, the Black Bat leaned forward to open the hatch cover wider. He heard a scraping noise behind him, looked once, then lunged. A man employed on the scow had stolen close. He was in bare feet and had made no noise a normal pair of ears would have detected. In one hand was a short piece of metal, and murder was in his heart.

Both arms of the Black Bat went around the sailor's legs. At the same instant the Black Bat lifted him. The sailor went up and over. He made one savage sweep with his metal bar, but missed by a yard. Then he was tumbling down into the hatch where two men were slated for murder and their killers were getting ready to leave.

Vanin howled a curse as the sailor crashed almost at his feet. He drew a gun. Then two shots smashed the gasoline lantern which illuminated the hold. Vanin heard the swish of what sounded like the wings of some huge bird. Then he saw a giant bird, silhouetted against the sky, swoop down. Vanin raised his gun, and despite the darkness, Jordan saw that gesture. He grabbed Vanin's hand, twisted it and the gun fell to the floor. Vanin reached behind his neck to draw a keen blade from a scabbard slung between his shoulders.

CHAPTER XIX

WATERY BURIAL

D R. VANIN'S aide was stumbling around, trying to locate something at which to shoot. Suddenly two powerful hands closed about his throat. Two thumbs moved experimentally for a second, seeking that nerve center from which the entire body can be paralyzed. The bulky killer tried to bring his gun close, but only succeeded in raising it a trifle before his world turned into a black void.

The Black Bat let him drop, and danced agilely away. Vanin made a leap, landed beside the form of his unconscious aide and crouched there like an animal. He kept swinging his knife and cursing bitterly.

"Vanin," an unruffled voice came out of the darkness, "drop that knife. If you don't, I'll drop you with a piece of lead."

Vanin's foot happened to touch the gun his aide had dropped. With a shout of triumph he bent down, picked it up, and began firing at random. A single shot answered him. Vanin's half mad grin faded into a look of awe. The kind of awe a man feels when he thinks he has discovered death. Blood ran down his face. He wiped a hand across his temple, felt the gore, and with a sigh he folded up like a toy balloon.

"You got Vanin all right," Jordan's voice announced from a corner. "I hope you killed him."

A match flared. There had been a second gasoline lantern unlit and swinging from a beam. As the hold was flooded with light, Jordan looked around in satisfaction.

"Vanin isn't dead," the Black Bat said. "My bullet just scraped his forehead, which I intended it to do. Vanin couldn't take it. His pal will be out for hours. Help me get these two boys free, will you?"

The intended victims recovered rapidly under the Black Bat's ministrations and they gladly told their story.

"We're washed up with that outfit," one said. "Both of us were on a freighter owned by Freuling's line. We listened to all this crazy talk of that gang that wants to take over our union—all about sharing the world's property and everything. It sounded good, but it has never worked out yet. Anyway, we scuttled that freighter, and it wasn't the first one either."

"What about the Adams boys?" The Black Bat was examining the irons that were linked about the men's wrists and ankles.

"The youngest one who was assigned to the radio room didn't like our theories, and said so often enough. The older brother was quieter and smarter. Anyway when we scuttled the tub, we tried to knock off the youngest Adams, just like other members of the crew who wouldn't have anything to do with this here foreign bunch. Those were orders. The oldest Adams brother waded in, put the kid brother in a lifeboat and stood over him with a gun. After we were rescued, somebody knocked off both of those brothers. It wasn't any member of our crew, because we were all below and not one of us went on deck or out of the big cabin assigned to us."

Jordan looked over at the Black Bat. "This time I will write a story that'll shock the whole country," he said. "Make them see what's really going on."

"No, it must wait," the Black Bat said, and turned again to the two sailors. "Now why were you brought here to become fish food?"

"Because we shot our fool mouths off," he was told. "We got sick of being ordered around. For guys who preach every man his own boss, they sure do a lot of supervising. We told one of the big shots we'd talk if they didn't lay off. That clinched it. So we were headed for this scow that's been used plenty for getting rid of saps who can't keep their mouths shut. Now what happens to us?"

"You go to jail. Certainly you didn't expect anything else. But Vanin and his pal will go with you. Jordan, pick up Vanin's gun and keep everyone covered. I'll send Captain McGrath here. And not a word of this to anyone. Soon as McGrath takes the real garbage in this scow to a cell, I'll give you some more instructions."

One of the sailors heaved a big sigh.

"I guess we are human scum all right, but bring on this cop and I'll give him an earful. But we still don't know who the big boss is."

AFTER McGRATH appeared with a squad and all the prisoners were removed, including the scow sailor who had tried to crush the Black Bat's skull with an iron bar, Jordan ambled casually up the street. The same quietly dressed man who had approached him near the newspaper office, came up again.

"Jordan," Silk said, "these are the orders you expected. We have discovered that the sailors who man the scow are not yet aboard. Therefore it will sail on schedule and nobody will be the wiser as to what happened on board. All who have been arrested will be held without publicity. Did you learn the place and time of the next executive meeting?"

"Vanin didn't know," Jordan answered. "There's to be an informal meeting of a few men in a little while though."

"Good. Go there. Act worried and hesitant. Tell them you had a date with Vanin and he didn't show up. You want instructions. Pretend interest in their theories—do anything, but get the date and place of that next meeting!"

"I haven't been a reporter nine years for nothing," Jordan said. "I'll worm the dope out of them. Thank the Black Bat for me, will you?"

Jordan hurried away and Silk turned the next corner. He got into the Black Bat's car.

"He'll get the dope if anybody can," he said. "Now what? Or do we call it a night?"

The Black Bat laughed. "Hardly, Silk. We're just beginning. In fact the last little cog of my plans has just slipped into place. I have a job for you—a highly dangerous one. Do you mind?"

"Not so long as it will help round up those skunks," Silk said. "But what about Brad Gibbons' kidnaped wife? Hadn't we better get her free before the leaders of the gang are tackled?"

"I'm aiming at exactly that target, Silk. We'll go back home first and I'll explain the entire procedure."

SAM BARNETT, exponent of peace at any price, studied the latest submissions to an essay contest about how to stop war. Minor, his straw-haired secretary, popped in and out of the room every few minutes and Barnett kept looking up with an annoyed grunt. Then Barnett became aware that there was a shadow across the manuscript he was reading. He swallowed hard and turned his head.

Two men were in the room. Apparently they had come through the window. One of his uninvited guests wore a black hood and a cape. He also gripped an automatic which Barnett liked least of all. The second visitor stood with his back toward Barnett.

"I'm afraid we startled you," the man in the Black Bat's hood and robe said. "Of course our visit isn't in accordance with the best rules of Emily Post—but then neither is treason or murder. Mr. Barnett, I'm the Black Bat. In the course of my investigation concerning activities of Communist, Nazi and Fascist spy groups infesting the waterfront, and murders committed through orders from these foul traitors, your name has come up as a suspect."

"Me—suspected of being a Communist—or a Nazi—or a Fascist?" Barnett roared. "That—that's the worst insult I've ever taken in my life! I'll call the police! I'll see whether you can burst in here and accuse me—"

"Quiet," the Black Bat snapped. "You've talked enough. How about it, my friend? Is the voice familiar?"

Sorokin turned around. "No, that is not the man, I am sure of it."

SUDDENLY MARK MINOR burst into the room carrying a sheaf of papers.

He spotted the tableau and froze in his tracks. The papers slowly fluttered to the floor.

"Ah," the Black Bat welcomed him, "I'm glad you came. You fall in my list of suspects also. You were a passenger aboard a boat where three murders were committed. What do you know about them?"

"Nothing," Minor snapped. "If I did, I wouldn't tell it to a masked man. Don't talk, Mr. Barnett! If he is the Black Bat, he's in league with Communists, at least, because that man with him is one of their higher-ups. I have learned that through some of my investigations into subversive activities for you. Refuse to answer."

The Black Bat glanced at Sorokin with a silent question in his eyes. Sorokin shook his head. The Black Bat stepped closer to Minor.

"While we're on the subject of suspects and suspicions, would you mind telling me why you dye your hair, Mr. Minor? A man doesn't usually resort to that unless he wants to change his appearance for an ulterior reason." Minor backed up, and suddenly whirled around. He made a dive for the hallway, opened the front door and took a header out into the night. The Black Bat could have cut him down a dozen times, but he made no such attempt.

Instead he bowed slightly to Barnett, took Sorokin's arm and started for the same door.

"We'll pay Freuling a little visit next," he said, as he passed through it. "Sooner or later you'll recognize the voice, Sorokin. It will mean quite a few years knocked off your sentence if you coöperate."

When they reached a car parked nearby, the Black Bat got behind the wheel. Sorokin was no longer dangerous. He'd had plenty of time to think while tied up in Butch's room. Sorokin began to realize that life in the United States wasn't so bad. The workings of a democracy gave a man an even break and the kind of living that made the whole world envious.

The Black Bat turned a corner and headed down a dark, narrow side street. Freuling's home lay at the extreme end of it. Suddenly two cars shot out of driveways. They swerved and swept straight toward the Black Bat's sedan. Sorokin yelled. There was a terrific crashing of fenders and running boards but the Black Bat's car kept on going. When those cars appeared, he had stepped on the gas, hard. The momentum of the sedan carried him through the crash.

Now the roar of guns broke the night silence. Sorokin whined and tried to merge himself with the rug.

The bullets came thicker and thicker. Then a hissing sound and the car lurched crazily. The Black Bat spun the wheel, mounted the curb, and drove straight onto a lawn.

"That does it!" he gasped. "They hit a tire. Run for it, Sorokin. They're after you, too!"

Both men leaped out of the car and raced away into the darkness. But this time the Black Bat's luck did not hold. Both cars, not badly damaged, and loaded with armed men were now streaking across the lawn to head off the fleeing men. One car slowed and four killers jumped from it. They spread out.

Sorokin tripped and fell heavily. He was promptly seized. Then two of the men closed in on the Black Bat. He tried to shoot, but it was no use. Other members of the murder party formed a circle around him. He dropped his gun, raised both hands and surrendered.

HALF A dozen guns were jabbed against his ribs. One of the men struck him across the face. Another kicked repeatedly at his ankles and cursed him. But Blinov came stalking over and took command.

"We must get away from here at once. The shooting will attract police. We go to the waterfront and the scow. It has not yet sailed and we shall give it another pair of passengers. Hurry!"

The Black Bat was whirled around and pushed toward the car. He took several steps and Blinov, bringing up in the rear, could no longer restrain himself. He struck the Black Bat on the head with his gun butt. The Black Bat went down with a crash.

"Throw him in the car!" shouted Blinov. "Do not forget Comrade Sorokin. He should be entitled to some special treatment if we have the time for it. Hurry, you stupid oxen!"

CHAPTER XX

FACE OF THE MAN IN BLACK

POLICE CARS arrived, and found nothing but one wrecked, bullet-riddled sedan. When they tried to check on it later, they found this to be impossible. The cars which the Black Bat used in his forays were specially treated so they could never be traced to Tony Quinn or anyone else.

Far down on the waterfront, Blinov, bursting with satisfaction, supervised the transfer of his prisoners to the scow. It was loaded now and ready to sail. Blinov flung Sorokin and the Black Bat onto the floor of the wheel-house. He bent down while his men clustered about him. Blinov seized the edge of the Black Bat's hood, then looked up at his cohorts with a triumphant leer.

"You will now see the face of the Black Bat, comrades. I understand the cleverest crooks and the smartest policemen in this country have never looked upon his features. You see—it takes a man with skill and courage to accomplish such feats."

Blinov gave the hood a violent wrench and it came free in his hand. He gazed down at the face of his victim. Then he sneered, stepped back and administered a kick.

"Get the irons. We have no time to waste on these carrion. So that is the Black Bat! It is too bad we cannot publicly announce our success."

The irons were quickly brought and clamped into place on the victims. Blinov barked orders. His men carried Sorokin and the man in black to the narrow deck. At a signal they hurled both onto the heaped-up garbage. Two minutes later the scow pulled away from the dock. Blinov, although in a hurry, decided at the last minute to remain and personally see those bodies disappear into the sea. Nothing else was quite so important.

They were two miles out when the engines of the scow began to throb. Slowly the steel dump bins began to move. The garbage slid into the water. Blinov saw both Sorokin and the man in black pitched overside. He walked to the rail and spat into the water. Then he ordered the scow to put back at full speed. Many triumphs had given Blinov great elation, but none quite so definitely as the Black Bat's death. Blinov felt expansive—something that had not happened since the day he had commanded his first firing squad.

As he stepped ashore, his men eagerly asked for confirmation of the Black Bat's death. Blinov confirmed it with an accompanying lurid description. Then he dismissed the men with a reminder they were to meet at a specified time.

BLINOV HAD himself driven to a modest, uptown hotel. He took the elevator to the ninth floor, sought Room Number 909 and rapped on the panels. A muffled voice answered him.

"I am the man about your new book—*The New Civilization*," Blinov said with a smirk.

The voice ordered him to enter. Blinov stepped into a darkened room. Someone, who had been standing beside the door, closed it gently and a key turned in the lock. A hand took Blinov's arm and led him to a chair. He sat down and then, without waiting for the Unknown to speak, he blurted the news.

"I have just watched the end of the Black Bat. There is no question about it. He is gone, and so is that traitor, Sorokin."

Blinov could hear the Unknown's sharp breathing in the darkness. Then the voice, elation-filled.

"That is the best news yet, Blinov. For your work I shall see that the proper superiors in Moscow reward you handsomely and, until our great coup is accomplished, you shall be my first lieutenant; perhaps confidante. Did you look beneath the Black Bat's hood? Did you see his face?"

Blinov shrugged. "Of course. It was that of a man I had never before seen.... But you have instructions."

"From this place," the Unknown said, "I go to a secret retreat where I maintain a short-wave wireless station. With it I can communicate with every ship at sea. Freuling's freighters are manned by a majority of our followers. Every radio operator believes in our Cause and will stand by to receive my orders. With one blow I shall wipe out one of the largest shipping lines, and put an end to most of the shipments of ore from South America and the sending of supplies down there.

"I shall arrange it so that the defense measures of the entire continent will hit a bottleneck that will keep them behind orders for weeks. By then our hold will be so strong everywhere that we can take over entire unions, subjugate business to our will, turn the rule of this fat and prosperous country over to our leaders.

"If there is resistance on the part of any fools with patriotic ideas, there will be a civil war, for followers will flock to us by the millions. We have a bait they cannot fail to swallow—that of more money and individual power. We shall give them a taste of it, too—until those who oppose us are beaten to the ground. After such triumph we can then manipulate the masses to suit our own wishes."

Blinov licked his lips in anticipation.

"I have looked forward to this for years. I came here just before the last war. I ran away from the draft then because I was not so foolish as to fight for swine. I remained away for years. Then I returned four years ago by jumping ship. Since then I have planned and worked hard, returning to Moscow whenever necessary, by way of Siberia, so that these people who have the best food in the world, more money than any other nation, more comforts and greater freedom, will learn how to bow their heads."

"Yes, yes," the Unknown agreed impatiently. "I've heard that before. Now for orders. Tonight there is to be a meeting of Independent Maritime Alliance men with their officers, which we must not fail to sway. Probably eight hundred of them will assemble at Union Hall. Our men have done their work well. Many of those who formerly were opposed to our Cause are now seeing eye to eye with us, and are willing to stand with us even against the arguments of their own American leaders.

"They are coming to believe that we are the ones who have their best interests at heart. Before the meeting is over tonight, I guarantee we will be in a position to control the entire union, to throw out their present officers and substitute others of our own—as we have hoped.

"It has cost a great deal of money, for there have been bribes to pay, and recompense for certain strong-armed individuals who have removed undesirables. But our investment will be a mere fraction of what we will get out of it. Gather our own executive committee at once. They will attend the meeting in a body and distribute themselves about the hall, to whisper encouragement to others who may seem afraid."

Blinov arose. "That is easy. We have often done it in the past. At the proper moment we will also encourage the speaker who represents our Cause. May I ask if that will be you?"

"You will know me soon, Blinov. Now on your way. There is much for me to do."

COMMISSAR BLINOV hurried away. Twenty minutes later a lone figure—still the Unknown—slipped out of the side exit of the hotel, stepped into a car and drove off.

The Unknown left the city and sent the speedometer climbing when he hit the State highway. Finally he turned off the road and stopped beside a fairly large building. Two men stepped out of the shadows, and moonlight glistened on their guns.

That man who had just arrived entered the house, and ran up a flight of stairs to a locked room. He opened the door with a key taken from his pocket. Inside was a complete radio room. The Unknown fished in his pocket, consulted a long list which he kept in a leather case, and sat down before the radio instruments. Using a code book he flashed signals for almost an hour. As each operator gave prompt acknowledgment, the Unknown's spirits rose.

Finally he was done. Leaning back in the swivel chair, he spoke to himself in a soft voice.

"It is done. Each ship will be scuttled at the proper moment—and all are loaded with supplies. Within a month we shall have them exactly where we wish them to be."

CAROL BALDWIN, her lovely young face grim, maneuvered a sedan up a narrow, deeply rutted lane. Butch sat beside her, an unlighted cigarette dangling from his lips.

"So we rescue the snatched dame, huh?" he mumbled. "Okay, but I hope she's got plenty of punks guarding her. I feel just like busting jaws and pushing in their funny faces. Where is this dump?"

Carol yanked the wheel hard and climbed over one of the ruts. She nursed the car beneath the overhanging branches of a poplar tree, backing it into place so that it would be ready for a fast getaway. All this took time and skill, for she didn't dare show a light.

"Now listen carefully, Butch," she whispered. "This job we're doing is just as important to the success of the case as what the Black Bat and

Silk are doing. We can't fail them. We know Mrs. Gibbons is a prisoner in this mountain lodge. We even know the room, but she is guarded
by five men. They are all armed and ready to shoot. Up here nobody will
hear shots. We can't expect help. That's why everything must be done
quietly and fast. There's a wrench on the floor at your feet. Take it along."

From behind a thick bush they surveyed the lodge and saw that it
was being constantly patrolled on all sides. Two men kept up a steady
march covering a certain beat, while two others were on fixed post beside
each entrance. Gaining entrance here was going to be difficult. Carol
tried to figure out what the Black Bat might do under the circum-
stances. It seemed to her that drawing some or all of these men from
their posts was the first essential.

"I'll take the wrench," she told Butch. "With fists like yours, you
hardly need it. Now listen to this. I'll sneak over as close to the back
door as possible. Give me ten minutes. Then you gather a small pile of
dry leaves and set them afire. Duck out of sight. When those tough lugs
come over to see what's happened—well, I'll be glad I'm not close by.
All set, Butch?"

He nodded his big head and grinned. Butch was always ready for a
party of this kind, but it was often best for him not to be taken into full
confidence. Carol dropped to all fours and gradually approached the
rear entrance. The door looked stout and was probably bolted from
inside. But there was a long porch with pillars of rough tree trunks which
invited an easy climb to the second floor windows and Carol reflected
that it was much easier and faster to smash a window than to force a
door.

CHAPTER XXI

THE MEEK TIGRESS

CAROL GUESSED the ten minutes of which she had spoken
was about up, and kept looking in the direction where Butch was
hidden. Then she saw a tiny flame and a column of smoke which looked
black in the moonlight. The flames spread rapidly.

One of the guards shouted a warning. Two of them went sprinting
toward a small shed at the rear of the place, and they were equipped
with brooms when they emerged.

Carol smiled, and wondered if Butch would try to wrap the brooms around their necks. She ran lightly across the cleared space until she reached the end of the porch. The guard at the rear door was still on duty, although he had left his post to get closer to the fire. Carol drew herself up on the porch railing, secured a grip on the roof eave and hauled herself up silently and easily. With hardly a sound she crawled across the roof toward a window that was partly open.

Carol wormed her way through the window, ran across the vacant room, opened a door which led into the hallway, and paused to listen. Someone might be downstairs, yet she had to risk it. There were several doors in the hall, only one of them closed. That would be the one! Carol tiptoed to it, tried the knob.

The door was unlocked. She flung it open. A gaunt, middle-aged woman who had been sitting beside a window, reading, looked up with startled eyes. Carol ran across the room to her.

"Mrs. Gibbons," she whispered, "I am here to help you! The guards have all been taken care of, but there's no time to lose. Come with me!"

"The guards have been—" began the woman, her very tone showing her deadly fear of them, and that she could hardly believe what Carol said. She tried to get to her feet, but fell back weakly. "My chance to get away!" she moaned. "Nobody here but you, my rescuer, and now I'm too weak to move, they've starved and ill-treated me so!"

"Never mind," said Carol promptly. "There are none of them to stop you now. I'll help you."

Instantly Carol had lifted the woman, with a surprising strength, and staggered out into the hall with her. At that precise instant the whole building shook as though a small earthquake had struck it. The earthquake proved to be Butch as he came through the front entrance, door and all. There was a screech of pain, and a thump against one wall. Carol knew what that meant. Butch always banged his victims against the most convenient surface when he was tired.

"Butch!" Carol called. "I'm up here with Mrs. Gibbons. Is the way clear?"

"If it ain't," Butch yelled back, "I'm losin' my strength. I got all of the mugs I could find…. Say, is the old lady hurt? I could wake up a couple of the bums and rock 'em to sleep again if they hurt her."

"She's all right—just weak and frightened. Come and help me carry her down."

Automatically the woman drew back in renewed terror when she saw Butch, but Carol soothed her.

"My friend is a bit overgrown, I'll admit," she said, "but his heart is as big as he is. If you don't mind staying with him, I'll run down and get a car. We'll have you back home in no time."

CAROL LEFT Butch to guard Mrs. Gibbons while she streaked down the road. In ten minutes she was back with the car. She helped Mrs. Gibbons into the rear seat and got in beside her, while Butch manned the wheel. During Carol's absence. Butch had dragged his unconscious victims into the lodge and tied them up. They were piled on top of one another like pieces of lumber.

Mrs. Gibbons took one of Carol's hands between her own.

"My dear, I don't know who you are, but I'm terribly grateful. My husband is a wealthy man. He'll pay you anything for helping me. Poor Brad—he must be half sick with worry. They told him over the phone that unless he obeyed them, they would kill me. I suppose they wanted ransom."

"More than that," Carol answered. "Why don't you just sit back and rest, Mrs. Gibbons? You've been through so much."

The older woman closed her eyes. "Yes, I am terribly tired. I will rest."

She leaned heavily against Carol's shoulder.

Butch, intent on driving, took a look in the rear view mirror, a habit he never neglected in his work with the Black Bat. No telling when a car might be trailing. Butch saw no car, but what his eyes did discern brought a yelp of horror from his lips.

"Carol! Look out! Duck!"

Butch's foot sought the brake, and he squirmed around in his seat. Mrs. Gibbons had suddenly raised one hand and in it was a short, wide-bladed dagger. Its point was aimed at the back of Carol's neck.

Carol, however, did not sit there in amazed terror. Her short jump carried her around to face the woman she had rescued. Carol's right hand balled into a fist, clipped Mrs. Gibbons squarely on the point of the jaw. She was thrown backward by the force of the impact and her slicing aim with the knife cut through part of the car's upholstery. Carol swung once more, then calmly removed the knife from the woman's limp hand.

Butch swallowed hard, and looked at Carol.

"Gosh! I couldn't have done better myself. Where'd you pick up a wallop like that?"

Carol smiled. "I don't waste my idle time, Butch. I went to a gym to learn how to fight."

"Hey—wait!" Butch eyed the unconscious woman. "You don't act scared or surprised either, Miss Carol. Kinda like you expected the dame to pull a shiv on you. Is there somethin' I don't know?"

Carol nodded. "The Black Bat warned me that her kidnaping was faked, that she might prove dangerous. Now drive back to the lodge, Butch, and release one of those prisoners. Make sure he's unconscious when you do it. Then we'll go back to town with our precious passenger. Hurry, Butch. I'm worried about the Black Bat. It's been hours since we've heard from him...."

UNION HALL, one of the largest in the city, was well filled. The orchestra seat were occupied by delegates from labor organizations interested in just what might happen to the Independent Maritime Alliance. There were rumors of a complete reorganization, with new officers.

The gallery was jammed, and on the platform, backgrounded by a black velvet curtain, were officers of the various unions.

Hans Freuling, ship line owner, was there on invitation, to give the employer's side of the strike. Sam Barnett, smiling benignly at the audience, sat beside Mark Minor, his bleached blond secretary. Minor was patently nervous.

Brad Gibbons, armaments manufacturer, slowly tore folded pieces of paper into shreds. He showed his worry and anxiety over his wife's kidnaping. In the wings stood Ted Jordan, ace reporter for the *News-Globe*.

As the auditorium filled, members of the combination Communist, Nazi and Fascist undercover executive committee filtered in, one by one, so as not to arouse suspicion. Certain sections had been assigned to them, surreptitiously, and at the proper moments they were to lead in the applause or the disapproval.

Each man of the committee who entered found that two total strangers followed close behind him. When the foreign trouble-maker sat down, so did the other two men—on either side of him. That same little act took place all over the meeting hall.

At last Blinov appeared. He was showing his true colors now, certain that there would be no interference. He rapped for order, raised both hands and proceeded to speak, though how it had been possible for him to usurp the chairmanship, it would have been hard to tell.

"Members of the Independent Maritime Alliance, and invited guests, the I.M.A. welcomes you," he boomed. "We are holding an open meeting tonight during which both sides of the present maritime strike will be heard. Our aim is to prove that, in spite of what some of the union's officers may say to the contrary, that we are in the right, that all other unions should also strike. Yet, to be fair, we have invited guests. Mr. Freuling will tell you why he cannot meet our terms. Mr. Gibbons, an armaments manufacturer of note and wealth, is backing Mr. Freuling—"

"Hey, this Freuling sounds German!" someone from the gallery called out. "Is he a Nazi? Is he, I'm asking?"

Blinov frowned, and quieted the wave of muttering that rose.

"What Mr. Freuling's political or international connections are, have nothing to do with this meeting. As I was saying, Mr. Freuling has suffered serious losses of late because he has manned many of his ships with inexperienced crews. We also have with us, Mr. Samuel Barnett, a leading exponent of worldwide peace, who has especially asked permission to address you. First let me present Mr. Freuling."

In the gallery, the various planted members of Blinov's executive council pursed their lips for long-drawn-out boos. The derisive sound was not emitted, because those strangers on either side of each Communist, Nasi or Fascist lieutenant, quietly bent toward him and each gripped one of the alien disturber's wrists.

"One squawk out of you," came the stern warning from one who spoke identically as did the others, "and you'll wish you were back in Moscow, Berlin—or even Greece. That goes for cheers or hisses. If you don't believe me, try it—but take a look at this first."

One of the strangers opened his hand and showed a badge of the F.B.I. Blinov, who expected a sustained series of boos when Freuling arose, was surprised. There should have been cheers for his speech, too, but they never even got started.

FREULING MADE a simple but impassioned speech, asking for unity between labor and capital while the whole world faced a grave crisis. When he sat down, he was applauded. He wiped his moist forehead. He had expected to be shouted down, instead of applauded.

Brad Gibbons took a long drink of water, then faced his audience.

"As you may know," he said in a voice that trembled slightly, "I have also been a loser when Mr. Freuling's ships sank, for many of them carried cargoes I shipped. The loss has been far more than merely monetary, for the cargo consisted of armaments manufactured by factories so hard pressed now that they are far behind. Those orders will have to be refilled, so of necessity orders for United States munitions and for British guns, planes and bombs, will have to wait.

"I have always believed in unions. I believe in collective bargaining—but not in strikes during a critical period, and this is one of the most serious in the history of our nation. You men are the backbone of our civilization. Your demands should be met. If there is any profit to be made during times like these, then you should have your share of it. I admire the working man. I am his friend. I—"

Blinov, who had gone off stage at a signal from someone in the wings, came back and hurried up to Gibbons. He whispered something, and Gibbons turned deathly pale. He took another drink of water, tried to say something to the audience, but instead strode off the platform.

He swept past Ted Jordan and several men acting as Blinov's bodyguards. Ten seconds after he disappeared, the bodyguards decided it might be best to change their affiliation, possibly surrender the guns they carried illegally.

Each man was hemmed in by several strangers.

CHAPTER XXII

REVEALING TRUTH

G IBBONS LOOKED around for a phone booth. Blinov had said he was wanted on the phone urgently. He spotted the booth at the far end of the big backstage area. The receiver was off the hook. He closed the door and spoke. The slightly befuddled audience had another shock as they watched the stage. The black backdrop parted and a figure dressed in jet black moved into view. The face was covered by a hood. The cape was that of the Black Bat, and two holstered guns were strapped to the thighs.

Blinov, eyes popping in amazement, reached for his hip pocket. Two men jumped for him. They extracted the gun he had intended to draw, and showed it to the crowd.

"I am the Black Bat," the figure in black said in a voice that rang through the hall. "I have little time to speak. You are all being taken as a pack of soft-headed fools by foreign agent who intend, eventually, to make serf out of you. You want proof of that. Then listen to the telephone conversation which our estimable Mr. Gibbons is now having. He doesn't know it, but his phone is hooked up to an amplifier. You'll hear the conversation."

Someone must have snapped a switch then because suddenly Gibbons' voice came out of the amplifier.

"Yes—yes it's Gibbons, you fools. What happened?"

"Gosh, Boss, some gorilla as big as a house walked in and grabbed your wife. I just got loose and I been tryin' to get you. I found out you was at this meeting so I thought maybe I should phone."

"Hang up, you stupid fool," Gibbons said tersely. "I've got an important call to make."

The sound of both receivers being cradled came to the audience, quiet as death. Then they heard the sound of dialing. Finally a heavily accented voice cut in.

"Comrade Zharky?" Gibbons said. "This is Gibbons. There is the very devil to pay. Someone has actually kidnaped my wife! Yes, yes, I arranged it so she disappeared or rather, she arranged things. She is a strong-willed woman. Now someone has really kidnaped her. It may be some of those White Russians. Or American Secret Service agents."

"What of the Black Bat?" that accented voice demanded.

"No—no! He is dead. Blinov had him killed and witnessed the disposal of the body. What shall I do?"

"You shall receive all the aid necessary," the other man said. "Control yourself, please. We are near the end of our work and not even the disappearance of your wife must stop us. You are certain no one can hear you phoning?"

"I'm sure of it," Gibbons said. "The meeting is progressing smoothly except that some of Blinov's agents need more coaching. They have not responded well tonight, but I am giving the union members a good talk. The sea of ignorant faces! I tell them in one breath that they should not strike against defense measures, and at the same time inform them that they should. Our men will sow the seeds of discontent among them."

"What of Freuling's ships? Remember they must be sunk—every one of them sent to the bottom and all members of the crews who do not adhere to our belief drowned. So far you have succeeded in sinking only a comparatively few."

"The ships are all taken care of," Gibbons said. "I radioed each wireless operator and all of them are on our side. At rapid intervals our men will take over the ships and kill those who cannot be trusted. When the big strike occurs here on land, we shall take care of others like them."

GIBBONS THOUGHT he heard a noise like thunder, but went on talking. In the auditorium a roar had gone up from the assembled men. They realized how they had been tricked—those members of the Independent Maritime Alliance who were learning only now of the evil that was masquerading among their membership. They heard the cool plotting of murder, the calm recital of past killings. The Black Bat silenced them.

"Gibbons has stated that I am dead," he said. "But the Black Bat lives. I've fought these disciples of a red Satan and other black dictators with everything I possess. But until I could convince you of what they actually intended despite their sugared words, my battle was lost. Now you have heard. Gibbons has controlled alien spies and agents, and is a capitalist. Does that make sense, according to the teaching of Lenin, you who have listened, for instance, to Communistic propaganda? His wife has been one of the most active members of that particular foreign party for many years. Her influence and domineering mind brought Gibbons into this, but he was out to get all the power he could. If he had won, what conquered nations of Europe are suffering would be a picnic to what he had planned for us."

"But those ships!" someone yelled. "You've got to stop the sinkings!"

"That has been taken care of," the Black Bat assured. "When Gibbons finished sending his messages in code, he carefully locked up his code books, but locks and I have a great deal in common. Ten minutes after his broadcast, I put on another, using the same code. I ordered each one of Freuling's radio operators to relay a message to the captain which would bring each ship either into port in the United States, or within sight of one of our neutrality patrol vessels. The Navy was also advised. None of Freuling's ships will be scuttled. No member of their crews will be harmed, except those who are in league with murder. They won't like the brig."

Ted Jordan ran on stage and waved his hand. The Black Bat stepped back, parted the curtains, and vanished. Gibbons strode back to the speaker's platform, faced the audience, and never looked once toward Blinov or the other men who belonged to his plan for revolt.

Raucous shouts stopped Gibbons cold. His jaw sagged, his eyes bulged. Then he heard a wild yell of hate, and saw Mark Minor of the straw-colored hair making a dive toward him. Gibbons tried to reach a hidden gun, but Minor got him first. He bent Gibbons over the speaker's table and sunk his fingers into the traitor's throat.

"You murdered my brothers! You tricked me into giving you information I was seeking for the government, making me think you could lead me to my brothers' killers! You told me Barnett was a radical, that he was the secret leader of this rotten bunch of cutthroats! And all the time it was you!"

Firm hands dragged Mark Minor away. One of the regular union officials on the platform took over the meeting. He made a stirring speech which Freuling followed up extemporaneously. Quietly dressed men took charge of Blinov, Gibbons and the executive council.

The man in the Black Bat's regalia disappeared in the night. Moments later, an intent observer would have noticed a man in black, with a wide-brimmed hat drawn over his eyes, walking swiftly along a quiet street. He stepped into a waiting car which drove away instantly.

THIS MAN in black pushed back the big hat and grinned. Tony Quinn was as satisfied as any man could be. In the front seat was almost his counterpart, but a rather sorry one. Silk, dressed in the flowing garments of the Black Bat, was soaked to the skin.

Butch drove, but kept his ear cocked for details. Carol rested her head on Quinn's shoulder, content.

"Sorokin has been punished enough," Silk said, and chuckled. "I hope the courts are not too hard on him. A few times I thought he'd blow his top and slip off those iron fetters you fixed so neatly. They clamped on nice and hard, but pressure in the right places and they fell off. We got rid of them as we slid into the water with the garbage. Which reminds me—I'm not hungry."

Tony Quinn laughed. "It was a tough assignment, Silk. Yet it had to be done. Gibbons wouldn't come into the open unless he thought all opposition from us was gone."

"I picked both of 'em up two minutes after they hit the water," Butch broke in. "Silk looked like a wet rat."

They rode on in silence for a moment or two. Carol raised her head.

"We're waiting, Tony. How did you guess it was Gibbons?"

Tony Quinn's eyes grew somber. "I didn't guess—I knew. But not until a great deal had happened. Gibbons killed the Adams boys to prevent them from talking. He murdered the ship's doctor to get his uniform for a disguise. I'm sure Gibbons wasn't always a radical because he built his business up well. He married rather late in life and his wife was, secretly, one of Moscow's most avid disciples.

"To divert suspicion from himself, Gibbons arranged for her to visit a country lodge he owned. The guards out there were so much stage property, in case the police should find Mrs. Gibbons. The guards themselves believed they were there protecting her.

"Then Gibbons fixed that phone call to Freuling's office, announcing the snatch. It struck me as odd that the kidnapers should have known Gibbons was there at that moment. Gibbons had gained a hold on many foreigners, claiming to help them to become citizens. They would therefore listen to him. So when I left them in the warehouse, Gibbons appeared almost immediately, and they took his advice to disperse quietly and go home.

"Soon after, they were visited by agents who impressed them with the idea that complete silence would insure the continued health of their relatives in Europe. Those men in the warehouse would hardly have listened to and obeyed anyone but a man they trusted—and Gibbons was the only one who filled that bill.

"He tried to dispose of Freuling by planting a bomb in his home. When Freuling didn't die, Gibbons went after him a harder way. He talked Freuling into letting him invest money in the shipping business. That gave Gibbons the right to study the books and to know just where each ship was. It also made things easier for him, if the firm should be forced into bankruptcy. Gibbons could take over cheaply, and force Freuling out."

"And Mark Minor, with the bleached hair?" Silk asked. "Where did he come in?"

"He is Mark Adams, brother of the two murdered sailors, and is the third man in that picture you found, Silk. He had always been worried about subversive elements in his brother Frank's union, and when he learned of the mess both his brothers were in, he determined to do something about it. He decided he could do that better by doing his part to break up the Communist, Nazi, and Fascist hold on men in the union than in any other way. He learned that Barnett, of the Peace League, was doing a lot of work to uncover subversive activities, so went to him with an offer of aid in undercover work—and got the job as secretary.

"Later, he thought he had made a mistake, for Gibbons got hold of him, made him believe that Barnett himself was in league with the foreign element in the Independent Maritime Alliance, and that by working against Barnett he would be going far toward uncovering the killers of his brothers. Gibbons promised to help Mark in any way in his power, and in return, Mark agreed to keep Gibbons informed of everything that Barnett was doing. He could have no idea, of course, that Gibbons' real purpose was to pin the rap on Barnett if things went sour.

"You can easily see now why Mark was so excited on shipboard. He had heard that S.O.S. from the sinking freighter, knew his brothers were aboard it, and also knew that other freighters had been sabotaged and sunk. He was nearly crazy, believing them doomed to death. Because of his undercover position, he could not go near them when they were rescued, believing that they were safe then. But when they were killed he renewed his efforts to show up the men who were trying to take over the whole union, and to get the murderers."

CAROL HAD a question for Quinn.

"Barnett, then," she said, "is just what he seems to be—a well intentioned man who has a job too big for him?"

"Exactly," Tony Quinn said. "He was aboard ship with Silk and me, too, but too seasick to show his face. We only saw his secretary, and he certainly did give us cause for suspicion. Especially with that bleached hair, though the reason for that was simple. Before he went with Barnett, he had tried some investigating along the waterfront on his own, so when he agreed to do it for Barnett, he knew, he had to change his appearance, or some of the men he had met on the waterfront would recognize him.

"He is certainly regretting now that he ever pussyfooted for Gibbons, for he had no idea that the details he reported aided Gibbons in setting the stage for sabotage, strikes, and riots. He believed he was gathering information that would go direct to the government. Why, he even snooped for Gibbons down at that book store to see if the placard was in the window, before Gibbons appeared there. He believed Gibbons' cock and bull story about going there secretly on work to wipe out the Communist and Axis threat.

"When Silk, disguised as the Black Bat, interviewed Barnett, Mark Minor ran out to advise Gibbons of the fact. From then on I kept Gibbons in sight, for I followed Mark. I arranged for the real kidnaping of Gibbons' wife so that he would become alarmed and phone for help to certain trading companies which masquerade as such while they really handle much of Moscow's espionage work here. The man Zharky, to whom he phoned, heads a trading outfit.

"I knew that when Gibbons talked to Zharky, or any man like him, that he would blurt out everything and if the men of the union could hear the truth, they'd realize that men like Gibbons have only their own ambitions in mind. That they exploit working men far more than any capitalist ever thought of doing."

He paused, went on:

"The methods of these Trojan Horse agents are as invisible, at first, as the borings of termites. But like the work of those insects they will eventually topple over our way of life, our freedom. The only cure is a counter-poison they cannot stand—exposure! Bring them into the light, and they and their schemes will be seen through like glass. Drag them from under cover so that their twisted, warped ideas can be seen in a true light as the workings of brains that want nothing but power—

worldwide power—no matter if they must climb over the mangled bodies of millions to attain that goal."

For moments the Black Bat was silent. The car stopped. He bent over and kissed Carol lightly, and laughed happily.

"Now for home," he said. "Stop in, in a few moments and have coffee—with Tony Quinn."

www.ingramcontent.com/pod-product-compliance
Lightning Source LLC
Chambersburg PA
CBHW032235010726
47494CB00002B/508